MW01134792

A Tale of Two Sides

A Novel on Vaccines and Disease

John Phillip Ryan

Copyright © 2018 John Phillip Ryan.

All rights reserved. No part of this book may be reproduced, stored,
or transmitted by any means—whether auditory, graphic, mechanical,
or electronic—without written permission of the author, except in the
case of brief excerpts used in critical articles and reviews. Unauthorized
reproduction of any part of this work is illegal and is punishable by law.

This is a work of fiction. All of the characters, names, incidents,
organizations, and dialogue in this novel are either the products
of the author's imagination or are used fictitiously.

The medical information in this book is not intended as medical advice
and does not replace the advice of a trained health professional. If you
know or suspect you have a health problem, consult a health professional.
The author and publisher specifically disclaim any liability, loss, injury, or
risk, personal or otherwise, which is incurred as a consequence, directly
or indirectly, of the use and application of any contents of this book.

ISBN: 978-1-4834-9002-1 (sc)
ISBN: 978-1-4834-9004-5 (hc)
ISBN: 978-1-4834-9003-8 (e)

Library of Congress Control Number: 2018909923

Because of the dynamic nature of the Internet, any web addresses or links contained in
this book may have changed since publication and may no longer be valid. The views
expressed in this work are solely those of the author and do not necessarily reflect the
views of the publisher, and the publisher hereby disclaims any responsibility for them.

Any people depicted in stock imagery provided by Getty Images are
models, and such images are being used for illustrative purposes only.
Certain stock imagery © Getty Images.

Lulu Publishing Services rev. date: 09/28/2018

Contents

Chapter 1

Nurses Know Best

"Push! Good! Now, breathe … that's it. Deep breaths. Now give me your hand."

Paulina felt her contraction subside as Dr. Goodman gently guided her hand down past her abdomen and … "Is that …?" Paulina asked.

"Yes, my dear. That's his head."

This was Paulina and Reuben's first baby. So far the labor was about what she'd expected … except for the pain. *Ugh. No one warned me about that. But isn't it almost over now?* she wondered through the mixed haze of pain, work, and joy. *And Dr. Goodman is so wonderful. The best OB in town,* she thought. *So glad we picked her. She's so warm, understanding, and confident.*

Reuben, on the other hand, doesn't look so good, thought Paulina, glancing up at her husband. *Oh, please don't faint … not now. Men. I can't believe I have to worry about him while I'm right in the middle of … Oh, dear God!*

The next contraction hit hard. Paulina tuned everything out again except for Dr. Goodman's gentle, reassuring voice. "Push, now breathe, push, now don't push. Relax." Paulina was focused and followed every suggestion and—

"Waaaaaaaahhhhhhhh!" The most joyful sound in the world. Paulina felt the warm, slimy, squirming body on her chest. She wrapped her arms gently around this little bundle of joy who instantly became her entire universe. Now all was right in the world.

Julianna loved being a nurse. All those years of training were hard but well worth it. She wasn't so thrilled with having to work labor and delivery over the past year, but, "You take what you can get," was her motto. She didn't have any kids yet, and this year had really done nothing to convince her she'd ever be able to go through what each of her patients had to endure.

She glanced across the labor and delivery room at the new mom and dad, both gazing at their one-hour-old baby, now sleeping in Mom's arms. *They look happy, especially the mom. What was her name again?* Julianna checked the chart on the counter. *Gonzalez. Paulina Gonzalez. That's right. Catchy name,* she thought as she prepared the vitamin K shot and hepatitis B vaccine Baby Gonzalez would need in the next few minutes. Julianna glanced around for the consent forms to make sure the parents had given their permission for the shots. *There it is. And of course it's not signed.* She rolled her eyes. *I hope these Gonzalezes aren't the type of parents who think they know what's best for their baby. Geeze.*

Compliant parents were what Julianna loved most about her job. And in labor and delivery, most parents listened to her. She was a nurse, after all. She knew way more about medicine than any of them. She had a checklist of medical procedures that saved lives. And anyone who said no to something on her checklist not only put their lives in danger but caused her way more hassle and paperwork. It's hard enough doing all the proper charting on a patient as it is.

Julianna picked up the two syringes and headed over to the family, making sure her best smile was showing. She'd worry about the consent forms later. She watched the new dad obediently move out of the way as she neared. *Now he's going to be a good father,* she thought. *He already knows what he's doing.*

"Time to give the baby his vitamin K shot and his first vaccine," announced Julianna, watching both parents for any telltale signs of "the look" that would warn her they'd require some extra convincing.

"We want to delay the vitamin shot until we ask our pediatrician about it," said Paulina.

She's surprisingly alert, thought Julianna. *After all that arduous labor, most moms are so out of it that I can usually get the shots in before they even know it.*

"But we don't want the hepatitis B vaccine."

Here we go, Julianna almost said out loud. Instead, making sure to keep smiling, she offered, "Your baby really needs this vaccine to save his life. It's important. Don't you want your baby to be protected?"

"Why does my baby need to be protected from hepatitis B? How exactly do you think he's going to catch it?" challenged Paulina.

"You never know," Julianna replied. "Plus, the doctor ordered it, and it's hospital policy. And ... it's mandatory, you know." *Plus I'll have to walk all the way down to the nurse's station an extra time to grab the refusal of medical care forms*, she added to herself. She liked to call these forms "the bad parent forms."

"Maybe we should just do it," caved good-patient Reuben. "It's only one shot."

"No, Reuben," Paulina answered calmly, her arms reflexively pulling her baby closer to her chest. "We talked about this. There's risk to this vaccine with absolutely no benefits since he's only a baby. It's for an STD for God's sake! Don't you remember reading about this?"

Julianna watched the confident and loving way her patient looked at her husband and knew she had her work cut out for her. *This* mom wouldn't be an easy sell.

Paulina knew her husband agreed with her, but he often found it hard to stand up to medical authorities. *Good thing I don't*, she thought. *And it's nice that Dr. Goodman wasn't too pushy about the vaccines she wanted me to have during pregnancy either. Maybe she'll help me get this nurse off my back before she leaves.*

"Dr. Goodman, what do you think?" she asked. "Does our baby need a hepatitis B vaccine?"

"Well," the doctor temporized, looking at the nurse holding the shots and then back at her patient. "You know I *do* recommend all vaccines. Didn't you did get the Tdap and the flu shot in my office during one of your prenatal visits?"

"No, you let me skip those shots. But yeah, I know you have a lot of patients and wouldn't expect you to remember that. But I was concerned about getting any shots during pregnancy because there wasn't enough safety research on them. You always told me to be very careful about what goes into my body during pregnancy, like the mercury in the flu shot. I know you didn't exactly agree with my decision, but you agreed it was *my* decision."

"Oh, yes, I remember. You know, I never could find any published safety research on the flu and the Tdap vaccines except for a few very small studies. And there was even one study showing a possible link between the flu vaccine and miscarriage. But now that they are giving these vaccines to every pregnant woman, they'll have proof it's safe pretty soon. As for the baby's shots, you'll probably have to ask the pediatrician. It's a little out of my area. But if it's recommended, it must be very important. Otherwise, why would it be recommended? Oh, and that reminds me, I have to check on your rubella immunity test. I forget if you were immune. You might need a rubella booster. I gotta run though. I'll check in on you tomorrow."

Paulina let Dr. Goodman go, but she was already leery about getting a rubella booster shot even if she needed one. She turned back to the nurse. "You said the hep B vaccine is mandatory. What exactly do you mean by that?" She knew it wasn't but was curious what the nurse would say.

"Um, well, your baby won't be able to go to school without it. Plus, this vaccine prevents cancer. It will save his life."

"Well, school is a long way off. And I can teach my child how to prevent hepatitis B when the time comes," said Paulina. "Right, Reuben?"

"Yes, you're right," he answered. "We'll skip the shot for now."

Paulina sighed as she watched the nurse leave the room shaking her head. She was used to that. It seemed to happen a lot to her whenever she went to the doctor. And now that she was making medical decisions for her baby as well, she suspected this nurse wouldn't be the last medical professional to shake a head at her.

"Well, if they don't want the shot, that's their choice. Just have them sign the refusal form and move on," instructed Joanna, Julianna's charge nurse. "You can't force them, you know."

Joanna liked being in charge of labor and delivery. Much of a labor nurse's job was guiding parents through various medical decisions, and the newborn hepatitis B vaccine was just one of them. Joanna had never really understood why they gave that shot to newborns, so she was OK when parents said no. Most of the nurses on the floor were. Medicine requires informed consent, and if parents want to opt out of an STD vaccine for their newborn, that was fine with Joanna and most of her colleagues. But there was something about Julianna that Joanna found odd—an unusual obsession with policy and procedure. Joanna suspected the nurse wasn't always following the rules, and she'd kept her eyes on her to make sure she didn't cross any lines. And proper consent documentation was one of the most important.

"Fine." Julianna grabbed the refusal form and headed back down the hallway.

"Bath time," announced Julianna as she paraded back into the Gonzalezes' room, the unsigned refusal form stowed away in her back pocket along with the hopefully soon-to-be-used hepatitis B shot. "I'm going to take Baby to the nursery for his first bath. That way you two can get some rest. You look exhausted!" *Always remind them that you're doing them a favor,* she reflected. *Works every time.*

It didn't.

"Oh, we don't want him to get a bath yet," responded Mrs. Gonzalez. "Tell her why, Reuben."

"Umm … yeah. The baby's supposed to keep the vernix and all the natural bacteria from the birth on his skin to help his immune system get off to a good start."

Paulina had an annoyingly satisfied look on her face, and Julianna suspected this man was just reciting what this woman had put into his brain.

Seriously? thought Julianna. She had heard that one before and had no idea where such nonsense came from. If it were even remotely true, she would have learned it in nursing school. Everyone knows you are supposed to sterilize a baby with antiseptic soap as soon as possible. A sterile baby is a healthy baby after all. *Well, I have more cards to play.*

"OK, I'll just take Baby to the nursery to check him out then. Gotta make sure he's healthy."

"Nope," answered Mom. "I thought this hospital had a rooming in policy? The baby can stay right here with us while you check him."

"Well, we need to do his hearing test then. That has to be done in the nursery."

"Don't you wait until he's 24 hours old to do that? I thought I read that in the hospital prenatal brochure," chimed in Dad.

Geeze. Whose side is he on anyway? Julianna didn't realize she was rolling her eyes for real. *What, do these parents think they know everything?*

Julianna left. Her shift was almost over anyway. *If these parents want their baby to get an STD, that's their business. Would serve them right.*

Paulina awoke the next morning to a commotion in the hallway. She heard a man's voice asking questions, and the sound of a woman crying. She glanced at her baby sleeping in the hospital bassinet, and at her husband sleeping in the chair. *Of course. He'll sleep through anything.* Curious, she got up and peeked outside the door in time to see a baby being wheeled down the hallway in an incubator. She assumed that the woman crying in the doorway next to hers was the baby's mother.

"What's the matter?" Paulina asked, putting her hand gently on the other's shoulder. "Is that your baby?"

"Yes," the other sobbed. "She has a fever and they are taking her to the NICU for treatment and observation. I don't get it. I had a fast labor. I don't have vaginal Strep. Everything was fine yesterday. Why would my baby suddenly get a fever?"

Paulina had a sinking feeling she knew the answer. She had read in the FDA's vaccine Package Insert for the hep B vaccine that between 1 and 10% of kids get a fever from the vaccine. *But of course, it might not be that. Maybe the baby does have a real infection after all.*

"I wanted Sage's life to start out right," the mom continued. "She was nursing well, and we were just getting ready to go home. She just passed her hearing test with flying colors, and went to the nursery for her first bath so she'd be healthy. An hour later, when they brought her back to me, she was lethargic and burning up. What the hell happened?"

Paulina didn't have the heart to tell this woman what may have happened. She suddenly felt like she needed to get herself and her baby out of here as quickly as she could. And screw the hearing test.

"Another one in the NICU," sighed Dr. Goodman. "That's the third baby this month. I don't get it."

Marissa Goodman liked eating lunch with Peter Tommaso, one of the local pediatricians who still came into the hospital to see his newborn babies. Marissa was the current head of OB, and she liked to pick Peter's brain from time to time about what was going on in the world of newborn medicine.

"How many of your febrile babies actually end up having a positive sepsis work up?" Peter asked. "Or do they all just end up getting the usual 48 hours of IV antibiotics and intensive care, then go home?"

"I haven't had a baby with a real infection here in years," Marissa answered. "I guess that's a good thing. But I sure wish I knew why so many seemingly healthy newborns are getting these fevers. What about you? You seeing a lot of rule-out sepsis cases in your patients?"

"Nope. Can't say that I have. I think the last one I had was about five years ago. But most of my patients tend to be the home-birthers anyway. I only have one or two each month who are born here at the hospital these days. No offense to you and your profession," Peter smiled, holding up his hands.

Marissa laughed. "None taken. You know I support home births, although I do think it's much safer to deliver in hospital. So, you really aren't seeing many fevers, huh? Maybe it's all the granola your patients eat."

It was Peter's turn to laugh. "No offense taken either, unless you are trying to imply there's something wrong with granola." They both laughed, and earned a few stares from the surrounding patrons in the hospital cafeteria. "But seriously, I get all the naturally-minded patients. They usually don't stay very long in the hospital. Although that still doesn't explain why they aren't getting fevers."

Marissa wondered if she should ask him about what was really bothering her, but wasn't sure she wanted to open herself up to any professional criticism. Although, from what she knew of Peter, if there was any pediatrician she could ask about this, it was him.

"OK Dr. Goodman. Spit it out. I can tell something's bothering you. You have that look."

"Do you know if the …" she lowered her voice and glanced around, "the hepatitis B vaccine can cause fevers?"

Peter knew the answer to that question. In fact, he'd known the answer for many years. The risk of fever was one of the reasons he stopped giving his newborn patients this vaccine years ago, despite the CDC recommendation that all newborns need it. That, and the fact that babies don't catch sexually-transmitted infections. He kept quiet about it over the years, but was recently re-thinking that stance.

And he liked having an OB like Marissa around. *Yeah, she is pretty mainstream, but at least she welcomes patients who want a more natural approach to their OB care. She's young enough to know she doesn't know everything yet. She's teachable, but like all good doctors she needs data. Research. You know, proof that makes something right.*

"Well, yes it can. It says right in the vaccine's Package Insert that between 1% and 10% of people will get a fever from the vaccine. And there is an interesting study published in 1999 from Israel that shows the year they started giving all their newborns the hep B vaccine as recommended, their NICU admissions for fever doubled, without any increase in actual newborn infections."

"What? Seriously?" Marissa was shocked. "If that's true, and based on my experience I'm beginning to believe it, why do we give that vaccine to newborns? Why not wait until they are a few months, or even years, old? Hell, why not just wait until they are teenagers?"

"That would make way too much sense, Marissa. Since when did you start expecting a government-based medical policy to be made based on logic and common sense? I was already practicing back in the early 90s when this all went down, and it's quite a story. Got a few more minutes?"

Marissa glanced at her phone. "Yes. I don't start back in the office for another half hour."

"Good. OK. So, the hep B vaccine was created back in the 80s. It was targeted at those who were at high risk of catching hep B – sexually-promiscuous adults and IV drug abusers. But, no surprise, they couldn't get these patients to line up for their shots. They also gave the shot to any newborns who were born to a hep B positive mom. Which makes sense, right?"

"Right."

"Well, that's where the logic of this vaccine ended, in my opinion. I wonder if people were pissed because they'd invested hundreds of millions of dollars to develop a vaccine that very few Americans were signing up for. Less than 1% of moms are hep B positive, and no one really makes any money vaccinating 1% of the country. So, two of the doctors who worked with the pharmaceutical companies teamed up with a few colleagues and published research that 'showed' about 30,000 American infants were mysteriously catching hep B every year."

"What's up with the air quotes, and the word mysteriously?"

"Well, there was no real evidence that that many kids were catching the disease. The easiest way to find out would have been to do a simple blood test on tens of thousands of kids and see the rate of hep B. But I think they didn't think that would work, because what would happen if they didn't find any hep B, which is what I suspect they would have found if they did a straightforward analysis like that. So, the way I see it, they decided to do the study backwards. Start with adults who were infected and work back to try to figure out when in their lives they became infected. They had data on the number of adult Americans who were chronic hep B carriers at the time: it was about 1.25 million people. Epidemiological analysis showed that in order to have that many chronic carriers, there had to be about 200,000 people catching new cases every year. So they interviewed a bunch of adults with hep B to figure out how and when they may have caught it, and they found that about 1/3 of adults didn't seem to have engaged in any high-risk behaviors - ever. The researchers concluded that about 1/3 of chronic adult hep B carriers *may be* (air quotes, again) contracting the disease during childhood. That 'may be' is the key. It's not a lie, because it 'may be' true. You see that a lot in medical research. But then, somehow, a 'may be' turns into 'probably' and then it becomes a fact. They did a little more fancy math and published some estimates showing that 'as many as' 30,000 American children were catching hep B every year through non-sexual contact. 'As many as' is another way to blur a statistic. As many as could mean as little as just one, or as many as 30,000. Anyway, doctors and policymakers convinced themselves that if 30,000 American kids were catching hep B non-sexually every year, it must be occurring either at birth or through casual contact during childhood. And these kids needed saving, and the best way to save them would be to give the hep B vaccine to every single newborn in America. You create a generation who will be immune, which sounds like a good idea, if the vaccine was harmless. But, as you can see, it isn't. Here, I'll text you the research. I keep it handy on my phone for times like this when I have a rapt audience who will need to read it for themselves later." A link to three research articles showed up on Marissa's phone.

Peter paused to let this all sink in. Marissa sat quietly, trying to process it. "OK, I have a million questions. First, hep B isn't a fun disease, right?"

"God no," agreed Peter. "Especially when kids catch it. Sadly, if a baby catches hep B from his mom during birth, he has about a 90% chance of becoming chronically infected if left untreated. About 25% will go on to liver failure or liver cancer. It's not a pretty disease. Glad I've never seen any cases in my 30 years of pediatrics. Fortunately, older kids who are accidentally exposed to it only have a 10% chance of chronic infection. And for adults, 95% of cases pass within a month or two without any lasting harm or chronic infection; most healthy adult immune systems kill off the disease. For the 5% who do stay chronically infected, about 1/3 will be cured with a chemotherapy-type medication. So, the fact that it *is* worse when babies catch it was probably a factor in getting the vaccine approved for all babies. They kind of just ignored the fact that babies don't catch it."

Marissa rolled her eyes. "That wasn't directed at you, Peter. It was aimed at whoever 'they' are. Second question: why did anyone believe this research, and didn't it bother anyone that two of the doctors who were involved in this research had previously done some work for the vaccine makers?"

Peter just raised one eyebrow at his friend and waited.

"Oh. Stupid question," Marissa answered herself. "No one in the medical community reads entire research studies. They only read the summary, so all they would see is '30,000 American infants are catching hep B each year' and freak out. And I imagine the Pharma doctors had to disclose their ties to those companies, but no one really cares when that happens, right?"

"Correct. It's right there in the author section of these studies. They have to disclose it, but yes. No one cares."

"Next question: How do you know that 30,000 children *aren't* catching hep B every year through non-sexual contact?" Marissa put a challenging look on her face.

"Well, let's see what the CDC says about how hep B is transmitted. This will take me about 30 seconds ..." Peter typed CDC hepatitis B transmission into the Google search on his phone, clicked on the first choice, then clicked on the transmission, symptoms and treatment link under Q and A For Health Professionals. "Here, read this."

Marissa took the phone and read all the ways hep B was transmitted, then read how it was *not* transmitted: *HBV is not spread through food or water, sharing eating utensils, breastfeeding, hugging, kissing, hand holding, coughing, or sneezing.* "So how do they think children are passing the disease to each other?"

"That's a good question," complimented Peter. "And the answer is they are not. Not passing it to each other, that is."

"Weren't there any real data on hep B in children before they recommended the vaccine?"

"Yes. I'll send you that study too so you can read it later." Peter's phone chirped and Marissa's chimed acceptance. "They were only finding about 1 infant case for every 100,000 children, or about 360 cases each year. These cases were virtually all kids who caught the disease at birth from an infected mom who didn't know she was infected because she didn't get prenatal screening."

"But that's nowhere near 30,000!" Marissa protested.

"Yeah, but it is somewhere between 1 and 30,000, or 'as many as' 30,000. So they weren't technically lying."

"But I still don't understand how this vaccine made it through the CDC's approval process to be put on the schedule for all babies. Why not just focus on universal screening for all pregnant moms and vaccinate all the babies whose moms are hep B positive?"

"Well, first, I don't know if they even looked at the real disease data to see how rare this disease really was in babies. I wasn't there, so I don't know. But it's my opinion that they may have had some unintentional bias toward studies that supported their agenda. And another reason this vaccine got approved is that some of the doctors who sat on the CDC's vaccine approval board back in the 90s had a financial stake in the success of vaccines. They were working for, or had stock in, or had previously done work for the pharmaceutical companies who made the vaccines."

"I suppose you are going to text me proof of that as well?" smiled Marissa, right before her phone chimed and Peter smiled.

"The U.S. government investigated the FDA and CDC vaccine-approval boards in 2000 and reprimanded them for allowing such conflicts of interest, and told them to start following the ethical rules that are in place to avoid such conflicts."

"And did they? Start following the rules, that is?"

"Nope. In 2007 they were investigated again and reprimanded because 64% of the doctors serving on the CDC's ACIP vaccine-approval board had financial conflicts of interest with vaccine manufacturers that should have banned them from taking part in the vaccine-approval process, but some took part anyway."

"Didn't anyone get in trouble over this?" asked Marissa.

"How would anyone get in trouble? The government tells the CDC to follow the rules, and the CDC, which is also the government, says OK. Then no one enforces the rules."

"How do you even know all this?" wondered Marissa.

"Welcome to my life," sighed Peter. "Think carefully whether or not you want to become a part of it."

A chime alert startled the computer operator out of his reverie. Or had he actually been asleep? He wasn't sure. He read the words on his screen.

"Ms. Donahue? Tony sent over a threshold alert from a small community hospital in ... let me see ... Washington State."

"What factor?" asked his boss.

"Looks like hepatitis B, again."

Francine Donahue walked over and stood behind Jim so she could read for herself. "Hmmm. Looks like a negative acceptance rate of 8% now. Get me some background data."

Jim clicked a few buttons and they both read what came up. "Steady newborn hepatitis B vaccination rate of 96% for many years," mused Francine. "Lower than the usual, but steady. Someone there doesn't like this vaccine. But why the sudden alert?"

They kept reading … "There it is," pointed out Jim Remington, trying to appear useful to his boss. "A sudden drop from 96% to 92% … in only one month. Someone *else* doesn't like that vaccine now either."

"Well, I'd like a state-wide report on this before end of day. I doubt just one community hospital will hurt uptake by more than 0.01% statewide. And as long as we don't fall below 95% for Washington, we'll keep the guys upstairs happy. Which makes me happy, which in turn lets you keep your job, Jimbo."

Jim didn't mind the brief shoulder rub that accompanied his boss's encouragement/threat. *Yeah, she's quite a bit older than me … but what does that matter?*

He was just glad there were vaccines for STDs these days. *Geeze, where would we be without them?*

Chapter 2

Saving Sage

D r. Stanley was tired. But, then again, he was always tired. He thought he'd have gotten used to working the ER night shifts by now – six months of trying to switch his days and nights around – but no. His brain still thought he should be asleep right now instead of being awake saving lives.

What time is it anyway? he thought, then groaned as the wall clock in the doctor's work room laughed at him that it was only 2:15 am. *Six more hours of this. Ugh. Well Jack, up you go. Step to it.*

His second wind sailed him out into the hallway while he pulled up the next patient on his iPad. *A seven-week-old with fever. That sucks.*

Jack liked being an ER doctor, but the pediatric side of the job wasn't his favorite, to say the least. He didn't have kids (yet), and he didn't really understand them. Parents confused him even more. *Why do they have to ask a hundred questions, even for the simplest of medical problems? And babies with fevers are the worst.*

Well, the parents *of babies with fevers are the worst*, he corrected himself. He had as much empathy for sick babies as any other doctor. But trying to explain to worried parents that their febrile baby needed an array of medical tests to rule out severe infection, and to convince the parents to consent to the testing, was a task Jack didn't relish. *Enough whining, Jack. You signed up for this.*

"Hello Mrs. Gonzalez, Mr. Gonzalez," he introduced himself as he approached the two worried-looking parents sitting in the exam area. "I'm Dr. Stanley, and I understand your baby has had a fever for the past six hours?"

"Yes Doctor, thank you for seeing us." The father stood up as his wife continued to try to nurse the baby. "We think our baby is pretty sick. He won't nurse, he's very lethargic, and when he is awake he's extremely irritable. Our pediatrician told us to bring him in and to not give him any Tylenol yet so he could be properly assessed."

Smart pediatrician, thought Jack. *At least for a baby this young.*

Jack proceeded with the exam, letting the baby stay in Mom's arms for most of it since he was currently so quiet. *Or extremely lethargic,* Jack corrected himself, his concern for this particular baby growing with every minute. He had Mom transfer the baby to the exam table so he could check out a few more things, and the baby lost it – back arching, screaming. Jack lifted the baby's head off the table to check for nuchal rigidity and … *damn. Yup. Here we go, the usual your-baby-may-have-meningitis-and-we-need-to-do-a-spinal-tap speech that I don't have to use very often but always works in the end.*

"We are worried our baby may have meningitis," offered Mr. Gonzalez, as his wife picked the baby back up. "We know it's so rare, and we didn't think it would happen to our baby. But he has all the signs."

Jack couldn't hide his surprise. *Smart parents, too.* He slid his speech back into its mental file and pulled out his spinal tap in layman's terms explanation, but Mrs. Gonzalez beat him to it.

"We know you'll probably have to do a spinal tap," Mrs. Gonzalez spoke up for the first time through her tears. "Do whatever you need to do. Just please make sure our baby is OK!" That's all she could manage before she broke down again, hugging her baby close.

"You are both right," Jack confirmed, realizing he could just get right to the point with these obviously-intelligent parents. "I am concerned about your baby. I will have the nurse start an I.V., draw some blood for testing, get a urine sample, and then I will do the spinal tap and we will probably start antibiotics right after that. And don't worry …" Jack put one hand on Dad's shoulder and his other on Mom's. "We'll do this as quickly as we can so your baby can get started on treatment, if it really is an infection."

An hour later, the spinal tap done and the Gonzalez baby's labs cooking, Jack was trying to catch a few minutes of rest in the work room before he expected the results to start coming in.

"Doctor, we have another one," said Lisa, the nurse who was also on the Gonzalez case with him, as she briefly stuck her head in through the doorway.

"Thanks, Nurse." Jack knew Lisa was one of the ER nurses with a sense of humor, and he liked to respectfully call her and a few others "Nurse," just as they liked to call him "Doctor" right back. He was smart enough to know who *really* deserved all the respect in a job like this. He caught up with her half way down the hallway.

"Another two-month-old, but I'm not as worried about this one," explained Lisa, handing Jack the iPad. "*This* baby has had all her shots. The Gonzalez baby, on the other hand, hasn't had his shots. He's a week too young to have had them yet anyway. Bad timing. But this new baby … Baby Johnson … the parents marked in the history that she's had all her shots so far."

"So it's probably *not* meningitis," Jack agreed. "Well, let's see what it is then."

Darla Johnson had never seen one of her children look this sick. Her husband was home with the other three kids, and this was her first time in an Emergency Room. Her arms, legs, and back were aching from having to bounce her child around all day and now half the night. She looked up as a middle-aged doctor approached her and introduced himself.

"Please help us," Darla begged. "She won't stop screaming!" She had to talk loudly to be heard over the baby's wailing.

"How long has she been like this?" asked Jack, watching the mom bounce back and forth, patting the baby in vain.

"Since yesterday afternoon. I don't get it. We just had her two-month checkup yesterday morning. The doctor said she was fine. As we drove home, *this* started, and she hasn't stopped screaming since. Nothing will console her. She won't take her bottle. She hasn't slept a wink, and neither have I. I just don't get it!"

"Maybe it's just colic, or gas," offered Jack. "But let's take a look ..."

Jack hadn't found anything wrong with baby number two on exam, except for the non-stop screaming. He'd discussed colic with the mom, but was now starting to rethink that diagnosis because two months was a little late for colic to just be starting. And this was way worse than just simple gas pain. He wondered ...

"The lab called with a preliminary finding on Gonzalez," announced Lisa, walking into the work room. "Gram-negative coccobacilli in the CSF. Lots of them. Consistent with Haemophilus. Full identification will take another 24 hours. And white blood cells too numerous to count. So it's definitely meningitis."

"Damn," muttered Jack, although not surprised. In fact, he'd told Lisa to get the I.V. antibiotics ready with the proper dosing just in case. "Hang the two antibiotics. I'll call the Peds floor and let them know we have an admission."

Two minutes later Jack finished explaining the case to the pediatrician hospitalist over the phone.

"Haemophilus influenza? Really? Haven't seen that in decades. Not since the HIB vaccine came out in the ... what, the late 80s?"

"Me neither," agreed Jack. "The lab isn't certain it's type B yet, of course, but we'll know tomorrow. But yeah, I don't think I've ever even seen a case of this particular bacterial meningitis. Figured it was pretty much eradicated."

"Close," said the Ped. "I was reading about it the other day. For the past decade there have only been between 10 and 25 cases of HIB meningitis every year in the United States. Not like in the 70s and 80s when I saw one every single month. Not to mention epiglottitis. Remember that? Babies coming in, barely able to breathe. That was almost scarier than the meningitis. Was really glad when this vaccine came out. Haemophilus is an interesting germ though. Type B is the strain covered by the vaccine, so we rarely see it anymore. But Haemophilus influenza type A, and nontypeable Haemophilus, are still around. They just don't make people nearly as sick. Would be nice to have a vaccine against those too."

"Thanks for the history lesson," smiled Jack. "And I agree. Not having to deal with HIB epiglottitis and meningitis anymore makes my job much easier. Although, the vaccine wouldn't have mattered in this particular case. The baby is about a week too young to have gotten it."

"Actually, you can give HIB vaccine as young as six weeks of age. But yeah, most doctors just start all the shots at the two-month checkup."

"Dang. Bad timing for this baby, I guess. I almost hope it's *not* type B. Might help the parents feel better knowing they couldn't have done anything to prevent it. Hey, speaking of 'all the shots,' can I pick your brain about a second case I have down here? I don't think it's an admission, but it's right up your alley."

"Fire away. I love talking about sick children at 4 am."

"So, I have a baby who *did* just get all her shots yesterday, and …" Jack explained the whole story.

"Sounds like a typical vaccine reaction. Happens all the time," answered the Ped. *A little too casually*, Jack thought. "Although, we don't like to call them 'reactions,' because that implies the vaccine may have actually caused what's going on. We call them 'adverse events after vaccination.' 'Cuz most of these are just coincidental anyway. Saw a lot of this back when I worked the clinic. Parents used to call back all the time because their babies were screaming. Tylenol usually did the trick."

"Well *this* particular baby is seriously screaming. Non-stop since she got here an hour ago, and according to the mom it's been over 12 hours now."

"Oh, parents always exaggerate this type of thing, you know," dismissed the Ped. "I mean, I rarely saw these babies when they were screaming 'cuz we wouldn't tell the parents to come back into the office, of course. Just Tylenol and call us in another day or two. They never did call back after that."

"I don't know if I could take this kind of thing in my own child, not that that's happening anytime soon. So, you think this could just be from the vaccines?"

"Yup. If there's nothing concerning on exam and no fever or other history of illness, just dose 'em up and ship 'em out," concluded the Peds doctor.

"Got it," agreed Jack. "And good luck with this meningitis baby. Gonzalez is the name. I'll be watching for the specific bacterial identification tomorrow because now I'm curious. See you."

Jack finished up the paperwork on the Johnson baby. He didn't know how to code the visit with a diagnosis of a suspected vaccine reaction, so he just put "colic" instead. *Close enough*, he figured.

Jim Remington was still learning the ropes in his new position as Chief of Section 2 of the Media Division at the Center for the Progress of Medicine. That downward trend on Hepatitis B vaccine uptake had kept him busy for another week, then he'd been promoted to a supervisory role, and Francine had scored the head slot for the entire Media Division. Jim much preferred delving into data and numbers himself rather than supervising others in their work to keep the public informed about disease outbreaks. But he also knew he needed to stay where the fun was, and following his boss up the ladder would keep him closer to the fun.

Jim had first scored this job here a few years ago right after Zika hit. This new and mysterious virus had been a windfall for the Center. The media division had expanded into five sections and hired on about 100 new employees, and they'd worked tirelessly to make sure the American public developed a healthy respect for Zika.

It's amazing how far one can go with a few brain-damaged babies at your disposal, Jim recalled Francine's comment when they'd chatted about this the first night he'd spent with her, which still surprised him now, even coming from her. *But she was right. The American public had bought it hook, line, and sinker. And Congress was even easier. Convince the public that their babies are in danger, scared moms start calling their Senators and Congressmen to save them, and bam! Another few billion dollars get routed to the CDC so they can go to work. Disease prevention, travel advisories, research to show how dangerous Zika is. Then several pharmaceutical companies, independently of course, begin preliminary research on a vaccine to meet the needs of the new market.*

And The Center for the Progress of Medicine was completely separated from all of that. Started in the early 90s as a small private endeavor to serve the public by keeping careful track of vaccination rates and disease trends in the United States, the Center had grown into a full-scale operation staffed by hundreds. And it wasn't government-run; it had no official ties to any government entity. It existed solely to collect data and pass it along to those who could make good use of it to serve the public good, like the media, government departments, and pharmaceutical companies. But that was controlled by the people upstairs. Literally. Jim had never met Francine's bosses, and he wasn't sure she had ever seen them face to face either. He'd heard her refer to a group called The Three, but didn't really know who or what that was. For all he knew, Francine was one of the people upstairs, but liked to work down here instead, where all the action was.

Jim had loved his prior research and stats work, and heading up a whole media section was new to him. He was a fast learner though. And Francine was amazing at this, like she was born for it. Jim suspected she'd seen to his promotion just to keep him closer to her, but he didn't mind. Not at all.

Francine had thought Zika was going to keep them busy much

longer than Ebola had. *Ebola*, reminisced Jim. *That was a few hundred million well spent, for a disease that had zero chance of spreading to the United States. But then again, fear reigns.*

And now people were beginning to realize that Zika might not be worth devoting billions of dollars to either. Much of Europe was laughing at Americans over this. The world had much bigger problems to solve: war, starvation, real actual disease outbreaks. Researchers published conflicting data: Zika causes brain damage to almost everyone who catches it; no it doesn't, it's harmless to virtually everyone. So some of the money had dried up, and the Media Division had taken a hit. They were now down to only three Sections (out of the original five). But there was still plenty of work for them. Media has never had fewer than two Sections. It's hard work to keep 350 million Americans informed.

Before Zika, there was measles, briefly. But the higher ups knew that measles outbreaks are very short-lived, even when they start somewhere like Disneyland. They tried to make the most of it, focusing on debunked autism myths and disgraced doctors. Then they got lucky with the Somalis in Minnesota. But that didn't end up going anywhere either. Only 70 or so had gotten infected, and they expected way more than that in such an unvaccinated population. And of course, no deaths. *Thank God.*

Francine had made another comment back then that had surprised Jim: *There's nothing like a good death or two to get all the nay-sayers to rush into the doctor to get their damn shots.* He knew she would never actually wish for any deaths, but wondered if she had a point. *Would an occasional death or two help keep vaccine rates higher?* Jim knew very little about any of this back when he was just a numbers guy. *Maybe this whole media thing is more fascinating.* Interesting or not, he had work to do. He browsed through the day's news stories but found nothing. *Is it too early for lunch?* he wondered. *Crap. It's only 11:30?*

Jim's phone rang. He waited until the fourth ring to pick it up so he'd look busy.

"Jim, it's Tony. I've got something for you."

Tony was still one of the underlings stuck in research and stats, and he was always among the first to know about any disease outbreaks.

"Lemme guess. More measles? Maybe chickenpox? A new flu strain?"

"Nope," answered Tony.

Jim could actually hear the excitement over the phone line. *What the hell?* "OK, just spit it out. I'm hungry and not in the mood."

"Meningitis," Tony revealed.

Jim rolled his eyes. "That's all? Dude, there are like a dozen different causes of meningitis, and we don't even have vaccines against most of them. And meningococcal meningitis is pretty much a constant in our country, although a very rare constant. Section 1 handles meningococcal disease anyway. So why are you calling me?"

"Not just any meningitis, Jim. HIB meningitis. I'm talking Haemophilus influenza type B."

"Hemi what? Influenza? You mean, the flu?"

"No. Haemophilus influenza is a bacterium. And type B is the most dangerous type, apparently. I didn't even know anything about it until I got the laboratory alert from Washington State. I had to look it up."

"So what does this have to do with me? One case of meningitis does not a news story make. Unless ..." Jim sat up in his chair. "Unless the baby died! Oh God, did he die?"

"Thank God, no. But it's still usable. The kid was unvaccinated."

Ahhhhh, there it is, Jim realized. The possible media angles were already starting to spin in his head, and he knew Francine would get seriously excited over this. And when she got excited ... Jim snapped out of it. He'd think about *that* later.

"I already emailed you the details," Jim heard Tony explaining. "But I thought it was worth a phone call too."

"Thanks buddy." Jim hung up the phone. *So much for a long lunch.* He'd schedule a group meeting for his people and Francine right away. They'd probably work all day on this and into the night. He just hoped Francine wouldn't be too tired when he drove her back to her place later. But then again, she seemed to have the *most* energy whenever a health crisis came their way.

"Ok people, listen up," Francine's commanding presence brought the room to order. "You've all read the summary on baby Pablo Gonzalez. He's out of the hospital and is doing very well. He was one lucky little baby. Apparently his parents are pretty smart, suspected he had meningitis, and went to the ER right away. As you all know, meningitis can be pretty bad, especially HIB meningitis, if diagnosis and treatment are delayed. Although it has one of the lower fatality rates of the various meningitis diseases, only about 5%, it does have a 25% complication rate. According to the hospital records, the baby didn't pass his hearing test in his right ear the day before being discharged. So we will definitely want to play up the hearing loss angle. It's been a while since we had any HIB to play with. Were any of you around in 2008 when this department last had to deal with it?"

A middle-aged man raised his hand. "Anthony Appleton, ma'am," he announced. "Been around a while. Back in '08 we had four kids die from HIB meningitis in Minnesota, including a four-year-old who wasn't vaccinated. We got national coverage for weeks with the message that HIB disease was on the rise and that it can spread like an epidemic. HIB vaccine acceptance went way up, especially in Minnesota and the surrounding states. But since then, it's been fairly quiet."

Francine wondered what Anthony was still doing here as a low-level media jockey. *Maybe he just has no ambition,* she thought. "OK. Well, for Gonzalez, we'll start with the local evening news. They should be headed out to the family's home as we speak. We'll play up the hearing loss, but we have to make a decision on two other competing angles. I'm not sure whether we paint him as an *unvaccinated* baby, or if we spin the angle that he is *too young to be vaccinated yet.* Both are true, although the second choice is more true. The HIB vaccine isn't really on the schedule until 2 months, and this baby was only 7 weeks old. But the CDC does allow early vaccination – as early as 6 weeks. So, he could have been vaccinated if he'd had an early checkup. But that may be pushing things a bit. Both angles have value, but in this case we have to pick one because we obviously can't say both. Jim, did you get anything useful from the focus group data?"

"Yes, actually," Jim sat up straighter. "This department tested the question on several different focus groups during Disneyland. The data I could find were very clear: people showed a lot more sympathy toward an infected baby who was too young to be vaccinated yet, compared to a child who caught the disease because the parents had chosen not to vaccinate. Although, these focus groups were dealing with measles, not meningitis. No one's ever run any scenarios on infant meningitis because it's too rare."

"And we don't have time to run a fresh focus group now." Francine looked a bit frustrated. She nodded toward Anthony, who had raised his hand again. *Geeze, what is this? Kindergarten?*

"I was part of those group sessions. And what was interesting, but I don't think made it into the summary analysis, was the anger factor. While it was true that the public had a lot more sympathy toward babies who were less than 1 and couldn't get the measles vaccine yet, they were also a lot more angry at whoever caught the disease and then exposed a young vulnerable baby. Angrier compared to their general feelings toward unvaccinated children. It was like, the public accepted the fact that some families choose not to vaccinate, and don't think it's a big deal, especially since they feel safe because their own kids are vaccinated. But throw a little baby into the mix who was too young to get a vaccine, and an unvaccinated kid infects that baby? Whoa. Watch out. That really struck some nerves. And people were scrambling to catch up on their missing MMR vaccines for over a year."

"Well HIB doesn't spread around like measles," corrected Francine, still wondering why Anthony, who seemed to know his stuff, was still in this low-level position. "And we don't even know who infected this baby. HIB usually just strikes randomly, out of nowhere, without a source. It doesn't cause outbreaks." Francine held up her hand for quiet so she could think for a minute. Anthony's hand interrupted her thoughts. "Yes Anthony?"

"The outbreak angle had a huge effect during the '08 HIB cases in Minnesota. The public really bought headlines like 'Worst meningitis outbreak in 20 years' and 'Resurgence of infant meningitis.'"

"Well, if we see more cases, we'll play that up of course," agreed Francine. "Maybe we'll plant that idea. However, parents are smarter than they used to be thanks to the F-ing internet, so we have to be careful. Let me think …

"For now, I think it's too risky to play the unvaccinated angle, as some may realize the age discrepancy. Let's play up the fact that this poor little baby was too young to have gotten his first shots yet. That should help us get more on-time vaccination compliance as well as an uptake specifically for HIB vaccine. Who covers the supply pipeline?"

Anthony raised his hand. *Hmmm,* wondered Francine. *I wonder if Mr. Appleton has his hand in the cookie jar and that's why he's stayed in his current position for so long.* "OK. You will let the pharmaceutical companies know to increase HIB vaccine production? I think they will be able to bank on at least a 10% boon for the next 6 months." *And so will you, you lucky bastard.* Although Francine knew she had her own ways to make bonuses as well.

"OK team. I will handle the local news story myself, just to make sure they get it right. We need to downplay some of the facts, like how rare HIB really is. And let's just call it 'infant meningitis' without trying to confuse people with medical jargon. Social media team, reach out to all your bloggers and have them start spreading stories about the dangers of meningitis. Broadcast news team, once the local coverage airs, get on the phone to the regional and national producers so they can run with it. Print news, you know what to do as well. By this time tomorrow, I want every little mommy in America who hasn't given her baby a HIB vaccine in tears. Real tears, people!"

Meeting over and back at his desk, Anthony called his stock broker. Gerry had always warned him not to send emails, since they were easier to trace back.

"Ger, it's Anthony. Can you see if you can scrounge up about 10K worth of stock in the top three? I have this feeling …"

Sara Sanderson held one hand over her ear as she listened intently on her cell phone in the passenger seat of the News 17 van.

"Infant meningitis … Used to affect 20,000 American children every year … Virtually eradicated since the vaccine's introduction in the 80s … Vulnerable infants … Check with your doctor to make sure your baby is up to date on all vaccines … Safe and Effective, of course … First reported case in Washington in over 5 years … Resurgence of this fatal infection? … OK, I got it. Pretty much the usual. Thanks for the heads-up, Francy."

Sara hung up and glanced at her notes, barely legible due to the rural road she found herself riding down on a Saturday afternoon. Tommy, her cameraman/driver/sound guy was probably hitting every bump on purpose during the phone call as he always liked to do when she was doing her homework on the way to a story. She sat back in her seat, unwilling to accuse him of sabotage because that would start up a conversation with the world's most annoying small-talker. Sara wanted to collect her thoughts and get this story right. She pulled up the Gonzalez's address on her maps app just to make sure Tommy knew where he was going. Her phone estimated she had about ten minutes until showtime.

Reuben Gonzalez turned the minivan into the rural neighborhood development, glad to almost be home. Although the past ten days in the hospital with baby Pablo had been trying, the course of treatment and his recovery had ended up feeling fairly routine. Paulina was a trooper and held the baby the whole time, nursing him so much that the nurses turned off the continuous I.V. drip the second day. After that it was simply a matter of twice daily I.V. antibiotics. Pablo perked up after two days and now seemed like nothing had ever happened.

Except for the failed hearing test in one ear, Reuben corrected himself. That came as a surprise. The doctor told them they do see it in a very small percentage of HIB meningitis cases. *But on the bright side, he only suffered about 50% hearing loss in that ear, and the other ear is fine.*

He looked at his wife in the rear-view mirror, sitting in the back seat next to the baby. He missed the days when she sat up front next to him in his Dodge Charger. *Getting rid of that for this minivan was still painful,* he thought. *But not as painful as losing Pablo would have been. I wonder if Paulina and I are making the right decision about vaccines?*

The couple kept their plans secret while in the hospital. They knew that none of the staff blamed them for Pablo's illness because he just so happened to catch it a week before his first vaccines were due. *I wonder what they would have said if Pablo caught this vaccine-preventable disease a few weeks* after *we'd skipped his shots,* he mused. He didn't even want to think about that.

Paulina and Reuben Gonzalez had spent months researching vaccines during their pregnancy. They read three books, and as much CDC information as they could, filtering out what was obvious propaganda and absorbing all the pertinent real medical information. They concluded that the risks of getting the entire schedule of 70 childhood vaccine doses, 24 of which were grouped into the first six months of life, were higher than the dangers presented by the diseases the vaccines were designed to prevent. In other words, the statistical likelihood of suffering a severe vaccine reaction was much higher than the statistical likelihood that baby Pablo would catch a severe case of a disease and be harmed, or killed, by it. At least that's what he and his wife concluded. They'd considered getting a few of the most important shots, one of which was HIB, but since it was so incredibly rare they'd decided they would opt out for the first year or two, then see how they felt.

So, how do you feel now, Reuben? he asked himself. *Did you make the right call? Did you make the right decision that would protect your baby from harm, or did you put him in danger by not vaccinating?*

It was easy to answer this *now,* since Pablo is basically alright. They could live with some moderate hearing loss. *But what I couldn't live with is a severe vaccine reaction if we rolled the dice that way and he suffered harm,* he told himself honestly. *We are making the right choice, and we are educated enough to recognize when our baby got sick. We sought treatment right away, and now he's fine. We are good parents who are just trying to make the best, safest decision we can.*

He knew Paulina felt less sure about their plan to skip all vaccines, given that Pablo had now caught one such disease. But she was still dealing with the guilt of 'letting her baby catch meningitis,' as she put it. *That's how she sees it. No one else blames her, especially me. But what mom wouldn't feel guilty when her baby has to go through something like this? It's good to be the dad, I guess. Less guilt, less work, but more responsibility.*

He looked forward to asking Dr. Tommaso what he thought about their choice when they saw him for a follow-up appointment in a few days. He already seemed pretty understanding of their decision when they asked about vaccines at their newborn checkup. But Reuben wondered if the doctor would …

"What the!" he exclaimed as he pulled up to their house.

Sara watched as the Gonzalezes, she assumed, pulled into the driveway of their mid-size suburban home.

"Here they are, Tommy. Start rolling."

Sara knew she technically wasn't supposed to follow the minivan up the driveway onto their private property, but she figured this family wouldn't know the law. Plus, they needed to get some close-up shots to really capture the human side of the story.

"Hello, Mr. Gonzalez," she started as the thirty-something man got out of the driver's seat of the minivan, making sure she stayed slightly to the side so Tommy could get them all in the shot. "I'm Sara Sanderson with News 17. Do you mind if I ask you a few questions about your baby's battle with meningitis?"

"Um, how did you …" Mr. Gonzalez trailed off, looking uncertainly from Sara to the camera and back.

"We received word that your baby caught what used to be a rare form of infant meningitis that now seems to be on the rise again. How is your baby doing?"

The sliding door of the minivan began to open, but Mr. Gonzalez put his hand out to stop the door from opening further.

"Thank you for asking, umm, Ms. Sanderson did you say? Our baby is doing just fine and we are happy to be home."

Quick recovery, Sara thought. *He seems pretty confident and comfortable in front of a camera, but I don't think he's going to give me very long.*

"I understand your little one is too young to have started his vaccines yet. How do you feel that someone, somewhere, must have exposed him to this deadly disease?"

"Ms. Sanderson," he seemed to stand up a little straighter and moved protectively in front of the gap in the door as Tommy swung around to try to get a shot of mom and baby inside. "Thank you so much for your concern. Yes, this has been a tough week for our family. We are happy to be home, and we would appreciate you respecting our privacy, and our property, and allowing us to get settled back into our lives."

Damn, she thought. *He said both "P" words.* Sara knew that nothing shot after this point would be legally usable, so she decided she'd better cut her loses so there'd at least be *some* humanizing footage. She turned to Tommy and gave him the "cut" sign.

As she started to back away down the driveway to demonstrate her good will, she followed up with "Your baby just turned two months while in the hospital. I assume you are looking forward to beginning his two-month vaccinations so that you don't have to go through something like this ever again?" *Bam!* She smiled.

"Good afternoon, Ms. Sanderson. And again, thank you for your obvious concern."

Darla Johnson was annoyed at the wait. Not only did she have to sit in the busy waiting room for a half hour, she then had to wait for the pediatrician in the exam room for another 20 minutes. She heard a knock on the door, and in walked Dr. Jones.

"Hello Mrs. Johnson. Let's see how Sage is doing."

Darla watched the doctor do a quick exam and consult the electronic chart on his laptop.

"Looks like Sage is doing well. About average size on the growth chart compared to other four-month-olds. Is she rolling over front to back and back to front?"

"Almost," answered Darla. "I see her trying every day."

"Ok. So today's vaccines are a repeat of the last visit: DTaP, HIB, Pneumococcal, Rotavirus, Polio, and hepatitis B."

"Umm, Dr. Jones. Do you think she'll scream all night again like she did last time? That was pretty rough."

"What's that now?" The doctor looked confused.

"At two months, the night we got the first vaccines, she ended up in the ER because she was so fussy. They told me it was a normal reaction, gave her Tylenol, and later she was fine." Darla was surprised he didn't know. *Didn't they call him? Didn't the ER send records so he would know?* She assumed they would have.

"Ok, start from the beginning. Tell me what happened." The doctor glanced at his watch as he said this.

Darla explained quickly how Sage started screaming within minutes of the shot on their drive home, screamed non-stop all afternoon and evening, and what had happened at the ER.

"How soon were things back to normal?" he asked.

"Well, she was fine about an hour after they gave her Tylenol. Then she slept for three days and barely took her bottle. That was a nice break. I got more rest in those three days than I have in the past four months."

"Yeah, that sounds pretty typical. Babies often react that way to their shots. It's nothing to worry about," Dr. Jones reassured her as he stood up.

"Ok …" Darla was a little doubtful. *But the doctor would know,* she told herself.

Darla waited another 15 minutes for the nurse to bring in baby Sage's shots.

God, I hope she doesn't scream all night again, she thought. *That was awful, and I don't want to spend another night in the ER. And they didn't even have to do anything. Geeze, I could have squirted that Tylenol into her mouth better than that nurse did.*

Darla was glad Sage became such an easy baby after that. For the first two months of her life she seemed hungry all the time and wanted to be held a lot. She'd been a lot of work … always wanting something. But ever since that night of screaming at two months, she'd changed for the better. The ER doctor told her the screaming was just an expected reaction to the vaccines and that she'd be fine in a few days. *And he was right!* She smiled. *More than right. Sage has been a piece of cake ever since. Could the screaming actually have changed something? Well, Dr. Jones isn't concerned.*

Her reverie was interrupted by a knock on the door, and in swept the nurse with a tray full of syringes.

Nurse Jamie Anderson preferred doing the shots for Dr. Tommaso's patients. She liked only having to give one or two shots at a time. But she was stuck with Dr. Jones today, and sighed as she carried the tray into the exam room.

"Hello Mrs. Johnson. And how is little Sage doing today?"

"Great. The doctor says she's doing just fine. Meeting all her milestones. Growing well. I sure hope she doesn't scream all night from these shots again. This time I already gave her Tylenol before we came in."

"Good idea," Jamie agreed. She knew that some crying was expected. She also knew that non-stop inconsolable screaming for three or more hours was *not* expected. In fact, it meant a baby was having an encephalitis reaction, or brain swelling and inflammation. *Well, Dr. Jones ordered the shots, so he must have figured the patient's first reaction wasn't bad enough to worry about. Plus, moms always exaggerate. And if the baby had an encephalitis reaction, or "screaming all night" like mom said, she'd probably have gone to the ER, and they would have told her not to repeat the vaccines. I don't want to worry her more by asking her about it.* "I'm sure she'll be just fine."

"Ambulance coming in," announced Lisa. "Wake up, sleepy!"

Jack lifted his head up off the desk. "I'm awake."

It was a quiet night in the ER. Jack preferred busy. It made the night pass more quickly.

"What is it?" he asked, jogging to catch up with the nurse.

"Little baby having a seizure is all I know."

Jack saw the ambulance bay double doors open at the end of the hallway to admit two paramedics wheeling a stretcher, followed by a woman whom he assumed was the mother. *She looks familiar.*

He followed the stretcher into the trauma area and took a look at the apparently sleeping baby. *Good color, steady breathing.* Jack let out a sigh of relief and looked up at one of the paramedics.

"Four-month-old female had an apparent febrile seizure. We estimate it lasted about 3 minutes. Was post-ictal but stable when we got there. Rectal temp was 104.7. We provided cooling measures on the ride over. Vitals have otherwise been stable."

Jack leaned in for a closer survey of the baby, listening and feeling around to confirm she was ok for now. *Muscle tone's a bit low, but steady heart rate and breathing. Pupils reactive. And arousable,* he confirmed as the baby started to squirm in response to Jack's prodding. Jack stood up and looked around for the mother.

"This is Mrs. Johnson," offered the paramedic, guiding the woman forward.

"Is she ok?" asked the familiar face.

Johnson. Jack remembered. *About two months ago. The screaming baby who was fine.* "Hello again, Mrs. Johnson. I'm Dr. Stanley. I saw you and your baby a couple of months ago. Yes, she looks fine now. We'll give her some more Tylenol to bring the fever down, then decide what more we may need to do. But first, start from the beginning and tell me everything that happened."

"We just had our check-up today, like the last time we came here. But this time she didn't scream or cry all day. She did the opposite. She just slept. Didn't even wake up for her dream-feed bottle at 11. Around 2 a.m. I heard something on the video monitor, but I couldn't really see her very well. So I went into her room and she was shaking from head to toe. I picked her up and she was on fire. My husband called 911. It took forever for them to get to us. The baby stopped shaking at some point and has just been sleeping until now."

"Sounds like an uncomplicated febrile seizure. I know it's very scary when it happens. But ultimately these things are pretty harmless. Let me do a full exam and we'll decide if we need to do anything." Jack was glad for something interesting to do. It sure beat having Lisa catch him napping again.

"Oh. My. God," vented Darla, sitting in the front passenger seat as her husband drove them back home a few hours later. "Why does this keep happening?"

Arthur Johnson was a calm person. Nothing rattled him. Being a father of now-four kids, he learned to let the little things go. And the Doc had assured them that this was, indeed, no big deal.

"Honey, the Doc said it's fine. These fever seizure things happen all the time. And they're harmless, right? Sage is fine now. Just look at her still sleeping back there in her car seat. The fever's gone. Just relax."

"But why did she get such a high fever? Almost 105! She's never had a fever like that, not even when she had that cold and cough last month. I bet it's those damn shots, that's what it is. Dr. Jones said she might get a fever, but he never said something like *this* could happen."

"Yeah, but the ER Doc said the vaccines aren't really technically what caused the seizure, remember? He said it was the fever. And he said the fever might not even be from the vaccines. The baby probably has a virus too. What'd he call it? Rosalia or something?"

"Roseola," corrected Darla, rolling her eyes. *Geeze, I'm the medical one in this family.* She already pulled up febrile seizures and Roseola on her phone when still at the ER after the doctor explained it all. "But febrile seizures usually don't start until 6 months, and neither does Roseola. And what, it's more likely our baby just happened to get sick tonight than it is that the vaccines caused the seizure? What if the doctor is wrong?"

"He was right the last time you rushed in just because she was crying." He knew it was a mistake as the last few words left his mouth, and cringed.

"Are you F-ing kidding me Artie? 'Just because she was crying?' She was screaming non-stop all day and half the night. That's not normal, and neither was this seizure."

Darla didn't feel nearly as smart as she used to be. She'd come to accept that fact after her second child. Motherhood seemed to have sucked some of the IQ right out of her. But she was determined to get to the bottom of *this*, because this involved her baby. She knew her inner genius wouldn't fail her now.

It had been a week since the seizure, and Sage still wasn't the same. She'd stopped smiling, the sparkle in her eye was gone, and what little eye contact she did manage was fleeting. On the other hand, she was still a great sleeper and was more calm and quiet than ever.

Arthur tried to reassure her that the baby was fine, but Darla knew better. And she had the pictures to prove it – pictures from before two months, from before that first ER visit … from before those first vaccines. She scrolled through her camera roll on the phone, reminiscing. The look on Sage's face in the pictures after two months was just … dull. Then after three months the sparkle returned, and Darla lingered on the series of smiles and shiny eyes from just a few weeks ago.

And now … Darla shook herself. *No. No more crying. I have work to do.* She opened up Google on her laptop and typed in "vaccines." She saw that a link to the Centers for Disease Control and Prevention was the first to pop up. *I know them – the CDC. They know all about vaccines.* She saw several articles that reassured her vaccines are safe, vaccines are effective, and that vaccines save lives. *I've seen that a lot on the news. So that's where those statements come from? The CDC? But that's not what happened to Sage. They didn't seem safe to my child. In fact, they didn't save her life, they threatened it.* Darla searched again, but this time "vaccine side effects." The first link, again, was from the Centers for Disease Control and Prevention. *Well, they are in charge of vaccines, I think. Let's see what they say about side effects.* She touched the link and a page opened up that read "Possible side-effects from vaccines," and seemed to list every vaccine.

She browsed through some of the vaccines that she was familiar with and was surprised to see the words "a vaccine, like any medicine, is capable of causing serious problems." She went to Hep A vaccine. *I think that was one they gave Sage, right?* "As with any medicine, there is a very remote chance of a vaccine causing a serious injury or death." And Hep B: "Serious reactions are also possible." MMR: "Is capable of causing serious problems … the risk of MMR vaccine causing serious harm or death is extremely small." *Small? How small? What do they consider extremely small? Is their definition of a small risk the same as mine?* Then more on the MMR: " …include severe allergic reactions and problems such as deafness, long-term seizures, coma, lowered consciousness, and permanent brain damage." *WTF?* Even chicken pox vaccine: "Other serious problems, including severe brain reactions and low platelet count."

Wait. How can they say vaccines are safe, vaccines save lives, and then have all this small print that warns about brain damage and death? So what exactly do they mean by "safe?"

And I don't even know what vaccines she had. Geeze, what's wrong with me? I let them give my baby a few shots and didn't even know what they were giving her? Just like I did with our first three kids. Oh yeah, the vaccine card! She reached for her purse hanging on the chair next to her at the dining room table. There was the folded yellow card, wrapped in a plastic sheath. She pulled it out and opened it up. On it she saw a series of vaccines with dates hand-written in, along with Valley View Pediatrics stamped next to each. The dates corresponded to Sage being two months and four months old. There was even a date from the day she was born, written in next to hepatitis B. *That's weird,* she thought. *I don't remember her getting a vaccine when she was born. And I certainly don't remember anyone asking me if I wanted her to have a vaccine. Not even during the few days she spent in the NICU because of that fever on the second day. Wait, isn't hepatitis B an STD? What the hell? I don't have hep B. Why would they give her that? Could Arty have hep B? Could the doctor at the hospital have ordered that vaccine because Arty has it?*

No, if Arty had hepatitis B, I would know it. So why? She chided herself to stay focused. *Vaccine side effects.* She saw HIB vaccine listed on the yellow card, then clicked on HIB on the website and saw the list of side effects. Redness, swelling, fever, nothing that seemed like any big deal. She went back and tapped on another vaccine – PCV 13. *What is that? Never heard of it.* She knew she'd have to go back and read more about the actual diseases. This shot had a slightly longer list of side effects: "About half become drowsy and have a temporary loss of appetite," she read. *No crap!*

She wondered why no one warned her to expect that if it was going to happen to *half* of babies. "Swelling … Fever … 1 in 20 will have fever over 102.2." Then, "8 out of 10 become fussy or irritable."

It's as if Sage read these side effects and decided to have them all. No wonder the ER doctor said at the first ER trip that this was all normal and expected. But why on earth didn't Dr. Jones even tell me? If half are going to stop eating and most are going to get fussy, why not tell me to expect that? Would have saved me that first trip to the ER.

Darla scanned through the rest of that page, not noticing anything pertinent, until one word caught her eye – seizure. "Young children who get the PCV 13 vaccine at the same time as a flu shot may be at increased risk for seizures caused by fever." She grabbed the card to see if Sage had also gotten a flu shot that day. But no, the flu section of the card was blank. *I gotta remember to not get a flu shot with this PCV 13 vaccine. But I'm sure Dr. Jones knows that, doesn't he?* She wrote the word seizure next to the flu shot and PCV sections of the card so she wouldn't forget. *But why did Sage have a seizure with* these *shots?*

She moved on to rotavirus vaccine, not knowing what that disease was either. There was the same warning about irritability. But then, *Intussusception?* She had to read the explanation a few times, and realized that Sage hadn't had any signs of intestinal blockage. But, "there is a small risk of intuss … whatever … from the rotavirus vaccine … may occur in 1 in 20,000 babies who get the vaccine." *I wonder how many babies* that *happens to every year? Wait, I can figure that out. I know we have about 4 million babies born every year in the U.S. How would I do that math? Divide 4 million by 20,000.* Darla pulled out her phone and swiped open the calculator. *200. Wow. 200 babies needing intestinal surgery to relieve a blockage every year? From a vaccine?* But Darla was no longer feeling "surprised" by any of this. What she was feeling was *anger.* Anger that she hadn't even once been informed about any of these risks. *And I gave all these to my first three kids as well, and didn't know a single thing about any of them.*

Stop that, Darla. You're not going to guilt yourself over this. It's not your fault. The doctor is supposed to warn you about all this, isn't he? Or the nurse? Darla knew she wouldn't be able to avoid the guilt forever. But it was anger that was her fuel now.

She kept reading to the end of rotavirus and was re-surprised all over again. "There is a remote chance of a vaccine causing a serious injury or death." *Remote again? How remote? If there is even a chance of that, why would anyone … People just don't know. They have no idea. I certainly didn't. Has Sage suffered a serious injury? Did she fall victim to this "remote" chance? And why didn't the other vaccine pages give the same warning?*

She scrolled back to the previous vaccines and was shocked to see that all the other ones also had the exact same warning and she hadn't even noticed. And she saw something else. "This information is based on the rotavirus VIS." *What's a VIS?* She tapped on it and continued to read.

And Darla Johnson hadn't yet even begun to unravel what exactly did happen to her baby. But she would, though, two vaccines later, right there in black and white on the CDC Vaccine Information Statement for the DTaP vaccine. A sheet she was supposed to have been given to read twice so far at her pediatrician's office, and wasn't. Darla was about to learn another new word … encephalitis. And she wasn't going to like it.

Arthur Johnson hit the snooze button on the alarm clock. He wasn't sure if this was the first or second snooze, and was just about to not care and go back to sleep when he realized he was alone in the bed. *Darla usually sleeps in later than I do. Maybe the baby woke her up early?*

He rolled out of bed and grabbed his bathrobe, knowing that if the baby was up, he'd better get up too. The rest of the kids should still be asleep on this Saturday morning. As he walked down the hallway, he saw the baby's bedroom door was still closed. Shrugging, he continued toward the kitchen. He noticed the absence of the bacon and pancakes aroma that used to waft through the house on Saturday mornings … a long time ago. Nowadays weekend breakfasts had become his job. Not that he minded.

Arthur noticed his wife sitting at the kitchen table, her head resting on her arms, her computer open, her purse lying on its side with its contents half-strewn about, and a half-empty cup of coffee within reach. She was asleep, as evidenced by the little puddle of drool on the table near her open mouth. He watched her for several long seconds, saw her shoulders rise and fall with each breath, and sighed happily. He tiptoed up and kissed her on the head. Then again, longer. He felt her stir slightly, stretch, then he had to jump back as she sat up quickly and looked around.

"Good morning, sleepy head," he greeted her, and leaned in for a hug. "You know, I think all the kids are still asleep ... the baby too ... and ..."

"Arty, you're not going to believe what I found last night!" Darla exclaimed, surprisingly awake, and completely oblivious to her husband's too-subtle hint. Or simply too focused on whatever last night's mission had been to think about anything else.

"Sit down, sit down. Let me show you," his wife continued. "Wait, you better have some coffee first."

Darla jumped up and strode over to the coffee pot, still half-full and warm. "You are right, honey, it *is* a good thing all the kids are still asleep, because I need your undivided attention."

You were going to have it, he sighed. *All kinds of undivided attention.* "Ok Princess, what is it?" he asked as he took the warm mug of coffee and sat down at the table.

Darla sat down next to him and pulled up the CDC website. "Here is what is called a Vaccine Information Statement. It's from the Centers for Disease Control, and it's a two-page summary of the pros and cons of each vaccine. It explains the risk of the disease, then the side effects of the vaccine, and any warnings you should be aware of regarding that vaccine."

"Why would there be any warnings? These things are perfectly safe and effective. You hear that on the news all the time."

"Good question. They say they are safe and effective out of one side of their mouths, then quietly provide dozens of pages of warnings and side effects. It's like the TV commercials: the guy that talks so fast and quietly about all the warnings of death if you take this drug, and to ask your doctor if this purple pill is right for you. And our doctor didn't tell us anything," said Darla angrily. "Sorry. I've been processing this all night, and you are just hearing this for the first time. Ok, so here is the VIS for what is called the DTaP vaccine."

"The VIS for the what vaccine?"

"The Vaccine Information Statement. Come on, Arty. Keep up. For the diphtheria, tetanus, and pertussis vaccine. This is the VIS version the CDC used since 2007 up through this year. They just updated it last week, so some of this is different on the CDC website now. Read this section titled "Some children should not get DTaP vaccine or should wait."

Arthur read on. "Don't vaccinate if your baby is really sick – *duh*. Don't vaccinate if there's been a life-threatening allergic reaction to a previous dose – *duh again*. If a child suffered a brain disease within 7 days of the vaccine – *seriously?* These are all so obvious reasons why someone wouldn't get the vaccine again. Why even bother having this as a warning?"

"Keep reading Arthur," Darla said patiently.

"Talk with your doctor if your child 1. Had a seizure or collapsed after a dose of DTaP, 2. Cried non-stop for 3 hours or more after a dose of DTaP, or 3. Had a fever over 105 degrees F after a dose of DTaP. Ok. Wait, Sage had a seizure. So what does it mean 'talk with your doctor if your child had a seizure?'"

"Keep reading below that."

"Some of these children should not get another dose of pertussis vaccine. So, sounds like we shouldn't do another dose of this vaccine then?"

"Arthur, I want you to reason through this yourself, and see if you can reach the same conclusion I did. Sage got this vaccine twice, once at 2 months and once at 4 months. Think about what happened each time, and read the warnings again."

Arthur did as instructed, reading through the list of … *Wait. Non-stop crying for three or more hours … Sage did that after the first dose. Some of these children should not get another dose … ask your doctor for more information …* "When you went in for Sage's 4-month appointment, did you ask Dr. Jones about this? Did you tell him about Sage's hours of screaming and your trip to the ER?"

"Yes," managed Darla, through the start of her tears. "I told him all about it. He said it was a normal reaction."

"But the CDC says right here some children are not supposed to get the vaccine again if that happens. Which children? How would we know? Wouldn't Dr. Jones know? Maybe he thought it through and decided Sage isn't in that group of 'some children who shouldn't get another dose.'"

"No, I don't think it's that at all, Arty," said Darla quietly. "I think it's that Dr. Jones doesn't even know about these warnings. I don't think he even knows what non-stop crying for 3 or more hours actually indicates, because I did tell him exactly what Sage did. I think he is completely in the dark about these vaccine side effects and warnings."

"Didn't he learn this stuff in medical school?"

"Obviously not. There's a federal law that mandates Dr. Jones was supposed to give us these forms to read. He didn't. And then he ignored the very warnings from the CDC about the danger of re-peating this vaccine in babies who have had such reactions. Even the vaccine package insert on the FDA website gives the same warnings. But that's not the only problem. The VIS that I just had you read was an older version. The CDC just changed it last week – last week! And they removed the warning about not repeating the vaccine if your child suffered three or more hours of non-stop screaming or fever over 105. They left in the warnings about seizures, but took out the non-stop crying and high fever, as if they don't want parents to know those are serious problems."

"If he broke federal law, can't we report him or something?"

"Absolutely. I am going to report him to the medical board for this. But technically he isn't required to follow this federal law be-cause most states, including ours, have a law that says doctors are not required to give informed consent for vaccines - specifically just for vaccines. Like, they have to give informed consent for every other medical treatment they provide, but not vaccines. So the state law gets them off the hook from the federal law. Even if I report him, I doubt anything will happen."

"But if enough patients report him for this, he'd get the message, right? Maybe start paying more attention to vaccine reactions."

"Good point."

"And what about all the rest of the reactions listed on this sheet below that?" continued Arthur, not really asking a question. "There are mild problems that seem to occur in about 1 in 4 kids: fever, redness, swelling. *That's* probably what you could call *normal*. Tired, poor appetite in 1 in 10 kids ... and Sage. Wait, seizures are only 1 in 14,000?"

"For this vaccine, yes. But another vaccine – MMR/Chickenpox – has a seizure risk of 1 in 1250, according to the old VIS. The new VIS, changed 6 months ago, doesn't have the statistic."

"Did Sage have those shots too?"

"No. Those aren't until 12 months. But there's no way I'm letting her have those, not with a seizure risk like that."

"And the seizure reaction that was supposed to be only 1 in 14,000 just so happened to hit Sage. But what's so bad with this 'non-stop crying for three hours' reaction that she had with the first shots anyway?"

"The CDC VIS form categorizes it as a moderate reaction, but just as serious as seizures," explained Darla, pointing to the screen. "That's because non-stop, inconsolable crying for 3 or more hours is a symptom of vaccine-induced encephalitis."

"Encephalitis?" Arthur looked confused. "That has something to do with the brain."

"Yes. It means brain swelling and inflammation," continued Darla. "It wasn't easy to figure that out. It took me about an hour of reading various medical websites. That's because there are many different infectious causes of encephalitis, like viruses and parasites. Those cases are much more severe and require hospitalization and advanced medical treatment. But vaccine-induced encephalitis is usually milder, so it is rarely recognized. But it's still brain swelling and inflammation, no matter how you look at it. And it's not ok, in my opinion. I even found a recent article in a medical journal called Pediatrics, July 2018. It's right here," she clicked on the next browser tab. "'Safer pertussis vaccines for children: trading efficacy for safety.' This article describes how the old DTP vaccine caused four particularly-harmful reactions: high fever over 105, febrile seizures, prolonged crying, and acute encephalopathy. It was so bad they had to stop using the vaccine and swap it out for the newer DTaP. The newer one doesn't work as well, but it's less likely to cause these severe reactions. But, even the DTaP vaccine can trigger these, and that's what happened to Sage: fever, non-stop inconsolable crying for hours, and febrile seizure. I'll show you a website that has a short video on how to recognize vaccine reactions like this later too - from Immunity Education Group or something like that."

"So why doesn't it just say 'encephalitis' or 'brain swelling and inflammation' on the CDC website, so people would know?"

Darla just waited.

"They don't want people to know. They can't say brain swelling or brain anything occurs, because no one would get the vaccine. And then Sage had an even worse reaction because we repeated the shot; the very reaction that it warns about right here – a seizure!" finished Arthur.

"Exactly," smiled Darla, through the tears, relieved that her husband saw the same thing she did. She watched her husband continue to read, and knew what part he was coming to.

"This encephalitis is one in a thousand?!" he nearly shouted. "If I had known they were going to give my baby a shot that had a 1 in 1000 chance of making her brain swell, I sure as hell wouldn't have let them do it. And I see they've totally removed that number from the new VIS on the CDC website. They want people to think it's extremely rare. And no wonder they only publicly call it 'non-stop crying for 3 hours.' That way they can get away with it seeming harmless, and they don't scare people away from the vaccine. But they are lying! And screaming and seizures are supposed to be warnings not to repeat the vaccine again!"

Arthur stood up and started pacing. "So Dr. Jones not only broke the law, he put our child in danger. Thank God the seizure was brief, and she hasn't had another one. Thank God Sage is ok."

Darla's tears started flowing more freely now. Because this next part would be even more difficult. She didn't want to break her husband's heart or make him any angrier than he already was. But she also needed his support in this. She needed him to be on her side and not just try to tell her everything was fine. They needed to get through this together.

Darla pointed to the 'Severe Reactions' list on the VIS form, and her husband read out loud as he followed her finger, "1. Long-term seizures, coma, or lowered consciousness and 2. Permanent brain damage. These are so rare it is hard to tell if they are caused by the vaccine."

"Arthur ..." the tears were streaming freely down her face now. "I don't think Sage is ok ..."

Dr. Alice Choi loved being part of a large pediatric group. She loved the business side of medicine, even more than the medicine side of medicine. So when Alan Goldstein asked her to help him as the co-business manager for the group, she was thrilled. He did insist that she continue to see patients part-time though, which she grudgingly agreed was necessary to keep her skills up and keep her up to date with advances in pediatric medicine. Which ultimately made her a better business manager, he'd said. And today was her day to play doctor, but only for the morning. Their quarterly group meeting was scheduled for lunch today, with all the doctors and office managers, and she and Alan were planning on making a major change to their practice – a change she was confident most, if not all, her fellow Peds would accept. *One more patient before lunch,* she sighed as she walked into the next exam room and greeted a mom with a toddler who was new to their practice.

⸺◇⸺

Mrs. Stewart was hopeful. *This is the pediatrician who is finally going to listen to me. To treat me as a partner in my child's health. To allow me an equal say in my baby's medical care.* She had done her homework on Dr. Choi: she was a mother herself, she apparently only worked part time, which meant her family must be important to her, she was a woman, and she was Asian. Mrs. Stewart assumed these four factors increased the likelihood that this doctor would be more open-minded, more child-centered, and more accepting of natural approaches. She was about to find out if she was right.

"Listen to me, Mrs. Stewart. Just because you heard Jenny McCarthy whine about vaccines on television doesn't make them dangerous."

"Umm … I never said anything about … who is Jenny McCarthy?"

"She's that Playboy centerfold who is going around trying to convince everyone that vaccines hurt her son. A Playboy centerfold? She has no business even having an opinion on …"

"Pardon me, Dr. Choi. I didn't get my information from someone on TV. I read all the vaccine package inserts, I reviewed disease data for the entire past century and examined when each vaccine was introduced and …"

"Just because you heard on TV that vaccines cause autism doesn't make it so."

"Autism? I never said I was worried about …"

"What, you read one book written by a chiropractor and suddenly you're an expert on vaccines?"

"Well, I did read a book – three books, all written by medical doctors. But I also …"

"What, you don't believe in modern medicine? You want your baby to die of meningitis or whooping cough? Measles? Are you some sort of religious fundamentalist who is against science?"

"Dr. Choi, I feel like you aren't listening to me. I am not against science. That's what I've been trying to tell you. All I've read is the science: the FDA package inserts for every vaccine, CDC information and medical research articles about vaccine side effects, statistics on the government's Vaccine Adverse Events Reporting System website …"

"Oh, the internet huh? Vaccine conspiracy websites? Did you get your doctor's degree from Google university? I got mine from the University of …"

"No, Dr. Choi. The internet is where everybody reads research now. You don't have to walk into a medical school library anymore. It's all online. I've researched public health department websites and CDC data on current disease outbreaks, how many vaccinated as well as non-vaccinated people catch and spread the diseases, and the Institute of Medicine's 2013 Report on the safety of our vaccine schedule."

"Just because you've talked to a few parents who said they don't like vaccines, you are going to trust *them* over the medical establishment?"

"I'm just going to ask one more question, Dr. Choi. I made a scientifically-educated decision that I have every right to make on be-half of my child, and I would like to know if you would be my baby's pediatrician without accusing me of child abuse, of blindly following pseudoscience, or of putting my child in danger."

"Well, even if I wanted to be your child's pediatrician, I couldn't. Not with our new office policy about patients who won't listen to science."

Dr. Jones hated these office meetings. *At least we only have them four times a year. And at least I don't have to do anything to prepare.*

Alex Jones liked being a pediatrician, but he didn't like the business side of managing an office. So he was happy to leave that to others. Drs. Choi and Goldstein really had a knack for business and seemed to enjoy running their large group of 15 pediatricians.

"Ok, so the last item on our agenda is our new vaccine policy," continued Alan Goldstein. "Alice and I agree that the safest thing for all of our patients is to make sure each and every one is fully im-munized. We can't have measles walking into our waiting room and infecting all our babies who are too young to have gotten their MMR shot yet. And you all know how whooping cough is going around. And that polio outbreak in California has me concerned."

"Polio-*like* outbreak, you mean." Alex heard the comment from the other end of the table and rolled his eyes. *That would be Peter, of course.*

"Right, Peter. Sorry. It was a different enterovirus, not actual po-lio, but some of our patients think it was polio. Back to the point. We feel it is our duty as pediatricians to make sure every baby gets every vaccine no matter what. Some of these parents are skipping some of the shots that they seem to think aren't as important. And we even have some who aren't getting any shots at all." Alan's roaming gaze rested briefly on Peter, whom Alex knew wouldn't be able to let it rest.

"Alan, I hear what you are saying. But doesn't it bother any of the rest of you that you are talking about mandating vaccines that don't even prevent the spread of its disease? Don't you all know that DTaP doesn't prevent the spread of whooping cough or diphtheria. Neither does polio, flu, or meningococcal vaccine. And hep B and HPV aren't spread in a waiting room. So why are you talking about mandating all vaccines?"

Several interested heads raised their eyebrows at this and turned toward Alan.

"Well Peter, I'm glad you asked. Because this isn't just about pa-tient safety. This is beginning to cost us money. Alice?"

"Right, Alan," Dr. Choi took over. "It's costing us in several ways. First, and I just found this out last week when a patient called us to complain, at least one insurance plan has decided they won't cover vaccination anymore unless it is done per the CDC schedule. One of your patients, Peter, called and said the insurance company was de-nying payment on the vaccines given at her baby's last two checkups because they weren't all given together. She said she was just following your advice, and you should have known they wouldn't be covered that way. So, she doesn't want to pay."

"That's news to me too, Alice," said Peter. "That must be a brand new change, because they've always been covered just fine no matter how we give them. That's a little scary to me – that insurance plans would now dictate how we give the vaccines."

"Well, that's not all. The same insurance plan now refuses to put our office on their Premier tier because of this 'anti-vaccination' policy, as they put it to me over the phone. They'll only keep us classified as Standard. Sure, most of our patients only use the Standard tier anyway. But some are Premier, and if they can't use those benefits here they'll go someplace else. Plus, lacking Premier status will keep new patients away. But there's more.

"You are all aware that most of the insurance plans keep track of their clients' vaccination rates, and they generously grant us a year-end bonus if we maintain 95% or higher vaccine compliance – complete and on-time vaccine compliance. Basically, we keep their clients healthy with vaccines, and it ends up costing the insurance less in the long run. It's their way of telling us thanks."

"How much money are we talking about?" Alex was surprised to hear his own voice asking the question. *I never ask questions – they prolong the meeting. But I'm curious.*

"I'm getting to that, Alex," responded Alice, looking even more surprised at Alex's participation. "It varies between 5 and 10% of annual payments. For example, for every patient we have, we generate about $1400 of revenue from their vaccines in their first year, and another $800 from all their checkups through age one. Add in a few sick visits, and we generate about $2500 or so per patient in that first year. The following years are less, of course, because almost half the vaccines are given in the first year, and we do fewer checkups as they get older.

"So most plans bonus us 10% of that revenue if the baby is fully immunized on time. That's $250 a head. Each of us sees between 50 and 100 new babies a year. Doing the math for all 15 of us, that's about 1125 new babies a year, times 250 dollars, that's about $280,000 in bonuses, just for the infants. Then it takes us about four more years to generate that much revenue for each patient, because we see them less as they get older. But there are more of them than there are babies, so it evens out. I'll spare you all of *that* math, but we get about another $500,000 or so for kids one through five years, then about another $300,000 for our cohort of patients six and up.

"That million dollars really helps our bottom line," concluded Alice. "You know we already struggle with how much insurance pays per visit. That's why we've had to stress the importance of timely patient flow and physician productivity."

That's a nice way to put it, thought Alex. *Sounds better than "keep your checkups as short as possible and see as many patients a day as you can." But where the hell are the insurance plans getting that type of money? I thought they were struggling too?*

"And as of this past month, mid-way through the year, our on-time and complete vaccination compliance rating for our practice as a whole just fell below 95%," announced Alan, re-entering the conversation. "Although many of us are above 95%, some are below – way below. Since the insurance plans bonus us based on the performance of our office as a whole, if we don't get it back up before year's end, well ..." He let the silence speak for itself.

The pin dropping in the corner was heard by everyone in the room. Then, one by one all eyes turned toward Dr. Peter Tommaso. Alan let the numbers sink in for several more seconds, and let everyone ponder who was to blame, before moving on.

"So, it's time to put this to a vote. We've talked about doing this for a couple years, and many of us have discussed and debated this issue over many lunches and between patients and hashed out all the arguments. Alice and I now feel we have no choice. Are there any more comments?"

"Well, for me it's not about the money, it's about the importance of vaccines," chimed in Dr. Tehrani. "Don't get me wrong, Alice and Alan. I appreciate that you two have a knack for the bottom line. But I think, for most of us regular doctors, this is simply about the fact that vaccines are important, and taking this stand sends that message to our patients and the community."

Nods of agreement from most of the table.

"Ok then," continued Alan. "All those in favor of implementing an office-wide vaccination policy that mandates the complete CDC schedule for all patients, raise your hand. Any opposed? Ok, the 'ayes' have it. We've drafted a patient-notification letter and some signs that we'll put up around the office. I think all our patients will be comforted knowing that everyone around them is infection-free and safe."

Alex Jones wasn't surprised by the vote's outcome, but he was surprised that Peter wasn't the only one who raised his hand in the negative.

"I don't know why you were surprised that I sided with you on this, Peter," confided Mike that evening as the two sat with their drinks overlooking the river. "Yeah, I do think vaccines are as important as the next guy. But mandatory vaccination? To not give patients any choice in the matter? What is this, *A Brave New World* or *1984*? Nazi Germany, maybe?"

Dr. Michael Jameson had emailed Peter after the meeting and asked him to join him for a drink after work. Peter had never really socialized much with the practice's founder over the years. Mike was a bit of a dinosaur – two or three decades older than Peter – but everyone loved him. He was pretty much the patients' favorite doctor, especially the long-timers. He'd even taken to coming to work in Bermuda shorts and Hawaiian shirts lately, which fit with his casual style. Most of the new patients coming in didn't even know Dr. Mike because he was all filled up, and his part-time schedule left little room for new patients. But Mike, like all pediatricians, loved newborns. So every now and then a young family who really begged nicely got in with him.

"I hear you," Peter agreed. "Alan and Alice played that very well. Start with patient safety and end with the threat of losing your very nice Christmas bonuses. Although, I wouldn't go around accusing Alan *Goldstein* of being a Nazi. And comparing coerced medicine today to what happened in World War II? Seriously? There's no comparison, Mike. Not even close."

"Point taken, and no offense intended. But we do hear some people refer to over-vaccinating and mandatory vaccination as a holocaust. Clearly there's no comparison to *The* Holocaust. But I think what medical freedom supporters fear is that if the people give up one basic human right, like the right to choose your medicine, that this is just the first step in eventually losing all freedom. Ten more steps later, all our health care choices are controlled by a Pharm-ruled regime that dictates every medical aspect of our society. That's what people fear. We should learn from history, not ignore it when it starts to repeat because we think there's no way that can ever happen again – not to *us*. Perhaps the lesson here is this: what early freedoms did the German people give up as the Nazis gradually took over? Freedoms that didn't seem like a big deal at the time. Dictates that seemed so right for the people, but then, nine freedoms later, it's too late. You're under the total control of a regime. I think that's what people fear with mandated medicine 'for the public good.' Are we supposed to ignore history until things get extreme? Or do democratic people stand up to any first step toward tyranny? I say we stand up.

"Anyway, I actually like Alan. I hired him, after all. He's been a real gem for the practice. And frankly, I don't think he would have pushed for this had it not been for Alice Choi. Maybe she's the … well, I won't say it again. But patient safety? Really? Does Alan really think any of us believe that safety is driving this decision?"

"Sadly, Mike, I think Alan half believes it himself. And most of the younger doctors in the group do as well."

"But half of the vaccines we give don't even prevent the spread of the diseases," complained the older doctor. "Sure, the vaccine will likely make someone feel less sick and reduce the complications of the disease for that one individual. But in many cases the vaccines don't keep a person from catching the germs, allowing the germs to replicate in their respiratory or GI tract, and passing the germs on to everyone else. So those vaccines, or a lack of them, have nothing to do with 'patient safety' and reducing the spread of those vaccine-preventable diseases." Mike paused to look down at his drink.

"Preaching to the choir, buddy. And I've told that to Alan over and over again. Believe me, I've spent hours with him showing him study after study. I even tried talking to Dr. Choi, but talking to her is like talking to a brick wall."

"More like the *Berlin* wall, you mean. Ok, ok. I'll stop." Mike actually looked chagrined.

"Anyway, I even showed Alan that 2014 FDA and NIH study that literally proved the DTaP vaccine doesn't prevent infection and transmission of whooping cough. All it does is reduce how sick a person feels, but fully vaccinated kids are going to spread whooping cough just as much as unvaccinated kids because that vaccine just doesn't work that way. Plus, the non-vaccinated subjects caught whooping cough once, but the vaccinated ones were more likely to catch the disease over and over. So they spread the disease even *more* than those who weren't vaccinated. It's as if the vaccine is making things worse, not better. Even the study's title spells it out in plain English: 'Acellular pertussis vaccines protect against disease but fail to prevent infection and transmission in a nonhuman primate model.' And you don't even have to read the whole article – the abstract summarizes that the vaccine triggers the wrong type of immune response, so it can't prevent infection. And this isn't some granola journal. This was the FDA and NIH."

"And what did Alan say?"

"He just shrugged and told me not to bother him with facts. We would be doing everyone a favor by making them vaccinate."

"That doesn't sound like Alan. *That* sounds more like Alice," murmured Mike.

"I do remember one DTaP conversation that Alice did jump in on. She said that even though the pertussis part of the vaccine doesn't prevent the spread, the diphtheria and the tetanus parts of the vaccine *do*. So we need to do our part to make sure those diseases don't spread around."

"Tetanus? Seriously? Exactly how does she think one patient is going to pass tetanus along to another patient in our waiting room? Did she even attend an immunology or infectious disease lecture in medical school? What is it with these younger physicians today? You know, my Grandpa used to tell me all kinds of stories about his days as a medic in World War I. Tetanus was all he would talk about. That and amputations, of course. Sounds like Alice could use a history lesson and an immunology lesson. Anyway, maybe she has a point about diphtheria though. You are too young to have seen that, Peter, but I saw my fair share during a stint in Alaska way, way back."

"The DTaP vaccine doesn't prevent diphtheria spread either," corrected Peter, surprised that Mike didn't know this.

"Wait, what? I just assumed that since we don't have diphtheria in the U.S. anymore ... Oh, wait, you are right! It's all about how the DTaP vaccine is made. For the tetanus portion *and* the diphtheria portion, all they put into the vaccine are the neutralized germ toxins, not the actual germs themselves. Our immune systems create antibodies against the germ toxins, so if we ever *are* infected, the real toxin is neutralized so we don't *feel* sick. But we still catch and pass the germ. And the same is true for the pertussis part of the vaccine. Although a bit of the germs are in the vaccine, our immune response is mostly against the pertussis toxin. That's why we don't become immune to the disease when vaccinated. And that's why we still have tons of whooping cough. But how'd we get rid of diphtheria then?"

"Better living conditions. Less poverty."

"Got it. Geeze, if even I forgot about that, how on earth would Alan, Alice, or any of the young ones know it?"

"Doctors know almost nothing about actual vaccine ingredients and how they work. They just assume that every single vaccine prevents infection, but many don't. This is also true for polio vaccine; the injected one we now use doesn't give you intestinal immunity. It only protects you from getting the neurological consequences if you do swallow the germs. So it doesn't matter who is vaccinated against polio anymore, at least from a public health standpoint. And some diseases have so many strains, like pneumococcal disease, HPV, and the flu, that mandating vaccination doesn't prevent much overall disease anyway. Then there are the diseases that aren't spread through casual contact, like hepatitis B. So there's no public danger there either. And meningococcus? Did you know that 10% of us carry that germ harmlessly in our nasal passages, regardless of vaccination status? Actual cases of meningitis from that are so rare, but vaccination doesn't prevent spread of that germ either. It only reduces severity of disease for the vaccinated individual, just like pertussis. But when it comes to making vaccines mandatory for the good of everyone around you, don't bother with the facts. All you need to know is 'vaccines good, diseases bad.'"

"Yeah, so it's easy to get mandatory vaccination policies implemented because they aren't based on any actual science that proves they will reduce disease spread and keep diseases from coming back. Instead, people just assume that all vaccines are equally good, safe, and effective. So it must be good to mandate them," summarized Mike.

"That's pretty much how they got the mandatory vaccine law passed in California. They got enough state legislators to just stop thinking beyond the mantra vaccines are good, they save lives, and all vaccines prevent all diseases. Glad our Washington legislators are smarter than that." Peter added. "But don't get me started on politics."

The two were silent for a minute, enjoying their drinks and the surrounding ambiance of the pub.

"So, what are you going to do now, Peter? You've got the most unvaccinated or partially-vaccinated families of all of us. You probably have more than all of us combined. I don't think the group is actually going to fire you, but I don't think your patients are going to just suddenly start letting you fully vaccinate them. I've seen a number of your patients over the years. I know how they think."

"I do have a number of patients who totally opt out. But some eventually get most of the vaccines. They just do them more slowly. The main vaccine some of my patients are behind on is just hepatitis B."

"Yeah, mine too, to tell you the truth," Mike confided again. "I haven't given that vaccine to a baby in years."

"Geeze, does Alice know?" laughed Peter. "But seriously, you are lucky to be a part-timer now. Your 'non-compliant' group of 'uncooperative' parents is too small to drag her precious rating down more than a fraction of a percent. Mine, on the other hand …"

"So, you are leaving?"

"I have no choice. Most of my patients will follow me, and Drs. Choi and Goldstein will be happy to see them leave, especially the ones who are completely unvaccinated. Talk about families who don't contribute to Alice's bottom line," chuckled Peter, smiling. "And it's not just about buying the shots. They also come in less often for checkups, especially when they've already had a child or two and know what they are doing. And their kids never get sick … or almost never, that is. At least they don't get sick enough to come in."

"Wait, what? Your unvaccinated patients are less sick? That seems ironic."

"Don't you notice the same thing?" asked Peter.

"I never really thought about it, honestly. But I have so few completely unvaccinated patients, I don't know that I could even comment on it."

Peter leaned forward a bit. "Here's my theory, and it is just a theory because there are only a few studies that corroborate this so far: I think that while vaccines work to provide specific immunity to the diseases they are designed to target, they also reduce our immune system's ability to fight off all the regular everyday diseases. Giving so many shots at such a young age has such an artificial effect on the immune system. These aren't natural germs being introduced to the immune system one at a time like in the real world; these are as many as nine genetically-modified or artificially-created germ components shot into the system all at once. Does our immune system really know what to do with all of that? And the bigger question is, do we actually know what all that is doing to these immature immune systems? No, we don't. The immune system is so complex, there's probably more that we *don't* know than what we *do* know. To assume that vaccines are safe and that we know everything about them is probably one of the most scientifically inaccurate statements anyone can make.

"Anyway, back to my point: it's a trade-off. You get some protection from rare diseases if you vaccinate, but your immune system is weaker overall. So you get sick more often from everyday illnesses that we have no vaccine for, and you get sicker when you catch them. But you probably don't catch any of the really bad infections that the vaccines can prevent. Or, at least that was the original intention. Now it seems like they are trying to prevent *everything*, including chicken pox, ear infections, and of course the dreaded flu. But there are some studies that show routine childhood illnesses make us healthier in the long term. So those who are not vaccinated probably have much healthier immune systems, they rarely get sick, and when they do it's mild."

"I know, but letting people purposely get sick isn't a popular idea."

"And I'm not suggesting we do that. You don't want polio, or meningitis, or tetanus. But where do you draw the line between what we *should* prevent with vaccines and what we *can* prevent. Just because we can prevent a disease doesn't mean we should, especially when it's harmless for virtually everyone who catches it. Like chicken pox. Why don't we focus on all the bad stuff, like vaccines were originally intended? I think that the push for mandatory vaccination policies that include vaccines that just don't make sense will end up hurting our vaccination system because more and more parents are going to protest against the stupid vaccines like hepatitis B, and then they are going to start questioning even the important vaccines. Like, 'Hey, the government is trying to force me to vaccinate my baby against a sexually-transmitted disease. What *else* is the government trying to sneak in there that I don't know about? Maybe I should investigate all vaccines.' And when people do *that*, you know what happens."

"Yes. They realize there's significant risk to vaccinating. And they start to question it. I bet they would have better vaccine compliance if they didn't try to force them and just kept quiet about it. Stir up less controversy."

"Who knows?" shrugged Peter. "We could go on and on about this. We are not going to fix this broken system any time soon. Meanwhile, we'll just go on with our lives and our practices and keep offering to educate our patients one at a time. That's all we can do, right?"

"You should send Alan a going-away email with some of the most pertinent studies you think he should see. Plant a seed before you go. Who knows?"

"That's a good idea. And thanks for the drink."

"No Peter, thank you for reminding me why I got into pediatrics in the first place. It's not for us, and it's certainly not for the money. It's for the kids, right? And the parents."

"I think that's all any parent wants in a pediatrician." Peter held his glass up to his old boss. "Speaking of which, how much longer do you think you will be doing this?"

"Who knows. I'm getting tired. And I've never gotten used to all this rain. I grew up in Texas, you know. My brother down there is an ER doc. I may wrap things up here in the next year or two and retire back down there."

"This place would miss you, Mike. I don't blame you. The rain here is a drag. But the trees though. They don't have trees like this down in Texas."

Arthur sat waiting patiently in the exam room with his wife and their youngest, now six months old. Baby Sage was sitting propped up in his lap, facing him, and he was enjoying the smiles and coos coming from his daughter – smiles and coos that disappeared at four months, and were just now starting to appear again. *She's back*, he thought thankfully. And now he could see what his wife was talking about. They had definitely "lost her" after that two-month vaccine reaction. She'd recovered, but then her spark had died out after the four-month seizure reaction. She'd lost all eye contact, didn't smile, didn't coo. She ate and slept. And they cried. Cried a lot. But then she came back, and Arthur wasn't going to let anyone harm her again.

The knock on the door preceded the "Hello Mr. and Mrs. Johnson" from Dr. Jones as he entered and washed his hands. "Let's see how Sage is growing."

Arthur let the doctor do his exam and listened as he and Darla discussed feeding, growing, and development. His wife described Sage's developmental regression and gradual recovery, but she and Arthur had agreed earlier that they weren't going to mention anything about vaccines and vaccine reactions. Maybe it was a bit unfair to test their doctor this way, but they wanted to give Dr. Jones a chance and see if he'd figure out there was a connection between the vaccines and Sage's reactions.

Arthur realized that he wasn't surprised when Dr. Jones concluded at the end of ten minutes that Sage looked perfectly healthy, and it was time for the third round of all her vaccines. *Should I be surprised?*

"Dr. Jones," his wife began. They'd agreed she would do the talking, because they both knew Arty would get way too angry too quickly. "We have some questions about the vaccines ..." and she proceeded to explain what happened after the first vaccine, reminding him that she'd mentioned this at the 4-month checkup. She showed him the CDC VIS form, and the warnings about the prolonged inconsolable crying. She moved on to the seizure after the 4-month vaccines, then described Sage's developmental regression that followed. She was concise in her description, taking only a few minutes to explain what happened. "We aren't sure what we should do now, and would like your opinion."

Alex Jones was glad that this was his last patient before lunch. It stressed him out to fall behind in his schedule, a schedule that permitted about ten minutes per checkup, maybe the occasional fifteen. But he was also reasonable, and he sensed that this appointment would take even longer, *and that's what the lunch break is partly for anyway – catch-up.*

Alex glanced back at the 4-month checkup notes. He didn't see anything about Sage Johnson's first reaction, and he certainly didn't remember Mrs. Jones having any concerns about a reaction at that time. *Plus, a lot of babies scream for hours after vaccines. We get those calls all the time.*

But Alex also realized that he had no idea that the CDC VIS form spelled it out so clearly as a warning about repeating the vaccine. *I wonder what the CDC means by "some babies shouldn't get this vaccine again" after having an extreme prolonged crying episode? How am I supposed to know if the vaccine should be repeated?* Alex knew they were supposed to let patients read the VIS forms before giving vaccines, and he assumed the nurse took care of that. He'd have to check.

"Well, let's discuss the seizure first," Alex began. "I see the ER record in her chart." *Now that you told me about it. I had no idea that Sage had that seizure.* "The record says Sage had Roseola. That *is* the most common cause of febrile seizures, you know. It probably had nothing to do with the vaccines. Coincidence probably. The ER record doesn't say anything about this being a reaction to the vaccines."

"But Sage never got the characteristic Roseola rash, and her fever only lasted a day. Plus she's young for Roseola, I read. If it is a known fact that these vaccines can cause a seizure reaction, and she had a seizure the evening of vaccination, why focus on a much-less-likely cause like Roseola? Shouldn't we first presume the obvious cause?"

"I understand your concern," continued Alex. "But it sounds like the seizure was ultimately harmless. I know you feel like she wasn't herself for a few weeks after, but babies will commonly do that anyway, regardless of vaccines." *I think. Do they? I don't have kids yet.*

"Dr. Jones, we have three other children. None of them lost all eye contact and went silent and stopped smiling for an entire month. Sage did these things twice, after each round of vaccines. I don't see how that is normal. But, yes, I am glad that now she is fine. So, the question is, what do we do now? Do we skip vaccines for a while? Do we skip only the DTaP, since that's more known for these reactions? And maybe the PC vaccine too?"

"I do recommend you continue the vaccines. They are so critically important – every one of them. Sage could die if you don't do them. Plus, the CDC lists this as a moderate reaction, not severe. Also, we had an office meeting the other day about how important vaccines are, and we now have a mandatory vaccination policy for our patients. So if you decide not to continue, I wouldn't be able to see you anymore."

"Even after having two bad reactions?"

"They were only moderate reactions. The crying, and the seizure, are not what we call contraindications. Babies who have a contra-indication, like a severe life-threatening allergic reaction, coma, or permanent brain damage, like it lists under severe reactions on your VIS form, those babies could be excused from the DTaP vaccine. But not Sage."

"But look at this DTaP VIS form I brought with me, where it says 'What if there is a serious reaction?' It describes a severe allergic reaction, like you just said, but then it also calls 'behavior changes' a serious reaction, not moderate. The MMR VIS form says the same thing: 'unusual behavior' is considered a serious reaction there too."

That's absurd, Alex thought. *The CDC can't possibly think that 'behavior changes' are a severe vaccine reaction.* Without even looking at the VIS form Mrs. Jones was pointing to, he said "Sage really needs to continue all vaccines. They are just so important."

Mrs. Johnson didn't look very happy about this. "What exactly do you think Sage is going to die of if I don't finish the vaccines? Here in America, with modern healthcare? For Sage, the vaccines now seem far more dangerous than any of the diseases. And you're telling me that we would have to wait until Sage is permanently injured before stopping vaccines, instead of considering all these 'moderate' reactions as warning signs that something much worse could happen if we do continue?"

"Yes. And it's not only for Sage's good. It's for the good of society too. I'll tell you what, though. I understand you are concerned. So, how about we do all the rest of the vaccines that are due today but leave out the DTaP. That way Sage is mostly protected, and we don't risk another seizure. We can see how she does with those, then come back next week for the DTaP."

Alex watched Mrs. Johnson nod her head and say ok. *Whew. That was fairly easy.* Alex ordered the Hep B, Polio, HIB, PC-13, and Rotavirus vaccines in the chart. *Oh, and the flu shot,* he realized, it being October and the start of flu season. He stood up, nodded good-bye, and left the room. *Lunch time,* he thought, noticing his stomach starting to rumble.

Jamie drew up the vaccines quickly. She was hungry too, and wanted to join the other nurses in the lunch room. She could hear them chatting down the hall and laughing. *Sage Johnson,* she read on the chart. *Isn't that the baby who had the encephalitis reaction with the first shots? Well, she must have ended up fine after the second ones.* Jamie looked at Dr. Jones's notes from the two-month visit, four-month visit, and today's notes as well. *Baby healthy. No problems. Discussed vaccines,* she read. There was nothing written about the two-month screaming, nothing about any reactions in the four-month visit, and nothing written today about any past reactions. *I must be thinking about someone else,* she thought, feeling even more hungry now.

Done preparing the vaccines, Jamie walked down the hallway carrying the tray of Hep B, Polio, HIB, PC, Rotavirus, Flu … and DTaP vaccines. In his haste, Alex Jones forgot to de-select the DTaP from the list of vaccines that was automatically ordered at 6 months. And Jamie had no reason to know that he'd meant to not order it. She knocked on the exam room door, her greeting to the Johnson family ready on the tip of her tongue.

But the room was empty. The Johnson family had left, for good.

Chapter 3

Seemed Like a Good Idea

The auditorium was full, and the back and side walls were lined with people. Jenny was pleased at the turnout. She had no idea so many people would be interested in this. Many of those standing in the back were women holding small babies in baby carriers. *I hope those babies stay quiet.*

Jenny was a grad student in chemical engineering, and this month it was her turn to host the community debate for her department at the State University. And no one ever had a turn out like this. *That's because most people pick boring topics.* She thought about last month's debate between the county director of sewage and water reclamation and a local environmental activist. They'd gone head to head over the topic of prescription medications contaminating our water supply – to an audience of ten people. *Talk about a snooze fest.*

But Jenny was also a little apprehensive about the topic she'd chosen. An argument she had with one of her friends had given her the idea, and she was glad to see her friend among the moms in the back. Jenny's own baby was at home with her husband, of course. She glanced at her watch. *Show time.*

"Good evening, ladies and gentlemen ... and sleeping babies," she began into the microphone. "My name is Jenny Martinsen, and I'm a graduate student here at State. Welcome to this month's discussion: Are aluminum adjuvants in vaccines safe? This topic is particularly important to me as the mother of a nine-month-old baby. Of course, vaccines are very important, and I wanted to take advantage of this opportunity to educate my colleagues and my community about vaccine safety, yet also provide a forum for debate and discussion. I've been seeing a lot of unscientific discussions online lately about aluminum in vaccines, so I thought I would bring in one of our nation's top experts on vaccine safety to represent the affirmative side of the topic. Dr. John Smith is the head of toxicology at University Hospital where he studies the toxic effects of chemicals. Welcome Dr. Smith." Jenny nodded to the red-haired middle-aged man sitting to her left on stage.

"And here to present the negative viewpoint of our question is a local pediatrician with whom most of us are familiar, Dr. Montgomery Ward. Dr. Ward is a graduate of the Charlestown University School of Medicine and trained in Pediatrics at Children's Hospital of Texas. He is a private practice pediatrician. Welcome Dr. Ward." Nod to the younger-looking man to her right.

"Let me establish the rules of this debate. First, we are not here to discuss vaccines in general, or the infectious diseases they prevent. So try to stay clear of those topics, if you can." She smiled at the doctor on her left and received a polite ripple of laughter from the audience. "We are here tonight to discuss one thing only: aluminum adjuvants in vaccines, and whether or not they are safe. What's an adjuvant? It's an ingredient added to a vaccine to make it work better. Aluminum is added to about half of our vaccines in order to create a better immune response to the vaccine germs; without the aluminum, our vaccines wouldn't work nearly as well," again glancing at John - Dr. Smith – and getting a smile and a nod back.

"However, some claim that the amount of aluminum in the entire schedule of vaccines adds up to too much, and that we do not yet have sufficient safety research to prove this aluminum is safe and effective ... sorry, I mean just safe. We aren't debating its efficacy." She didn't glance to her right toward the pediatrician, trying to avoid looking embarrassed at her slip.

"We are all aware of the growing controversy over vaccinations. Even though science has settled the question of vaccines and autism, some still worry about vaccine ingredients. There was a lot of concern about the minuscule amounts of mercury in vaccines; and although extensive research proved that the type of mercury in vaccines was safe, vaccine manufacturers removed mercury from vaccines in 2002. But some continue to question vaccine ingredients. And tonight we will put our focus on the controversy over aluminum.

"Each speaker will be given 15 minutes to present his position. Then each will have a 7-minute follow-up. Then I will direct some questions to each speaker, sticking to just this particular topic, until the hour is up. We won't take questions from the audience, in the interest of time. We begin with the Affirmative. Dr. Smith."

"Thank you, Ms. Martinsen, and thank you to the University for hosting this event," Dr. Smith began after adjusting the microphone. "I would like to start by correcting one thing Ms. Martinsen said. The topic of vaccine aluminum is *not* a controversy. There is nothing controversial about aluminum. It is safe, and we've proven it is safe, and by the end of this evening I trust that all of you will agree that there's nothing controversial about it.

"We've been using aluminum in vaccines for over 80 years. That alone proves the trace quantities of aluminum in vaccines can't possibly do harm. It is absolutely safe. But let's look at exactly how little there actually is.

"Some vaccines have as little as 0.125 milligrams. The most that any one vaccine has is 0.85 milligrams. Let's compare that to the milligrams of something you are familiar with – Tylenol. For a headache we all pop two 500 mg pills of extra strength Tylenol. That's a thousand milligrams. So the most aluminum any one vaccine has is less than 1/1000th of a dose of Tylenol. Less than a milligram. That's how little there is. But the next logical question that anyone would ask is how much does a baby get in total throughout the entire vaccine schedule? That's the real question. I have calculated how much a baby would get in the first six months of life, and it comes out to about 4 mg. Again, a tiny amount.

"Perhaps one of the most obvious proofs is looking at Mother Nature. Aluminum is the most abundant metal on our planet. It makes up almost 10% of our earth's crust. It's everywhere: in our kitchens, our medications, household products, our construction. And traces of aluminum are found in our food and water. So we can't avoid it. Aluminum is actually a light metal. It's not a heavy metal. You hear a lot about the dangers of heavy metals, like lead and mercury. Well, aluminum isn't even in that same chemical category. As a light metal, we can take in a certain quantity of it and our bodies know how to handle it.

"Now let's talk about how much aluminum we get, as humans, every single day. Most adults will ingest about 8 mg of aluminum every day in food and water. In six months, that's 720 mg. Now I already told you that babies only get about 4 mg of aluminum in their shots over 6 months. That's less than an adult gets in only a day. Babies ingest more in their breast milk and formula. That's right, baby formula contains aluminum, and so does breast milk. That's because all moms have aluminum in their bodies, and the milk and plant substances we use to make formula also have it. A breastfed baby will get about 7 milligrams of aluminum total over six months. That's almost twice what they'll get in vaccines. Formula has more: regular formula gives a baby about 38 mg of aluminum in six months, and soy formula gives a baby about 117 mg. And the good thing about all this aluminum is that it passes out of our bodies harmlessly through the stools and the urine.

"The bottom line is that babies ingest way more aluminum than they ever get from vaccines. The amount in vaccines is trivial. That's how we know it is safe.

"It's a good thing we can use aluminum in vaccines because it helps each dose work better. If we didn't use aluminum, we'd have to give babies 2 or 3 times the number of injections just to achieve the same level of immunity that we can get with aluminum-adjuvanted vaccines. So this lessens the amount of all the other vaccine ingredients that babies get.

"But let's discuss the science on aluminum safety, because even though Mother Nature tells us aluminum is safe, we still need to rely on science. Let's start with the FDA. The FDA declared aluminum to be in the Generally-Regarded-As-Safe category in the 1970s. The FDA just last year released their updated guidelines on the use of aluminum adjuvants in vaccines. And I quote, 'An adjuvant shall not be introduced into a product unless there is satisfactory evidence that it does not affect adversely the safety or potency of the product.' So the FDA has stated very clearly it can't be used unless we have evidence it is safe. They also say 'the amount of aluminum in the recommended individual dose of a biological product shall not exceed 0.85 milligrams.' The FDA also says vaccines may contain '1.25 mg provided that data demonstrating that the amount of aluminum used is safe and necessary to produce the intended effect are submitted to and approved by the Director' of the FDA. All vaccines comply with these guidelines. So, the FDA has set a safety limit, and no vaccine exceeds that limit.

"In 2004, *The Lancet*, one of the world's most respected medical journals, published a study by Dr. Jefferson, one of the members of the Cochrane Review, an independent group of researchers and doctors who look at health care issues around the world, entitled 'Adverse events after immunization with aluminum-containing DTP vaccines.' They didn't find any indications that the aluminum in the vaccine caused any aluminum-related problems. They concluded that no further research should be undertaken on this topic. Another 2004 study in the *Journal of Environmental Monitoring* by Priest actually tested injected aluminum in humans and found it to be safe. Two years before that, Keith published a study in *Vaccine* titled 'Aluminum toxicokinetics regarding infant diet and vaccinations,' the very subject we are discussing right now, and proved the level of aluminum in vaccines is harmless. The AAP journal, *Pediatrics*, also published perhaps the most thorough look at this issue in 2003, titled 'Addressing parents' concerns: Do vaccines contain harmful preservatives, adjuvants, additives, or residuals?'

"The World Health Organization, The Institute of Medicine, The Centers for Disease Control and Prevention, The American Academy of Pediatrics, and The American Medical Association have all confirmed that aluminum in vaccines is perfectly safe. Every major medical and scientific organization in the United States and the world agree it is safe.

"Now, what do we know about the health effects of aluminum from other sources besides vaccines? We do know that if we get too much aluminum in our bodies, it can cause harm, even though it is only a light metal. This can't happen from vaccines, but it can happen from other sources. Aluminum toxicity can happen in hospitalized patients, especially if their kidneys don't work well. We know that kidney dialysis patients can develop brain disorders if they ingest too much aluminum in medications like antacids and in other intravenous treatments. We also know that dialysis patients used to develop weak bones because aluminum prevents them from absorbing phosphate, which is needed to make bones strong, along with calcium of course. Children who take aluminum-containing antacids for long periods of time can also develop weak bones. It can also cause anemia. Hospitalized patients who are given intravenous feedings, called parenteral nutrition, used to get too much aluminum, but now we know how to filter out aluminum from this so it rarely happens. We've also found that people with Alzheimer's disease have more aluminum in their brain tissue after they pass away. We don't know if this aluminum causes the disease, or if the aluminum is a result of the tissue damage in the brain from the Alzheimer's disease itself.

"Plus, you have to also understand the chemistry of aluminum salts. The aluminum in vaccines isn't the same as the aluminum we get in food and water. Vaccine aluminum is converted into a salt form; it's attached to either phosphate or hydroxide molecules. This stabilizes it so it can safely be used in vaccines and processed by the body.

"Now, I will admit that there is one, and only one, risk from vaccine aluminum that we have discovered and that the data do support. I assume Ward is going to touch on this too. There is an extremely rare skin reaction that has been reported in the medical literature called macrophagic myofasciitis. It's essentially an allergic reaction to the aluminum salt in the vaccines. The white blood cells in the skin, called macrophages, over-react to the aluminum and cause ongoing pain, inflammation, and weakness in the muscle where the vaccine was given. Because some of the aluminum remains deposited in the muscle, this reaction continues for weeks or even months. Some people will improve with treatment. A similar reaction, called pseudolymphoma, has also been reported. This skin rash occurs when another type of white blood cells, called lymphocytes, over-react to the aluminum in vaccines. The rash is ultimately benign. Thankfully, severe allergic reactions to vaccines are extremely rare. About 1 in a million. Such rare events need to be treated and handled properly. That's why it's important to get vaccines in a safe medical environment under the care of trained medical professionals, so that when a rare allergic reaction or skin reaction does occur, the patient remains safe.

"So, to summarize, aluminum has been around ever since we began our modern vaccination program in the 1930s. Decades of use without harm proves it is safe. The amount we do inject is tiny compared to how much we eat and drink. Aluminum protects babies from getting two or three times as many vaccine doses. Every medical organization on the planet agrees it is safe. There really is no question. The amount of aluminum in vaccines can't possibly do harm. In fact, it does the opposite. It does good. The science is settled on this. Thank you."

Dr. Smith turned and walked back to his seat and sat down as the audience gave a polite applause. Jenny got up from her seat near him and stepped up to the mic. "Thank you, Dr. Smith. We are a little ahead of time, which is rare for a doctor presentation. And now we will hear from Dr. Ward." She turned and nodded to the pediatrician who stood up and approached for his turn.

Wow, thought Jenny. *That was amazing. It's so obvious that aluminum in vaccines is safe. And that everything about vaccines is safe.* Jenny scanned the crowd in the back, hoping to lock eyes with her friend. *I wonder what Paulina is thinking right now. Probably embarrassed to even talk to me. I can't wait to chat afterwards. Ah, there she is. Glad her baby is still sleeping so she could hear all this. But …* Jenny could tell even from this far away that her friend didn't look chagrined, embarrassed, or confused at all. Her look was more … eager. No, that wasn't it. She looked as if something wonderful was going to happen … something that she could barely wait for … like a mama lion watching her pride-mates about to pounce on their prey – prey that would feed her young. *What the heck?*

Dr. Ward knew vaccines better than anyone. And he *knew* that he knew them better than anyone. Not in an arrogant way, but simply because it was true. He loved reading about vaccines, studying all the data, looking at all the research, and formulating science-based opinions about vaccines and the diseases they prevent. The basis for this confidence is that he'd spent his entire pediatric career, over 20 years now, studying vaccines, and giving them in his office every day. Most pediatricians simply learn just enough in residency to understand vaccines and to know a bit about their side effects, then spend the rest of their careers giving vaccines without reading anything new about them. Or, reading the occasional update about how safe they are in the medical media. Most pediatricians, sadly, know almost nothing about vaccines beyond the idea that they are safe and effective.

But Dr. Ward had read every vaccine Package Insert – three times. He'd read every safety study, both from the initial FDA approval process for each vaccine and its follow-up research. He'd read everything anyone has ever written about vaccines. And although he gives vaccines in his office to those parents who want them, there has always been one thing about vaccines that he never quite felt good about … aluminum. He simply could never find an actual speck of real evidence that vaccine aluminum was safe. Well, that's not quite true. There is a speck. But what he would expect, and what he would expect any reasonable person to expect, is that there should be a plethora of evidence that proves something is safe if you are going to be giving it to every single baby in the country. No, in the world. If you are literally going to inject every single baby on the planet with 70 doses of *anything* over their childhood, you'd really, really want to have a pretty large safety study that proves it is safe. Or even one that almost proves it is safe. But in all his reading, a speck is all he could ever find. And that's why he was here tonight. To challenge the assumption that vaccine aluminum has been proven safe. *Dr. Smith sure made all his "research" sound compelling. I wonder if he really believes it, or if he knows every single one of the studies he quoted actually didn't really look at aluminum safety or prove anything at all. Just because we've been using it for 80 years, my ass. That's not a scientific argument, it's a media sound bite.* Monty dwelt on these thoughts during the three seconds it took to walk from his chair to the podium. *This is going to be way too easy. And I can't believe that the University even agreed to put on this debate in public.* He glanced down at his several pages of well-organized notes and began.

"Thank you, Jenny, for organizing this important discussion. And thank you, Dr. Smith, for joining us. I know that the information you presented reflects the understanding and opinion of most doctors, researchers, and policymakers. But I am going to challenge your information. And I promise you and the audience, and anyone who views a recording of this debate, that I will only challenge you with published research and scientific data that I know is factual. If I have an opinion or two to share that isn't backed by science, I'll give a disclaimer.

"The basis of my objection to the use of aluminum in vaccines is that we only have three very small research studies that have been published that actually looked at injected aluminum in human subjects. Only three. Two were studies of IV infusions, and one used vaccinations. And Dr. Smith alluded to two of these studies, although he didn't tell you all the details about what these studies found.

"Dr. Nick Priest published a review of the two very old IV infusion studies in 2004 in the *Journal of Environmental Monitoring*. The first study was done in 1993 and involved six adults who were given intravenous aluminum. The pertinent question was this: do adults quickly excrete aluminum from the body when it is injected, or do they hold onto it? What they found was that about 60% of the aluminum left the body within 24 hours. But then it took another five days for only another 10% of the originally injected amount to clear the body. It mostly came out in the urine. Then the study ended. They didn't check clearance after that, so they don't know what happened to the remaining 30%. Dr. Priest then discusses a second study that was done long before the 6-man study, a study in which a researcher injected himself with intravenous aluminum. He found that 90% of the aluminum had left his body after 100 days. He continued to monitor his aluminum output and found that after a thousand days, 95% of the total amount of aluminum had left his body.

"The third study is more recent, and it is what we call a pilot study – a small preliminary study to test a theory. It doesn't provide conclusions. It is supposed to lead to much larger studies if its results are concerning. Movsas and her group published 'Effect of routine vaccination on aluminum and essential element levels in preterm infants' in *JAMA Pediatrics* in 2013. They gave 15 preterm babies, who were still in the hospital but had reached two months of age, their regularly-scheduled two-month vaccines. They measured the blood and urine levels of aluminum before the shots and again 24 hours after the shots. Their conclusion was that there was no significant change in urine or blood levels of aluminum in these babies. One criticism of the study is that they didn't disclose what the rise in aluminum was. They only said there was 'no significant change.' The pre-vaccine levels of aluminum in these babies averaged 11 micrograms per liter of blood. They didn't say exactly what it was 24 hours after vaccination. And they didn't study it after that to see where the aluminum went.

"That's it, ladies and gentlemen ... and babies in the back. That is the sum total of the live human research we have that involves direct injection of a measured amount of aluminum into real people and measurement of how it came out. Seven adults and 15 babies. So, as a scientist and practicing physician, it concerns me that we inject 4 million babies in our country with aluminum every year based on only having studied it in 22 people.

"But aren't there hundreds of studies published about aluminum, you ask? Yes there are. But except for the three I just mentioned, all of the other studies only looked at the external side effects that can be observed on the outside of the body. For example, the 2004 Jefferson study mentioned by Dr. Smith only looked at observable side effects from the DTP vaccine. That's all. They didn't investigate any other aspects of health. They didn't look inside the body for internal toxicity. They didn't monitor how much aluminum was cleared from the body. And they didn't look for any long-term side effects. In fact, they didn't even do a study themselves. They simply reviewed the original safety research done by the company that made the vaccine for the FDA approval process. Plus, they only looked at one aluminum-containing vaccine. There are six. They didn't study the side effects in people who received all six. And you know what? They actually did find that the one aluminum-containing vaccine caused more skin and muscle-related side effects than the non-aluminum vaccines. They found a problem. But what was their conclusion? Dr. Smith told us: 'No further research should be undertaken on this topic.' They didn't even study the aluminum at all, in my opinion.

"But let me update you with the latest published information from the Cochrane Review on aluminum in vaccines. And Dr. Smith, I must apologize if I have you at a disadvantage here, because this study was only recently published, so you might not have seen it yet. It is titled 'Aluminum adjuvants used in vaccines versus placebo or no intervention (Protocol),' and appears in Issue 9 of their 2017 *Cochrane Database of Systematic Reviews*. On page 4 they discuss four reasons why they consider it important to re-look at aluminum in vaccines: First, they admit that the 2004 Jefferson study 'was based on poor-quality evidence.' Second, the FDA and WHO do not require genotoxicity or cardiotoxicity studies of new aluminum adjuvants, and several new ones have been introduced since their 2004 review on only one aluminum adjuvant. Third, aluminum was used as the placebo control injection 'in the vast majority of randomized clinical trials on HPV vaccines, thus masking its potentially harmful effects. Clinical trials designed to administer vaccine adjuvants to the experimental group as well as the placebo group do not compare an intervention against a true placebo, and therefore, do not adequately assess safety.' Fourth, six studies have found that the reactions to HPV vaccines may be due to the aluminum. Plus, a 2016 study by Inbar showed behavioral abnormalities in mice injected with the aluminum-containing HPV vaccine. Inbar studied three groups: one given the vaccine, one given just aluminum (matching the vaccine amount), and one given a true benign placebo, something the human HPV safety studies failed to do. The results showed that both the vaccine and the aluminum can trigger autoimmune and neuro-inflammatory reactions, leading to the observed behavior changes. Page 4 of the Cochrane Review concludes with this: 'Indeed, aluminum adjuvants, new or old, should be evaluated for benefits and harms on their own merits. Aluminum is the most frequently used adjuvant … no systematic review has been conducted to assess the effects of aluminum adjuvants across vaccines … remains to be properly assessed using Cochrane methodology to determine … if they are causally linked to the numerous adverse events following immunization.'"

Dr. Ward paused to let that sink it. He didn't need to turn and look at Dr. Smith to know what expression he had on his face.

"Then there's the next study Dr. Smith referred to: Keith in *Vaccine*, 2002. He told you the study helped prove vaccine aluminum is safe. Guess what, this wasn't a live study either. It was a mathematical exercise that calculated what they think is probably happening to the aluminum they inject. There wasn't a single live measurement of anything. And something Dr. Smith forgot to mention is that Keith calculated that the amount of aluminum used in vaccines actually does reach toxic levels following injection for a brief period of time, but that the level quickly drops down to being harmless again and there's nothing to worry about.

"So, when a doctor, researcher, or policymaker tells you that they have proven without a doubt that aluminum in vaccines is harmless, it's important for you to understand that the scientific basis for this statement is primarily based on mathematical models, studies of observing people externally for symptoms, and 22 people who volunteered for actual injected research.

"The reason I chose to start by explaining the history of this research is that I am now going to tell you what we do know about aluminum. And what I didn't want you to do, while I tell you all this, is to sit there and say to yourselves, 'That's ok. We've researched this and know it's safe.' If 22 test subjects are enough for you, then go ahead and tell yourself that. If you think we should have tested it in more people before adopting aluminum in vaccines as standard operating procedure, then keep listening.

"Let's discuss what we do know about what aluminum does when too much gets injected into us. Dr. Smith also touched on this. But let's not just touch on it. Let's really *learn* it. Because you want to know. And you *need* to know."

What the hell? Thought Jenny. *This can't be right.* She glanced at her watch. *He's only been talking for 6 minutes, and he's already torn apart John's science. And look at all his notes – so well prepared. It's almost as if he knew exactly what John was going to say and started with his direct rebuttal. Well, maybe that's the worst of it. John obviously proved that the amount in vaccines is much less than what kids eat, so we know it's safe on that basis. So, we haven't really studied it well enough. It's not like they can take a bunch of kids now and do aluminum clearance studies on them, right? Hey, maybe they could do that. I should make that a follow-up question and see what they say. I can fix this.*

But Jenny had no concept of what she was about to hear.

"So the danger that injected aluminum poses to babies was first discovered in a neonatal intensive care unit in the 90s. A group of doctors at Cambridge were concerned because a growing body of research over the preceding decade had demonstrated that aluminum was a toxic metal after all. Others had already discovered that injected aluminum can and does build up to toxic levels in the brain, bloodstream, and bones if too much is given, and that this toxicity can cause progressive dementia in adults. Then, a preemie baby who suddenly died for no explainable reason was found to have high aluminum concentrations in the brain upon autopsy. It was also known that people with reduced kidney function won't clear aluminum out of their bodies, and preemie babies definitely have reduced kidney function. So, this Cambridge group decided to figure out if aluminum really was harmful to preemie babies.

"Back then aluminum was a naturally-occurring contaminant in preemie IV feeding solutions. It wasn't put in on purpose, but no one had thought to filter it out. These preemies were getting about 50 micrograms a day of aluminum in their IVs. What's a microgram? It's 1/1000th of a milligram. Or, there are 1000 micrograms in a milligram. Micrograms are used in the literature when a substance is so toxic in tiny amounts, they don't want to write 0.00 something to describe it in milligrams, because that's confusing. So most researchers use micrograms when dealing with aluminum. It lets us call a particular amount 100 micrograms, instead of calling it 0.1 milligram. Sorry for the chemistry lesson. Let's get back to Cambridge.

"So preemies were getting about 50 micrograms of aluminum a day in their IVs. They randomly assigned 100 of their preemies to get IV feedings that had 90% of the aluminum filtered out. These 100 babies only got about 5 micrograms daily. Their results showed that the 100 babies who got the regular amount of aluminum had impaired neurological and mental development at 18 months of age compared to the lucky 100 who had the aluminum filtered out. This landmark study, published in 1997 in *The New England Journal of Medicine*, prompted all NICUs to begin filtering out aluminum and led to other sweeping changes regarding the use of aluminum in all areas of medicine. Wait, sorry. I should say all areas of medicine except for one.

"The FDA immediately stepped in and created new policies to limit the amount of aluminum in injected therapies. The FDA had originally declared aluminum to be Generally-Regarded-As-Safe in the 1970s, as Dr. Smith said. But that GRAS term means that they didn't actually study it. They just assumed it's safe until proven otherwise. And with this new finding, they realized they'd better place limits on its use. There were two aspects to this policy: 1. No intravenous solutions were allowed to contain more than 25 micrograms of aluminum per liter of solution, and 2. All such solutions had to have a warning label that said 'This product contains aluminum that may be toxic. Aluminum may reach toxic levels with prolonged parenteral administration (parenteral means injected) if kidney function is impaired. Premature neonates are particularly at risk because their kidneys are immature, and they require large amounts of calcium and phosphate solutions, which contain aluminum. Research indicates that patients with impaired kidney function, including premature neonates, who receive parenteral levels of aluminum greater than 4 to 5 micrograms per kilogram of body weight per day accumulate aluminum at levels associated with central nervous system and bone toxicity. Tissue loading may occur at even lower rates of administration.' Does that sound generally safe to you?

"This 4 to 5 micrograms per kilogram measurement comes from the Cambridge study. Most of the preemies who had the aluminum filtered out of their IVs got less than 5 micrograms per kilogram of body weight, but 5 mcg/kg was the most any in this group got. So they determined this cut-off was probably safe.

"Right around the same time, the American Academy of Pediatrics published a policy statement called Aluminum Toxicity in Infants and Children. Their findings were 1. Aluminum can cause neurological harm; 2. There have been reports of infants with healthy kidneys showing elevated blood levels of aluminum from taking antacids; 3. People with kidney disease who build up levels of aluminum greater than 100 micrograms per liter in their bloodstream are at risk for toxicity; 4. This toxic threshold may be even lower; and 5. Aluminum loading (which means tissue buildup) has been seen even in patients with healthy kidneys who receive IV solutions containing aluminum over extended periods.

"A few years later the American Society for Parenteral and Enteral Nutrition published their agreement with the FDA guideline in 2004, re-stating all the worries about the harmful effects of aluminum and extending the warning label to all injected products, not just IV feeding solutions. Or again, all injected products except for one."

Oh my God, is he ever going to stop talking? shuddered Jenny, trying not to slouch in her chair, and way too afraid to look over at John for fear of seeing daggers in his eyes. Her watch informed her that Dr. Ward was still allowed another 5 minutes for this part of the talk. *Well, thank God babies barely get any aluminum, like John already said. I can't wait to hear his rebuttal.*

"So basically we know, for sure, without a doubt, that aluminum can cause serious brain toxicity if someone with impaired kidney function gets too much. That's not in dispute. The established safety limits as to what should be given parenterally are basically set up so that someone with impaired kidney function doesn't get too much.

"Let's discuss how much aluminum all of our healthy babies do get – babies who have healthy kidneys. Dr. Smith has already told us that babies get about 4 milligrams from their vaccines in the first six months. That would be 4000 micrograms."

Dr. Ward paused again to let that sink in.

"In case you are trying to remember some of the earlier numbers, the babies in the NICU who got 50 micrograms per day over 10 days in their IVs showed impaired neurological and intellectual development or, in layman's terms, brain damage. I sure hope giving 4000 micrograms over 6 months is safe though. And when I add up the total for all the childhood vaccines, I get 6600 micrograms.

"Next, let's look at how much aluminum a baby would get in just one day of shots. On the CDC-recommended schedule, a baby gets between 700 and 1225 micrograms of aluminum all at once, at 2 months, 4 months, and 6 months of age. The amount depends on the brands of vaccines used by the pediatrician.

"Plus, newborns, who are barely peeing yet because they are

waiting for mom's breast milk to come in, which is a close comparison to the kidney function of preemies although it's still not the same, get 250 micrograms in the hepatitis B vaccine within hours of birth. But even this number far exceeds what we know is safe for preemies.

"But let's re-touch on the FDA and ASPEN safety guidelines that were set up for all intravenous and injectable products – besides vaccines – that state they should not have more than 25 micrograms. They limit daily aluminum in an adult to 25 micrograms, but will give a two-month old baby 1225 micrograms? Then the AAP guideline that says people with kidney disease who have more than 100 micrograms per liter of blood in their body can be toxic. But somehow we know that giving 1225 micrograms is just fine if their kidneys are healthy?

"Dr. Smith mentioned the new FDA limit placed specifically on vaccines, and he did so accurately: 850 micrograms. My problem with this policy is that it's brand new. We've been using this amount of aluminum in vaccines for decades, and the FDA just now makes a policy that places a numerical limit that just so happens to match the highest amount that's currently in a vaccine? The FDA didn't look at any evidence at all that shows 850 micrograms is some sort of safety cut-off. They looked at all the vaccines, found that the one currently with the most had 850 micrograms, and made a new policy stating that no vaccines could exceed that. Then they added that they could exceed it if they got special approval from the director of the FDA. They have no idea if 850 is safe; they just made the policy so that no one would exceed it. They couldn't make it lower, because that would have forced some vaccines off the market, and everyone would ask questions. And, why limit all other injectables to 25 micrograms, but limit vaccines to 850? Why the difference?

"Here is what I think has happened, and why our medical community finds itself in an indefensible position on this, and then I will be done with my opening statements. Basically, some of our original vaccines were developed with aluminum, before we ever had any clue that aluminum was risky. Back when the FDA gave it the GRAS label. By the time we figured out aluminum was harmful in the amounts we were using in vaccines, our vaccine program was way too established and accepted to pause. No one in their right mind could say anything against vaccines by the 90s; anyone who did would lose their jobs and their careers. And no one will research it, for the same reasons. They know what they will find if they do. And we can't just stop vaccines, right? Can we?

"Thank you."

The auditorium was silent. Jenny sat there, not even noticing. Dr. Smith, eager to get back on top of things, stood up and walked slowly to the podium as he collected his thoughts. He glanced down at the few notes he'd made, points that he obviously wanted to counter.

"Ward's analysis of aluminum in vaccines has completely ignored two critical factors that prove the aluminum is safe. I focused on one of these facts already, but I will say it again. It doesn't matter one tiny bit that babies get 4 mg of aluminum in their shots because they get ten times that much in their baby formula. So adding a little bit more aluminum into a baby through vaccines, aluminum that we do know eventually gets cleared from the body as proven by the human research you pointed out, just doesn't matter. It's relatively so little.

"But the second critical factor that makes vaccine aluminum safe is that babies and children have healthy kidneys. Every single warning and problem that Ward points out here, including the warning labels from the FDA, only apply to people with kidney problems. Yes, I agree that we have to be careful with aluminum in kids with kidney disease. And since we know to be careful with them, aluminum poses no risk to all the healthy babies and children.

"And listen, it's not like we are all ignoring this. Every major research body in the world has looked at this issue and determined that the aluminum is safe. And we can't make many of these vaccines without it. Plus, our Vaccine Safety Datalink system monitors the health of over 5 million vaccinated children over their entire childhood to make sure we don't see any ill effects from their vaccines. If these children were having problems from aluminum, we'd know it.

"I want to conclude with the simple reminder that vaccines are safe and effective, and they've been proven so for decades. Yes, vaccines have to contain some chemical ingredients, but each of these has been thoroughly researched for safety. And aluminum, in particular, has stood the test of time. All of these chemicals occur in tiny quantities that the human body can handle. The amount of additional aluminum in vaccines is nothing compared to what all humans ingest. Thank you for being here tonight, ladies and gentlemen, and thank you again to the University for hosting an event where we can provide valuable education to the public."

Dr. Smith returned to his seat, pausing to shake Jenny's hand along the way, and keeping a thoughtful smile on his face. Dr. Ward stood up and approached the mic.

"Well, first the FDA warnings and guidelines don't only apply to people with kidney disease. They apply to all patients. It's one guideline, one limit, and it applies to all injectable forms of aluminum for everybody. What does only apply to people with kidney disease is that we know even a small amount is dangerous for them. What we don't know is how much is safe for people with healthy kidneys because we haven't tested it.

"And I want to address the Vaccine Safety Datalink, since Dr. Smith brought it up. If we are giving all the same vaccines, and aluminum, to 5 million babies in a database, and there's no comparison group of children who are not getting those vaccines, how would you even know if the vaccinated kids are having any problems? The VSD is pretend research, in my opinion, because it doesn't have a control group. It makes the policymakers feel better that someone is monitoring these kids, but it's not real science.

"How any true scientist can claim to know vaccine aluminum is perfectly safe, based on limited research in 22 people, I just don't know. Plus, there's a very strict rule when it comes to studying medications and side effects in medicine: medications and toxins act differently in adults compared to children. Babies handle things very differently than adults. That's why virtually every prescription and OTC medication has the warning 'not studied for safety in children under two. Ask your doctor.' So, scientifically we shouldn't even be using the research from those seven adults to determine aluminum metabolism in babies.

"But let me move on to the second of Dr. Smith's main points: the claim that we know it is safe because babies ingest, or eat, way more than we inject. Here is what Dr. Smith doesn't want you to know: When we swallow aluminum, 99% of it passes out harmlessly in the stools. In fact, it's actually 99.7%, according to the Who Health Organization, which has studied ingested aluminum worldwide in order to prevent toxicity in developing countries.

"So, when Dr. Smith tells you a breastfed baby swallows 7000 micrograms of aluminum in 6 months, what he really means is that only about 20 micrograms is getting into the baby's circulation. That's 0.3% of 7000. And out of the 38,000 micrograms (38 milligrams) swallowed by a baby on formula, only about 115 micrograms goes into the bloodstream. All the rest comes right out in the stools.

"So, to say that the 4000 micrograms over six months that gets injected into the body from vaccines is safe because we know that the 20 or even 115 micrograms that get into the bloodstream from feeding over six months is safe, is perhaps the single most invalid scientific statement I have ever heard anyone say.

"Let's also look at what happens in just one day of vaccination, compared to one day of eating aluminum. A breastfed baby eats about 40 micrograms in a day, and a formula fed baby eats about 200 micrograms. Of this, only 1 microgram gets into their bloodstreams every day, at the most. On the day of vaccination a baby is given as much as 1225 micrograms. Even those getting the lowest aluminum brands get 700 micrograms all at once. There's no parallel whatsoever in the safety of injected versus ingested aluminum.

"The whole argument that since we swallow so much, what we inject doesn't matter, is invalid. So what proof does that leave us with that aluminum in vaccines is safe? Everybody says so? The FDA Generally Regards it As So? That's all the proof we have. The AAP, the CDC, the FDA, the WHO, the AMA, and Dr. Smith all say it's safe, and they base their belief on 7 adults studied decades ago, and 15 infants who were barely studied for 24 hours.

"Let me summarize the current FDA guidelines on how much injectable aluminum is allowed to go into a person in the hospital: a 25 microgram limit in a day for adults, and 4 to 5 micrograms per kilogram of body weight for babies, which also comes out to about 25 micrograms for large newborns and average two-month-olds. But, we will inject 250 micrograms in the hep B vaccine the day babies are born, and another 1225 micrograms at two months, four months, and six months. We think much of it clears out quickly, but we don't know because no one has thoroughly studied clearance in babies. We know too much is toxic and causes brain and bone damage. That's the current state of affairs, and I am still waiting for evidence that doing this is safe. Thank you."

Jenny composed herself, put a smile on her face, stood up and walked to the podium. "Thank you, both, for sharing your information and opinions with us. This was a lot of information. So many numbers." She knew her smile probably looked as fake as it felt. *Just a little bit of Q and A, then it will all be over.*

"Let's start off with a question for Dr. Smith. Have safety studies been done that looked at giving multiple vaccines with aluminum together? If, as Dr. Ward suggests, giving too much aluminum all at once is somehow risky, what have they found out in research when 2, 3, or 4 of these are given together?" Jenny assumed this was a safe question.

"Well listen. There really is no limit to how many vaccines a child could safely get all in the same day. You could literally give a thousand vaccines to a baby, and the baby's immune system is equipped to handle each and every one of those germ components. Think of it. Babies, and all of us, are exposed to millions of germs every day, and our wonderful immune systems process them and fight them off. And yes, we have studied more than one aluminum vaccine given together and see no increase in adverse events."

"Dr. Ward? A response?" *Ha. Gotcha.*

"I'm not even going to respond to the aluminum part of this question, because that was covered repeatedly in my earlier statements. But I will address Dr. Smith's answer. There are two reasons as to why he is completely wrong about how many vaccines an infant could safely handle at once. The first reason is that no one has studied giving more than 9 simultaneous vaccines to a human infant. So, if we are going to use science, as Dr. Smith likes to do, as we all like to do, there is no scientific basis for claiming we could safely give a baby 1000 vaccines. There are no data upon which to answer this question. So, I'm not going to claim that we do know how many are safe … or not safe.

"But I will tell you that the millions of germs that Dr. Smith says we handle every day all enter our bodies through the natural layers of defense: our eyes, nose, respiratory tract, intestinal tract, and skin. Each of those entrance points has a first-defense layer in our immune system that processes these germs naturally, and presents them to the full immune system for processing and destruction. Or if it's a beneficial germ, our immune system welcomes it. That's nature at its best, and I agree with Dr. Smith that it is, indeed, awesome.

"Now, consider a vaccine germ. It bypasses the first layer of our immune system and gets injected through the skin into our muscle. And it's not a natural germ. It's an artificial genetically-modified germ in a chemical solution that now hits our immune system in a very un-natural way. What happens when natural germs enter this way? When they get punctured through our skin and get imbedded into our deep tissues? We often suffer a deep tissue infection. We need medical care for it: wound cleansing, antibiotics. We need help with it. And wow, if 1000 different germs were presented this way, what would our immune system do? We don't know. That's why operating rooms are sterile. That's why we clean wounds. It's because our immune systems don't handle germs that way in the normal course of life. We breathe them in or swallow them. That's how we handle millions at once.

"So, to say that we know a baby could handle 1000 vaccines in this artificial way, because they handle natural germs the same way, is comparing apples to … not even oranges. It's more like comparing apples to tacos. Dr. Smith has no business making such a non-scientific statement, and the fact that he feels comfortable doing so is partly why so many people don't trust those who promote unlimited vaccination."

Jenny moved on quickly so people wouldn't have time to think about that too carefully.

"Now a question for Dr. Ward, and I think many of you may be wondering as well. You state that we don't have enough research to show that aluminum in vaccines is safe. Are you aware of any research that proves it is harmful?" Jenny didn't notice the sharp look and head-shake from Dr. Smith. "After all, it is not a heavy metal, it is ubiquitous in our environment, and we are all exposed every day. And the only research showing harm that you presented was from IV feeding solutions in babies. So how do we know that there is any harm from aluminum?"

Jenny thought this was another safe question to ask, because she assumed that there couldn't be such research. If there was, the government and CDC would have probably done something about vaccine aluminum a long time ago. And if there was research proving harm, he would probably already have shared it. She watched as Dr. Ward approached the podium, leafing through his notes and landing on what she could now see looked to be a list of research article titles. Her heart sank. He was obviously prepared for, and probably even expecting, this very question.

"Thank you for asking, Jenny. Of course there would be no way to explain all of this research, so I'm just going to summarize one main point, then read you the titles of several more articles. Stop me when you think you've heard enough.

"I want to address the assumption that most or all of the injected aluminum harmlessly makes its way out of the bodies of our children. I've already told you it doesn't, but where does the remaining aluminum go? Does it just sit in the muscle where the shot was given, or does it go somewhere? Numerous researchers have examined this and found that it eventually makes its way inexorably into the brain. Gherardi and his colleagues wrote one of the most comprehensive reviews about aluminum vaccine adjuvants in *Frontiers in Neurology* in February 2015 called 'Biopersistence and brain translocation of aluminum adjuvants of vaccines.' They present over 50 scientific studies that show how our immune cells absorb the vaccine aluminum at the site of injection, move it into nearby lymph nodes, then take the aluminum throughout the body and into the brain. It doesn't just flow into the blood stream; it moves through our lymphatic system and within the immune cells in our blood stream. This explains the delayed, but serious, neurotoxic effect on the brains of our children. Given all the research cited by Gherardi and others, we now don't simply *think* vaccine aluminum goes to the brain, we *know* it does. And here are more studies:

"'Effects of aluminum on the neurotoxicity of primary cultured neurons and on the aggregations of beta-amyloid protein,' *Brain Research Bulletin*, 2001. They found that aluminum causes nerve degeneration and Alzheimer's-like changes in rat brains.

"'Aluminum-adjuvanted vaccines transiently increase aluminum levels in murine brain tissue,' *Pharmacology and Toxicology* 1992. They injected vaccines into mice and found that aluminum levels rose in the brain tissue, peaking at day 3 after injection.

"'Aluminum hydroxide injections lead to motor deficits and motor neuron degeneration,' *Journal of Inorganic Biochemistry*, 2009. Mice were injected with just the aluminum adjuvant used in vaccines and suffered behavior impairments, dementia, and damage to the brain and spinal cord.

"'Long-term persistence of vaccine-derived aluminum hydroxide is associated with chronic cognitive dysfunction,' *Journal of Inorganic Biochemistry*, 2009. This *human* study showed adults who suffered macrophagic myofasciitis (the skin/muscle reaction from aluminum that Dr. Smith discussed) also suffered cognitive impairment, not just skin reactions.

"There have also been three rat studies in 2001 and 2002 published in the *Journal of Inorganic Biochemistry, Food and Chemical Toxicology,* and *Pharmacological Research,* all showing that feeding rats aluminum over an extended period of time harmed the glutamate and GABA pathways in the brain and also caused brain degeneration.

"But let me conclude with one more recent study entitled 'Systematic review of potential health risks posed by pharmaceutical, occupational, and consumer exposures to aluminum, aluminum oxides, aluminum hydroxide, and its soluble salts,' *Critical Reviews in Toxicology,* 2014. This group of ten researchers from the University of Ottawa, Canada, looked at all types of aluminum exposure – food, water, consumer products, IV solutions, and vaccines – and reviewed all available research over the preceding 7 years. They concluded that adverse effects to vaccines with aluminum adjuvants have occurred; immune responses to some aluminum vaccines is no greater, and is sometimes *less,* compared to the same vaccines without aluminum; the scientific literature on the adverse health effects of aluminum is extensive; and that we need better justification for routine addition of aluminum to vaccines. They also concluded that research has demonstrated a link between Alzheimer's disease and aluminum in the brain, that these patients have way more aluminum on autopsy than would be expected from diet and deodorants alone, and that there must be a third source.

"And two final human studies that build on this last study are 'Aluminum in brain tissue in autism' from Mold, Umar, King and Exley, just published this year, which found higher-than-normal levels of aluminum in the brains of five deceased people with autism upon autopsy, and 'Aluminum in brain tissue in familial Alzheimer's disease,' published last year by King, Exley, and colleagues, which found extremely higher-than-normal levels in the brains of 12 individuals with Alzheimer's upon autopsy.

"There's a lot more than this, but I will end here in the interest of time."

Jenny tried to salvage things one last time. "Dr. Smith, what do you think about the new Cochrane Review that Dr. Ward referred to. Should they bother with any more safety research on aluminum? And have you spoken with anyone from Cochrane, since you know a lot of people in this field?"

"Yes, Jenny, I speak with my colleagues in the Cochrane group from time to time, and I don't believe that any of them feel that aluminum poses any risks at all. I look forward to reading that new Review."

"Dr. Ward?"

"Let me clarify. The new Review doesn't say any of the researchers think that aluminum is dangerous. And that would be a matter of their opinion anyway, which they wouldn't include in such a review. Their review is completely, 100% based on a look at the pure science of aluminum safety. And they concluded only this, again: 1. The HPV vaccine safety research didn't include a true placebo control group, because the placebo was aluminum, 2. Animal research on HPV vaccine that did include a true placebo demonstrated some serious concerns with both vaccine aluminum and the aluminum that they injected into one of the control groups, 3. Animal research has shown some serious concerns about autoimmune and neuro-inflammatory reactions, and 4. No systematic human review has been conducted to examine the effects across all six aluminum-adjuvanted vaccines. In light of the fact that several new aluminum adjuvants have been developed since the Jefferson review in 2004, which was only done on one adjuvant, Cochrane has decided if anyone wants to earn the right to say aluminum in vaccines is safe, it actually has to be studied, and that's what they are going to do."

"Dr. Smith, your response to this?" Jenny knew/hoped he had a good one.

"Most of the research that Ward is showing you are animal studies that link aluminum to brain toxicity. We don't have the same research in humans. I mean, we couldn't actually inject aluminum into people like that anymore, and study their internal toxicity. It would be unethical. It's too ..." He stopped talking, seemingly at a loss for words.

"It's too what, Dr. Smith?" asked Dr. Ward. "Too ... toxic?"

Chapter 4

Compliant Patients Are the Best

Tim liked working for Prestley-Churchill Medical Group. Although it was not the nation's largest HMO, it was thriving, and provided him with a steady job in Pediatrics. The only thing he didn't like was their vaccine policy. Not that he didn't like vaccines. Dr. Tim Ellington was as pro-vaccine as every other pediatrician. But, like a growing number of doctors, he also felt that nowadays there were too many vaccines too soon. Babies didn't need hepatitis B vaccine. Skipping vaccines for mostly-harmless diseases like chicken pox and rotavirus was fine with him. And there was no harm in delaying vaccines for things that were eliminated, like polio, especially since polio vaccine didn't prevent the spread of the disease. As long as people eventually got all the important ones, flexibility was fine with him. And when he'd first started working for Prestley-Churchill, there was no company-wide policy. But ten years ago that had changed. The higher-ups had decided to group as many doses into each infant and toddler checkup as they could, and to no longer allow any flexibility for their patients.

For the 2, 4, and 6-month checkups this new policy was no different than what every other doctor did, and that was fine. DTaP, HIB, PC, Hep B, Polio, and Rotavirus each time. That's what the CDC schedule called for, and that's what all doctors did.

But ten years ago the Prestley-Churchill policy-makers, headed by Dr. Jack Thompson, initiated a change that mandated all the toddler vaccines be grouped into one visit at 12 months of age. And this was something very different than what most non-Prestley-Churchill doctors did, and it was different than what the CDC recommended.

The standard CDC schedule had always been MMR, Varicella (Chicken pox), and Hep A at 12 months, HIB and Pneumococcal at 15 months, and DTaP and Polio at 18 months. And that's what most pediatricians, nationwide, did. They spread them out. This also allowed for more checkups during this second year of life. But the CDC also had "flexible age ranges" on their schedule, which allowed doctors to give these vaccines as early as 12 months, and that's what Prestley-Churchill decided to implement for all patients. So they gave MMR/Varicella, Hep A, HIB, Pneumococcal, and DTaP/Polio all together at the 12-month checkup – vaccination against 11 diseases. And the patients had no idea. Since these 11 could be grouped into just 5 injections, patients didn't think it was that much different than the earlier infant shots. They weren't offered alternatives, and they didn't know that vaccines were spaced out in most medical settings outside the HMO.

And since that time he'd seen more toddlers react poorly to this 12-month round of vaccines than he'd seen in the first part of his career when these second-year vaccines were all spread out. He'd seen more seizures, more temporary developmental regression, more encephalitis-like reactions (screaming and high fevers), more chronic and recurrent illnesses in the toddler population, than ever before. So many of these toddlers spent the next year or two suffering recurrent ear infections and colds, and developed allergies and eczema. Of course, he couldn't prove this was due to the vaccine policy. But he knew it from his daily observations of life as a Prestley-Churchill pediatrician. He was angry that this grouping of vaccines had never, ever, not even once, been studied for safety. When the FDA approved them, they were spread out. But Prestley-Churchill decided to give them all together anyway. For convenience, they said. Get them all done at 12 months and we don't have to bother with any at 15 or 18 months. Each patient was simply reassured that having a seizure, screaming for hours, high fever, and shutting down for a few weeks was normal and expected. And getting ear infections and allergies in the weeks to follow was simply coincidental.

And their clientele, the patients of Prestley-Churchill, were completely clueless. The minority who did ask for vaccines to be spread out were simply told no. Sure, patients could refuse any vaccines they didn't want for their children, but the harassment they had to endure from the Prestley-Churchill nurses was inhuman. He'd heard the nurses yelling at non-compliant patients through closed doors. Doctors too. And he'd watched nurses roll their eyes in a huff as they grudgingly gave fewer shots to those who stood their ground. Then there were the constant phone calls and emails sent to patients who were behind on their shots. And there wasn't a thing he could do about it, because he had to follow orders in a group like this.

And today was the annual policy meeting for his branch of Prestley-Churchill. Tim was on the policy board, and he'd tried, subtly, to prevent this vaccine policy from being enacted, but to no avail. He dreaded what Dr. Thompson would try to add to the vaccine schedule this year. *Not that there's anything left to add … is there? If there is, Jack will find it.*

As the meeting came to order, Tim would discover he was wrong, and right.

"And so, I propose that we add the flu shot to all 12-month checkups that occur during flu season, which would be from October through April. And as you know, babies need two doses of the flu shot the first year it's given, so they'll have to come back a month later for the second dose. But if we mix it in with the other five shots at 12 months, the parents won't even notice, and we'll raise our compliance numbers up above 95%, at least for the first dose. Currently we are below 70% on the flu shot, and that's because when we ask parents if they want their baby to have a flu shot, most say no, because most parents don't bother with one for themselves. This new approach gives them less opportunity to say no. Oh, also, we are going with the same mandatory face-mask policy this year again for anyone who doesn't want to get the flu shot. Not the patients. Just the medical staff. Us. I'd like to hear if anyone has any concerns about these changes."

Tim felt all of the two-dozen eyes at the table turn toward him, since they all knew he was the only one who ever objected to past vaccine consolidation. He already knew it would be futile to argue with the mask-wearing policy, and it didn't affect him anyway. He'd had several conversations about this with his sister, Anna, who was an ICU nurse. *I can't believe she's willing to wear a mask for six months out of each year.* He knew her reasons for not wanting the flu shot; their grandma had had a severe Guillain-Barre reaction to one decades ago. But Tim figured the shots were harmless to him now, since he hadn't had any problems with the first few. As for this new flu vaccine policy, he also knew it wouldn't do any good to voice his observations about what he thought the current 12-month vaccines were doing to their clients. And he noticed the way Jack called it "five shots" at twelve months, instead of the "eleven vaccines" that were in those five injections. *Eleven, now twelve with the flu, sounds like an overload. Five just sounds like a routine.* But there was one very valid scientific argument he could make, not that it would do any good either.

"My main concern, Jack, would be seizure-related adverse events," he began. "We already know that the MMR/VZ combo shot we give has a higher seizure rate compared to giving these two separately – a seizure rate of 1 in 1250, according to the CDC. We also know that other vaccines feature seizure reactions in their product inserts, like Hep A vaccine and DTaP, of course. But the CDC also warns about seizures when we combine the flu shot with pneumococcal vaccine at the same visit. That warning is on their VIS forms. The data show a seizure rate of about 1 in 1600 when you give both shots on the same day. I think we are already seeing more seizure reactions than we should, and throwing the flu shot in there will give us more. And any of my patients who have had seizures with these shots don't want any more. It really interferes with future compliance."

"Well, that's an even better reason to give them all at 12 months and get them over with," Jack countered, letting out a genuine laugh. "Then there wouldn't be any more shots for patients to argue about until the two-year visit when we give the next Hep A vaccine. By then they won't be as scared. And despite the seizure risk, the CDC still allows this grouping of shots, and they do not advise *against* grouping PC with flu shot. So we are just following CDC recommendations on this."

Then why the hell don't all other pediatricians out in the real world do this? Tim didn't say. "But we may see a drop in compliance with the second dose of the flu a month later if parents see their baby didn't do well with the 12-month shots."

"Well, they'll be in plenty of times for ear infections and such in the months to come, so there will be opportunity to fix that. You know how toddlers like to get sick. But speaking of compliance with vaccines in general, we also have a new staff member who's going to help with that. I'd like to introduce Lisa Goodman," nodding toward a new woman in the room whom Tim hadn't noticed yet. "She is a social worker and will be helping with all family-related problems among our patients: domestic disputes, family dynamics, you name it. She's here to help. Every single Prestley clinic nationwide will have one by the end of this year."

"What does that have to do with vaccine compliance?" Tim asked.

"Well, for one, she is going to start meeting with every prenatal family in the OB department to make sure everyone around that little baby-to-be is vaccine-compliant: the pregnant mom's Tdap and flu shots, the grandparents' and dad's Tdap, MMR, and flu shots, the sibling's vaccines, everyone. Lisa will help identify any holes in a family's 'cocooning' strategy – you know, the idea that if we surround every newborn with a 'cocoon' of vaccinated people, that newborn will be safer. She will advise the parents on how they can best keep any non-compliant family members away from the new baby for its first year or two of life. Believe me, any grandma, aunt, or god-parent who has to choose between compliance and family is going to make the right choice. No one wants to miss out on holding that precious little baby in their arms, right? We hope to achieve 100% compliance with all cocooning vaccines."

"But we all know the cocooning strategy was shown to be ineffective because the Tdap vaccines and flu vaccines don't prevent disease transmission," objected Tim. Looking around the table he saw a few others nod their heads. "Are the OBs still actually telling their patients that these vaccines protect a newborn?"

"Well, yeah. Of course they are. Once we institute a system-wide policy like that, and everyone starts following it, we can't just call it quits when a new study or two shows it might not work. Besides, even if the flu and Tdap vaccines don't provide any real cocooning effect for a newborn, they are still important for all people to get. Bottom line is that encouraging all family members to get all their vaccines so they can be a part of a new baby's life works. The reasoning behind it shouldn't matter."

Tim didn't even know what to say to that. Back when 'newborn cocooning' was first proposed, and government agencies began advertising flu and Tdap vaccines to expectant families, everyone just assumed that the vaccines would prevent disease transmission. When follow-up studies showed that vaccinating grandparents, dads, and siblings against whooping cough and flu doesn't actually prevent disease transmission, Tim assumed everyone would have gotten word to stop promoting the vaccines that way. But then he realized that was a foolish assumption. *Of course they'll keep promoting them as beneficial. Why wouldn't they? But to tell a family not to let other family members around, just because they know enough to not get the shots? That was just cruel.* But Tim wasn't prepared for what his boss said next.

"But that's only part of our new Social Service department's role. Moving forward, every family who refuses vaccines, or asks to get them done outside of our set schedule, will be informed that they are going to meet with our on-site social worker. Lisa will discuss the concerns they have, then inform them that she will be keeping a file open on them in case they'd like to discuss their vaccine concerns again at a later date."

"What good is that going to do? It sounds like it's just some extra paperwork and expense."

"Well, it's all in how you present it to your patients, Tim. I plan to tell each one of my patients who refuses vaccines that I would like them to discuss the situation with our social worker, who is in touch with the Department of Child and Family Services. I will let them know that if our social worker has any concerns about how the family feels about vaccines, she can pass her concerns onto Child Services, and a social worker from that government department can come out to the family's home and talk with them about vaccines too."

"Wait. What? You are going to report non-vaccinating families to Child Protective Services? Seriously? Like, for child abuse?"

"Listen Tim, I'm not the only doctor who feels that failing to fully vaccinate constitutes child neglect. I'm just letting these patients know that I take the well-being of their children seriously. Believe me, any patient who is on the fence about vaccines and is thinking about refusing them will certainly cave when they realize that they'll have CPS at their door."

"But legally speaking, refusal to vaccinate is not even a reportable offense. CPS wrote that into their rules a few years ago. Even if you, or Ms. Goodman here – nice to meet you, Lisa – file a report, they aren't going to even do anything about it. They aren't going to even call the parents. You know that."

"Yeah, but the patients don't. Compliance, Tim ... it's all about compliance. Oh, and that reminds me about the other policy change that will increase compliance. We are doing away with the CDC VIS forms."

Silence around the table. *Silence of agreement?* Tim wondered. "What do you mean 'doing away' with them? They are from the CDC. We can't just ..."

"I mean, we are no longer going to provide them to patients," finished Jack. "No more informed consent process prior to vaccines. It's a waste of time, and it only scares the patients and leads to more questions. But most importantly, we aren't required by law to provide them."

"Yes we are," countered Tim. "The National Vaccine Injury Compensation Act instructs doctors to show patients the VIS forms before ..."

"It 'instructs' us, Tim. It can't make us do it. Vaccine informed consent is under the jurisdiction of each state, *not* the federal government. Our state doesn't demand informed consent for vaccination, so we aren't going to do it anymore. The patients can just read the damn forms on their own at home if they want to."

Tim, again, was at a loss for words.

Chapter 5

Of Disease and Men

Peter Tommaso liked talking about vaccines. He could do it all day, and sometimes he did. Since he was one of the only pediatricians in the area who was open-minded and welcoming toward parents who didn't want to follow the entire CDC schedule, most such patients in the county and beyond ended up at his office. So he was glad to finally have his own solo practice where he could do whatever he wanted, and he decided to start giving a vaccine information lecture once a month in his office waiting room. This was his fifth one, and he was happy to see seven couples from his practice eagerly waiting to learn.

"Welcome everyone. We have a lot of information to cover, so let's jump right in and get started. I'm first going to give you an overview of every disease that we vaccinate against so you'll have a general understanding of the risk that each disease poses and why the vaccine was put on the schedule. I'll also comment on the relative importance, or lack thereof, of that vaccine.

"Hepatitis B is the first vaccine, scheduled to be given on the day of birth, 1 month, and 6 months of age. This is mainly a sexually-transmitted disease. It can also be passed by sharing IV drug needles or any type of accidental blood exposure.

"The only realistic way a baby will catch it is if mom is a chronic hep B carrier and she passes it to her baby during birth through all the blood exposure in the birth canal. The number of babies who become infected this way is about 30 every year. By the way, all disease stats we are going to discuss are based only on the United States, not the world. Just FYI. Another 30 or so preschoolers and about 70 elementary age children are diagnosed with hep B every year as well. These occur either from accidental blood exposure or were acquired at birth but had delayed onset of the disease.

"Hep B is very severe for babies who catch it during birth: about 25% of such cases are fatal, and most who survive will have lifelong liver problems. It is less severe for toddlers and preschoolers who catch it by accidental blood exposure: they have a 35% chance of chronic disease. Elementary age kids have a 10% risk of chronic disease.

"For adults it's a different story. Ninety-five percent of exposed adults will clear the disease without any lasting effects. The 5% who do become chronic carriers can be treated with strong medications that cure about one-third of these. The remaining victims will have varying degrees of liver disease. It's estimated that about 1% of American adults are chronic hep B carriers and about 4000 adults die from this each year.

"By the way, if a parent has hep B, and it's not passed to the baby during birth, then there's about a 35% chance the child will catch it from a parent from accidental blood exposure just from living together over the years of childhood.

"Bottom line on this disease is that while there are some situations in which this vaccine may be useful for American babies, for the vast majority there is no particular benefit to getting this vaccine during infancy or young childhood.

"Moving on to disease number two: HIB, or haemophilus influenza type B. This bacteria is transmitted like the common cold. It can cause a wide range of symptoms from just a mild cough and runny nose to pneumonia to blood stream infections to a severe throat infection called epiglottitis to meningitis. Before this vaccine was made available in the late 80s, there were thought to be about 20,000 severe cases of this disease every year. Now it's pretty much eradicated, with only about 10 severe infections being reported nationwide every year.

The fatality rate for the most severe form of infection – meningitis – is about 5%. So, it's a very bad disease, but thankfully it's extremely rare. The vaccine is scheduled at 2 months, 4 months, 6 months, and 15 months to provide ever-increasing levels of immunity during the early years when the disease poses the greatest risk. Kids older than 2 years of age rarely catch HIB, although it can technically occur at any age. Parents who wish to delay vaccines can get their toddler just 1 HIB dose at 15 months or later, and that one dose gives just as much immunity as if you had done all four along the way. This one dose works much better on a more mature immune system.

"Bottom line: it's a really bad disease, and thank God it's now so rare.

"Disease number three: pneumococcal disease. This bacteria causes the same conditions as HIB (except it doesn't cause epiglottitis), and it can be just as mild or just as severe. But when an infant or young child catches a severe case, like meningitis, the fatality rate is higher – about 20%. Like HIB, it's also treatable with antibiotics. But unlike HIB, PC disease is not rare. There are an estimated 2000 or so cases of severe infections – meningitis, bloodstream infections, or severe pneumonia – in kids under 5 each year. And there are probably hundreds of thousands of mild cases each year in kids and adults that don't even get diagnosed and just get better with antibiotics, or often even without treatment. The vaccine is given on the same 4-dose schedule as HIB. Those who don't want vaccines during infancy can just get two doses after age 1, or 1 dose after age 2, and get full immunity. The vaccine helps prevent 13 strains of this disease, but there are almost 100 strains out there. So it's still possible to catch PC even if vaccinated.

"Bottom line: Most cases are mild, but severe cases can happen and this is not rare.

"The fourth disease is diphtheria. This disease has been eradicated from the U.S., so there's really no risk for American babies now. But it was a horrible disease way back when. It causes a severe throat infection that makes it difficult to breathe. It's transmitted like a cold. There is treatment available if someone does happen to catch it.

"The fifth disease is tetanus. You all know what tetanus is. Fortunately it's extremely rare. Each year in the U.S. there are about 1 baby or young child diagnosed with tetanus, about 5 teenagers, and about 50 adults nationwide. About 10% who develop the neurological symptoms of tetanus will die. If you've never had a tetanus shot, and you get a very serious dirty wound (not just a simple clean cut that needs a few stitches – something really deep and dirty), getting what's called a TIG shot – tetanus immune globulin, which is different than the vaccine – can neutralize tetanus germs so you don't come down with it. Getting the first dose of just the regular vaccine doesn't help at the time of injury unless you've already had at least one prior vaccine dose.

"Bottom line on tetanus: It's just not a disease of infancy, and it is so rare in children. It's really bad when it does happen, but the chance of it happening is extremely small, and there is a preventive treatment if your baby or child gets injured but doesn't yet have the vaccine. Plus, thorough wound cleansing virtually eliminates the chance of tetanus, even in a high-risk wound. It's not like every unvaccinated person who gets impaled by a dirty, rusty spike will get tetanus.

"Disease number six is whooping cough, also known as pertussis. This vaccine is mixed with diphtheria and tetanus vaccines as the DTaP vaccine. It's given at 2, 4, and 6 months, then again at 18 months, 5 years, and 12 years of age. Adults can also get one dose as a booster. You can't get just a plain whooping cough vaccine; it only comes with tetanus and diphtheria. Whooping cough is very severe if a young infant catches it. About 20 infants die each year from this disease, and virtually all of these are 3 months and younger. It is almost unheard of for an older infant or child to die from this disease. About 1 in 200 reported newborn cases are fatal. The germ infects the throat and upper lungs and causes extremely severe coughing spells. It can be treated with antibiotics only if the disease is recognized early and antibiotics are started within several days of the onset of severe cough.

"Bottom line on the DTaP vaccine is that honestly babies don't need tetanus and diphtheria shots. But, also honestly, whooping cough is a bad disease to catch in the first few months of life. And it's no fun for older babies and kids, with weeks or even a few months of severe coughing fits. But there is little to no risk of dying from it once your baby is about 4 months and older.

"This vaccine is offered to pregnant women in order to pass some immunity to a baby through the placenta in hopes that the baby will have some immunity during the first two months of life before his own shots can begin. Research has not yet proven that this trans-placental immunity works well. So it's just a theoretical benefit. Due to a lack of safety research, I don't recommend any vaccines during pregnancy, by the way.

"I want to say that there is a lot more that could be said about this vaccine and all the ins and outs of whether or not to get it. This is just a brief introduction to the diseases. We will spend more on this shot later.

"Ok, so is your head spinning yet? Mine too. To briefly recap, we've discussed hep B, tetanus, and diphtheria, which are all very bad diseases but pose little to no risk to babies. And we've talked about HIB and PC meningitis, and whooping cough, which do pose some risk to babies. Now let's push on for a bit more then we'll take a break.

"Polio. This disease has been eradicated from the United States for over 35 years now. No one has caught the disease in the U.S. in all this time. We still give the shot at 2, 4, 6, and 18 months, with a booster at 5 years, in order to give people immunity in case we ever do have an outbreak. But again, this hasn't happened in over 35 years. We used to give people the oral polio vaccine, which worked much better and makes people pretty much immune to the disease; but about 8 American children were being paralyzed every year form this live oral vaccine. So in the late 90s we switched to the injected vaccine to avoid the paralysis reactions. This injected vaccine, by the way, doesn't make us immune. It only gives us internal immunity in our bloodstream so that the infection can't invade inside and get to the brain. But we would still catch the infection in our intestinal tract if exposed, and can pass it along to others. You just won't know you are sick with it because you won't have neurological symptoms.

Ninety-nine percent of people who do catch it won't even know it anyway because the infection only causes neurological problems in less than 1% of cases. And that's how it was way back when polio was everywhere; 99% of people who caught it didn't even know they had it. It was the unlucky 1% who suffered nerve damage.

"Bottom line is that this disease is pretty much zero risk to Americans, and the disease is virtually eradicated worldwide now except for a few small pockets of disease in Central Asia (Pakistan and Afghanistan).

"Ok. Now for rotavirus. This is a vomiting/diarrhea disease that is virtually harmless to almost everyone who catches it, especially if breastfeeding. The vomiting and diarrhea are certainly no fun, but you get through it. Every baby or child catches this disease by the time they have been in daycare or preschool for a year or two because it spreads easily in those places every winter. Before this vaccine came out in the early 2000s, the U.S. did have about 50 reported fatalities from the dehydration complications of this disease each year. These deaths were mostly in babies who didn't get access to IV fluids in time. This still, sadly, happens to about 10 babies each year. One brand of this oral liquid vaccine is given in just two doses – at 2 and 4 months - and it only protects against the one most common strain of the disease. The other brand is 3 doses and protects against 4 strains. There are more strains out there that the vaccine doesn't cover.

"Bottom line on this one is that it's a harmless disease for most babies and toddlers. It's certainly not a fun disease though; some will have diarrhea for weeks, and some will need IV fluids, especially if young. But if not in early daycare, then the risk of catching it while young is small. And if you catch the disease as a preschooler, it shouldn't be a big deal.

"Now for disease number . . . what is it, eight? The flu. This is another complicated disease and vaccine that deserves a longer discussion later. But here are the pertinent disease facts.

"Of course, most cases are ultimately harmless, even for babies. However, each year in the U.S. there are about 20 deaths from the flu in babies, about 20 in toddlers/preschoolers, another 20 in children and teens, and about 40 deaths in young adults. Then in the elderly, 65 and older, about 1300 deaths are reported each year. All of these deaths are tragic, of course. But realize given the enormity of our population, the risk of dying from the flu is miniscule. The shot is now recommended for every child every year between 6 months and 18 years at the start of each flu season.

"And the shot is also recommended for pregnant moms. I don't advise it due to the lack of safety research, like with the Tdap. The media has spread the false idea that the flu is extremely dangerous during pregnancy. But the research doesn't support this. At most, flu may be a tiny bit more risky during pregnancy than for other healthy adults, but this difference is negligible, and in my opinion, not worth vaccinating for during the one time in your life when you are supposed to be the *most* careful about what goes into your body.

"So everything we've discussed so far is started within the first six months of life. Twenty-four vaccine doses, actually. What's interesting is that we used to give that many vaccine doses throughout all of childhood, up through the late 1980s. What we give now grouped into the first 6 months of life is quite an escalation from the old days. Now onto some of the later shots.

"MMR vaccine is for measles, mumps, and rubella. This live-virus vaccine is given at 1 and 5 years of age.

"The rates of measles infection have varied between 55 cases each year to as many as 600. Children don't die from measles in a modern, healthy nation like ours. The only childhood fatality from measles in recent decades was back in 2003. The fatality rate from measles is about 1 in 10,000 cases, although there's some debate over that that we will discuss later. It's very contagious and easily spread like the common cold. It's certainly no fun to go through, but it's not the deadly disease that the media tries to portray during the small outbreaks that we have.

"Mumps is another mostly-harmless disease. It causes sore throat, fever, and swollen cheeks. It makes you look like a chipmunk for a week or so. We see between 200 and 6000 cases each year. It's not nearly as contagious as measles, so it doesn't easily spread. Mumps isn't fatal, but very rarely it can cause sterility if an adult catches it.

"Rubella is the "R" in MMR vaccine. It's been pretty much eradicated from the U.S. It's a harmless virus that causes fever and a rash. The reason we vaccinate against it is that if a pregnant mom catches rubella, the virus can cause birth defects. So we've eliminated the disease from our population so that pregnant moms and their babies don't have this risk. Each year, however, there are 1 or 2 or 3 babies born with a rubella-linked birth defect. So the risk isn't zero, but it is very, very small. There is no treatment for rubella. Oh yeah, that reminds me – treatment.

"I told you earlier which diseases can be treated. Knowing that a disease does have a treatment makes you feel a little less helpless. Rotavirus doesn't have a specific anti-viral treatment. The flu does. Mumps and rubella don't. But, measles *does*. That may surprise you, because you rarely hear the news warning people to go out and get their vitamin A preventive treatment during a measles outbreak. But taking high-dose vitamin A for two days greatly reduces the chances of suffering a severe case of the disease. It doesn't stop you from catching measles, but it can make the course milder. And if you are already sick, it can still help. Sorry, forgot to include treatment in these last few, but there it is.

"Ok, so chickenpox. This is another live-virus vaccine given at the same times as MMR – age 1 and 5. In fact, doctors can buy them together so they are in the same shot. I don't do this, though, because the combo shot has ten times the amount of chickenpox as the separate vaccine. Much of the virus dies off when mixed and stored with the M, M, and R viruses, so they have to put in a lot more when they first make it. Plus, the combo vaccine has a much higher rate of seizure reactions – 1 in 1250 kids – compared to if you give the two shots in separate injections. But that's vaccine info, sorry. We are focusing just on diseases right now.

"Chickenpox is a harmless disease for most kids. The chance of dying from it is about 1 in 65,000 cases. Back when everyone caught it, about 50 people died each year. Now about 5 Americans die from it each year. There is an anti-viral treatment that may reduce the severity of the disease, although it's not recommended for healthy people. This disease is worse if you catch it after puberty, by the way, but it's still manageable and virtually never fatal.

"Now for our last childhood disease – Hepatitis A. This barely deserves mention because it's a completely harmless type of food-poisoning if young kids catch it. It occurs as small restaurant-based outbreaks. When older kids catch it, like elementary age and up, it's a little tougher, with some vomiting and diarrhea. But not a big deal. If an adult catches Hep A, it can cause several days of vomiting, weeks of diarrhea, and some jaundice from liver inflammation. But no one dies of Hep A unless you already have severe liver disease. San Diego had an outbreak in the homeless population last year, many of whom had alcohol and drug-abuse problems, so their livers were already shot; about 20 people died. But this doesn't happen in healthy people. We vaccinate against it at 1 year and 18 months (or two years – the timing of the booster is up to each office). The idea is to get some immunity so that kids aren't caught up in a restaurant outbreak. But these rarely occur, and when they do, healthy people aren't harmed. There is no treatment other than supporting the symptoms.

"Ok. Take a deep breath. That was a lot of info. Yeah, it's second nature to me because I live these facts every day. But how do you, the parent, take all this in and make sense of it all? Oh, by the way, I didn't go over the last two diseases we vaccinate against, meningococcal disease and HPV, because those are teenage vaccines, and all of you here are making decisions for your babies. So I don't want to confuse you more by throwing in facts that you don't have to think about yet. Anyway, let's take a short break, and then we'll jump into the decision-making process."

"Ok, break's over. So let me summarize and break it down in a way that I think you, the parents of a young baby, should understand these diseases so you know why vaccines are recommended by the CDC, what the disease risk is, and what risks you are taking if you don't vaccinate for one or more of these. I'm going to assume that all of you are here because you don't just want to automatically get your child all of the 70 vaccine doses on the CDC schedule. You are here because you want to understand which vaccines your baby really needs. You don't want to get vaccines just because some scientist sitting on a committee somewhere decided that your baby needs them. You want to get vaccines only if your baby really does need them.

"The most straightforward way to describe a vaccine that your baby would need most is to consider the two criteria that make a vaccine most important: 1. The disease has to be common enough that your baby is somewhat likely to catch it, and 2. The disease would have to be severe if your baby did catch it. It would have to threaten your baby's life, or likely cause permanent harm if your baby does survive. Now that's a disease worth vaccinating against, right?

"So, what diseases fit both of these criteria? Actually ... none. Not anymore, anyway. We are all very fortunate that living in a modern society, with good hygiene, healthy living conditions, proper sanitation, and advanced medicine which, yes, includes vaccines, has brought us to a point where no dangerous disease is common, and no common disease is dangerous. Let me say that again. Regarding these two disease criteria, all the dangerous diseases are extremely rare, and all the diseases that are still common are not likely to be dangerous or deadly.

"Now I know what you are thinking. What about whooping cough? What about meningitis? What about measles? The flu? Tetanus? Hep B? Each of those can be deadly. But what I'm saying is that the chance that your baby – your one individual baby – born this year among the 4 million other babies born in America, the chance that your baby is going to be harmed or die from one of these is statistically extremely small. It's tiny. It's way less than 1%. In fact, it's way less than 0.01% - 1 in 10,000. No one really knows exactly what that statistical risk is, but you can easily calculate it based on the fatality rates of diseases that kill babies every year.

"Here are a few examples. Whooping cough: 20 out of 4 million babies die every year of this. That's a 1 in 200,000 risk. And virtually all deaths are in infants 3 months or less, so the window of risk is short.

"Meningitis: from HIB, 1 or 2 die every year, but let's just count all cases of HIB as serious, because they are. That's 20 or so cases out of about 20 million kids, if we are just counting kids in the first 5 years of life because that's the primary age range for this disease. So that's about 1 in a million risk. PC meningitis? We don't have very solid numbers, but experts estimate there are about 2000 or so serious PC cases in the U.S. each year in children. If we use the same 5 year age group, that's about a 1 in 10,000 risk, which is higher than the others. But this estimate really has its limitations, because we really don't have solid data on how many severe PC cases occur nationwide each year.

"Measles: No children die from that in the U.S., but an adult did die a couple years ago. So that's a risk of 1 in our population of what, 350 million? The last child to die of measles in the U.S. was in 2003.

"Tetanus: 1 child case among about 20 million 0 to 5-year-olds. Including teens, it's about 5 cases in 72 million kids 0 to 18, or a risk of 1 in 14 million.

"The flu? We have roughly 100 fatalities in our group of kids 0 to 18 years. So that's a risk of 1 in 720,000.

"You can do the math on any disease, and you will see that the statistical danger to your one little baby is tiny. So if you choose to not vaccinate, what risk are you taking? The highest risk I see is that 1 in 10,000 risk of pneumococcal disease. All the other risks are lower.

"Please realize that I'm not saying you shouldn't vaccinate. Many of my patients choose some vaccines. But what I want you to understand is that the disease danger is relatively small, and the decision to not vaccinate is not a dangerous one. It's all about understanding the disease risk, comparing it to the vaccine risks, and deciding which risks are you more comfortable with as a parent.

"Now let me tell you what I've seen among my patients who don't vaccinate, over these 30 years that I've been a pediatrician. In other words, if you don't vaccinate, what will your baby likely catch, and what will that be like?

"First, of course, is the flu. I'm not going to waste time on that. Virtually all cases pass without harm, as I said before. But, you can't come crying to me if your baby is pretty sick, wishing you'd gotten the flu shot that year. Be ready to go through a few flus during childhood. Plus, the flu shot doesn't work very well. Last year it was only about 10% effective. Some years it's as high as 60%.

"Next in commonality comes rotavirus. But we'll skip that 'cuz it's virtually always harmless.

"Next is whooping cough. It's pretty common, as I said. Now as long as your baby doesn't catch it in the first few months of life he or she will be fine. But your older baby or child might catch it because it's everywhere, and he might be stuck with a very tough cough for 2 or 3 months. It's no fun. And it is somewhat likely to happen. I see at least one case every month. If you identify it early, and get on early antibiotics, the course may be relatively short. Plus, there's a high dose vitamin C protocol that you can find online that works surprisingly well for whooping cough. Consider following that protocol if your child does catch it.

"Then there's PC disease – pneumococcal. I've had to put two kids in the hospital with PC pneumonia, a couple with bloodstream infections, and one with meningitis. I've seen one HIB meningitis too. One parent said, 'I had no idea my child could catch pneumonia like this. I wish I'd vaccinated.' Even though I do warn parents, many assume it won't happen to their child. It can, and it does.

"Your child might catch chickenpox, so you have to accept that he or she may go through that. The fatality rate for it is, again, only about 1 in 65,000 cases.

"I will also say that in my 30 years of pediatrics, not a single patient has ever been permanently harmed by any of these diseases. And I probably have the lowest vaccination rates of all Peds in the state. No one has died and no one has suffered a severe complication. I've seen a few complications that were moderate, like some hearing loss from meningitis and some minor nerve complications from chickenpox, which was unfortunate. These parents may wish they had chosen the vaccine, but it's easy to say that after the fact.

"Am I just lucky, or are the diseases just so unlikely to be dangerous today? You ask an ICU doctor or an Infectious Disease specialist, they'll say something very different. They've seen the kids die, because they are the ones who care for all the complicated serious cases. But in the life of a regular private-practice pediatrician, I just haven't seen it. Maybe that makes me less proactive about pushing vaccines. But I try to not be too casual about the diseases. I just present all the facts so you can make an educated decision.

"Now I know there are other reasons to vaccinate against a disease besides just protecting your one child, such as doing it for the good of the public health. We'll discuss this in more detail later, but the reality is that very few vaccines prevent the spread of a disease. Many just protect an individual from feeling sick and reduce the severity of the disease for only that individual. But a vaccinated person will still catch the germ and spread it to others. This is especially true of whooping cough. So, this public health argument is not valid for most shots. For the few shots that do help reduce the spread of a disease, you have to decide if you are willing to put your baby's health at risk from vaccine side effects by doing vaccines you think your baby doesn't really need so that you can help protect others. Is that your responsibility, or do you have the right to choose to not risk those side effects? Of course, you aren't risking anyone around you who is vaccinated, unless their vaccine doesn't work. But that's the fault of the vaccine, not your fault. And even if you did vaccinate, your child's vaccine could fail and your child could catch and spread the disease. And if you spread the disease to someone who purposely didn't vaccinate, that's a risk that they already freely accepted. So it's my opinion that you, as your baby's parent, do have the right to opt out of a vaccine that you decide your baby doesn't need, or you decide the potential side effects aren't worth the disease protection.

"This brings me to a side point. Do vaccines even work? I've talked a lot about why we vaccinate and how these vaccines can prevent disease. You may have read that some people claim vaccines don't work, so why are we even talking about doing them? Well, I believe they do work. Some work better than others. Some don't work very well at all. The way I like to explain this is to understand how each vaccine works so you know what gains you can expect by getting it. Some totally prevent the disease. But some allow you to catch the disease, and spread it to others, but just not feel as sick. It's this second group that people will point to and say, 'Ha! The vaccine doesn't work.' Well, yes it does, but it's not expected to prevent infection. It's just expected to prevent disease complications so you are less likely to be harmed by that disease. So, it did work in that way. It just didn't work the way you thought it should.

"I will say, however, that there's a misconception in the media and in the public, and among some doctors who aren't educated about vaccines, that all vaccines completely prevent infection and prevent the spread. These people are wrong, and the harm that comes from this misconception is that they then blame people who don't vaccinate for spreading the disease. They don't realize that many of these vaccines don't prevent that spread. So, which is which? And how do you factor these ideas into your decision? Don't worry. We'll cover that later.

"But in regard to your social responsibility for the few vaccines that do reduce disease spread, it's worth mentioning that one reason we do these shots is to protect the babies who are too young to be vaccinated yet. Measles and chickenpox are two such diseases because we don't give shots for those until age one. The media really shines a spotlight whenever that happens, and casts blame on unvaccinated kids. That's why you have to be very responsible if you don't vaccinate against something that is very contagious. Don't sit in your doctor's waiting room with a fever and a rash, or huge severe coughing fits, for God's sake. Be smart. If your child is sick, don't go out. And that's true whether you are vaccinated or not. We all share that duty.

"But one thing I do find ironic in regard to the MMR and chickenpox vaccines and vulnerable babies less than one year old is this: back when everyone caught measles, mumps, rubella, and chickenpox when they were kids, and the diseases were mostly harmless, they developed lifetime immunity. So, all moms were immune and their babies were born immune, and were therefore not vulnerable during this first year of life when the diseases can be more serious. Now that we vaccinate, the moms growing up in this generation don't catch the diseases. They have no natural immunity, their childhood vaccines wear off and they don't pass immunity to their babies. It's really our public health policy of vaccination that has created these vulnerable infants. So when such a baby does get sick, who do we blame? Or, do we simply blame no one and say that sickness and disease are nobody's fault and they are just a part of life?

"This ties into the concept of herd immunity, which I was going to cover later, but hey, let's just jump into it right now.

"So, some people think that herd immunity is a myth, or a lie. I disagree. I look at it not in terms of whether or not we have herd immunity, but as what type of herd immunity we have opted for as a society. Herd immunity is the concept that if virtually all people in a 'herd' are immune to something, then the few who aren't immune will still be protected. The disease can't enter the herd and take hold, because most are immune. Maybe a few get sick, but overall the herd survives. That's herd immunity.

"We used to have what could be termed 'natural herd immunity,' but it was very different than what we expect out of herd immunity from vaccines today. Prior to vaccines, everyone caught the diseases when they were the most routine – during childhood. Measles, mumps, rubella, and chickenpox used to be rites of passage; everyone caught them at the age when complications and deaths were least expected. Everyone grew up immune, including moms. This immunity was passed to each baby to protect them for the first year or so, as I've already said. Parents' immunities were re-boosted when their kids caught the diseases. And pregnant moms were immune to chickenpox and rubella during their pregnancies. Adults didn't get sick, which was important because that's when disease complications occur most.

"And that's one of the keys to how this natural herd immunity worked: people caught the diseases when they were designed to be caught – when they were handled best by the herd. Chicken pox is one example of a disease that's mild for most people during childhood, but more severe for adults. Measles is too, as is mumps and rubella. Hepatitis A is another good example: in third world countries every child catches it when it's harmless and goes mostly un-noticed. But it's a bear of a disease when you are older, especially if you have liver problems already. So, parents in those countries want their kids to catch it young. Side note, sorry. That doesn't really apply to us here because we barely have hep A. Anyway, moving on.

"Whooping cough is another example. When kids catch it naturally, it's certainly no fun but it is ultimately harmless in virtually all cases. And they become immune for life. They won't catch it and spread it around again and again. Yes, if newborns catch it it can be very serious, as I've already said. But new research at the NIH and FDA has shown that when kids who are vaccinated catch whooping cough, they don't develop long-term immunity. So they will catch the disease again later. Yes, these vaccinated individuals will feel less sick, but they'll also spread the disease more. So there's a trade-off when a society opts for artificial herd immunity from vaccination.

"But there's a cost to this natural herd immunity. Some fatalities and some complications from diseases occur. Back when everyone caught measles, about 400 kids died every year. Some babies were born with rubella-induced birth defects if the rare mom wasn't immune and she caught it during pregnancy. About 50 people died of chickenpox each year. Twenty young infants still die of whooping cough every year. That's a tough cost for a society to bear, especially when presented with a solution like vaccines.

"So, we opted to shift over to artificial herd immunity. The vulnerability to diseases was turned upside down, or inside out if you will. Here's what I mean. We started vaccinating all the kids, so eventually they all stopped catching the diseases during childhood. We stopped losing the 400 kids to measles every year, or the 50 to chickenpox. No more rubella birth defects, or very rarely so.

"By the way, I know that 400 deaths from measles in a modern country like ours sounds terrible, and it is. But, this death rate would have been much lower if we'd known back then how to treat it, and reduce complications, with high-dose vitamin A. So, nowadays, if measles came back, I don't think we'd have such a fatality rate.

"Anyway, now kids don't catch the diseases, and they grow up without natural immunity. Their vaccines wear off, so they spend the rest of their adult life susceptible. The moms start having babies, but don't pass immunity onto their babies. Consequently, babies spend the first year vulnerable. That's why people who are against mandatory vaccines will say vaccine-induced herd immunity is a myth; most of the 'herd' is technically not immune.

"Think back to natural immunity for a moment: babies and adults were safe, and kids got sick. With artificial immunity, kids don't get sick, and babies and adults are vulnerable. Interesting, huh? Well, I think so at least.

"Why do people look at this artificial herd immunity as a good thing, if it leaves so many vulnerable? Well, it's because these four diseases are no longer around among children. So the vulnerable are rarely exposed. But here's the catch: when the vulnerable *are* exposed, they are put in more danger than they would have been under the natural immunity model. For example, a baby who has no immunity catches measles and could get very sick. A pregnant mom catches rubella and her baby gets birth defects. A fifty year old man catches chickenpox and dies, or a college kid catches mumps and becomes sterile. None of these things happened, or happened so rarely, under the natural immunity model, because virtually all kids caught the diseases at the ages when these things didn't happen. The baby, the pregnant mom, the fifty year old man, and the college kid would all have been immune.

"So, which is a better model? I'm not going to answer that. I think as a society we've opted for the artificial. And it would work just fine if it wasn't for one thing: vaccine side effects. The rare, but serious, or even fatal, vaccine side effects make some people opt out of the artificial model. And that leaves holes in the artificial herd immunity, holes that the vaccinated blame the unvaccinated for. But the unvaccinated aren't the only holes in the herd immunity. There's vaccine failure too. So, vaccinated and unvaccinated alike could be 'guilty' of starting an outbreak. In the natural herd, there really weren't outbreaks. Everyone just accepted disease. But in the artificial herd, outbreaks stand out like a sore thumb.

"So that's how people who don't vaccinate claim that herd immunity is a myth; it's because vaccines aren't effective enough to completely protect the herd, especially because they only protect the children of the herd, leaving the babies and adults vulnerable. Plus, unvaccinated people factor in the cost of vaccination into the equation. Not the financial cost, but the cost of severe side effects, and any long-term problems that vaccines may be responsible for. It's that cost, which may affect everyone who vaccinates – the many – compared to the cost of the comparatively few who die from a disease they didn't vaccinate against, that makes supporters of the natural herd immunity model criticize artificial immunity.

"So, there it is. My take on herd immunity, without telling you what the 'right' answer is. But this raises two questions: are diseases on the rise because we don't have enough herd immunity, and what about immunocompromised kids in the herd?

"First the disease rise, or lack thereof. The media really hit this fear button hard when they talk about vaccines. They portray measles, mumps, meningitis, pertussis, and even polio as diseases that are all on the rise. The fact is, none of these are rising at all, except for pertussis. Measles occurs in small isolated outbreaks, with no continuous rise. Mumps has always been around here and there, with no rise. Meningococcal meningitis is very rare, with no increase. And yes, polio is not coming back, despite the media's best efforts to convince people it is. Pertussis is the only one, but it's not because of lack of vaccination. More on that later, though, because that's a complicated discussion. But the media have to blame someone or something for any disease outbreak, and they have to keep the impression that these diseases are a threat in order to encourage people to continue their vaccines for the good of the herd. But the reality is that we are in the same place with diseases as we've always been since we reduced or eliminated them in the 80s and 90s. And at this point, the fact that some families opt out of vaccines isn't changing that at all.

"We also hear a lot about protecting the immunocompromised kids. That's another aspect of herd immunity. They say we need everyone in the herd to cooperate with vaccination in order to protect the immunocompromised. If your unvaccinated child spread a disease to a child who is immunocompromised, that can be very serious. But this can also happen when a vaccine fails and a vaccinated person spreads a disease. Even the live-virus vaccine germs themselves can make immunocompromised kids very sick. But no one blames people who comply with vaccination, and they never blame a vaccine when it fails; they only blame the unvaccinated.

"Here is how I consider this issue. First, kids who are severely immunocompromised aren't even in school or out in public much because they could die of any disease, not just the few that are vaccine-preventable and still common. So there's little chance your child would infect someone who is immunocompromised. Plus, they are way more likely to catch something dangerous that we don't vaccinate against. Also, immunocompromised kids have had virtually all of their vaccines already anyway, so they are protected because previously-given vaccines still work even if you become mild to moderately immunocompromised later. Under the natural herd immunity model, these kids would have caught the childhood diseases when younger, and would then be immune during their immunocompromised days, so one could blame the artificial herd immunity model for any vulnerability they now have. The immunocompromised are indeed an issue, but I don't like to see them used as pawns in a game to mandate vaccines.

"Then there's the opposite side of that equation; the vaccine-compromised kids who have suffered severe reactions and are permanently disabled. Don't they deserve some consideration as well? Don't they have rights? And doesn't it matter that if you vaccinate, your child could become one of the vaccine-compromised? Don't you have the right in a society to not choose that risk? Are these kids less important than the immunocompromised? We see a child with leukemia at school and our heart goes out to them. We see a mentally and physically disabled kid in a wheelchair from a severe vaccine injury, and we ignore them. They don't deserve that.

"I feel like we, as a society, should work together to keep all kids safe and healthy, while also accepting our differences. We don't have to discriminate against a certain group who thinks differently. We don't have to consider one group as having more rights than another. We should all get along better because of our differences, not in spite of them.

"Ethically speaking, what's interesting is that the natural herd immunity group was here first. So, should they be forced to participate in the artificial immunity project? Or should they be able to opt out? Again, all those with artificial immunity are protected from them, as long as their vaccines work. But they wear off, or sometimes don't work as expected, and then the blame game starts.

"Why can't we all just get along? Ha-ha, but seriously, too. Why does this have to be a fight? Anyway, there are so many ways to look at this. And you, as the parent, have to consider them all.

"And that brings us to vaccine risk. What exactly is the risk if you choose vaccines? What are the risks of each individual vaccine? What are the risks of the program as a whole? Do we know everything about all these risks? Have we studied vaccines well enough to completely understand the risks? What do we not know yet? And what about all those strange vaccine ingredients?

"I can see many of you starting to panic, because your brains are now pretty full. Let's take another 5-minute break to stretch. There are snacks in the back, and coffee. I need some coffee. Then we'll jump into vaccine risk."

Paulina and Reuben Gonzalez were silent for the first few minutes of the ride home, each trying to process what they just learned. Finally Reuben asked, "Do you think he portrayed HIB accurately?"

"Yes, I do. I think in hindsight, if we could have vaccinated for it early I would have. And for our next baby, I'm pretty sure I'd want to do it."

"Or, we could delay it and just rely on the one dose at 15 months," offered Reuben. "What happened to Pablo was an anomaly. Statistically speaking it would be virtually unheard of for our second baby to catch HIB. But that's years away. Who knows when the next child will come along."

"Yeah," chuckled Paulina, patting her belly. "You aren't going to be putting a new baby in here for a long time."

"So, wow, what about the whole section on vaccine risks and side effects? That was very interesting. I mean, we kind of already knew a lot of that, but I had no idea about some of the risks Dr. Tommaso presented. And I like how he pretty much only presented the solid risks that the CDC acknowledges. The real risks that are backed by science. Like seizures, encephalitis, and other severe neurological injuries."

"And the arthritis for teen and adult women from the MMR vaccine," added Paulina. "One in four have an arthritis reaction, and an unknown percentage of those go on to suffer lifelong rheumatoid arthritis. Not so much when babies or young kids get the shot, but for women. That's a high risk. Remember when our OB told us I was not immune to rubella anymore on my bloodwork, and I should get an MMR shot after Pablo was born? You know, 'cuz they don't make plain rubella shots anymore. She never mentioned I could get rheumatoid arthritis. And my mom and grandma both have RA – it runs in families. Imagine if we hadn't known better and I'd gotten that shot? Remember how that nurse looked at me in the hospital? You know, that young pretty one who kept trying to give Pablo the hep B shot?"

"Yeah, I don't remember her ..." Reuben tried to shrug, earning an eye-roll from his wife.

"And I remember you trying so hard to pretend you didn't notice her. Ha-ha! You think I didn't notice? We girls see all, my husband."

"But the best part of tonight for me was what Dr. Tommaso said about the overall statistical risks of vaccines compared to the risks of suffering a dangerous case of a disease. All based on CDC data. Like the risk of brain swelling and inflammation from the DTaP vaccine is 1 in 1000, but the risk of dying from pertussis as an infant is only 1 in 200,000. Plus tetanus risk while young is only what, 1 case in about 20 million young kids? And diphtheria risk is zero. So why would any parent ever risk the DTaP vaccine with their young baby? Plus, that's a shot that doesn't prevent the spread of the disease to others, so you can't make a public health argument. And for every single other vaccine – all of the 15 others – the risk of suffering harm from a vaccine reaction seems greater than the risk that you'll be harmed by that disease. By far. Dr. Tommaso didn't really emphasize that point, though. I got the feeling that he expected his audience to kind of figure that out for themselves. If more people knew that, they'd be more careful with vaccines."

"And that's why the government, the media, Pharma, and the mainstream medical community are working hard to make sure people don't find that out," finished Paulina. "See? You have learned so much in these past few months. I know you accepted my beliefs on this early on, and you weren't quite so sure about not vaccinating at first, but see? I was right. And you know it."

"Yeah," Reuben grinned. "You'd read so much about it, and I barely knew anything. And I was man enough to admit that and trust your instincts. I think a lot of men just blow their wives off and blindly accept that doctors must know what they are doing with vaccines. And they are too busy to do any reading themselves, and too proud to admit ignorance."

"But not my husband," Paulina smiled back, grabbing his hand. "Not my husband ..."

Peter was tired. He liked giving these talks, but they were tiring. Even after he'd put all this into book form, and even shot a video version, parents still wanted to hear it live, to talk it through person to person - the human connection. But he also knew he couldn't keep giving these talks every month for the rest of his life. *There has to be a better way to present this information live to these patients, a way that doesn't just involve me. Something that could be presented to parents all over the country. No, all over the world.* Peter would put a lot of thought into this idea in the months to come.

Oh wait, darn it! I totally skipped talking about vaccine ingredients tonight. He made a mental note to email the attendees his one-pager on that. And as tired as he was tonight, he was kind of glad he'd forgotten. *Ingredients are the most boring part of the talk. I have to figure out a way to spice that part up.*

Chapter 6

Who Doesn't Like Cake?

Emily Shawna was nervous because her turn was next. This wasn't her first oral presentation in front of her class. *But it might be my last*, she worried.

Emily's dad was an environmental toxicologist, and his passion for chemistry had rubbed off on her. Her young childhood so far had been all about home experiment kits instead of dolls. She'd played with test tubes and Bunsen burners (under supervision, of course) instead of a soccer ball. And now, at eight years of age, she was already determined to rid the world of toxic chemicals, like her daddy was trying to do.

So when the class had been tasked with presenting an environmental report on what chemicals posed the most danger to children, her dad had gotten a funny gleam in his eye, like he'd thought of a wonderfully witty practical joke to pull on someone. Not on her, of course. *My daddy wouldn't do that.* But on someone or something, that was for sure. And even at her young age, Emily knew that the topic she'd finally chosen with her dad's help was a hot one.

She remembered hearing her parents argue that night when they thought she was asleep:

"She can't present on *that*! Are you crazy? And in front of all the parents, eh?"

"Why not? It's the truth."

"It's *your* truth, Chris. Sorry, that's not fair, I know. But if it's the truth, why doesn't anybody else believe it? No one up here in the north does, and it's even worse down in the States. Despite all the studies published in the medical literature, people just aren't listening."

"More and more people are starting to listen. And she doesn't have to go all crazy on the topic, just present the facts. Straightforward facts. Leave the commentary out. The facts speak for themselves, eh?"

"But she's eight years old. She won't even be able to pronounce half the stuff."

"Wanna bet?"

"Ok mister. I'll take that bet. A back rub for me – no, a full body massage. One hour. Not just one of your half-hearted shoulder rubs."

"You're on. And if I'm right, and she nails it, I get ..."

Daddy's voice had quieted down by that time, as it often did when daddy smiled at mommy and gave her a kiss and whispered in her ear, so Emily didn't know what her daddy would get. *Mommy will probably bake him a chocolate cake, or something like that. My daddy loves cake ...*

"And that is why we should never sniff glue."

Emily was brought back to the present by the polite applause, and a few giggles, from the class and the parents as Jamie sat down proudly.

"Thank you, Jamie. That was excellent," said Ms. Tomlinson. "Emily? Why don't you go next."

Emily picked up her paper, walked to the front of the class, cleared her throat, and began.

"The Chemicals in Our North American Vaccines: Toxic ... olog-ical Classification and Potential Risks."

Whew! I did it! thought Emily. She'd been worried about pro-nouncing the title just perfectly. She didn't think that brief pause in the middle would cost her daddy his cake; she hoped for a piece too.

Mrs. Shawna looked over at Emily's teacher. Mrs. Tomlinson nodded at her with raised eyebrows. *Wow. Impressive topic.*

She gets it from her dad, she gestured back, glancing sideways at her husband.

"Shots are an important part of our health and our safety from in-fec … tious diseases. And it is important to understand the ingredients we use to make vaccines so we can know they are safe for all of us." She'd practiced the gesture with her left hand to arc across the whole room from right to left.

"First, some vaccines have mercury. Mercury is a known neuro … toskin … toxin that kills brain cells by … disrupting the electron … transport chain in our mito … our mitochondria. This results in … cerrular … cell-u-lar death, especially in our brain cells. Mercury is also found in old fashioned glass thermometers and some new light bulbs, so be careful if you break one. It should be carefully disposed of as toxic waste.

"Second, most vaccines have alum … ninum. Alumninum sounds harmless, but if we get too much of it, it is also a neurotoxin. Its toxic effects are also syner … gistic when given at the same time as mercury, so be careful not to get them together."

This time Mrs. Shawna felt a different vibe from Emily's teacher. She glanced over and saw that 'impressed' had been replaced with a frown.

"Next, many vaccines have formaldehyde. This chemical is a known carc … carcinogen. That means it causes cancer. It also causes kidney damage. But these dangers are known to mainly happen when you breathe it in, like if you work in a chemical factory or with cadavers – those are dead people that scientists study. No one has studied injected formaldehyde for safety yet.

"Vaccines also have polysorbate 20 and 80. Some people worry about these pres … ervatives, but they are classified as GRAS, which stands for Generally Regarded As Safe, which means it is safe – probably. But we haven't studied it yet.

"Gluta … glutaraldehyde is another chemical, and it's like formaldehyde. It is fatal if you breathe too much in. So don't. It is also corrosive to body tissues.

"Mono … sodium … glutamate is MSG. It is what makes our Chinese food taste yummy. It is an exciting … an excito-toxin. This means it isn't good for our brain. But don't worry. Vaccines only have a little bit."

Now Mrs. Shawna felt the stares from the other parents as well. Her husband, of course, was oblivious. He simply stared proudly at his daughter.

"Where did she …?" she whispered.

"It wasn't me," quietly. "Seriously. I just showed her the FDA website – the American site – and how to find the vaccine product inserts on it. Oh, and the description section of the inserts that list the ingredients. The rest is all her."

"2-phenoxyethanol is a preservative for some vaccines. It is known to cause reproductive defects, which means someone can't have more babies. But vaccines only have a little bit.

"Octoxynol is also a chemical that makes people not have babies. I don't know why." Giggles from the kids in the room.

"Oct … yl … phenol and nonyl … phenol ethox … ylate are harmful if swallowed, so don't eat them. They also can cause cancer.

"Cetyl ... trimeth ... ylam ... monium bromide is also something you shouldn't eat. It also burns body parts.

"Also, glysophate ... I mean, gly ... pho ... sate is a chemical that kills weeds. So farmers use it. People think it causes cancer. A man won 289 million dollars because he got cancer from it. People who make vaccines don't try to put it in, I think. But independent tests show it contaminates five of our vaccines."

Deep breath and a smile on Emily's face. All the hard words were done.

"Also, scientists use parts of animals and of people to make vaccines. Here are some of the parts: protein from your blood, called albumin, cells from little babies that didn't get born, cow blood, cow hearts, and other cow parts, kidney cells from monkeys, parts of chickens and eggs, baby guinea pigs who were never born (with another hand gesture to the class pet in its cage in the corner of the room) ..."

Two of the little girls in the room started crying.

"But it's all accurate," Chris whispered to his wife. "Every word. It's in kid-speak, but it's all true."

They both saw Ms. Tomlinson stand up and start moving toward the front of the room. Mrs. Shawna sensed her husband was about to start forward to intercept her. She put her hand on his arm, gently. He'd learned to listen to her over the years. To trust her. *Emily can handle this,* she said with her eyes. *She's all you, after all.*

"And so, in conclusion, vaccinations are very important and they are very safe. The good news for you (a sweeping gesture again) is that you have already had almost all of your shots. We don't need anymore until Grade 4. But only six of them. Then two more when we are teenagers. But that's all. If you want to know more, you can read about these chemicals on the websites of these places (deep breath – more big words): The Environmental Protection Agency, Occupational Safety and Health Administration, Consumer Product Safety Commission, and The Federal Drug Administration. Thank you."

Emily didn't understand why only her parents were clapping, five kids were crying, and Ms. Tomlinson looked very different than she did earlier that day.

Emily had never been to the principal's office before. It was nice. Although, she wasn't exactly in her office. *Mommy and daddy are in her office. I'm just out here in the waiting room. I wonder why the principal wanted to talk to them.*

"Emily, dear, would you like a chocolate?" This from Ms. Jones, the secretary. She was always nice to Emily when she helped on field trips.

"Oh, yes please!" She reached into the candy bowl on the desk and picked one of the gold-wrapped ones.

The door to the office opened and her parents came out. Mommy looked angry. Daddy looked … like daddy always did. Proud of her.

"Let's go, Emily. We are taking you home early today," said Mommy.

"To make cake Mommy? Does Daddy get to have his cake?"

Chapter 7

Subjective Truth

"Mom, I don't feel very well. My throat hurts."

"Oh, you're probably fine. You have that test today. If you feel worse after that I'll come pick you up." Evelyn Harding also had an important day at work that she couldn't afford to miss. At least the first part of the day. She heard her daughter coughing at the table and looked up. Jamie hadn't touched her food. She looked a little peaked, but no worse than the usual cold.

"Come on dear, we're going to be late. Bring your breakfast. You can eat in the car." Evelyn grabbed her coffee and work bag and headed for the door.

"Welcome back, Jamie," greeted Mrs. Jefferson. "How was Europe? Find any time to study for ... hey, are you feeling ok?"

Jamie knew she had to somehow avoid getting sent to the nurse's office ... at least not until after her math test. Her mom had told her to try to hang in there until at least 10:30 and she could come get her then.

"I'm just tired. I think I caught a cold on the plane home. But yeah, it was amazing." Jamie plopped down at her desk near the front of the class just as her best friend Allison came in.

I don't know how Allison does it, Jamie thought. *Coming to school with a bandanna covering her bald head. I think I'd opt for a wig. I'd go blond. Long blond. No, red. But Allison likes to keep it real.*

"Oh my God Jamie, how was Europe? I can't even imagine!!!" bubbled Allison, heading for the desk next to Jamie. "Tell me everything!"

"Wait until lunch, girl. We have a math test to kill. And, actually, I'm not feeling very well. You might want to stay clear of me today."

"Oh, that's fine. I'm not due for my next chemo cycle for another couple weeks, and right now my white counts are up. So, a little cold won't matter. But you know, Jamie, I appreciate you watching out for me."

The bell rung and the girls got to work.

Mrs. Jefferson looked at Jamie as the kids shuffled out at the end of class. Now her eyes were red and she looked flushed. And that cough had started to get a little distracting.

"Jamie dear, I think you should go see the nurse."

"Ok, Mrs. Jefferson," Jamie managed, glad that she'd made it past 10:30.

"Oh dear, yes. You definitely have a fever. Would you like me to call your mom for you?"

"That's ok, Ms. Ramirez. I already texted her. She's on her way."

Samantha Ramirez washed her hands and pulled Jamie Harding's record up on her computer. She was required to check the immunization status of every student who came through sick. This seemed like a flu, but … yes, sure enough Jamie had had her flu shot this year. Everything else was up to date too. So, nothing to worry about.

Dr. Tommaso liked his new office. Although the space was much smaller, it better suited his low-key style of practice. And since it didn't need to accommodate a dozen other pediatricians, nurse practitioners, medical assistants, office managers, front office clerks, and 6 patients an hour per doctor, it didn't need to be large. These last few months had brought a much-welcomed change to his professional life, and he was happy to be comfortably busy as virtually all of his patients, and a number of his partners' patients, followed him here. He had enough office space to bring on another doctor and figured he'd have to do that soon if things got any busier.

"Hello Jamie," greeted Peter as he walked into the next exam room for his first sick patient of the day. "Looks like you have some flu symptoms?"

"We just got back from Europe," explained Mrs. Harding. "I picked her up early from school, took one look at her, and came right over. She seems way more sick than usual."

"It's just a sore throat and mild cough, Mom."

Peter smiled at the unspoken eye-roll that his patient managed to suppress.

"And fever, and now your eyes are red, too. Dr. Tommaso, what do you think?"

Peter had begun looking at Jamie, feeling her neck glands, looking in her ears, listening to her lungs, and finally ending with "say ahhhh." *Hmmmm, her throat looks a little strange. Light-reddish spots. Not really red enough to be Strep. No pus.* "It could be just a flu, although we haven't really seen much of that quite yet. Could be another virus. It could possibly be Strep, but I don't think it is. I'll have Heather run a rapid Strep test just to rule it out. Basically, I don't think it's anything that's going to need antibiotics, unless it does show Strep. It should clear up within a few days."

Peter moved on to his next patient, an eleven-day-old who was in for the first checkup. *Those pink spots in Jamie's throat ... where have I seen those before?* he wondered. He washed his hands extra well before examining the next baby, whose cuteness quickly made Peter forget all about it.

———◦———

Another busy day in the office, sighed Peter as he looked at his schedule a few days later. *I guess it's good to be busy, when you are self-employed.* But he often felt more tired now compared to when he'd first started doing this a few decades ago. *And I can't complain about the slower pace now – 3 checkups an hour is really nice.*

Heather, his new medical assistant, walked up to Peter's desk. "Mrs. Harding is on the line. Her eleven-year-old woke up with a strange rash this morning and she's really worried."

Peter remembered seeing Jamie a few days ago. *Maybe it's a Strep rash – scarlet fever.* He pulled up her chart just to make sure. *Strep test was negative. Maybe the test missed it though – it isn't a perfect test.* "Tell her to message us some pictures and I'll look at them."

An hour later Peter checked his inbox of messages on his laptop and saw the message from Mrs. Harding. He clicked on the pictures and instantly felt a sinking feeling in the pit of his stomach. *Damn. That's what those spots in the throat were.* He leaned back in his chair so he could catch Heather's attention over at her work station. "Heather, call Mrs. Harding. Tell her to bring Jamie back in, but have them drive up and just wait outside by our back door. I'll see her outside. And tell her not to stop anywhere along the way."

Peter checked Jamie's immunization status. Yes, she'd had her MMR vaccine when she was one year old. One dose usually gives immunity to about 95% of kids, so Peter didn't usually push his patients to get the second dose at age 5. *But those pictures do look just like the measles rash. And yes, now I remember what those pink spots on her throat and inside cheeks were – Koplik's spots. Stupid, stupid Peter. Should have recognized those.* Peter had a hard time focusing on his next few patients, and couldn't wait to see Jamie so he could, hopefully, decide it wasn't measles. But he had a sinking feeling that it was.

Yes, it's measles alright, Peter said to himself as he looked at Jamie in the small parking area behind his office. *She looks pretty good though.* According to Mrs. Harding, Jamie was coughing less and feeling slightly better, but still had a fever. *But that rash is very obvious. Started on the face and neck, then moved down the body. Scattered red bumps and splotches, as mom put it, but has now coalesced into darker red patches. Plus there's the recent travel to Europe.*

"Well, it looks like measles, Mrs. Harding. I know Jamie did have the MMR vaccine, but it's not 100% effective. She probably caught measles in Europe."

"Is she going to be ok? I've heard measles is deadly." Mrs. Harding looked very concerned, and Jamie suddenly looked scared.

"No no, Mrs. Harding, Jamie. You have nothing to worry about. Although measles can be serious, fatalities are extremely rare – about 1 in 10,000 cases. There can be some complications, but mostly just ear infections and diarrhea/dehydration. Occasionally pneumonia. But these are easily handled, especially in a country like ours. And Jamie looks fine. She has a very routine case. She'll have to stay home for another few days – four days from the onset of the rash. Just give her lots of fluids and some healthy foods. Oh, and Vitamin A drops. High-dose vitamin A is recommended for hospitalized patients with measles complications, but I like to give it to any patient who has measles." *Not that I've seen that many. Just that one family, what, 8 years ago?*

But Jamie still looked very concerned. "When do you think I started being contagious, Dr. Peter?" she asked.

"About four days before the rash started. So, that would be probably the day before you came to see me."

"Oh good," said Jamie's mom. "That means you weren't contagious on the flight home."

"Yeah, but I was contagious at school that day. Sure, I've been at home ever since. But mom, the math test … and oh my God, Mom. Allison!"

Peter saw the concerned look on Mrs. Harding's face. "Who's Allison?" he asked.

"She is Jamie's best friend. And she has leukemia. Well, she *had* leukemia. She's kind of in the recovery phase. Still on chemo though. But can't something like measles be very bad for someone like her?"

"That depends on a lot of factors. It depends if she is currently immunocompromised. But listen, we are getting ahead of ourselves. We don't know for sure yet that this is measles. We first need to confirm the diagnosis, and I'd suggest you go to the public health department for testing. They will get us the fastest result so we'll know what to do, and what this means for your friend. I'll call the health department right now to confirm they can see you, then I'll come back out to let you know."

"Wait, the public health department?" Mrs. Harding grabbed Peter's arm, and he inwardly flinched. *Stop that, Peter,* he told himself. *They don't have leprosy. Mrs. Harding would actually have to be sick to pass it, and it doesn't just pass through a casual touch like that anyway.* "Why do we have to involve them? Are they going to investigate us? The house is a mess. We haven't even fully unpacked yet. I heard they like to take your kids away if they get really sick with something and it was your fault."

"Ok, Mrs. Harding. Listen. First, this wasn't your fault. You vaccinated her. But even if you had chosen to not vaccinate, you still couldn't be found at fault simply for choosing a more natural approach to raising your child. No one takes your kids away for that. And yes, I would like to involve them so they can help us prevent an outbreak. In fact, legally I *have* to call them. We all need to work together on this. I'll be right back."

Peter knew he was in for a long day – no, a long week. Before calling the health department, and after washing his hands and his arm (he couldn't help it), he checked his schedule from when Jamie was in 3 days ago. *Damn. That newborn baby was here. And a host of other kids. Many probably unvaccinated since that is the majority of my patients these days. If this is measles, there are going to be a lot of scared parents … and angry health department authorities. Stop that, Peter. Don't you go getting all conspiracy here. The health department is here to help, and you know you are legally obligated to involve them. So, buckle down and do your job.*

Peter picked up the phone.

—◄◇►—

"Mom, Jamie says she thinks she has measles."

Mrs. Harrington didn't hear her daughter at first. She was trying to find a parking spot in the medical center's outpatient lot and, as usual, the place was full. "What did you say dear?"

"I said, Jamie just texted me that she thinks she has measles. Hold on …" Allison tapped away on her phone some more.

"Wait, did you just say measles?" Sally Harrington said, her daughter's statement finally registering. *Ah, there's a spot – right near the entrance to the clinic,* she though triumphantly. With their life such a nightmare this past year, it was the little things that helped keep her going. "Oh that's terrible. Is she ok? What do you mean she *thinks* she has it?"

"I said hold on. She's sending more info now. She and her mom are on their way to the public health department to get tested. She's been sick all week. She didn't look good on Monday when I saw her for the math test. She said she had a cold."

"Geeze, Jamie. We are lucky that your white counts are up right now. Otherwise, I think measles could be really bad for you. Plus, you were vaccinated for it anyway, and your doctor already told us we wouldn't have to worry about measles or chicken pox, even when your counts are down. It would be things you weren't vaccinated against that we have to worry about. We'll double check with the doctor though. You aren't due for chemo again for another ten days, but we might have to postpone it. Let's go, we're late."

Peter got to the office early the next morning. The county health department lab had called last night and let him know about the positive result. He'd expected it, but it was still a bummer. He read up on what would be expected of him and his office as far as notifying any exposed patients who were in the office when Jamie Harding was there and for about an hour afterwards. He identified about 14 potentially-exposed patients during those couple hours. Some had been there for checkups before Jamie, but hadn't left yet before Jamie got there. A few had just come into the front office area to ask some questions. Then several had come through the office in the next hour during his busy sick time.

That's the challenge with measles, he reflected. *You think you just have a cold, but that's the most contagious period. It spreads through the air from coughing. By the time you realize you have measles, as evidenced by the rash, you've exposed a lot of people. And it passes easily through the air.*

He knew he was immune. He had both his and his medical assistant's vaccine records on file and they'd both had 2 doses of the vaccine. He also had a titer checked a few years ago because he was curious to know everything he was immune to before his trip to Africa, and he was very immune then. He was glad his wife/office manager wasn't there that day. She was probably immune too, though.

Out of his 14 exposed patients, 6 were unvaccinated, including a six-year-old who had been in the room right after Jamie had left. Six were vaccinated. One new patient's vaccine status was unknown. But the one that worried him the most was that newborn baby. He was too young to have been vaccinated. He had spoken with the parents that day about starting vaccines at two months and they'd told him they were planning to vaccinate, but weren't going to get every vaccine – just the more important ones.

Heather was already calling the unvaccinated families to come in so they could get all their questions answered. Peter didn't want to spend an hour on the phone with each family listening to them panic. Not that he didn't care, but he just didn't have all day to spend on the phone. He'd counsel them all as a group at lunch – outside the office. He knew none of them could get sick for about 7 days from exposure, and some may not feel sick for up to 21 days. But he'd keep them outside. *Half of them probably don't want to step foot into the office right now anyway.*

Peter knew it was too late for anyone who was not vaccinated to go ahead and get the vaccine now. It had to be given within 72 hours of exposure in order to try to prevent the disease from taking hold.

That's the other thing about measles. By the time you know someone has it, more than 3 days have usually passed so unvaccinated exposures can't benefit from the vaccine. Then again, they chose not to vaccinate. So they knew the risks. The key now is to keep all of the unvaccinated exposed people at home during the 7 to 21 day post-exposure period. You don't wait for them to feel sick; you just ride it out at home starting maybe on day 5. And the public health department will make sure they comply.

He was going to have his staff call the vaccinated patients next, just to let them know. They will be assumed to be immune if they've had both doses of the MMR, or just one dose but not yet old enough for the second dose at 5 years of age. He planned to offer them all high doses of vitamin A anyway, as he was going to offer it to the unvaccinated families at lunch. *I'm glad I keep a good supply of it in the office. High doses of the liquid drops once a day for two days.* And he'd give it free of charge; it wasn't worth charging the few dollars it cost him to buy it. He knew vitamin A reduced the risk of severe complications, according to the World Health Organization and the AAP. *That's why they give it every year in many poor countries. It's literally an immunization against severe measles.* What research wasn't positive on was whether or not the vitamin helped prevent the disease itself. *But that's ok; reducing complications is useful, although severe complications are already rare.*

But Peter wanted to talk with the parents of the newborn baby himself. He dialed their number.

"Hello Mrs. Jalinski. This is Dr. Peter Tommaso, the pediatrician." He always found it more instantly recognizable for people when he reminded them which 'Dr. Tommaso' was calling. "How is the baby doing?"

"Oh, the baby's fine. These newborns always are. Seriously, why doesn't anyone ever ask how the mama is doing?" The laugh in her voice told Peter she was kidding around ... mostly.

"I know. These first weeks are the hardest part of the already-hardest job in the world ... or so I'm told." That got a sleepy-sounding laugh from the other end of the line.

"Anyway, the reason for my call is …" Peter went on to explain the exposure, and the preventive treatment that is recommended for young babies and immunocompromised people who have been exposed to measles: measles immune globulin. This is an antibody shot that neutralizes any live measles virus in the system. It's very different from a vaccine, which stimulates the body's immune system to attack measles. The immune globulin, instead, is actual live anti-measles antibodies filtered out from donated blood units and processed for injection in situations just like this.

"I appreciate you calling, Dr. Peter … Dr. Tommaso."

"It's Dr. Peter, to my patients."

"I appreciate it. I know quite a bit about vaccines and diseases after reading up on this whole controversy while waiting for the baby to come. And you know what makes me the most angry? I, this baby's mom, am supposed to be immune by going through the natural infection when I was a child. But I was vaccinated, along with everyone else, and that vaccine wears off. So most of us adults aren't immune to measles anymore. And we don't pass vaccine-induced measles immunity to our babies so that they can be born immune. If I had caught natural measles as a child, when it's mostly harmless, I'd be immune now and I'd have passed all my wonderful antibodies to the baby and we wouldn't even be having this conversation."

"Wow, Mrs. Jalinski. I'm impressed. Very few people would even know that. You are right. In the old days, all kids caught measles, and rubella too, and all women grew up immune so they'd be immune through pregnancy and pass about a year's worth of very effective immunity to their babies. Then that immunity wore off, the kids caught the diseases themselves when they were safe, and the cycle continued."

"So, ironically it's the vaccine's fault that my baby was exposed to measles." Again, another laugh.

"It's more the fault, or, fault isn't really the right word. It's more of a change in mindset in a modern country like ours and how we decided to approach the normal childhood diseases. Our medical policy-makers decided we would be better off eliminating these from our population. But the drawbacks? We lost natural herd immunity. And the artificially-induced herd immunity we opted for doesn't work nearly as well. And these live vaccines don't work in young babies. So now a lot of babies are susceptible to these diseases, as are most adults. It was a trade-off."

Peter briefly explained his take on artificial versus natural herd immunity, although he suspected this mom already knew all of that. He concluded, "I think there are good arguments on both sides, especially when you factor in that we know getting all the childhood diseases during childhood provides some significant benefits against allergic disorders, asthma, autoimmune diseases, and even some cancers. Our immune systems were designed to be challenged during childhood to give us better protection from a lot more than just the diseases as we age. But again, fatalities from diseases are a tough pill to swallow for any modern society."

"But we are causing more long-term health problems in everybody by depriving them of these diseases just to save a few lives," challenged Mrs. Jalinski.

"Well, those deaths are immediate and tragic. The long-term health consequences of not catching these diseases aren't immediately apparent to people, although they have a huge impact on society as a whole: cost of healthcare, quality of living, etc. Anyway, wow, that was quite a digression. Back to the point. I do recommend the baby get the immune globulin shot. The window in which it's effective is within 6 days of exposure. And it's been four days. The theory is that the antibodies will neutralize any measles that got into the baby before the infection takes hold. The public health department can deliver the dose to us today, free of charge. They keep a supply handy, and the government pays for it because it's very expensive."

"Damn right they should. It's their fault my baby isn't immune. OK, Dr. Peter, I'll let it go. But it was nice to be able to vent. I'll bring the baby in at the end of the day."

Wow, thought Peter. *That was ... interesting. She's one of the smartest moms I've met lately.*

---<o>---

"We've got measles! We've got measles!"

Jim rolled his eyes at the phone. He should have let it go to voice-mail. He could picture Tony jumping up and down at his desk down the hallway. And Jim prayed that none of Tony's female co-workers were currently sitting near enough to hear Tony's not-so-subtle 80s movie quote. Not that he expected any of them to get the reference, despite the fact that many of the women in that department were nerds too. It was definitely a guy's movie. But if or when any of them did, the HR department would have their hands full with sexual-harassment charges.

"Nice. Where?"

"Washington State, again. Near where that one HIB case occurred a while back. So far all we have is that it's an eleven-year-old girl with recent travel to Europe. Vaccinated too, although we haven't confirmed that with records yet."

"Well, hopefully there will be more to the story," Jim said, bored again. "People aren't biting on just regular measles outbreaks anymore, since we have about a dozen or so small outbreaks every year, and each of them are so quickly contained. No one dies. Francine is worried that the public is going to realize we really *aren't* in any danger from measles and what that might do to vaccine rates."

"I'm thinking I'm going to call my stock guy anyway. Get me some more shares. The value always goes up a least a blip, even with normal outbreaks. You sure you don't want in on that?"

"Yeah, I'm sure Tony. I'm just not really a stock market guy. I enjoy other perks of this job. I'll at least put out some local media alerts on this, but we won't go national until we have something more. Like, an exposed baby or the mother lode – a kid with cancer." Jim almost said, '*But one can only hope, right?*' but caught himself. *Geeze, have I been working for Francine for too long?*

---<o>---

"Dr. Tommaso, that's the fifth call we've gotten from the media today. They really want to talk to you."

"Sorry, Heather. You'll just have to keep telling them that our patient care is confidential, and that the public health department should be able to answer their questions." *And I wonder how the hell they even know?* wondered Peter. He wasn't surprised that the media knew about the case, just that they'd found out so quickly. *And once it hits the news tonight, we'll be flooded with patient calls tomorrow. And if some parent dares to page me tonight after the news broadcast in a panic because their child happens to live in the same county as this measles case, I'm going to … Now Peter, you know you won't tell them how you really feel about their ignorance in buying into the fear-mongering the media like to stir up. You'll be patient with them, like you always are. Yeah, but I still won't like it.*

"I'm going to post the "What to Do in Case of a Measles Outbreak" flyer on our homepage and put in a request on our voicemail for patients to first read that before calling us. That should help with the patient calls tomorrow. And by then, the media will probably have moved on once they learn there's no story here."

Peter was a smart guy, if a little naïve.

"Jim?"

"Yes Tony." Eye roll.

"Guess what?"

"What Tony."

"Aw, come on. Guess."

Tony never played guessing games before, Jim realized. *That meant …* "Wait, are you messing with me? Someone who matters was exposed? What, cancer? A baby too-young-to-be-immunized? What?"

"Yes."

"Yes which? Wait, you mean *both*?"

"Yup."

"No way. Francy … Ms. Donahue is going to be happy … I mean, this will give her … us … some more angles to work with. No one died, I hope?"

"No. And this is straight from the local public health department after their first day of tracking down all the known exposures, and it's all preliminary. Nothing's been confirmed yet. Oh, and by the way, you can call her Francy when you're talking to me, you know. You two aren't fooling anybody. Anyway, here's what I know …"

Francine held her hand up for quiet in the room, and the team quickly settled down. "Ok, so we have about 17 exposed in the doctor's office – 6 unvaccinated. One newborn baby. So we push those two angles as usual. And another 50 or so exposed at school, with 3 of them unvaccinated. But we also have an exposed pre-teen with leukemia. According to what we could manage to see in her electronic medical records, she isn't currently immunocompromised. In fact, her oncologist isn't even giving her immune globulin because she's had both her MMR doses. So, don't share any details with the media besides the fact that Patient Zero's best friend, who is suffering from leukemia, is working closely with her oncologist to make sure she survives the exposure. And of course the usual: measles is preventable with vaccination, make sure your child has had two doses of the MMR vaccine which has been proven to be the best safe and effective protection against measles, measles is on the rise, Disneyland outbreak, unvaccinated kids, vaccines save lives, etc. You know the drill."

"Do we know if the Prevention Department is going to be talking about Vitamin A this time?" The question came from near the back of the room.

"They are not, as usual. We want to focus on getting people immunized, and the vitamin A prevention protocol detracts from that. In fact, they are putting out a press release reminding the public about the dangers of overdosing on vitamin A. Since it's a fat-soluble vitamin, people *can* overdose on it and cause harm. Sure, they can't cause harm with just the two-day measles dosing protocol, but we don't want to confuse anybody.

"Oh, wait, I almost forgot. We've got to spread the all-important word out to adults as well. Adults can catch measles, and it's way more serious when they do. They should talk to their doctors about updating their MMR vaccine, especially if they live in a county with a measles epidemic. I spoke with the manufacturer this afternoon and they have a nice stockpile ready to ship out wherever needed. So, make sure your media contacts focus on that as well. Adult vaccination is the new black.

"I know it's late, but it shouldn't take more than an hour to get this out to all your national sources in time for the eleven-o'clock news. Check in with me before you leave to go home. I'll be in my office."

Ninety minutes later Jim followed Francy out to her car. It had been a long evening, and he was seriously tired. But he saw the spring in Francy's step and knew she was the opposite of tired. In fact, she was glowing. *What exactly is it about these outbreaks that gets her so excited?* he wondered. *Is it the simple satisfaction of a job well done? Of saving lives? But none of my doctor friends get excited over disease outbreaks – they actually hate them.* He saw her pull out her car keys and click the car unlocked as they approached. He tried to decide if she wanted him to drive home so she could relax, or … Francy opened one of the rear doors of her car, set her briefcase down on the ground, turned around and grabbed Jim by his shoulders, pushed him into the back seat, and climbed in after him.

I might be getting too old for this, he wondered briefly before deciding he didn't care.

"We are live in front of the Harrington home where little Allison is fighting for her life after being exposed to measles several days ago. What makes this deadly disease especially dangerous for this young teen is that she also suffers from leukemia and is currently undergoing chemotherapy. With her system possibly immunocompromised, measles is expected to be even more dangerous for her than it already is. We've also been told that, fortunately, Allison did receive all of her vaccines when she was younger, including both doses of her MMR vaccine, and that this safe and effective vaccine could end up being particularly life-saving for this young woman. We won't know if Allison is out of the woods for three more weeks, which according to the Centers for Disease Control is what is called the incubation period for this disease. The family has so far declined to comment on their only daughter's condition, but we will keep you updated in the weeks to come. Meanwhile, ask your doctor if your children are up-to-date on all their vaccines. And adults can get a booster dose of the MMR vaccine to make sure their measles immunity is up to date as well. Measles spreads easily; even being in the same store or shopping mall with someone who is contagious can put you at risk. This is Sara Sanderson reporting live for News Chanel 17."

Sara had gotten the call just in time to get out to the subject's home for a live shot and commentary for the late-night news. She wasn't happy about cancelling her evening plans, but a job was a job. They were the only station here tonight, a fact that she owed to her connection back East. But she knew the place would be swamped in the morning, both here and wherever the baby lives. Sara had chosen to go with the immunocompromised angle tonight, and leave the new baby angle for Bob on the morning crew, who hadn't been able to get over to the baby's house in time for tonight. *Oh well, you snooze you lose. We'll open with both angles again in the morning,* she knew, *and spend as much time on it as we can. Because the public really needs to know when these things go around so they can decide whether or not they should stay home, too.*

"What do you think, Tommy? You want to stay parked here tonight so we have a front-row seat in the morning?" she asked her cameraman.

"Yeah, I probably should. Steve will chew us out if we give up this spot. Why don't I call you a Lyft and you can stay in that inn we passed a couple miles back. No reason why we both should get a bad night's sleep in the news van. Plus, you are the one who needs to look pretty and all."

Peter clicked off the news, ready for bed after the long day. His wife patted his hand.

"About what you'd expect," she consoled. "Do you know the immunocompromised child?"

"No, she's not my patient. Although the Harding's mentioned Jamie's best friend was in remission from leukemia. That means she should be fine. I'll ask the Hardings when I see them. But it's amazing how cleverly that reporter summarized all the right points to scare people. Only the intelligent would see through it, and there aren't enough of those in the audience to matter. Let's go to bed, although I doubt I'll be able to sleep."

Paula Jalinski decided this would be the morning to resume her routine walk. *Gotta get back in shape.* The baby seemed fine after getting the measles antibody injection yesterday at the doctor's office. Dr. Peter seemed so apologetic. But she knew it wasn't his fault. She knew it was nearly impossible to recognize measles before the rash. But any doctor worthy of his profession would still feel bad, which means she'd picked the right doctor. *And I better take the baby outside while I still can,* she realized. The day 6 quarantine would start tomorrow. Even though she and the baby technically should be able to just walk around the block without infecting anybody, especially without even having symptoms, she decided she'd play by the rules and not risk it. The health department might be watching. *Oh, stop that Paula. You're being paranoid.*

Baby in stroller, running shoes on – or rather, very-slow-walking-shoes on – she opened the door and stepped out ... to a street full of news vans and reporters. *What's going on?* She looked up and down the street for some sign of commotion – police cars, fire engines, something that would explain why ...

She froze. All the cameras were pointing at her, and multiple voices erupted in unison.

"Mrs. Jalinski, is your baby ok?"

"Mrs. Jalinski, do you have a few minutes to answer some questions?"

"Mrs. Jalinski, how old is your baby and has he started his vaccines yet?"

"Pardon the interruption, Mrs. Jalinski. It's Bob Stevenson from Chanel 17," said the closest reporter. "We understand your baby was exposed to measles? How is he doing? Is he ok? How are you holding up?"

He is a she, thank you very much, she thought to herself as she ducked back inside and closed the door behind her. *Well, at least that last guy was polite about being rude and intrusive. How the hell did they even know?* Then she started laughing. *Of course they would know. And of course they'd try to make a spectacle of it. Scare the public. Stir up the mob. There'll be torches and pitchforks by tonight because of my unvaccinated baby. Never mind that she wouldn't even get an MMR vaccine until she was one year old, and the only shot she's missed so far is her newborn hep B.*

Maybe I should go back out there and let them know how it's their own fault that my baby doesn't have measles immunity. Let the public know that there is a trade-off to vaccinating, and maybe getting every single vaccine isn't always a good idea.

No, her smarter half restrained her. *There's no easy way to explain something so complicated to a camera, and they'd just edit it to make me look crazy anyway.*

But she could still hear some of the commentary through her open window. "Well Steve, I was unable to confirm the status of Baby Jalinski. It would appear that he is alive, although I cannot confirm just how well he is doing. We will keep the News 17 audience updated as events unfold here at the Jalinski residence. Back to you, Steve."

Taking a few deeps breaths, Paula wheeled her baby into the

family room in the back of the house where they kept the elliptical machine. *So much for a nice morning walk outside in the fresh air. At least I can still get in some 'walking.' And look on the bright side. I can catch up on Grey's Anatomy while I get this body back in shape.*

Four weeks later Peter and his wife were relaxing at a resort in the Bahamas for a very well-deserved vacation. Four of the toughest weeks he'd had in a while. *But it had all gone smoothly,* he summarized to himself, sipping his rum punch and watching his wife nap next to him in her pool lounge floaty. *Napping during the day. Must be nice.*

His patient, Jamie, was just fine, although the several phone calls he'd gotten from Mrs. Harding that week about the high fevers and the body aches left him with the impression that it was anything but easy on Jamie. Fortunately, no one in her family had gotten sick. Her friend with leukemia in remission was fine, too. Two unvaccinated kids from Jamie's school had come down with measles, but they were already in quarantine when symptoms started. A fully vaccinated child and the school nurse had also come down with it, but the nurse had started a self-imposed quarantine on day 6 and so hadn't gotten anyone else sick. The vaccinated child exposed the kids in Jamie's class a second time, but had only been at school that first day of having a runny nose and cough before her mom pulled her out, so the health department wasn't concerned, as everyone in the class was likely immune. They'd still be vigilant for another couple weeks just to be safe. But all in all, just a routine measles outbreak, as they almost all were.

And he still couldn't believe none of his patients caught it from that morning of exposure in his office. The newborn was fine. The 6 unvaccinated kids were released from home quarantine after 21 days and none of them had gotten sick. They'd all come in for vitamin A dosing, and he wondered if that was why. And none of his fully-or-partially vaccinated patients had caught it. *Either measles isn't as universally contagious as they say it is, or vitamin A really does help prevent it, or we just got lucky. I should publish these data. Yeah, as if! I'd probably only get it picked up by Joe's Granola Journal of Science, or some such publication. No mainstream medical journal is going to publish a case series of vaccinated and unvaccinated children exposed to measles in a doctor's office in which none of the kids caught the disease. They'll accuse me of making it all up.*

The medical community really plays up how contagious measles is. Ever since one person caught measles from being exposed to a contagious person sitting on the opposite side of a stadium in the mid 90s, everyone says you will catch it by simply breathing the same air that an infectious person breathed even an hour before. Well, not in my office they didn't.

But the media had been another story. The "epidemic" had received national attention. The plight of the poor girl with leukemia on death's door. The fragile newborn baby cooped up in her home. The fear of measles continuing to spread nationwide. The media lies that reminded us that measles had been eliminated in 2000 (a year that had 85 reported cases in the U.S.). The lies that measles has a 30% complication rate and a 20% hospitalization rate, even though that's not even close to true. And the complete and total silence about the other way people can help prevent measles complications. Nope, the vaccine is the only thing you can do - should do - and you are a bad parent if you don't do.

Then there were the bloggers and tabloid writers. Casting blame on a doctor for daring to accept unvaccinated patients into his office, conveniently forgetting the fact that Patient Zero was vaccinated. *As if it was my fault that a patient would choose to not vaccinate against one thing, and then they catch that disease. Like, I didn't do my job well enough if a patient left her appointment with me failing to convince her to vaccinate her kids. If doctors start getting blamed for their patient's illnesses, people are going to stop becoming doctors. A doctor's job is to provide informed consent, educate the patients, share their opinions about treatment options, urge patients to accept treatments, and ultimately respect a patient's right to chose. The ethics are very clear on that. And I'm sure virtually all Americans would agree. But when it comes to vaccines, the vocal minority and the very vocal media look at things differently. The only right choice is to vaccinate.*

The real truth about measles, as Peter saw it, was that it really was a routine illness for virtually every child who caught it in a modern country like the United States. The real fatality rate was about 1 in 10,000. Peter knew that the 1 in 500 or 1 in 1000 fatality rate often quoted in the media was misleading; those numbers were the fatality rate in *reported* cases, not in *all* cases. And they came from the last large outbreak in the United States from 1989 to 1991. During that outbreak, thousands of cases had shown up at hospitals and doctor's offices, and out of those, about 1 in 500 to 1 in 1000 died.

But, that's really just out of all the people who felt sick enough from the measles to seek medical care. Decades earlier, back when everyone caught measles, research showed that only about 10% of people felt sick enough to seek medical care. When measles became a mandatory-reported disease, the data showed that only about 10% of cases were being reported, even though every child was catching it. Bottom line was that about 90% of people who catch measles don't feel sick enough to seek care. So all the stats on fatalities and complications are overblown because they are only based on people who feel the most sick. And when the media warn that measles has a 30% complication rate, they don't tell you that statistic comes from only the reported cases as well, not from all cases. The true complication rate out of all cases is only about 3%. Plus, most of those complications are simply diarrhea and ear infection. The serious complications are extremely rare. And it's not on the rise. The 600 cases a few years ago was an anomaly due to the single large outbreak among the Amish in Ohio. You take out that year, and it's been steady for the past 20 years. But that doesn't stir up fear.

Then there's vitamin A. Almost every third-world country uses it as an "immunization" against measles complications. Some even give it as a yearly dose to all kids. That's because measles is very dangerous to anyone with is vitamin-A deficient. Or malnourished. But that's not America. Yet, the media, and the medical community, are unwilling to push that angle. Why? Because no one makes any money from vitamin A? The only solution is the vaccine. Why not publicize both? That way you reduce the disease spread and reduce complications for those who do catch it. Vitamin A for measles isn't granola medicine; the research is extensive and clear on that.

The Disneyland outbreak really gave the powers-that-be the ammunition they needed to make vaccines mandatory for school in California, he reflected. *Even though not a single case of measles was transmitted in any school during that outbreak, and over half of the cases were in adults, they still managed to pass a law to make vaccines mandatory for the one place that measles didn't happen.* The irony frustrated Peter, and he was very thankful he'd been able to help keep the tiny outbreak at the local school from spreading. Otherwise, his state might be facing the same new law.

The media had, thankfully, stopped calling his office. He'd called one of them back, once, thinking they wanted him to come into the studio for a live interview. But, as it turned out, all they wanted was any information over the phone that they could get to use against him. He realized that they were too scared to let him appear live on the news. *No one has doctors like me on live TV anymore. Ever since Dr. Ward tore Dr. Smith a new one on what ended up being a live debate about aluminum filmed by a number of people in the audience on their phones and posted online, very few mainstream shows want to talk about this live on TV anymore. They want control. They want to do prepared pieces that they can frame to forward their agenda. Maybe that means we are finally getting under their skin, but it also means it's getting harder to reach the mainstream public who aren't investigating these issues themselves.*

Wow, that was a ramble. What even got that started? Oh yeah. Measles. I'll just have to keep on keeping on. Tell the truth. That's all I can do. Like in that movie – Concussion. Will Smith just kept asking people to 'tell the truth.' And they eventually did. One can only hope.

But I'm tired. I can't do this forever. I know I'm not the only doctor who thinks this way, and who gives long talks to his patients about vaccines. I still need to figure out a way to make such talks available to everybody. *Objective, neutral, science-based talks that help people make an educated decision. If I could just clone myself … like Arnold Schwarzenegger in that movie. Ha. That didn't turn out well for him. Although …*

An idea planted itself in Peter's mind. Not actual cloning, of course. But along the same lines. *What if …?*

Stop that, Peter. It's vacation. You can worry about saving the world when you get back to it. Geeze, my glass is empty. I'll just paddle over to the pool bar for another and be back here before my wife wakes up. And then … it sure was nice to finally vacation without the kids.

Dr. Rosen was also reflecting on the last few weeks, but for a different reason. She was a Rheumatologist. Joint aches and pains were her specialty, and the elderly population in this Washington State community was keeping her busy enough. But this past week her office had gotten a couple dozen calls from young adult women complaining of sudden onset of severe joint pain and swelling. She'd seen a few of these already, and each one had looked like rheumatoid arthritis. Lab tests were still pending, but she knew RA when she saw it.

So what the heck is going on? You can't have epidemics of an autoimmune disease. Unless there is some sort of environmental factor. Like a toxin or something.

She was aware of the small measles outbreak at one of the local schools. And she also knew measles could be a trigger for RA. But so far none of the three new women she'd seen had any symptoms of measles. And none of them had even been exposed. She'd added a measles IgM and IgG titer to their blood work out of curiosity, but she didn't expect to find that they'd caught sub-clinical measles.

Wait. I wonder if any of them went and got the vaccine. I can't believe I didn't even ask. I'll have to follow up on that with some phone calls tomorrow. But surely no one would have been dumb enough to give adults the MMR vaccine unless there was a confirmed exposure and they weren't immune from their childhood vaccines. Because the

MMR is risky in adults. That's why we don't give MMR boosters to most adults. Even the CDC warns right on their vaccine warning statements – a 1 in 4 risk of suffering an arthritis reaction, some of which will become severe and chronic. Meaning, RA. But they don't spell that out on their warning sheets because that would scare people. But every Rheumatologist knows this. The problem is, family practice docs and internists don't. They just give whatever vaccines they are told to give.

And I bet they've been giving it out left and right during this outbreak. Without informing their patients of the risk. Sure, get the MMR vaccine if it's important. I agree with vaccination. But with adults it's trickier … and often riskier, especially when giving a live-virus vaccine that was supposed to have been a childhood disease. The disease, and the vaccine, are both more dangerous for adults. That's why we safely use these in kids only.

I'm going to ask Sara if she'll do a news report on this. Warn people to consider the risk of adult MMR vaccine before they get it. She likes doing medical pieces. RA sucks. It means drugs for life, and a life that's less fun to boot.

I'd take measles over the MMR vaccine as an adult any day. And I'm a doctor.

Chapter 8

The Moral Politician

It was the beginning of a new legislative cycle, and Tom Landon wasn't looking forward to all the long nights and weekends ahead. His boss, Senator Charlene Emerson (D), was on a mission again – a mission that had failed here in their state last year. And she wanted to take another bi-partisan stab at it this year, again with Senator James Korsen (R). Tom hated bi-partisan bills. *Republicans were so ... republican. Their brains worked so differently than normal. Talking with a Republican was like talking to someone on drugs. They'd stare at you blankly as if they had no idea what you were talking about.*

Although, Tom did like Korsen's Chief of Staff, Elena. She was smart. Smarter than Tom was, he admitted. Her body was so-so, but her red hair made up for it. But Tom liked brains over body anyway. And admitting his intellectual inferiority made it so much easier to work with her, and do all the other stuff he'd gotten to do with her. It was good to be single in politics. For him, anyway. Obviously being married didn't stop some politicians from living it up. But he didn't think he'd be that way when he eventually settled down, even if he did end up running for office.

Ultimately they'd had to pull their bill last year. Too much public opposition. And too much Republican opposition, despite Korsen's help. It was hard living in a state with a Republican majority in the Senate. The House was just about evenly split, which gave Democrats more of a chance to do some real good. But this year would be different, Charlene had told him. This year they had help from Doctor/Senator Donaldson.

Ahhh, to live in her state, Tom day-dreamed. *To live in a purely Democratic State with a Democratic majority in both State houses, with a Democratic Governor to put his signature on everything that was right (Democratic), and to veto everything that was wrong.*

Senator/Doctor Jane Donaldson, who got the mandatory vaccination law passed in her state, was touring the country to share her brilliance with fellow Democrats everywhere on how to get the same law passed in their own states. Donaldson had watched her fellow Democrat in California, Senator/Doctor Richard Pan, get the job done in the Golden State, and she'd come up with an even better plan in her own state. So she was now sharing her expertise with the rest of the nation. And tonight was the welcome dinner to kick-off their weekend of revitalizing their own bill and planning their next steps. Four senators and their staff, plus two members of the House and their staff, would be there. All people who had already signed on to the resurrection of the new bill. They didn't need any convincing, but they all needed training in this issue.

Yeah, it's going to be a lot of work. But at least Elena will be there too …

"And so, my fellow Americans, we have a health crisis in our country, and it affects every state," the visiting senator concluded. "You saw what happened in California when measles was allowed to take hold and spread among the pockets of unvaccinated children. This epidemic didn't just harm that state and endanger Dr. Pan's constituents; it spread nationwide and threatened us all. And other diseases are on the rise: whooping cough, mumps, meningitis, and even polio is threatening to make a come-back. These diseases used to be eliminated and have now returned. We must put a stop to it as a nation. Our herd immunity is being threatened by too many anti-vaccine families, whose fears are fueled by a few rogue anti-vaccine doctors who spread lies about vaccines. We all know that vaccines are safe and effective, and they are the right choice for every child. And it concerns me greatly when parents decline this life-saving treatment. It makes me wonder if they are even fit to be parents.

"Because vaccine laws are under the jurisdiction of each state, we can't rely on the federal government to make vaccines mandatory. We have to do it ourselves. They were victorious in California, and I won this battle in my state as well. I would like to introduce you to the man who made it all possible. He is the head of my state's medical association, which represents the interests of over 10,000 physicians, and he, along with his team, are really the ones whom you should thank for this success and for saving the lives of so many children. Ladies and gentlemen, Mr. Jackson Jones."

Emilio Sanchez clapped politely along with the rest of the intimate group of 20 or so gathered in the private dining room of the steakhouse. He certainly loved these dinners, but this particular one had taken even his appetite away. He glanced sideways at Elena, his boss, and saw the genuine smile on her face as she watched the Senator sit down and the well-dressed, middle-aged man stand up from the adjoining table and take the podium.

She really believes this stuff, he thought. *They all do. They actually believe it.*

He looked past Elena at *her* boss, and his – Senator James Korsen. *He does, too, although he doesn't look quite so enraptured. More calculating. Probably calculating votes: the votes that this endeavor will bring him versus the votes that he will lose over it. Or, calculating the funding his campaign will receive from the State Medical Association for his role in helping to pass this law. Not that they haven't paid him enough already.*

Emilio Sanchez had worked hard to get where he was. Despite graduating in the top 10% of his class at UVA Law, he still couldn't shake the feeling that he was hired onto Senator Korsen's staff as the token Mexican they'd been missing for a while. He knew he deserved it though. He was good.

But when this mandatory vaccine law came up last year, and

Senator Korsen decided to co-sponsor it, Emilio found himself torn. Legally, and ethically, he had to represent his boss and support his endeavors, no matter how he personally felt. But he himself did not like vaccines. After what happened to his little brother, ten years his junior, nobody would. So he found himself in a moral dilemma. He'd opted to follow the ethics that had been grilled into him in law school and do his job, and try to do it well enough to keep his conscience clear. *But that's the thing about conscience: it cares a lot more about morals than it does ethics. Plus there's my Hispanic Catholic mother in the forefront of my mind making sure I follow my morals. And when I don't, she shows up in person.*

That had been an interesting evening, just a day after his boss had publicly announced his support of the bill for the first time last year. His mom showed up at the door to his little studio apartment overlooking the river, conveniently located within walking distance to the Capitol Building, and also, unfortunately, within driving distance of the house he grew up in. They'd talked, and cried, long into the night. She'd eventually left, accepting their compromise that he'd stay in this job for now. They'd both been thrilled when Senator Emerson had pulled the bill later due to lack of support. And they thought it was over.

But now it's back. I shouldn't be surprised. In fact, this bill will probably hit every state eventually, and there won't be any legislator's office that will be safe. But working for a Republican should have been safe. Mandatory medical laws were much more of a Democratic agenda, and he'd been surprised when Republican Korsen had thrown in his support. He'd bought the "all medicine is good, and vaccines are even better, so it's okay to force them" argument. Emilio had done his best last year to subtly steer James's thinking in the right direction, but to no avail. He hadn't wanted to show all of his cards and get fired.

And now he knew he had to be careful again. Not just to keep his job, but to avoid breaking any actual laws that would either land him in jail, prevent him from ever sitting for the Bar, or from ever working in politics again. Because this year, Emilio would follow his Hispanic, Catholic, and mother-instilled conscience and do the right thing.

Making that decision had been quite a relief. Even though it added some stress to his life, the moral peace it brought his heart and mind more than made up for it. His morals also wouldn't allow him to break the letter of any laws, although he knew he'd be bending the spirit and intent of his legal obligation to represent his boss. But he thought he'd found a way to do it, and both James and Elena had loved the idea.

Emilio was going to play devil's advocate in all their discussions. Challenge every idea and point that anyone put together in support of the new version of the mandatory vaccination law. Present the arguments that he knew the opposition would put forth so that Elena and the senator could plan the right counter-arguments.

Emilio was worried that by doing this he might be helping them instead, but he balanced that by realizing all of these counter-arguments would be heard by every legislator they talked to. He'd be able to plant the right seeds, make them think, challenge the pro-mandate way of thinking right there out in the open.

And he promised himself, and his mother, that after this particular fight was over, whether they won or lost, he would find another job. He was thinking Texas. That was closer to his family's roots, and they valued medical freedom down there much more than some of the other states. He'd miss his mama, and his brother, who needed full-time care at home and would so for the rest of his life. But they had a lot of family support here, family who helped take care of his little – well, not so little any more – brother.

Emilio suppressed the tear that always formed when he thought of his brother. His once-happy-playful-smiling-talking-walking baby brother who had gone in for a checkup one day, and had come home screaming and screaming and screaming, and had never been the same again. The encephalopathy diagnosis hadn't been confirmed for about another year, but the sudden change that occurred the day after his one-year checkup had Emilio and his whole family convinced that something had triggered Arturo's change. It wasn't coincidence, like the doctors had told them. It didn't just happen for no reason. And Emilio knew that the only right thing to do was to help make sure that no family in America was ever forced to accept the risks of what had forever damaged his baby brother.

Emilio sat up straighter as all of this flashed through his mind, sitting there at dinner. He'd missed whatever Mr. Jones had been saying, but from the laughter in the audience it sounded like just some warm-up comments. He was now getting to the good stuff.

"So here are some of the main issues we are going to look at tonight, then break down further throughout the weekend. First, let's take a look at how the vote went down in California, then I'll share what happened in my own state.

"Out of the combined California Senate and Assembly, totaling 120 members, they needed 61 yes votes to pass it, and they got 70. Only 58% of the Legislature voted for it. So, this law just barely passed in California, and in my own state the numbers were very similar. Which is interesting, and I asked myself why something so safe and good for our health would get so much opposition? More on that later.

"The votes were also very much along party lines: In the 80-member California Assembly, only 44 Democrats voted for it, and 8 voted against it or abstained. Virtually all Republicans voted against it – 25 of them – and only 2 voted for it. They got 24 yes votes in the 40-member Senate, again along party lines. And in my own state it was about the same, but even a little closer.

"So here in your state, you have your work cut out for you. Senator Emerson will spend some time securing most of the Democrat votes, then focus more time meeting with Republicans. It was our experience that most Democrats who were already morally opposed to any mandatory medicine laws wouldn't be swayed. One of Senator Pan's Democratic colleagues had the nerve to call the law 'draconian' – in public, if you can believe that. So let's not waste much energy on the few Democrats who aren't on your side already.

"Senator Korsen will start in with his Republican colleagues, and here is what I would suggest: start with the Senators who don't have children. In California they found that these were much more likely to support the bill. Legislators who do have kids are much more in favor of parental rights to make medical decisions for their children, and are unwilling to put such decisions into the hands of the State. At the time of this vote, in the 120-member California legislature, 83 had children, and only half of those voted for this bill. Whereas with the 37 who didn't have kids, 29 voted yes and 7 voted no. Legislators without kids were 4 times as likely to support this bill as those with kids.

"So it should be easy to get the non-parents onto our side with the simple 'vaccines are safe and effective, they are for the good of society, they save lives, etc.' message. The simple arguments. Once they are convinced, and we get some momentum, then it will be time to start working on the parents. Senator Korsen – James – you have kids, and so does Mrs. Emerson. So you'll both really have to chat it up with the other parent legislators.

"You'll all have to be prepared for an in-flux of phone calls once this goes officially onto the agenda. Our friends from The People for Mandatory Vaccination have volunteered to help man your phones. This is a fairly small volunteer organization, so they may only have enough people for one helper per legislator. Our experience in my state showed us that the number of calls to legislator's offices in opposition to the mandatory vaccination law was between 4 and 10 times greater than the calls in support, and the same was true in California. Basically, virtually all of the public opposed this bill, but the medical organizations – at least the mainstream ones, which also happen to be the ones with money – supported it, of course. So, we'll team up a volunteer with each legislator who throws in his or her support of this bill, because that's where all the phone calls are going to start coming in.

"Here is why we think we saw such little support from the lay public. We think that most Americans are opposed to any laws that make any type of medical treatment mandatory, no matter how good the treatment is. They just don't want to give up their autonomy in making medical decisions for themselves and their children – especially their children. That's why it's our job to also focus on the 'good of society' argument. That, yes, medicine should be decided by individuals, but sometimes the good of society comes first. Herd immunity, which we also like to call 'community immunity' because it's catchier, the danger of unvaccinated children, the rise of diseases, and the fact that the science is settled on vaccine safety. These are the four pillars of our argument.

"Now, you and I would agree that it's okay for a government to mandate something that is both necessary and harmless. And that's what vaccines are, so that's why it's okay for the government to step in where some parents have failed to make the right choice and vaccinate their children. But let me caution you not to go into that argument. Stay clear of it. Senator Pan introduced a children's bill of rights in California last year, a bill that basically gave all children the right to have medical care, and that the government would guarantee that right. But the opposition saw this as a stepping stone to making vaccines not only mandatory for school, but just plain mandatory period. And not just vaccines, but any aspect of health care that their legislature, guided by the medical societies, decided was in the best interest of children. That's how they saw it anyway. Surprisingly to all of us, almost all the support Dr. Pan had gotten for SB 277, which made vaccines mandatory for school, completely vanished. Very few would touch this new bill. Maybe he acted too soon. We'll see. He may try to figure out another way to go at it in the future. Senator Donaldson and I plan to as well, after we see how Pan's turns out. So, be careful. Don't discuss with your legislator colleagues that we are trying to step in and interfere with parental medical decisions because that's unpopular. Just focus on the four pillars.

"And let me caution you: you don't want to dive too deeply into the medical side of these issues, because they are complicated. Don't let yourself get drawn in when someone tries to argue medicine. You aren't doctors, so you won't win any medical discussions with any of your legislative colleagues or constituents who oppose this bill. Your whole job over the next few months will be to have conversations with your colleagues that focus on the four pillars. When they try to sidetrack you onto other issues, like vaccine reactions, conflicts of interest in our vaccine safety research, parental rights, government overreach of police powers, and medical freedom, just go back to the four pillars. Again, what are they? Community immunity, the danger of unvaccinated children, diseases are on the rise, and vaccine safety science is settled."

Emilio put himself at the back of the line so that he could be the last to greet Senator/Dr. Donaldson. He wanted to ask her a few questions to get a measure on her intelligence and basic knowledge on vaccines and infectious diseases, and figured he'd get more time if there was no one behind him. He watched Elena leave the dining room with Tom from Emerson's office. *Lucky bastard. If Tom shows up tomorrow morning for our first session with a big grin on his face, I'm going to punch him.* Emilio had hoped he would have a chance to get to know Elena better, but now thought maybe it's a good idea that he didn't, with her being his supervisor and all. Plus, he didn't want her watching him too closely. And he wasn't really the casual sex type anyway. He just wished he could keep a serious girlfriend for more than a few months, but …

"Hello, I'm Jane."

Emilio stared at the hand that was being offered to him, and he froze for a second. *I really have to shake this person's hand?* He did so, and hoped his true feelings didn't show on his face.

"Hello, Senator. Thank you so much for coming to help us. Emilio Sanchez, with Senator Korsen's office." Emilio saw the lobbyist, Jackson Jones, standing a few steps away working on his phone. "Can I ask a couple of tough medical questions I've gotten lately that I'm not sure how to answer? I know we'll probably learn all this tomorrow but I wanted to pick your medical brain on this. First, I thought all vaccines prevented the spread of diseases, but I'm hearing that some do and some don't. Can you tell me which is which?"

The doctor stared at Emilio for what turned into an increasingly uncomfortable ten seconds before she answered, "That's a good question. Let me see. Well, of course the measles vaccine does. And whooping cough. Diphtheria vaccine, too – we definitely don't want diphtheria to come back. Polio vaccine, of course. Chicken pox, too. Let me think, the list of vaccines that don't prevent the transmission of its disease is very small. I think only the tetanus vaccine doesn't prevent someone from passing tetanus onto another person. But wait, I think that's because tetanus isn't even contagious anyway."

So why the hell did you include tetanus vaccine in your list of vaccines that schoolchildren needed in order to help keep other kids around them safe? And polio, whooping cough and diphtheria vaccines don't prevent spread either, Emilio didn't say out loud. "That makes sense. Thanks. Next is hepatitis B. I get a lot of questions about how we can justify making this vaccine mandatory for daycare and school when it's a sexually-transmitted disease and doesn't seem like a risk to babies and children."

"I get that a lot, too. But I like to look at all vaccines as equally important. They are all critical and life-saving. So they simply all should be mandated for school and daycare. I think Jackson is right on this – steer away from arguing medical logic with people. Just keep it simple."

"I like that, Senator. Thanks. Last one, if I can ask. Which diseases are on the rise? When I try to find data on that, I can't find a continuous increase in anything. Just some occasional ups and downs of whooping cough, but that's it. Can you help me out?"

Emilio wasn't sure why, but he suddenly felt someone's eyes on him. He glanced a little to his right, past Emerson, and saw Mr. Jones looking at him with intense interest. But with a very blank expression, as if Emilio didn't matter but also seemed to matter greatly at the same time. *I thought I was keeping my voice down, but this guy apparently has excellent hearing.*

"Well, Emilio, obviously whooping cough, but also measles and polio are on the rise too. But yes, you'll pick up more on that tomorrow."

Yup, that's what I thought. This woman has no idea what she's talking about. And this is the person who is leading the nation into mandatory vaccination? Hey, maybe this is a blessing. Someone who is clearly so clueless about vaccines and disease trends couldn't possibly sell this idea to an entire nation, could she?

But Emilio had the sickening feeling that yes, she probably could. With smart people like Jones to do all the real thinking, and the amount of Pharma money this woman had behind her, she could.

"So how long have you been a pediatrician, Dr. Donaldson?" Emilio was genuinely curious.

No pause this time. "Oh silly, I'm not a pediatrician. I'm a real doctor ... I'm a surgeon."

That explains why you don't know jack about vaccines, Emilio would have given his left hand to say out loud.

Jackson Jones dialed one of the numbers listed under his "favorites" tab as he stepped away. "Bob, it's me. I have a name I want you to look into. I want to know if he or any of his family show up in our system ... yes, a few days is fine."

Elena Moretti shook the business-owner's hand, allowing her hand to linger in his slightly longer than necessary, and thanked him for his support and for informing her about the new business park that the city planners were proposing in his city – a business park that would cut deeply into his own business. And his wasn't a small business. Over 2000 employees. And he'd also been very supportive of James's campaigns over the years. Elena assured him she would let the Senator know right away and work with him to see what they could do.

She looked at the next appointment on her schedule, then rolled her eyes. *Not another one. How many of these crazies do I have to sit with before this vaccine bill is done?* But she didn't really have a choice.

Every constituent had the right to be heard, and hear them she would. *I just don't have to* listen *to them. Especially because they aren't donors.*

She stood up and walked out to the small reception area and approached the group of 3 women and one man, sizing them up as she went. They were well-dressed, young to middle-age adults, each with a small stack of handouts on their laps. They stood as she approached and polite introductions went around. Elena gestured for them to follow her down the hallway to the conference room. She poked her head into Emilio's office along the way and told him to sit in on this with her.

The group took chairs at a long table in a somewhat cramped conference room, Emilio trailing in after them.

"Hi, I'm Emilio Sanchez, one of Ms. Moretti's assistants on this particular bill. And you four are ...?"

"I am Barbara Highfisher, one of Senator Korsen's constituents. I have brought with me today three of my friends: Sophia from the Immunity Information Center, Kimberly from Vaccine Voices, and Dr. Montgomery Ward, a pediatrician. We want to chat with you about the new mandatory vaccine bill."

Elena sat politely through their spiel. What was interesting with this group is that they didn't focus on the dangers of vaccination, how vaccines cause autism, how the diseases aren't deadly, or about how their own children had been harmed by vaccines – all the stuff she'd had to sit through over the last couple weeks with every other group.

Instead, these three – she didn't include the constituent at first, because it was obvious she was just there to get these other three non-constituents a meeting – seemed intelligent, well-informed, and well-spoken. And some of their points were refutations of the four pillars that Jackson Jones had trained them on during their weekend seminars, so she was prepared with the packaged responses. But then they went beyond that and said a number of things that Elena hadn't heard before. She usually didn't take any notes at these meetings. She knew Emilio knew these topics and he'd be able to walk her and James through them later. But she did jot down a few new things these people brought up that Jackson Jones had left out:

First, the California measles outbreak hadn't touched any schools. Not a single case was even transmitted in a school. It was all in restaurants, stores, medical centers, and homes. That surprised her. And their point that having a mandatory vaccine law for schools wouldn't have changed the course of that measles outbreak was valid. The doctor made a point that if they really wanted to prevent measles everywhere, what they really should do is not let any unvaccinated children in public anywhere, make everyone show their immunization papers everywhere they went – *that* would keep measles away. But Elena knew that they also knew how ludicrous that sounded, and would be political suicide for any legislator who tried it. Other than a driver's license, free Americans don't need "papers" to show anyone.

Then he made a point of saying that most vaccines don't prevent the spread of the disease they are intended to prevent, which couldn't possibly be right. The doctor obviously sensed her doubt, and he offered a very convincing example of how the tetanus vaccine only makes your body generate antibodies against the tetanus toxin, so that if the germ ever invades your body the toxin gets neutralized so it doesn't paralyze you, but the tetanus germs are still there. That made sense, but that was only one vaccine. The doctor, rightly so, said that he didn't want to spend the entire time with a lecture on immunity, and he gave her a handout that summarized which vaccines don't prevent person-to-person spread of its disease, adding that this list included diphtheria, whooping cough, flu, and polio vaccines. He emphasized the point that mandating a vaccine that doesn't even prevent the spread of the disease is unnecessary because it won't reduce infections in schools at all.

Then the one woman's point about how "pockets of unvaccinated children don't correlate with disease outbreaks" was also surprising. She gave Elena some data to back up her statements, which she'd probably just throw away. Apparently LA County had one of the lowest vaccine exemption rates – only 1.6% of schoolkids had registered a personal belief exemption (PBE) from vaccines; meaning they'd opted out of vaccines. Yet they had 29 cases of measles. Marin County, with a much higher PBE rate of 6.5%, only had 2 cases.

Looking at whooping cough in California, counties with some of the highest numbers of whooping cough had the lowest numbers of PBEs – between 1.6 and 1.9%. Her point being that schools with a higher proportion of unvaccinated kids don't have more disease.

Then she went on about how a senator, during his campaign to pass the California vaccine law, had claimed that some schools had PBE rates as high as 25%. And that such schools with that many un-vaccinated kids are outbreaks just waiting to happen. But many of the schools with high PBE rates are very small schools. So a small school of 100 kids with a 25% PBE rate would only mean 25 unvaccinated kids. A large public school with 2000 kids, with only a 5% PBE rate, would mean 100 unvaccinated kids. So there would often be more unvaccinated kids at schools with the highest vaccination rates. But, again, there was no scientific correlation between disease trends and PBE rates.

And finally (*would she just shut up already?*) someone with a PBE could possibly only have opted out of just one vaccine, like hepatitis B. Many would be fully immunized against all the real contagious diseases. So claiming that the high rates of PBEs puts everyone in danger just isn't accurate.

Geeze, I'd love to have this girl on my team. She could talk circles around anyone. It's a good thing for us that no one really cares about that much detail on this issue.

The third person, the other woman, then went on and on about all the conflicts of interest in vaccine safety research. And Elena knew this lady must be making most of this up.

There's no way that the former head of the CDC, who was in charge of all vaccine safety research for almost a decade, would have been allowed to own stock in one of our nation's largest vaccine manufac-turers. No one would have allowed that. Especially not over $4 million dollars worth, according to some financial newspaper in the Dakotas as this lady claimed. And there's no way that vaccine company would openly hire that head of the CDC to lead their vaccine division. Sure, she could see the CDC head owning some general stock in pharmaceu-ticals, like the most recent head did before she resigned after just nine *months. Many people who devote their lives to public service in the government hope to land a cushy job someday, but $4 million seems too outrageous.*

Then she claimed that another doctor who headed the CDC's vaccine approval board in the 90's also held stock in a vaccine company, and that some of the doctors who served on those approval boards had financial ties to vaccine makers.

Then there was this new secret group at the CDC that called themselves SPIDER. What did that stand for? She had to write it down: *Scientists Preserving Integrity, Diligence, and Ethics in Research. This group had lodged a formal complaint that their own CDC is compromised by corporate and government interests and has lost its mission to objectively safeguard the health of our community.*

But she didn't stop there. The CDC whistleblower – Dr. Johnson was it? – who was part of the largest CDC study that proved vaccines didn't cause autism was now saying the research was faked? What is she smoking? Elena wondered. *I'd like some of that.*

Finally, it was the doctor again who brought it all home with another claim, one she knew for sure just couldn't be true. The claim that the recommended CDC schedule had not been adequately tested for safety. He said something about an Institute of Medicine – she'd have to look up who that was – claiming back in 2013 that, and he quoted, which she tried to write down quickly, "studies designed to examine the long term effects of the cumulative number of vaccines have not been conducted," "existing research has not been designed to test the entire immunization schedule," and "the committee generally found a paucity of information that addressed the risk of adverse events in association with the complete recommended immunization schedule."

She'd have a long de-brief with Emilio about all this, then let James know, just so he wasn't ever caught off guard when he talked to someone smart. She'd pass this along to Tom as well. She knew most of this couldn't be true, but they all needed to be prepared to counter any of it that is true. Especially if any of this came out in the hearings.

We spent a whole weekend with the Doctor/Senator who is supposed to know it all, and her lobbyist who seemed to be the real brains behind the success in their state, and all they focused on were their four bloody pillars and how to promote them. They didn't get into any details on the medical arguments or any of these ideas I am hearing now. What a colossal waste of time that weekend had been ... well, except for the nights. Tom was never a waste of time.

And then the constituent, Barbara something, whom she didn't think would have anything important to say, ended up saying one of the most interesting things of all: "Who has the moral authority to deny anyone the right to follow their conscience or religious beliefs when making a decision about a pharmaceutical product that could brain injure or end their lives or their children's lives?" *Finally, the 'vaccines are dangerous' argument.* "Utilitarian health policies that force everyone to be treated the same are cruel and immoral. Without flexible medical and religious exemptions to vaccination, enforcement of a one-size-fits-all vaccine law creates fear and distrust of government and doctors."

Wait. She's not really saying vaccines are too dangerous. She's saying that because they can be dangerous to some, a government does not have the right to mandate them. We don't have the right to force all of them on everyone. There has to be some flexibility.

Elena realized that the last woman had come to the end of her point, so she took the opportunity to bring an end to the meeting. She thanked them for coming, and assured them she'd let the Senator know about their concerns. *Why did they even bother to come in and try to argue against a bill that our office sponsored? It's not like we can change our minds now. They should be focusing on all the other members of the House and the Senate. They are the ones they need to convince. I better give Tom a heads-up so he can help me spread the word to the other Chiefs of Staff and their schedulers. We can't let people like these three get in front of too many legislators. We'll dig up some dirt on this doctor, too, and spread it around so our colleagues have the right preconceptions about him.*

"I feel like that was a waste of time," said Kimberly, as the three women waited for the elevator. "Their office co-sponsored the bill. It's not like we are going to change their minds."

"I agree that we weren't going to change their minds," Sophia countered. "But I think it's also important that we be able to tell *other* legislators that we met with Korsen's office and shared our concerns with them."

"Well, that makes sense," Kimberly agreed. "But I've been told by a few friends who are big donors to some of the senators that when it comes to trying to educate a legislator about an issue, it's money that talks, not logic or data. If you aren't a donor, they don't listen. They vote yes or no based on who they owe favors to, or who owes them a favor. Like, 'you vote for my bill and I'll vote for yours.' It's all about money and influence, not about what's right and wrong."

"Do you think that's really true?" asked Sophia. "They can't all be that way."

"No, they aren't all that way, in my experience," chimed in Barbara, the constituent. "Some do have ethics; and, for some, being their constituent has more weight than being a donor. The important thing is to know who is who."

"And that's where relationship-building comes in," Sophia continued. "I've been told by a number of experienced friends that the most important way to have an ethical legislator's ear is for them to know who you are because they see you around in their office and at their events. Be friendly and respectful and let them know you are a voice for medical freedom and parental rights. You aren't there just for one issue. You are there to be a source of valued information. Then, when a vaccine-related issue comes up, you have an 'in' to share your two cents as their constituent. You aren't just some crazy lady who shows up once talking nonsense. You are that intelligent, friendly, well-spoken supporter who's often around. And you are a voter. Maybe a financial supporter, too, but not in a way that looks like you are trying to buy your way in. The more legislators we can build relationships with, the more impact we will have over the years as vaccine issues come up."

"But that takes time," added Barbara. "Time that many moms don't have. So those of us who do have the time, and are good at it, spend our time focusing on relationships. And don't forget about lobbyists. I know some people view them as evil, but when you hire a lobbyist with a good reputation whom the legislators already know and trust, that's another way to get their ear."

"Too bad that takes money that many of us don't have." Sophia again. "But you are right. If we were more organized, and pooled our resources to do this right, we'd be more effective."

"And don't forget," finished Barbara. "When you are dealing with medical legislation, you have to get a doctor in the room if you want to be taken seriously. Where is Dr. Monty, by the way?"

"A couple of moms grabbed him for a picture I think. Now they're chatting," explained Kimberly.

Sophia rolled her eyes. "I think he secretly enjoys the celebrity attention, even though he'll swear to you he doesn't. But it really helps to bring a doctor along for something like this."

"Well, he knows we have another meeting in five minutes, right?"

Dr. Ward jogged up. "Sorry. I was just …"

"We know. Taking a picture," Sophia said.

"Oh, Dr. Monty," smiled Kimberly, winking at the two other women and moving over next to him. "Can I take my picture with you? The girls in my group back home won't believe I actually got to meet you!"

The doctor blushed.

"I think you're right, Sophia," observed Barbara. "He does like being a celebrity."

The doctor blushed even more. "You're the celebrity, Barbara. Why didn't you introduce yourself to that staffer as being the head of NCIV?"

"I think, in this case, I'd get more credibility just being Korsen's constituent since I live in his district. Oh, and can I get a picture too?"

"Stop teasing him you two," Sophia decided the joke was over. "Ok, so you don't like it, Monty. But that's what you get for doing the right thing. For standing up for others who need your help. They love you for it. I wish my husband and I had met you before what happened to my Arabella."

"I feel like I'm not doing enough," admitted the doctor, changing the subject. "And I'm not sure we are going about this the right way."

"We were just lamenting the fact that we haven't built the proper relationships with any of these elected officials," agreed Sophia. "So they don't really have any reason to listen to us because they don't know us."

"And we are only here for today," continue the doctor. "What I should have done is taken a whole week off and tried to get into as many of these offices as I could. So they could get to know me, see that I'm an intelligent, humble, informed doctor who knows a heck of a lot about vaccines and is there to answer their questions, not just preach at them. I feel as if it matters less what I say, and more how I say it and what impression I leave them with."

Barbara jumped back in. "Plus, we should have been doing this months ago – influencing these guys *before* the hearing and the vote. People think that bills are decided in the actual hearings. They're not. They are decided long before that as legislators and their staffers meet, discuss, and negotiate. *That's* the time to shut these bills down. Once they make it to a hearing, the game is mostly over. The deals are done. We try to present an educated defense in the hearing, as if that's suddenly going to change all the legislator's minds. It doesn't. More of us have to build bridges with each legislator in our home districts so when we need to bring in an expert they are ready to listen. And all this has to happen at the first hint of a vaccine bill, not after it's already on the legislative agenda."

"So we are playing catch-up, trying to let them know the medical facts and why this law is wrong. I have so much to say to these legislators, but there just isn't enough time and opportunity to say it all. And I don't even know if they're listening, because they don't know me from Adam. I'm just some doctor they don't know. I wish we could make them all read a simple five-page summary that has every important piece of information in it. They *think* they are getting that in the Legislative Summary that's supposedly written for them as an objective presentation of both sides, but we all know that's bogus."

"And no legislator is going to read even two pages late in the game, let alone five," agreed Sophia. "That's why we make all these one-page flyers and graphics with simplified points on them as a last-ditch effort. But I have a sinking feeling that this whole fight isn't about convincing any of these guys with facts and logic. From what Barbara is saying, and what I've heard from others, it may be more about the relationships you build for some, and how much money you've donated for others, and we haven't done enough of either. If we lose this vote, then we may have to turn our attention to the public. To the *voters*. Convince them that mandatory vaccination laws are wrong, just as all laws that mandate medicine, or penalize the non-compliant, are wrong."

"Well, we have to keep talking to them for now anyway," finished Barbara. "Who knows? We may get lucky and reach some."

"Yeah, pretty much everything they said was true," Emilio told Elena when she cornered him later that day. "I had to look up some of what they said, because some of it was even new to *me*. But yes, it's all true."

"Even that bull crap about the 4 million dollars of Pharma stock and the head of the CDC?"

"It was reported in a news story, apparently. I have it pulled up right here online." Emilio showed her. "I couldn't find the original source yet, just this article from Health Impact News – some granola news site. They claim she sold 2.3 million worth of her stock in Merck once she left the CDC, but held onto the other half. But their link to the original source isn't live anymore, so I can't verify it. But if this is true, then the head of the CDC was basically overseeing almost ten years' worth of CDC safety research on the vaccines made by the very company she held this stock in. Some might look at that as a conflict of interest, others as just business as usual."

"Well, don't mention these issues in our mock hearing presentation tomorrow morning. With all these possible arguments against this bill, we need to make double sure James and Charlene are well prepared for any questions, *if* they come up. But I don't want these issues to get out if we can help it. It would have been nice if Jackson Jones or Dr. Donaldson had given us a heads-up on some of this. They must have had to fend off all of these same questions."

Jackson Jones answered his phone and listened to the report from his contact.

"I had a feeling something was up with this kid. Brother is a Vaccine Injury Compensation Program recipient, huh? When ... Back in 1995? Severe encephalopathy ... $3.2 mil, huh? That's just great. Yeah, well this victim's brother is actually working in Korsen's office. Yeah, Korsen in the state where I was a few days ago. Yes, *that* Korsen to whom you've been so generous ... I've no idea how he got hired there. Not everyone has access to your list ... Yes sir, I'll make sure to let them know."

Jackson glanced at his watch. *Midnight here on the West Coast. That's three a.m. back east. I'll send an email now, then call James's chief of staff in the morning. Half a day can't hurt.*

"Members of the committee, colleagues, and the people of this great State, I bring before you a petition of great importance. We have a health crisis on our hands, one that threatens the lives and well-being of our most precious citizens – our children. Our nation faces disease outbreaks we haven't faced in decades. And it is due to the negligence of only a minority of our people. Despite the overwhelming evidence that vaccines are safe and effective, some parents still do not choose to vaccinate their children. Yet, these kids, who can carry infectious and contagious diseases, are given the same rights and freedoms as healthy children who do take part in the vaccination program – children who not only are vaccinated for their own good, but for the good of society. It's time that we, the legislators who are responsible for the well-being of all our citizens, take matters into our own hands and enact legislation that will protect all of us."

Tom Landon looked around at the audience in the hearing chamber. There were seats for 300, but only about 20 of them were filled with staffers from various offices. No legislators, of course. They would have to sit through the real hearing in a few weeks, and no one in their right mind would want to also sit through this practice hearing. But Tom's boss, Charlene, needed the practice. And a junior staffer – Emilio, he thought, from Korsen's office – was going to play the role of the opposition and challenge her with some tough questions. This would be interesting. *So far so good,* he thought. *Charlene was managing to appear as if she wasn't reading her presentation, which was important in order to show she understood and believed everything she was standing for. It had to come across as authentic and original, and nothing put legislators to sleep like someone reading a prepared statement to them.*

"Let me first start with the crisis," Charlene Emerson continued. "Measles is at an all-time high, and it continues to rise. This serious, potentially fatal disease was declared eliminated in 2000. But in recent years we have been plagued by outbreaks. In 2012 we only had 55 cases nationwide. By 2014 that had jumped to 667. And now we have almost 70 cases in one state alone – Minnesota. And our state has not gone untouched. Measles is deadly, and those who do survive it don't go unscathed: 30% of victims suffer complications, and 25% get hospitalized. And it spreads so easily that one person can expose an entire school just by walking through it. And that's just the United States. Measles kills over 100,000 children every year worldwide. To allow this disease to take hold again is unconscionable. And we have the authority to stop it.

"But that's not the only crisis. Whooping cough is also at an all-time high. And infants in their first year of life are the most vulnerable. Every year about 20 American babies die from this disease. Whooping cough was nearly eliminated decades ago, but we now have as many as 50,000 cases reported annually. This highly contagious disease spreads easily through child care centers and preschools, putting infants and young children in harm's way.

"These disease outbreaks happen because of unvaccinated children. What's alarming to me is that some schools have as many as 25% of their student population who aren't fully up to date on their immunizations. This puts other students at significant risk.

"But I also want to focus on the kids who are the most vulnerable: immunocompromised children. Children with cancer who are on chemotherapy must also attend school. So do children with HIV. Some kids with chronic medical problems must take medications that suppress their immune systems, leaving them vulnerable. So diseases that might not harm a healthy child can kill an immunocompromised one. You will meet little Red today, and his father will share their story about how they had to live in fear when a case of measles was reported in their county last year.

"You will also hear today from Dr. Sampson from the university about how safe vaccines are. The FDA and CDC, as well as countless medical schools around the world, have been studying vaccine safety for decades. And the science is clear. Vaccines are safe. Vaccines don't cause autism. The one research study that claimed there was a problem years ago was debunked and retracted, and the British doctor who published that false study lost his medical license for committing this fraud. Yet some parents still listen to him and to a few other rogue doctors and celebrities who claim vaccines are dangerous. They are not. They are safe.

"The government and the courts have the authority and the right to protect their citizens from the threat of infectious diseases. Jacobson vs. Massachusetts in 1905 set this precedent in the Supreme Court, which ruled that one man did not have the right to refuse the smallpox vaccination for his children during a smallpox outbreak. The State of California took this step two years ago to help ensure every schoolchild was fully immunized and protected so that children would no longer be put at risk. And last year another state made the same decision. Now it is our turn, here in our state, to protect *our* kids. I ask for your support to help end this health crisis and save our children. Thank you."

Tom stood up and stepped over to the lectern, turning off the mic so he could confer with the Senator. "Excellent, Senator Emerson. And this would be where you introduce Red and his dad. He's been given two minutes to share their experience. Although I sure wish we could have found an immunocompromised child who actually *was* exposed to measles instead of just one who *could have been*."

"Of course. But no one around here has for a while. So we go with what we've got. Mr. Jones said presenting a live face to the Members of the Committee was key. And then I introduce Dr. Sampson and he will present his vaccine safety facts. Two minutes as well. Then I'll wrap it up with the closing we've prepared."

"Yes. And now, I want to introduce you to Emilio Sanchez, from Korsen's office. Emilio?"

The young Hispanic man got up from his seat at the table next to the lectern and introduced himself.

"Don't go easy on me, Mr. Sanchez," smiled Charlene. "Bring it on. I will need to be prepared to counter anything that the anti-vaxxers throw at me in a few weeks."

"Fair enough, Senator Emerson. I've done my homework on this, and I think I have a good handle on what the opposition will say. Just do *me* a favor: don't shoot the messenger."

The three laughed quietly, two of them genuinely.

Tom and Charlene sat down as Emilio stepped up to the lectern and reached down to push the button to turn on the mic.

Elena Moretti thought Tom's boss had done a decent job. He'd obviously prepped her well. Although why on earth they insisted on starting so early this morning was beyond her. *Nine a.m.. The West Coast is just waking up for God's sake.*

She scrolled through her list of emails on her phone and saw she'd gotten one late last night from Mr. Jones. *I'll look at that later.*

He's probably thought of a new pillar of brilliance or something, she smiled at herself.

Then her phone buzzed with a text message. Jackson Jones again. *Need to speak with you. Urgent. Call me.*

Well, yeah, I'm a bit busy right now, she thought. Elena had considered telling the lobbyist about their practice debate and asking him to look over Charlene's presentation to see if he had any suggestions, but figured he was too busy. And that's what the training weekend had been for anyway. *We don't need him to hold our hands.* She decided to ignore the text for now; she'd share the good news about the success of the practice debate after they were all done.

"Members of the Committee, I am speaking today in opposition of proposal 999. Exercising our governmental police powers by requiring vaccinations for all schoolchildren in our state is problematic for three reasons: 1. It is unnecessary, as there is no health emergency as my respected colleague would have you believe, 2. It won't work, as most vaccines don't prevent the spread of diseases, and 3. We don't know, scientifically speaking, that the full vaccine schedule which we propose to enforce is actually proven to be safe. Given what Senator Emerson just told you, you are probably thinking I am crazy. But I will show you CDC data that prove I am correct in all three of these reasons. Bear with me.

"First, this law is unnecessary. There is no increase in infectious diseases in our state, and there is no overall increase in our country either. There is no health crisis, therefore there is no reason to act with police powers by mandating medical intervention.

"Allow me to elaborate …"

Tom was getting a little nervous. He heard one of the legislator entrance doors open behind the raised section of desks where all the committee members usually sat, currently empty during this practice debate, and saw a senator enter and sit down facing the proceedings. *That's odd. What is the senator from Orange County doing here.* Tom turned around to study the staffers sitting in the audience seats. Most of them were busy texting, and a couple were speaking very quietly into their phones. All except for the staffer from the Orange office, who was nodding her head at her boss and pointing toward Emilio. *Did that staffer call her boss to come and watch?*

"Let's start with the supposed measles epidemic that Senator Emerson is warning us about. According to the State Department of Health, our state has been virtually measles-free for over a decade. Between 2006 and 2010 we had between 1 and 3 cases every year. In 2011 we had a larger outbreak of 7 cases, but this has not happened again since that time. In 2014 we had two cases, one of which was fully vaccinated. In 2015 our one and only case was also in a vaccinated child. We even had zero cases in 2012 and 2013.

"Now let's talk nationally. CDC data from the past 20 years show us that we have had an average of 128 cases each year nationwide. And contrary to what my esteemed colleague says, and with all due respect, measles was never eliminated from the United States. In the year 2000, when the Senator claims it was eliminated, the CDC reported 85 cases that year. And since then, we have never had a zero year. So, to state that measles was eliminated, and now it's back, is not a true statement. That's because the CDC defines an 'eliminated disease' as one that no longer persists continuously in our country; a disease that only exists in small isolated outbreaks that are quickly contained and don't spread unabated. For example, chicken pox is present somewhere in our country each and every day, and it spreads every day. It's not eliminated, obviously. Measles is 'eliminated' because it does not have a continuous presence here. But it was never gone, and it's not 'back' because the CDC still considers measles to be eliminated here in the U.S. by their definition. And this ongoing 'eliminated' status highlights the truth that it is not a rising threat in our country.

"Measles is not on the rise. Annual cases have ranged from 55 in a low year to 220 in a higher year. In 2014 we had an anomaly: two large outbreaks, one in an unvaccinated Amish community in Ohio of almost 400 cases and another in Texas of over 100 cases, brought our nationwide total to 667 that year. But what is very telling from these two outbreaks is that they were isolated and quickly contained. Yes, partly because those outside their communities were vaccinated, but even more so because of our effective public health quarantine measures which worked like they always have, and voluntary vaccination for those who were exposed. And the total number of measles cases nationwide outside of those two areas was just like any year. The very next year measles was back down to 188, even with the Disneyland outbreak. And in 2016 we only had 86 cases and 118 just last year. My point is that measles was never gone and it's not on the rise. Measles is simply measles, as it has been for decades now.

"Furthermore, measles is not a deadly disease that kills indiscriminately. In all of these outbreaks that we have every year, we've only seen two fatalities in almost 20 years. One adult in 2015, who had already been hospitalized for many months for a chronic, unrelated severe illness, was found to have evidence of measles in her lungs on autopsy, although the infection was never identified during her hospital stay. The only other case, and yes, both of these cases are tragic as all deaths are, was a child in 2003 who passed away from measles complications. This is not a deadly epidemic that warrants extreme police medical powers be exercised now. In fact, CDC data tell us that back when everyone used to catch measles here in our country, back when it was considered a routine childhood illness like chicken pox, the fatality rate was 1 in 10,000 cases. So even an outbreak much larger than any we have seen here in the U.S. in over 20 years is not likely to cause any real harm.

"Allow me to pause for a moment and address what I know you are all thinking right now. The reason we are all safe from measles is because of the vaccine. And I'm not arguing against that, because I agree with you. And I'm not asking you to discount this one particular vaccine or its benefits. And that's a common strategy employed by those who propose mandatory vaccine laws – to paint anyone who argues against such a law as being anti-vaccine, so that you won't listen to anything else they say. Well, I am not arguing against the vaccine at all. I am showing you, legally and scientifically, why we don't need to make vaccines *mandatory for school attendance*. That is all. The debate over vaccines in general is a completely separate one, and isn't even on the table here as far as I'm concerned. It's only about whether or not we should employ police powers and make them mandatory for school attendance."

By now, 5 more senators had taken seats up front to listen in, and 3 more were sitting in the audience. And they weren't busy reading other materials in front of them or speaking quietly with their staffers and each other, as they usually did during real hearings. They were actually listening. Tom wrote down the names of those he recognized. They might need some significant de-programming after this.

"Ok, moving on to the second disease that the honored senator describes as a nationwide and state health emergency that warrants mandatory vaccination: whooping cough, otherwise known as pertussis. Now, I would agree that whooping cough *is* a national problem. It can be a very severe disease for newborn babies. We do tragically have about 20 young infant fatalities every year in this country, and we do have more whooping cough now than we did decades ago. Those facts are scientifically irrefutable.

"But this particular disease and vaccine pair highlights my second point: mandatory vaccination laws won't work. There is a misconception that all vaccines do two things: protect individuals from getting sick, and prevent individuals from passing the infection on to others. All vaccines help with the first statement, but most of them don't actually keep the person from acquiring the germs and then passing them on to others. So, most of us benefit from getting a vaccine in that if we are later exposed to the germ, we won't feel as sick, and possibly won't feel sick at all. That is an individual benefit to that one person. But many injected vaccines only give us immunity in our bloodstream. The infectious germs will still enter our GI or respiratory tracts, multiply in the body, and then pass on to others, even if we don't have any symptoms. In other words, a vaccinated person will still be contagious. This is true of our current polio vaccine, the diphtheria-tetanus-pertussis vaccine, the flu vaccine, and others. Therefore, such vaccines offer no public health benefit, and mandating them in school won't change anything.

"And the whooping cough, or pertussis, vaccine is a particular case in point, and it's worth focusing on because this *is* a disease that we are having problems with, as both of us have already stated. But what is scientifically irrefutable is that the whooping cough vaccine does not reduce whooping cough cases. It does not prevent the infection, and it does not prevent someone who has it from passing it on to others. Our own FDA did a study in 2013 which clearly demonstrated that the vaccine only reduces the severity of symptoms in those who catch the infection. But they still get sick, stay contagious to others just as long, and pass the infection on to others just as easily as those who are not vaccinated. Furthermore, those who are not vaccinated and catch the disease develop better and longer immunity, and don't get sick a second time, compared to those who are vaccinated. And I quote, the observation that the vaccine 'fails to prevent colonization or transmission provides a plausible explanation for the resurgence of pertussis and suggests that optimal control of pertussis will require the development of improved vaccines.' This is from researchers at our own FDA. And the CDC agrees. The pertussis FAQs on their website state that pertussis is increasing due to increased awareness, surveillance, and reporting of the disease, improved testing, more circulation of the bacteria, waning immunity, and genetic mutations in the germs that help it resist the vaccine. The CDC also says unvaccinated children are not the driving force behind the large scale outbreaks.

"And other researchers share their concern. Study after study, which I have provided to you in your information packets, make it clear that our current vaccine doesn't prevent the disease or reduce outbreaks. And I quote, from Clinical Infectious Diseases 2012 in a study done at Kaiser-Permanente, 'The current schedule of pertussis vaccine doses is insufficient to prevent outbreaks of pertussis. The vaccine effectiveness was only 41% for kids ages 2 to 7, 24% for ages 8 to 12, and 79% for teens.' And in another study from the AAP in 2015, 'This teen vaccine protection from the 12-year-old booster shot wears down to only 34% effectiveness within 2 to 4 years.' And keep in mind that what they mean by 'effective' is simply a reduction in disease symptoms, not actual prevention of the spread of infection.

"In 2014, California had an increase in pertussis, and the CA Department of Health tracked all pertussis cases in schools and found that out of the 9000 kids who caught it, 90% of them were vaccinated. How are we doing here in our state? Well, our whooping cough rate is way below the national average. The CDC pertussis surveillance data show the U.S. national average rate is 10 cases per 100,000 people. In 2012, our state's rate was 7 per 100,000. In 2015 it had dropped to 4. In 2016 it was 6. And just like in California, most of our cases are in vaccinated children. Whooping cough continues to wax and wane, and the vaccine doesn't impact this at all.

"The fact is, this particular vaccine only helps protect each person from severe symptoms, but it doesn't stop them from catching and spreading the disease. So, there's no public health benefit. Vaccination rates in a school won't impact its spread. So there is no group benefit from mandating vaccination against this disease. The disease does and will spread even through a fully-vaccinated school. And when it does spread through school-age children, it is not deadly. It's only dangerous if a newborn sibling catches it, something that vaccination status in the school-age child doesn't prevent.

"Therefore, we can talk about our nation's, and state's, problems with whooping cough all day, and how important that vaccine may be for parents to consider with their doctors for their individual children, but that won't change the fact that vaccination status in schools won't change a thing. A law which makes this vaccine mandatory for school won't do anything to reduce whooping cough at all. And ladies and gentlemen of this committee, with all due respect to your service and position, if you don't question Senator Emerson about this and demand a satisfactory answer as to why she is proposing to mandate a vaccine that won't reduce a disease, then you aren't doing your jobs. Again, will all due respect. Because none of you asked this very question to another senator who got a similar law passed that mandated flu shots and whooping cough vaccine for all day-care and preschool workers and parent volunteers in preschools. That's right. Several years ago, this very body of lawmakers mandated two vaccines for parent volunteers - moms and dads who just wanted to help out and be a part of their preschoolers' lives. You mandated two vaccines that don't even prevent disease spread. So now, parents who don't want a flu shot, and don't want another pertussis shot, can't step foot into their kids' classrooms anymore. Because none of you thought to ask if the flu shot and pertussis vaccine would even stop these parents from bringing the flu and pertussis into the classrooms.

"I would like to pose a question, and offer an answer, an answer I know all of you will agree with. What is the duty of our legislature when it comes to enacting laws to safeguard the public health? One essential requirement for any law that infringes directly on the rights of a portion of our citizenry, even to the benefit of a larger part of the citizenry, is that the status quo isn't working; that the laws and procedures currently in place are ineffective and there is a clear and present danger to our citizens. If, on the other hand, the status quo *is* working, and there is no danger, then it is our duty as elected officials *not* to overstep our bounds and enact any extreme measures upon those who have elected us. And in the event of a health crisis, if one should present itself, it is in our own state constitution that when it comes to exercising police powers, we must do so using the least restrictive means necessary to keep our citizens safe. And a law which basically mandates that unvaccinated children must stay home, a law which essentially labels children whose parents embrace a more natural approach to their medical care as unclean, unsafe, and unsuited to be allowed in public – as if we are saying what? That they have cooties or something? – such a law is a most restrictive and inappropriate use of our police powers. We as a nation have done that before to small proportions of our people for unfair and unjust reasons, as other nations have done in centuries past, and some still do today.

"The status quo of voluntary immunization which most people take advantage of, and proper quarantine measures enacted by our medical professionals and public health officials, have helped keep measles and all other diseases at an all-time low in our state. And again, in order to pass a law, there must be something wrong with the status quo. There must be a problem. And there isn't. Furthermore, for a government to step in with what is essentially an exercise of police powers for the safety of the citizenry, there must be an emergency. And there isn't. Not to mention the fact that stepping in this way won't even work for most vaccines.

"It's not enough to simply believe vaccines are good, so we need to mandate them. There needs to be a reason.

"And this brings me to my third point as to why this legislature should not support this bill. If it isn't enough for you to consider that mandating the CDC vaccine schedule is unnecessary, and that it won't even succeed in reducing diseases in schools, the fact that the CDC schedule of vaccines has not been proven to be safe, and will harm some children, should matter to you.

"Now, before you accuse me of saying vaccines are unsafe, allow me to clarify exactly what I just said. I didn't say vaccines are unsafe: I said that the current CDC *schedule* of vaccines, which the bill will require you to mandate, has not been proven to be safe.

"The Institute of Medicine, which is our nation's most authoritative and respected body of researchers, reviewed all available safety data on the CDC schedule of vaccines in 2013. They concluded that the CDC schedule of vaccines has not been proven to be safe. Here are some key quotes from their conclusions:

'Studies designed to examine the long-term effects of the cumulative number of vaccines ... have not been conducted.'

'Existing research has not been designed to test the entire immunization schedule.'

'The committee generally found a paucity of information that addressed the risk of adverse events in association with the complete recommended immunization schedule.'

"I have given you each the entire IOM 2013 report so your staff can verify this information. But I know what you are thinking. We hear it all the time in the news: vaccines are safe and effective, vaccines save lives. We know they are safe. The science is settled. But what does that mean? It means that individually, and in some combinations, vaccines have passed the safety testing process in our FDA and have been found to be safe enough for use in our country. Like all medications and medical devices, vaccines do undergo rigorous safety testing individually before they are approved. And the IOM findings support this. And the IOM is not saying that individually vaccines are dangerous.

"What the IOM is saying is two things: 1. We don't have studies that show giving all 70 doses on our CDC childhood vaccine schedule is safe, and 2. We don't have studies that have even looked at the CDC schedule at all. Quote, 'These studies have not been conducted.' They haven't studied the long-term effects and they haven't studied the risk of adverse events from the complete schedule. The IOM actually says one more thing: they also say they recommend the CDC schedule anyway. Don't worry that we don't know it's safe – do it anyway. That last is not a quote, just my opinion.

"So, you can say vaccines are safe all day long, and you can believe it. But there is not a single scientist in the world that can show you a study that demonstrates the CDC schedule of vaccines is safe. To support the FDA's safety approval for individual vaccines is one thing, but to legally mandate the CDC schedule is completely different.

"This legislative body has an opportunity to send a very clear message to its citizens and our federal government: that we hold ourselves and our federal medical policy-makers to the highest standards of scientific integrity. And that a complex medical intervention that involves injecting every child with 70 doses throughout their childhood cannot, by any reasonable ethical, moral, or medical standard, be mandated without safety testing.

"It is for these reasons that I and my colleagues oppose this unnecessary bill. Thank you, ladies and gentlemen, and I look forward to your questions."

Tom Landon couldn't remember a time when the silence in this council chamber had ever been so … loud before. He had stopped turning around to count the number of staffers and Senators, not to mention the dozen or so members of the House, that had flooded in over the last ten minutes. He could feel them all staring silently. Even his boss was frozen. Tom knew he had to do something, anything. He stood up and stepped over to the microphone.

"Thank you, Mr. Sanchez, for that interesting analysis. You have raised a few points that warrant looking into. This was very helpful, as we now have a better understanding of how the anti-vaccine activists may try to plant misinformation into our ranks. And thank you, Senator Emerson, for presenting this important life-saving bill in this practice session. Let's adjourn back to our offices and prepare to move forward."

At least this disaster was just practice, so it wasn't recorded like all the regular sessions were, Tom mused, trying to keep an unconcerned look on his face. *Many of these people didn't hear most of the first part. That last garbage about safety was total bull crap, but Emilio presented it as believable. We will definitely have to do some damage control on that.*

Terry Wong was usually bored to near death during most legislative sessions. All he had to do was push "record" when they started and "stop" when they ended. And check the sound level from time to time. He'd been surprised when Emilio had asked him to record this practice session, something that usually wasn't done. But a hundred dollars was a hundred dollars. And Emilio was a straight-up, down-to-earth guy. He'd talked to Terry on several occasions in the past, and treated him as an equal. Not like most of the other staffers. To them Terry was just the nerdy Asian tech guy who sat in the booth all day. So he probably would have done Emilio this solid even for free. And seeing what Emilio just pulled off, and pulled off so well, was worth every penny. Terry didn't really care one way or the other about vaccines. He didn't have kids, and he didn't remember having any bad side effects as a kid. But "sticking it to the man" was always fun. And doing so on film was even better, something that Terry was very good at.

He popped the flash drive out of the computer and slipped it into the inside pocket of his blazer. He thought about deleting the footage from the hard drive, but then realized that he had to pretend as if he'd thought this was a regular session that he was supposed to record. So he clicked the "publish" button so it would go live on the state government website. He'd play dumb when someone asked. He was just doing his job, recording everything that happened in that chamber as he always did. They'd delete it then, of course. Possibly after all the legislators had viewed it, which was what he assumed Emilio wanted. When that happened, Terry would surprise him with the copy that he could then continue to distribute if needed. Maybe they'd laugh about it over beers or something, as Terry consoled the staffer for losing his job. *Yeah, there was no way Emilio was keeping his job after this, no matter how innocently he tried to pretend he was just playing devil's advocate. Smart guy. Yet naïve. Oh well. At least this would be the most fun I've had in a while.*

The three staffers cringed as they heard the high-pitched yelling coming from Senator Korsen's office. Fortunately, most of it was muted by the thick door. Two of the staffers glared at the third, who tried his best to look innocent and neutral. Several minutes of muted discussion followed, then Korsen's door flew open and Charlene Emerson stormed past, snapping her fingers for Tom to join her.

Tom looked back at Elena as he followed his boss out through the front office and made a "call me" motion with his hand.

Elena Moretti stood up and strode toward James's office. Emilio started to follow her in, but Elena stopped him.

"You might as well start clearing out your desk, Mr. Sanchez. I'll let you know if Senator Korsen wants any final words with you." Elena closed the door behind her and approached the Senator's desk. James was standing behind it, looking out the window.

"He knows he's fired, right?"

"Yes Sir. Although I'm going to see if he'll agree to a resignation instead. Less paperwork, and fewer potential legal issues. We can't technically fire him for being good at his job."

"Where the hell did he get all that information? He has obviously been working on that for weeks. And to present it all in front of other senators, staff, and even some representatives, and in such a well-resourced way, we'll have a hell of a time bringing enough people back onto our side. We had this bill in our pocket. We had all the votes we needed. Why did Charlene even need to practice? She knows the real hearings are just for show anyway. But you can imagine the earful I got from her. She's accused me of sabotaging the whole bill."

"I'm sorry sir. I should have looked over his materials first, and ..."

"We both should have. Well, Charlene is the one who insisted on practicing in chambers, so it could feel more real. And then to find out it was recorded, and who knows how many legislators got to play back the whole thing before I had it deleted. At least no one else will be able to see it."

"So, what's the plan now? Did Senator Emerson have any bright ideas?"

"She thinks we'll just have to ignore all the medical reasoning, stay away from vaccine and disease data as much as we can, and simply push the idea that vaccines are good, diseases are bad. The four bloody pillars, only we'll scale it back down to three: herd immunity, the danger of unvaccinated children, which we can still sell despite that hogwash Emilio spouted, and that vaccines are safe and effective. She thinks we stay away from any discussions on the CDC schedule and just talk vaccines in general, and all the good they've done in the past. And steer clear of claiming a rise in disease, although we can shift it a bit to include the risk of diseases worldwide. Use statistics from other countries, where children do die from these infections. But no more debates, no more public discussions, just focus on the good of vaccines. She thinks that if we just play it as a yes vote is a vote for vaccines and children's health, then we'll get it done."

"But how are we going to convince other legislators to go along with this now, especially if a copy of the practice session leaks out to the public?" Elena asked.

"Well, it will cost the pharmaceutical donor foundations a lot more money. They'll have to pitch in to a number of campaign funds for next year. But we should be able to get enough votes, and to get enough senators who won't be bought to pass the law simply because vaccines are good. And it won't hurt us at all to have Pharma spread their money around to more people besides Charlene and me. We already get enough bad press for being the largest recipients of Pharma donations every year. So let's get to it. We have children to save. And call Jackson Jones. See if he has any ideas for damage control."

That's right! Mr. Jones, Elena remembered. She'd forgotten to call him back amid all the chaos. *Well, he's not going to be happy about this. But he'll know what to do.*

"That was some crazy stuff you threw at that senator today," said Terry loudly over the din of the lively bar crowd. "The whole thing has already been deleted off the hard drive. I checked. They must have gotten someone on that right away. But it already had over 3000 views. Funny thing is, a lot of it sounded real. Like, you really believed it. You really had me going there."

"It was true, Terry. Every word of it," countered Emilio, pocketing the flash drive that Terry had just handed him and leaning in more closely so he didn't have to raise his voice. "I've been studying this issue for a very long time, gathering data and information, knowing that this would eventually come up as a political fight. When I got hired on by a Republican, I assumed I'd be helping my Senator *fight* a bill like this. I didn't know how much Pharma money Korsen had received though. Believe me, I almost quit when he first came on board with Emerson on this. But then they asked me to play devil's advocate, and I couldn't walk away. I didn't plan to have it go down this way in a live practice session, but they asked me to challenge them with what I knew, and I did. And as for what I said in there? It's all true. Trust me on this, Terry. I know what I'm talking about."

"But, I always figured vaccines were so good!"

"Well, I'm not saying they aren't good. Ha, that was one of my points in the speech. What I was saying was a mandatory law isn't needed, and it won't really work to lower disease. And what I said about the lack of safety proof in our full schedule, that was absolutely true – every word of it. And what I didn't really go into was exactly what the vaccine risks can be. That's an even scarier story. And it gets complicated, so I wasn't sure if it would be useful to throw too much information into that setting."

"I was fine after all my shots though. My sister Samantha, too."

"Yeah, me too," said Emilio. "But you know who wasn't fine? My little brother. He got all the same shots I did, but the night that he got several shots together when he was around 1 year old he started screaming … and convulsing. We rushed him to the ER. His seizure went on for hours. They couldn't get it to stop. When it finally did, he was brain damaged. They called it encephalopathy. He never walked or talked again. Before that, he was a babbling, talking, happy little toddler, running around tearing up the house, just like I did. Now he's a 28-year-old in a wheelchair who might smile at you on a good day. It broke my parents' hearts."

"Dude. Did you guys sue or something?"

Emilio raised his eyebrows at his new friend. "Seriously? You don't know? Terry, you can't sue doctors or vaccine makers for injury, not in the United States anyway. You have to go through a government vaccine court. We did that, and we won. They awarded my parents over 3 million dollars for the injury."

"Three million? Wow. That's a lot of money. But … I guess it goes without saying, you would much rather have your little brother back, huh?"

"Damn right. The money helped us take care of him. But I added up all our bills and hardships over the years, and you know what? We've spent most of that taking care of him up to this point. What are we going to do when he has to go into an institution or something? My parents will never be able to afford that. And we were lucky to even win our case. Most people lose. It's a totally screwed up system. And you know who pays for it? We do. The injury compensation fund is generated by a surcharge on every single vaccine. So it's government-controlled money, but it's not government money. It's the people's money. The vaccine makers don't have to pay anything.

"But that isn't really the worst of it. What really made my parents angry was the denial from all the doctors. Every single one of them, without exception, from the doctors in the ER that very first night to the doctors testifying against our case in the vaccine court hearing, all said that the vaccines couldn't have done that to my little bro. They all said it was coincidence – that it would have happened anyway. All except the actual vaccine manufacturers themselves, that is. They have warnings about brain-injuring reactions and much more right there in the fine print that they send out with every vaccine package. So does the CDC. They even tell you to report any severe injuries like this to the government – a program called VAERS: Vaccine Adverse Events Reporting System – and to apply to the government's injury court – called the VICP: Vaccine Injury Compensation Program – if you are injured. It's right there in the paper that's wrapped around the vaccine vials in every doctor's office. Seems like the only people that know about these risks are the people who make the vaccines and the small percentage who are injured. Everybody in between, from the doctors to the patients to the parents and the entire public, is totally clueless. Ha, and you know what else the vaccine paperwork says? It tells doctors to warn patients about these severe reactions before administering the vaccines, and to make sure they haven't had a prior severe reaction before you give any more vaccines. But our doctor tried to talk my mom into giving Arturo vaccines again when he was 18 months old. And again at 5 years. By then my mom knew better, of course."

"You should have told *that* story in the hearing today."

"Nope. No one ever believes it. They just don't believe it. Even though the government has paid out over $3 billion to over 3000 families, no one ever thinks it will happen to their own child, and they don't believe it really happened to yours. Vaccine-injury victims are some of the most invisible people in our society. They are a reminder of what can happen, so everyone ignores them. They are too scary to think about. And their families – their voices – are ignored as well. If I speak out as a family member of a vaccine-injured child, I get ignored. If I speak out as anything else – a doctor, a lawyer, a government worker, anything besides a victim – then people listen."

"And at least your family got compensated, right? I mean, that's better than losing your day in court, right?" asked Terry, genuinely interested now. "What if they didn't even have that compensation program? You guys would have been financially devastated, right?"

"On the surface, you would think so. But those of us in this fight see it differently. Back in the 1960s and 70s, and even the 80s, many people were injured by vaccines, and some of them started suing the vaccine manufacturers, and they won large settlements, just like with any other pharmaceutical product that can cause harm. There were so many severe injuries that vaccine makers told the government, 'We can't keep making vaccines anymore because we can't afford the lawsuits.' Usually when Pharma makes a drug that starts killing or maiming people, it gets taken off the market, right? But nobody wanted vaccines to go away, so the government had to figure out a way to keep vaccines going without vaccine makers having to cover the cost of the occasional severe reaction.

"Meanwhile, victims of vaccine injury had gotten together and asked the government to set up the Vaccine Injury Compensation

Program so that future victims could be more easily compensated without having to go through expensive and prolonged court battles. But what nobody saw coming was that Congress decided to blend the two ideas into one: The 1986 Vaccine Injury Compensation Act set up the program we have today, but they also gave pharmaceutical companies immunity from being sued for vaccine injury. None of the injured activists knew Congress was doing that until it was too late."

Terry jumped in. "Let me ask you Emilio, as someone looking at this from the outside. That seems like a good thing. It allows them to keep making these much-needed vaccines, and lets some injured people get compensated. Yeah, it doesn't sound perfect. But it's something, right?"

"I get what you're saying, Terry. Most non-victims would look at it that way. But here's the catch: if no one is liable for severe vaccine reactions, then there's no incentive to try to make them safer. And there's no incentive to carefully investigate why some vaccines cause more reactions than others and why some kids suffer severe reactions and most don't. No *financial* incentive, that is. Sure, there should be a humanitarian incentive to make vaccines safer, to try to make vaccines that injure nobody. But, I'm sorry to say, when it comes to private enterprise in pharmaceutical companies, it's more about money than humanity. I'm not saying that's wrong either. Pharma has every right to make every dollar for their shareholders that they can. But if you are a pharmaceutical company that gets to make tens of billions of dollars every year on your products without any risk, and all the doctors and patients that keep using your products actually believe there is no risk, *and* the government provides you with a law that guarantees you no risk, and the victims of your product get paid off by the public's money, not yours, what are you going to do? Just keep providing the same products, or devote billions of your own personal dollars to investigating why your products do occasionally hurt somebody and figuring out a way to make them safer? So far, no pharmaceutical company has yet to sign up for the humanitarian option. They do keep making new vaccines, but using the same techniques and ingredients they always have, with the same rare but serious reactions that continue to harm a minority of kids each and every day. And they aren't doing enough to try to fix the older vaccines.

"And as if that wasn't bad enough, some of the doctors and researchers who work for the FDA and CDC who approve these vaccines have stock in the pharmaceutical companies that make the vaccines, including an ex-head of the CDC, according to a story put out by a financial magazine. So do you think they, and all the other stockholders, want their companies to spend billions in safety research when they don't have to? So, most people who are in this fight to prevent mandatory vaccine laws are also trying to repeal the 1986 Vaccine Injury Compensation Act so that Pharma becomes liable again. That *would* force them to start making safer vaccines, and it would force doctors to start being more careful when they have patients who do have bad reactions. And there are so many vaccines today, and so many opportunities to make newer ones, that pharmaceutical companies are not just going to stop making them, like they threatened to do decades ago when there were only a few. They'd keep making them, but this would force them to do something about the vaccines with the worst reactions. Even if it meant stopping production on one or two, or changing how many they give and when they give them, it would make the whole system safer for everybody. And today, in a modern country like ours, no vaccine is so critically important that it's worth continuing if it causes a lot of harm and could be made in a safer way."

"That's a lot of heavy stuff to process, amigo," offered Terry. "But I get it now. You make a lot of sense. So what are you going to do now? I mean, job-wise?"

"I thought I'd be screwed, but I've already gotten three offers from Republican offices who don't take Pharma money, or who don't take *much* Pharma money that is, who naturally oppose most mandatory medical laws, who believe in the general principle that less government is better government, and who want to bring me on. Richardson's office even offered me the chief position, would you believe that? So I'm good. But let me ask you, Terry. Do you have kids? Are you married? Have you ever thought about all this stuff before?"

"Nope. Single. But hey, my sister has a baby. She and her husband just moved away from here. I wonder what she thinks about all this."

"How old is her baby?"

"Just about to turn nine-months-old. Why?"

"You better call her, Terry. Call her right now and let her know she needs to do some reading before her next doctor's appointment. Those one-year shots are what did my brother in. I'm not saying don't vaccinate. I'm just saying, she needs to know the risks."

Emilio signaled the bartender for another round as his new friend stepped away to find a quiet place to make the phone call. *I got your back, little brother,* he mused into his empty bottle. *Wish I could have had it 28 years ago bro, but ... I have it now.*

Chapter 9

Cleaning Ladies

Samantha Chen was nervous. This was going to be her first time coming to the new play group. She was happy that Ming-Mae was going to finally get some social time with other kids her age. Nine months and crawling, Ming was getting harder to keep entertained. Once-a-week for a couple hours in the park with other babies would do her some good. And Samantha, too. She and her husband were new to the area, didn't have any friends yet, and she was looking forward to meeting, and hopefully befriending, some other moms.

Ming's little cough brought her out of her reverie. Thankfully it was still very mild. Not like her husband's cough. *What is going on with him? Has he started smoking again behind my back? No, you can't hide smoke breath. He's been hacking and hacking at night for weeks now, with 30 to 60-second fits of non-stop coughing, but surprisingly doesn't even feel sick much of the day. And of course he's not going to go to a doctor unless he's actually dying. Ming isn't sick like him. She's probably just teething.*

Some moms are good at denial.

Wow. So glad we went! Samantha reminisced that evening. *And Ming barely coughed at all. Those moms were so nice and welcoming. And I'm so glad I got a pediatrician recommendation from them. A solo doctor, not part of a large group,* which Samantha liked. *I'll call for a nine-month check-up. I don't think she's due for more vaccines. She had all those at the last few checkups, and her old doctor said no more shots until 1. Even though her brother had recently tried to warn her about vaccines, what did he know? He doesn't even have kids yet.*

"Hello, Mrs. Chen. I'm Dr. Peter Tommaso. You can call me Dr. Peter though. Welcome to my office. I understand you just moved."

Peter chatted with this new patient's mom for a bit more, then did the exam. Little Ming-Mae – what a pretty name – looked great. The mom said something about her having a cough, but he didn't even see any signs of illness. "Everything looks healthy to me. She's growing well. I see you did all the vaccines early on. I want to let you know that I like to do vaccines a little more slowly than most doctors. There's nothing due today, but next time you have the option of …"

He was interrupted by a choking cough suddenly erupting out of little Ming. "As I was saying, at age one …" But the baby continued to cough and cough … and cough and cough and cough. The mom just sat there looking at Dr. Tommaso, patting her baby gently on the back and expecting him to continue talking. Then, there it was …

"Whooooooooooooop!" A gasping inhalation of air that seemed as if it was unsure whether or not it really wanted to enter into Ming's airway. Then more coughing. Then whoop. Then cough again … and finally a gag, burp, another gag, drool, then a nice normal breath again.

"Umm …" stammered Peter. "Mrs. Chen, how long has Ming-Mae been coughing like that?"

"Oh for a couple weeks now. But it's only a few times a day. Well, maybe about once an hour or so. And at night. But she doesn't even seem sick otherwise. I thought she was just choking on her drool from teething or something. She did have a runny nose at the start, but that's gone."

Peter checked the baby's vaccine record. *Yes, she'd had her three DTaP vaccines already.* "Is anyone else sick at home?"

"Yes, my husband. He's had a similar cough for about six weeks now. But he's starting to get better. I would have brought her in sooner, but I decided it could wait a week or two until we had this checkup since she had no fever and she seemed happy – when she's not coughing that is."

Peter knew whooping cough when he saw it. Every pediatrician did. The problem was that most parents didn't know what whooping cough looked like. Many cases act just as Mrs. Chen described. A cold and regular cough that turns into the classic fits. But there's usually no fever, and the kids usually seem completely fine in between fits of coughing. That was a clue that distinguished whooping cough from other respiratory illnesses – the lack of looking sick. But that's also what prevented many parents from going to the doctor.

He wasn't worried. He knew whooping cough was pretty harmless unless it hit a baby in the first few months of life, as he'd explained to his patients over and over again during talks. So Ming would be fine. Peter explained his suspicion to Mrs. Chen, who seemed taken completely by surprise that her baby could have whooping cough.

"But she's vaccinated for it, right? I did give her all her vaccines so far."

"Yes, but this is one particular vaccine that doesn't prevent some-one from catching the disease. It just makes kids appear less ill when they do catch it. It probably came from your husband, from what you are telling me. At this point, antibiotics aren't going to help. They only help if started within several days of the onset of severe cough. She's contagious for about 3 weeks from when the severe cough first began. We could give her antibiotics now to shorten the period of being contagious, but if you are willing to just keep her home for another week or so we don't need to treat it. She was more contagious before the severe cough set in, during the initial runny nose and mild cough. But, of course, you wouldn't have known it was whooping cough at that point. But now you know, so stay home. She might cough like this for about three months total. But again, not contagious after the bad cough has been running for about 3 weeks. Have you been around any other families or children during these weeks?"

Mrs. Chen, for some reason, suddenly looked very worried/guilty. "Umm, yes actually. And they are not going to be happy about this."

"Well, can you do me a favor and call anyone you know who she was around and tell them about this? You'll be able to reach them sooner than the public health department will, and …"

"Public health department?"

"Well, yes. I'm legally obligated to report this case to them. They will probably call you and ask you to keep her home for the three-week contagious period. Your husband is already not contagious since he's had it so long, so they probably won't ask him to stay home from work. Now you, on the other hand, aren't even sick yet, right? I can prescribe you antibiotics so that you will likely not even get sick. The health department will probably want you to take them, but they can't force you to. I'd recommend it for you though."

Samantha Chen scrolled through her contacts looking for her new friend's number - Paulina Gonzalez. There it was. Her baby Pablo was so adorable, and Ming-Mae really liked him. *She is going to kill me.* Paulina had already told Samantha the story of her baby's meningitis. *And now he might catch whooping cough too.*

"Hey Sam, what's up?" came Paulina's always-cheerful voice over the phone. "Wait, hold on … Pablo's choking again."

Samantha cringed as she heard "cough, cough, cough, cough, whooooooooop" over the phone. After about a minute, Paulina picked back up. "Ok. Sorry. He's been doing that for that last couple days. I think it's probably whooping cough, and I'm going to see Dr. Tommaso this afternoon. He probably needs antibiotics."

Samantha thought quickly. *Do I tell her? She's going to get help anyway. Pablo will get treated, and he'll be fine. So, she doesn't really need to know where it came from, does she?* But Samantha wasn't like that, and she knew it. She couldn't start a friendship with lies. It would eat her up inside. Plus, they needed to make sure the other moms in the group knew too. *But wait, we've all been meeting the last few weeks, and Ming has barely even coughed while there. Maybe they'll all blame it on little Pablo ...* But no, that would be even worse. Samantha's Chinese upbringing just wouldn't allow it. She wasn't capable of such dishonor. Plus, the public health department might be calling the whole group anyway, and Paulina's smart enough to piece it together ... maybe.

"Paulina ... there's something I need to tell you."

"So, whooping cough, huh?" Darla Johnson wasn't surprised. Well, she was surprised that Mrs. Chen had the guts to call her up and tell her. She didn't think she herself would be capable of such honesty. Baby Sage was vaccinated against it, although she of course regrets doing that now. At least she'd have a milder case if she did catch it – probably. But she wasn't surprised to hear that Pablo had it. She'd heard him coughing at the last play date and was thinking about saying something. "Little Ming-Mae never seemed that sick."

"I know. Dr. Tommaso told me that's how it usually is, and why it often goes undiagnosed for so long. Ming barely coughed at playgroup, but she was contagious. And the fits got pretty bad at night. I should have known. It's so obvious ... now, anyway."

"Don't sweat it, girl. I'll check with Dr. Tommaso to see if Sage should be treated preemptively. But she's not even sick yet, so maybe her vaccine worked after all. But have you called Sherrie yet? Her two-year-old is vaccinated, I think. But she has that brand new baby. That could not be good."

"Yes, I'm calling her next. I don't think she goes to Dr. Tommaso, but I'll make sure she sees her pediatrician tomorrow so they can decide whether or not to start preventive antibiotics. Dr. Tommaso told me he thought the little baby definitely should, when I told him about everyone I'd exposed."

"Listen, Samantha. Don't feel bad about this. Whooping cough is everywhere. In fact, I've done a lot of reading about infectious diseases lately, and about vaccines. There are some things I think you should know. You've probably done all the shots so far, I think you said, right?"

"Right. For all the good that this one did Ming."

"Well, let's get together when the kids are done coughing. I really think you'll want to do some more reading before you move on to the next vaccinations."

"My brother Terry has called me twice and tried to warn me not to vaccinate, but I thought he was crazy. But yes, I am open to hearing more about what you think. Oh, there's one more thing, Darla. The public health department might be calling you. Dr. Tommaso said he had to report it to them. They'll be calling me first, and they'll want the names of everyone we've been around so they can try to contain this as best they can."

"Well, that's just lovely." Darla looked around at her kitchen, then into the living room, rooms that fed and entertained four young kids now. Well, five kids if you counted her husband. And one tired mommy who'd decided long ago that being a mommy was more important that keeping the house clean.

"How long do I have, do you think?"

"How long do you have for what, Darla?"

"Before CPS ... I mean, before the public health department gets here?"

"I've no idea. Why?"

"When the public health lady sees the conditions my kids are living in, they'll probably call CPS on me. She'll probably forget all about the whooping cough."

"I could come over and help ... my husband isn't going to work today and he could watch Ming."

"Don't you need to clean your own house first?"

"I am Chinese, Darla. Haven't you ever been to a Chinese house before?"

"Ha-ha. You just wait until you have four little ones running around, then you'll see how it is. But you know what, Samantha? I'm going to take you up on that offer!"

———◇———

"Wait, what?" Sherrie Williams said loudly. "Whooping cough? Are you serious?"

Now that's more the response I was expecting, thought Samantha. *That's how I would probably react if someone got my baby sick. We can't all be as decent and understanding as Paulina and Darla. When something threatens your own baby …*

"I am so sorry. Believe me. Ming is fully vaccinated. I confirmed this with the doctor. She had three shots to prevent this already. But my doctor said this particular vaccine doesn't work very well at preventing the spread of the disease. Your two-year-old is protected, I'm sure, having had four DTaP doses already, right? But the baby … whooping cough can be serious in newborns."

"You're F-ing right it can be, Samantha." Then there was silence.

"Hello?" asked Samantha, making sure her new friend – well, maybe x-friend – was still there.

"Yes, I'm still here. Look …" Sam heard a deep breath. "I know this isn't your fault. I'm just venting. But I'm obviously worried. Newborns die of whooping cough, you know. Lots of them."

"Darla said about 20 die each year … here in the United States, anyway."

"Yes, I've heard Darla's spiel about vaccines too, and how few die of whooping cough compared to how many babies have a severe reaction to the vaccine. Did she tell you about what she thinks happened to Sage after her DTaP vaccines?"

"No, she said she wanted to talk more about it later."

"Well, she thinks Sage had a bad reaction. Personally, I think it was all just a coincidence. But you know, I don't like to judge. To each her own, right? Anyway, I'll check in with the doctor. My three-week-old actually does have a runny nose and a tiny cough. Hey, wait, I was vaccinated against this near the end of my pregnancy. My OB said they vaccinated all moms-to-be now so that a newborn will have some immunity. So, maybe all she has is a normal cold. We'll see though. I'm going to the doctor tomorrow for sure. I just hope she'll be ok. Seriously, Samantha. This really sucks. But listen, again, I know this isn't your fault. I'll get over it, and I apologize for adding to your guilt. I'm sure this wasn't easy for you either. I guess play group is off for a few weeks, right? I'm sure we'll all be emailing to plan when we can all get together again."

That night baby Williams had his first coughing fit.

"Yes, I heard him coughing and coughing and coughing in his cradle next to me. When I turned the light on to check on him his face was red, he was struggling to get a breath in, then he turned a little blue, and finally gasped in some air."

Jack Stanley had seen whooping cough before. In fact, he saw it about once a month, mostly routine cases in kids who just needed an antibiotic prescription and five days of quarantine at home. It was never serious in older babies and kids. But he knew how serious it could be in a newborn.

"Well, Mrs. Williams. We will test your baby for whooping cough with a nasal swab, just to confirm he has it. But based on the known exposure that you've told me about, and the fact that he turned blue, we'll start him on the antibiotics right away and admit him here to the hospital so that he can be closely monitored during the fits, and be given oxygen if he needs it."

Sherrie Williams sat at her kitchen table, reflecting on what she'd discovered during the past five days in the hospital with her baby. The coughing fits had been pretty bad the first two days. The oxygen didn't even seem to help prevent his cyanosis – the word for turning blue that the nurses kept using. He threw up a lot and needed some IV fluids. But then he turned the corner on day three as the antibiotics kicked in. They had to stay one more night just to make sure he wasn't turning blue when he coughed anymore. And now they were back home.

She had used all this down time in the hospital – when her baby wasn't coughing, that is – to read everything she could about whooping cough. When she saw the possible fatality rate – about 1 in 200 newborns who caught whooping cough died – she'd burst into tears and it took three nurses to calm her down. Then she was angry at the failure of the vaccine and started digging into even more research. What she found had surprised her.

The original whooping cough vaccine – DTP – had been very effective in reducing the disease in the 80s and 90s to the point where there were only about 10,000 cases reported each year. But that vaccine caused some very serious reported reactions – suspected brain damage – so they had to pull it off the market and replace it with the current DTaP vaccine. The 'a' was for acellular, meaning they didn't put the whole pertussis germ into the vaccine like they used to. So while it didn't cause as many severe reactions, it also didn't work as well. Now there were 30,000 or more cases each year. And the CDC even reports that some strains of the disease are becoming resistant to the vaccine. Then she was surprised to learn that this particular vaccine doesn't work by preventing the disease. It doesn't make you immune enough to completely fight it off. The vaccine mainly just reduces the severity of the disease when you catch it; it helps neutralize the germ's toxin that causes the severe cough, but it doesn't really neutralize the germ itself. A brand new study confirmed that the vaccine helps reduce the severity of the disease if you do catch it, but it doesn't prevent you from catching or spreading it; among the 10,000 kids in this study, 3 out of 4 whooping cough cases occurred in fully-vaccinated kids. She was also surprised to read the statistics from the 2014 California pertussis outbreak from the CA Department of Public Health: 90% of the kids who'd caught pertussis that year were vaccinated.

So that's why my pregnancy vaccine didn't work, and that's how Samantha's child caught it even though she was vaccinated. But maybe my baby's case would have been much worse if I hadn't gotten the vaccine during pregnancy? Sherrie knew she was just guessing at that, trying to find some benefit of having accepted an untested, and she now realized possibly ineffective, vaccine during pregnancy. That had made her angry – reading that the CDC had started recommending that all pregnant women get the vaccine during each pregnancy without having first done any safety testing or even knowing if it would help. That seemed reckless to her. *You can't even take Tylenol when pregnant without calling your doctor, and they want to* inject *something without testing it?* She read some of the published studies that the CDC had now done *after* the fact, studies that showed no increased pregnancy or birth complications in women who had the vaccine, *but what did that prove? They aren't actually testing the babies. And how would you even test a young baby to know if the vaccine and its chemicals had caused any harm?* Then there were a couple studies that showed that newborns showed some pertussis antibodies in their bloodstream if the mom got the vaccine during pregnancy, but they didn't yet know if those antibodies were effective. *Well, they're not, as far as I'm concerned.*

But given what was happening to her own baby, she could understand why everyone was so worried about pertussis in newborns. But she found one thing ironic: in recent years virtually all of the 20 annual fatalities from whooping cough occurred in babies 3 months and younger. Older babies and children don't die of whooping cough. Giving babies the vaccine at 2, 4 and 6 months doesn't even achieve protection during the age range when babies need it most; by the time they have some protection, the disease is past the severe age. We give pregnant women the vaccine in order to try to provide some newborn protection, but we don't know if this works and we don't know if it is safe. So then people argue that giving it to all babies, children, dads, grandparents, and any moms post-partum who didn't get it during pregnancy – the so-called cocooning strategy that the CDC began promoting a few years ago – helps protect all newborns by preventing the disease in everyone who is around that newborn. But, the vaccine doesn't do that. It doesn't prevent the spread, and there isn't a single research study that shows it does. So some newborns are going to catch the disease no matter what we do, and you can't blame people who don't vaccinate, because vaccine status doesn't impact the spread. *So what's the benefit of the vaccine? Oh yeah, it reduces the severity when you catch the disease. That may be worth it. But, what did Darla say happened to her baby after the vaccine? Seizures and encepha-something. She had to go to the ER twice.*

Sherrie started to realize that her friend Darla might not be as crazy as she thought. *Maybe there is more I should learn about vaccines and how well they work or don't work. And side effects. If that old DTP vaccine could cause brain damage, and even the new DTaP can cause problems, how do we know all these new shots can't do that as well? I'll have to ask Darla more about this.*

Sherrie's train of thought was interrupted by something strange on the muted television in the adjacent family room. *Some sort of Little Red Riding Hood commercial? I gotta see this.* She un-muted the TV and re-wound back to the beginning. A grandma, with a cough. Her head turned into a wolf's head – the big bad wolf from the fairy tale. And she's holding a newborn baby. *OMG, is this a whooping cough vaccine commercial? For grandparents?* Sherrie felt like throwing the remote at the TV, but realized it wasn't worth a berating from her husband. *But the vaccine doesn't even prevent the spread. How can they ...* She rewound and listened again. *OMG, they never actually say that grandma getting the vaccine would prevent her from passing the disease to the baby, so they aren't technically lying. But still ...*

Her cell phone rang and she looked at the caller ID. It was her mom calling. *Probably wants to know how the baby is doing.* She paused the TV on the very creepy-looking grandma wolf.

"Hi mom."

"Oh dear, it's all *my* fault," Sherrie heard through the phone, followed by sobbing.

"What is, Mom? What's your fault?"

More sobbing, then "The baby ..." sob. "I didn't get that vaccine ... and I came to visit, and ... and I have this tiny little cough now. I must have given it to ..." she trailed off in a burst of tears.

The throw was perfect. Hit the wolf right on the nose. And it was well worth it.

Chapter 10

The Fourth Branch

"So, you are sure they are not going to air it?"

"Yes, I'm sure. She promised. She was trying to do an objective investigation into why some parents choose not to vaccinate. But when she heard everything this doctor had to say, she thought she better call me and let me see the footage. So we scrapped it, of course. Although it still somehow made it onto YouTube."

"Ok. Thanks." Francine hung up the phone.

And some interesting footage it had been. Accurate too, which is even scarier. Although this lady wasn't a medical doctor. Really just a mom. And she lives in freaking West Virginia, which takes her down a few notches on the IQ curve. So what if she's also a toxicologist? That doesn't make her an expert on vaccines.

But Francine was concerned that even a lay person like this could have pieced all this science together. *Ha, and that was one of her main points: the science is out there, you just have to want to look for it.*

Speaking of "looking for it," Francine was frustrated that YouTube hadn't agreed to start censoring vaccine information like this particular video. *So what if the 50 mountain folk that would have watched the KGRL News broadcast didn't get to see this bull? Over 1000 people on YouTube have so far, and who knows how many tens of thousands on Facebook. Plus, that f-ing Health Freedom West Virginia group has it on their website, so even if YouTube started cooperating with The*

Center's version of free speech, people could still get to it, and thousands of other videos, about the negative side of vaccines.

Well, at least the mainstream news outlets are finally playing ball. All the major networks have finally agreed to stop giving the anti-vaxxers any air time – at least not live air time. Ever since the other side changed to tactics that more closely matched, ironically, her own, she'd had to shut down all the live, on-air interviews with anyone who seemed like they knew their stuff. Sure, interview people as a taped piece, then see what you can cut and splice into usable material. That was just fine because you can make people appear to say whatever you want them to. That was now S.O.P. for all the "news" shows, and it was helping. And she'd gotten all the most popular news commentators to do pieces on the anti-vaxxers. She especially loved the one that HBO recently did. *I wonder if John Oliver really knows anything about vaccines? He has a huge following, so everyone just assumes he knows what he is talking about. I wonder what they did before teleprompters? And before producers? What, did people just report the actual news?*

And the print media was no different. She'd been able to gradually corral most of them into the fold as well, and promote a handful of writers to the front lines where they could really control the 'free' press and make sure everyone now only tells the right side of the story. *Especially that one writer – what's her name again? Something earthy. Used to only write for a gossip magazine until I got a hold of her. Now she has all kinds of Pharma-funded medical outlets she can dip her pen into. I just wish she would come across more intelligently in her writing. But I'll take compliance over intelligence any day. Much easier to control. And she's the best one-sided writer we have, and most people just want to be entertained now, not informed. We don't need reporters who will investigate and be objective anymore. That was the old days. We just need reporters who will report what their producers tell them to.*

And the free market system of advertising provided a dependable deterrent to any producers who remembered that objectivity was the original goal of the fourth branch of government. *Virtually all news sources have pharmaceutical advertisers they need to keep happy. Both in print media and on television. There's an ad for some drug in virtually every commercial break. There's no way that any outlet is going to piss off their main source of income.*

It had taken a lot of work to get to this point, but it was now pretty much on autopilot. Francine didn't have to micromanage so much anymore. That left her plenty of time to do other things.

She picked up the phone and dialed her boss for an update. Not her boss on paper. Her *real* boss. The one who signed her real paychecks.

"Charlton. It's Francine. What's new?"

Chapter 11

Something To Live For

Samuel was tired. He was old, and he was tired. And he was drunk, for the first time in a year.

Dr. Samuel Livingston was retired, and he lived alone. He had for a long time. He'd spent his whole life in a laboratory, and by the time he realized there was a real world out there, and a wife and three kids living in it, it was too late. His kids had grown, and his wife was leaving. The vaccinologist had continued to work in his company's vaccine development division for a few more years, then he'd retired.

And that's when he got a second chance on life. His middle daughter had a child. They lived only an hour away, and they needed someone to watch the baby from time to time. So he had sobered up and jumped back into his daughter's life, and it was the happiest he'd been in … yes, probably decades.

Once or twice a week he made the drive out to spend the day playing with the new joy of his life. But today, his reason for living came crashing down. Angela had turned 1 on Monday, and he'd enjoyed celebrating with her all day long. His daughter had taken the child in for her one-year checkup on Tuesday. Samuel had driven down today – Friday – to watch the baby again. But the granddaughter he had spent the day with just four days ago was gone. The lively, laughing, and talking child who had warmed his heart every week for the past year was no more. Angela's light had turned off. The eye contact was gone. The 'ga-da' she always greeted him with wasn't there. She sat staring at the spinning wheels on the toy car he bought her for her birthday. And she ran around on her tiptoes flapping her hands half the day. One day she's fine, and four days later she's ... what? Can it happen so quickly? Just like that?

Samuel had put on a positive face when his daughter came home earlier this very evening. He asked her about the doctor's appointment from a few days earlier, and she'd proudly announced that the doctor said Angela was doing great. He asked to see the yellow vaccine card, almost too afraid to look, pretending like he was just curious about what vaccines were like these days. But he knew. He knew.

His daughter pulled the card out of the diaper bag and handed it over, then walked into the kitchen to start dinner, leaving Angela sitting on the floor staring, again, at the car's wheels.

Oh please, God, no. Please! he begged. But there it was. In black ink. Tuesday's date stamped next to the Varicella vaccine, the MMR vaccine, the Hepatitis A vaccine, and ... the card dropped out of his hand.

He'd quickly kissed his daughter goodbye, kissed and hugged his granddaughter, who didn't even notice, and drove the hour home in silence, stopping at the liquor store on the way.

And now he sat at his desk in his study. An old LA Times newspaper, yellow with age, sat open in front of him. The date was February 08, 2005. The staff writer was Myron Levin. The title of the article on the front page was all too familiar to him, as was a printout of a memo written almost 14 years before the Times piece. A memo that he'd watched his boss write to the president of the company's vaccine division in 1991. A memo that was then buried for almost ten years. He picked up the memo and scanned it again.

"Infants are getting an elevated dose of mercury in vaccinations ..."

"6-month-old children who received their shots would get a mercury dose up to 87 times higher than guidelines for the maximum daily consumption of mercury from fish ..."

"The mercury load appears rather large ..."

All his boss's words, although the discovery had originated with Samuel himself.

It was an honest mistake. Anyone could have made it. Actually, everyone had. The mistake had been to label the amount of mercury in vaccines using *millimoles* per liter. No one except the nerdiest of chemists even knew what a millimole was. For decades they'd put a certain number of millimoles per liter of mercury into vaccines as a preservative, and everyone had always said it was fine.

Then the FDA had come out with a new guideline for how much mercury people could safely consume in fish – in *micrograms*. That was a unit of measurement that everyone could understand. And out of curiosity, Samuel had one of his chemist buddies convert the *millimoles* per liter of mercury in the vaccines into *micrograms* so that they could compare that amount to what the FDA was saying was okay in fish. He hadn't believed his friend when he revealed the conversion and had walked over to the next building and watched his friend do the calculations on paper. But there it was. Every American baby getting vaccines at two months, four months, and six months was being overdosed with mercury. And not just a little – 87 times the known safety limit. Samuel took the findings to his boss who then wrote the infamous memo to the head of their division.

And that was in 1991. The memo caused quite a stir. He and his chemist friend were pulled into meetings with the higher-ups. And then nothing. Nothing happened. Nothing changed. The company went right on making vaccines with mercury, as did everyone else. And when the flu vaccine went into routine use, that added even *more* mercury.

Then in 1999 federal health officials disclosed the mercury overload. Numerous research studies were published to reassure everyone that this mercury was safe; it was 'different' than the mercury in fish and not as toxic. What bull. It wasn't until 2002 that virtually all the vaccines that had mercury were used up, in the United States anyway. They still used mercury in many of the third-world vaccines. All American vaccines made after that were mercury-free. *Except for the flu shots. And even today, 27 years after we knew it might be dangerous, about half of our flu shots still have mercury. Flu shots we give pregnant women. Flu shots we give babies. California even passed a law banning mercury flu shots in babies and pregnant women. But dammit, half the years they run out of mercury-free flu doses half way through the flu season and they just put a hold on the law so that all the companies that make the cheaper mercury-filled flu shots can ship them out.*

And that's what Samuel saw on his little granddaughter's vaccine card. The flu vaccine. And he knew that, it being February, there was no way anyone still had mercury-free flu shots around. Plus, he recognized the vaccine's lot number as a multi-dose vial – the only place mercury still showed up in American vaccines. And he knew what had been done to 'his' little baby girl. Sure, she got other shots too, and he knew those were perfectly safe. But he knew the symptoms of mercury poisoning because he'd studied it decades ago during his early work with vaccines. The symptoms were, ironically, very similar to the signs of autism.

And he knew he was responsible. It was his fault. Now, almost 27 years later, his very work on vaccines, and his failure to make them listen, had now hit home. And he couldn't deal with it. The pain, even numbed by alcohol, was too much. He felt bad for his daughter. Letting him back into her life, and now he would leaving again – for good. But he knew little Angela wouldn't remember him, especially now. She'd be ok in her own little world.

The newspaper, the memo, his empty glass and empty bottle of whiskey. Those weren't the only items on his desk. Samuel stared at the loaded pistol he'd bought a long time ago. For safety, just in case. Ironic, considering what he was about to do with it.

He glanced at the photo of his daughter and granddaughter, then looked at the gun again. It would just be so easy to be done with all of it. No more pain. But ...

What if there was something he could do? For his precious little girl, and for other children? Samuel turned on his computer, for what he thought would be the last time, just to see what others were doing. What was that web site he'd seen before? Run by a son, or grandson, of a former president, or someone like that. World Mercury Project, or something? He Googled it and found they had changed their name to Children's Health Defense. He started reading, and continued long into the night. And the more he read, the more he realized there was something he could do to help bring change.

Chapter 12

If I Had a Penny, Or Ten

Cheryl was nervous. Not because she hadn't done this before. She'd sat in the hot seat hundreds of times over the years. She was pretty good at it, but not the best. Very few people were willing to sit in that seat, however, so she took every opportunity she could.

But this time was different. Instead of playing defense, she was trying a new tactic. Every interview she'd done over the years was simply an exercise in defending herself against very predictable questions. She had the answers down pat. But the game had changed, and she decided to change along with it. This was her first try with a new playbook, and she realized that if she nailed it, it would likely be her last. *Why not go out in a blaze of ...*

"Dr. Penningten, we're ready for you," the stage intern said, peeking her head through the green room door.

"Thank you." Cheryl stood up and followed her into the studio and sat down in the offered seat next to the television host. A lapel mic clipped onto her collar, a last touch of powder applied to her forehead, and a quick sound check while a commercial was running and she was all set.

"Hi, Dr. Penningten," the host smiled and turned toward Cheryl. "Thanks for being on the show today. We'll have a two-minute segment to start with, take a quick break, then come back for another three minutes or so. Sound good? Oh, and I'm John, by-the-way." He didn't offer his hand.

John Sebastian wasn't nervous at all. He was looking forward to this. He and his producer had spent several hours the day before going over the questions, anticipating the doctor's answers, and formulating appropriate counterpoints and take-home messages. *Got to remember to focus on attacking her and not her arguments. Discredit her as a person. Don't get bogged down in science. Stick to the scripted questions. Throw autism in there for sure. Get her on the defensive. Vaccines are safe and effective, after all.*

Others had tried to nail this heretic to the wall and failed, but John was ready. He was going to get the job done. The fact that he and his producer had been ordered by the higher-ups to stop giving any live air time to anti-vaxxers didn't worry him. Once his boss, and his boss's boss, and whomever bossed his boss's boss around saw how expertly he put this heretic in her place, John was certain he'd enjoy whatever his reward was. He was an investigative journalist, after all. He knew how to bring out the truth.

"We're live in 5, 4, 3 …" he heard the producer standing next to the camera count him down.

"We are here tonight with a very special guest. Many of you know her and her work, and we are going to chat with Dr. Cheryl Penningten today about one of the most important aspects of every child's medical care – immunizations. Doctor, thank you for joining us."

"Thank you, John. I appreciate you having me on the show."

"Let's get right to it. The anti-vaccination movement is growing because of misguided fears and unscientific arguments propagated by a few doctors, actors, and parents. Anti-vaxxers, such as yourself, focus on the …"

"Pardon me, John. I have to interrupt you right there. I see what you are doing and where you are trying to go with this. You just called me an 'anti-vaxxer.' You are calling me names and trying to label me as something negative. Bullying and public shaming are very effective tactics when trying to make a point and counter someone else's position. But let's be grown-ups here, John. This isn't elementary school. Nowadays, parents, like you and I, are trying to teach our kids *not* to be bullies. *Not* to use public shaming as a way to put others down and build themselves up. We are trying to build a society that is *more* accepting of our differences, not *less*. So let's put the playground tactics aside and talk about the real issues. How does that sound to you, and your audience?" Cheryl, who had been looking at the host this whole time with her very best friendly-but-serious face, turned to look straight into the camera as she finished her opening salvo.

"Umm … well … I hear what you are saying, Dr. Penningten, and …" the host trailed off, unsure of what to say.

"How do you even know I am anti-vaccine? Have you even met me before? Have you asked me my position? I've given vaccines to my children, and I have given vaccines to my patients. Does that sound like someone who is anti-vaccine? But let's put the name-calling aside and forget about me. This is about the information and the science. It's about vaccines and what parents need to know. Let's focus on that."

"Ok, Doctor. Let's talk about vaccine science. I want to address one of the biggest fears that parents have, and one of the myths about vaccines that science has proven to be wrong: autism. We know vaccines don't cause autism because science has settled that controversy."

Cheryl knew this was a favorite topic that the news loved to focus on, because they thought they had the science behind them. Reassure parents that vaccines don't cause autism, and they have nothing else to worry about, as if vaccines can't cause anything else – just autism. She preferred to not even go there, but knew a response was needed. So, she just went with the science.

"Well, to be scientifically accurate, as you put it, no, John, science has not proven that vaccines don't cause autism. Science can't prove a negative. No study in the world can prove vaccines don't cause autism. The scientific method can only prove a positive or see if there *is* a link between two factors, but they can't disprove a link. Do you follow me so far, John?"

"Yes, Doctor, I do, but …"

"Knowing that," Cheryl continued, "Science has looked at two aspects of vaccines – the MMR vaccine individually and the mercury that used to exist in other vaccines. Virtually all mainstream studies done on vaccine mercury, MMR vaccine, and autism have failed to show a link between them. They've concluded that there's no association between vaccine mercury and autism, and between the MMR vaccine and autism. My concerns with this are two-fold: 1. Most of the mercury was taken out of vaccines almost 20 years ago, and autism continues to rise – it's now 1 in 36 kids, and 2. The MMR is only 1 of the 12 vaccines we give kids today. So, scientifically speaking, research has not shown a link between only two very minor aspects of vaccination. What parents today want to know is whether or not there's a link between getting *all* the vaccines and autism. We give 70 doses to kids today. Forget the MMR; parents want to know about *all* of them. Not a single scientific study has even started yet to address that question."

"But we don't know that there *is* any link either, would you agree Doctor? Scientifically speaking?"

"When someone actually does the study, I'll let you know, John."

"We are here with Dr. Cheryl Penningten talking about children's immunizations. We'll be back with more after this."

Will we? Cheryl wondered. She wasn't sure.

———◇———

John listened intently into his ear as his producer told him how to take the reins back. He nodded, then turned back to his guest.

"Good start, Doctor. Interesting angle on autism. We'll pick up after the commercial with some other controversial aspects of vaccinations, and I look forward to what you have to say."

———◄○►———

Cheryl felt her cell phone buzz in her pocket. She pulled it out and looked at the text. *Not just one, but two so far during this break. And one actually on vaccines during the break leading into your first segment. Thumbs-up emoji.* Cheryl smiled.

"And we are back with Dr. Penningten, talking about childhood vaccinations. Doctor, some anti-vaccine …" John paused for a beat … "Rather, some parents who worry about vaccines are concerned about vaccine side effects. But science has repeatedly determined that vaccines are safe and effective. Vaccines save lives. How do you, as a doctor, reassure your patients about vaccine safety and get them to stay on the CDC schedule?"

Cheryl recently learned to focus on the part of an interviewer's question that mattered the most, instead of letting a host lead her down a scripted path of his own design. "What exactly does 'safe and effective' mean, John? It means that each vaccine individually passes the FDA's standards to allow it to become an approved product in medical care. The company does its own proprietary and confidential safety and efficacy testing, shows that research to the FDA, and the FDA says OK – you pass. It doesn't mean it is 100% safe for everyone, or it works 100% on everyone. Just that it is safe *enough* for general use. When you hear a doctor, or a news commentator, say 'Vaccines are safe and effective,' they imply 100% reassurance. But, scientifically, they can't. The 2000 or more severe, debilitating, and even fatal vaccine reactions reported to the government every year are proof of that."

"But severe vaccine reactions are extremely rare, Doctor. There really is little to no risk in our vaccine schedule."

"I'm glad you asked about the CDC vaccine schedule, John, because it's important to understand the science we have, or don't have, behind it. The Institute of Medicine, one of the world's leading organizations that study medicine and health care, looked at all the safety research that has been done on vaccines and found that safety studies have only been done on individual vaccines and in some groups, but that we don't have any research on our complete CDC vaccine schedule. And that was five years ago. No one has yet to embark on a safety study of the complete schedule. So, you can say 'Vaccines are safe and effective' all you want, but you can't scientifically say that the CDC vaccine schedule is safe. You can't say that at all because no one has looked at it yet. And that, John, is what most parents are worried about."

"But every expert in vaccines says otherwise, Doctor. You are in the minority here. Who is our audience supposed to believe? Objective science, or a few nay-sayers."

Again, with the public shaming, John, but I'll let it slide because I have more important things to say. And it's my turn to lead you. "Well let's talk about objectivity. The conflicts of interest that exist in vaccine safety research, vaccine policy-making, and the public promotion of vaccines are huge. They're huge, John. The majority of doctors and researchers who approve vaccines and promote the CDC schedule have a financial stake in the success of vaccines. So, is it any wonder why parents question vaccine safety? Parents would much rather these policies be controlled by objective people who have no financial stake."

"Avoiding all conflicts of interest in government is impossible, Doctor. And that's one of our jobs in the media – one of *my* jobs; to hold the government accountable when real conflicts of interest exist that put the public at risk. And I can assure you, and our viewers, that there is no such conflict of interest when it comes to vaccines. The science is settled."

Bingo. "You are an investigative journalist, John. I agree it's your job to discover the truth about things, to investigate major conflicts of interest in our government, and to inform *your* public about it. And when there's a controversy, to tell *both* sides of the story. Both sides. I rarely see any media give air time to anyone who discusses potential problems with vaccines. But I understand your position. You have people to whom you are beholden as well. Pharmaceutical companies are your biggest advertisers. Why, during the two commercial breaks surrounding this interview there were three Pharma commercials, one of which was for a vaccine. If you were to report on this issue objectively, you'd lose money. And you'd eventually be out of a job. No one bites the hand that feeds him. So, John, you asked me earlier, 'Who is our audience supposed to believe?'" Cheryl, again, turned toward the camera. "I'll leave that up to them."

Francine stared numbly at her TV screen as those two brown eyes bore into her for a long three-count before the show cut away again to commercial.

"What the F-ing hell were they thinking?" she said out loud in her empty office. She knew John and his producer personally. They'd received their orders just like everyone else. *But no, they thought they knew better!*

Francine picked up her desk phone and dialed the phone number she knew by heart. The TV commercial droned on in the background ... *"Side effects include dizziness, numbness and tingling, vomiting and diarrhea. Tell your doctor if you have ever tested positive for tuberculosis or have any other chronic infection before taking ..."*

John sat at the studio desk trying, unsuccessfully, to play it off like a win. He didn't even hear the doctor thank him as she left. He saw his producer through the control room window walk over to her work area and pick up her phone. Even from where he sat he could see her cringe, and he knew who was on the other end of the line. This was confirmed when he saw her hang up, sit down in her chair, and bury her head in her hands. *Is she crying?* He wondered. *Should I be worried about my own job?* Then he shrugged. Nope, he was too popular. Producers were a dime a dozen, but quality investigative journalists like himself were rare gems.

Chapter 13

The End of Discrimination

"**O**k people. This week we are hitting three topics: bullying, prejudice, and anti-vaxxers."

An audible groan was heard around the conference table from all directions, so the chief editor of the online news magazine couldn't know exactly who was complaining.

"Listen, I know these are boring topics, but the higher ups want them covered. Prejudice and discrimination, because of the recent events in our neighboring state, North Carolina. Bullying, because cyber bullying continues to rise. And unvaccinated kids, because one of the bosses said we have to. Peter and Janet, you two will take racism and prejudice. What are your thoughts?"

Peter Donelley spoke up first. "I'd like to build on the very definitions of prejudice and discrimination, but instead of focusing on race, feature other ways in which we exercise these hateful and ignorant practices against others. Prejudice is defined as unreasonable feelings, opinions, or attitudes, especially of a hostile nature, regarding an ethnic, racial, social, or religious group. Discrimination is the unjust or prejudicial treatment of different categories of people or things. So prejudice is how people think and feel, and discrimination is how they act – the result. So, we examine three ideas, beliefs, or lifestyles that a majority tend to have prejudice towards, look at why these prejudices are unreasonable, per the definition, explore what makes the discrimination turn hostile, and discuss how this majority should examine themselves and their pre-conceived notions, and instead of embracing division, create more understanding and acceptance of minority opinions and beliefs."

"I would like to add an historical example into the mix, although it does involve race," Janet chimed in. "My angle could include a look back at how Californians treated the Japanese Americans during World War II, since that's unique compared to our usual examples of how we treated the native Americans and blacks. Start with the prejudicial belief that because they were Japanese by background, Californians felt they had good reason to fear them. So they discriminated by interring all of them into camps. They excluded them from society by wrongly assuming all of them were dangerous because of their background. They wouldn't even let their children come to school. All because they thought they posed a danger to society."

"I like both of those angles," said the editor. "In fact, I remember a piece from an LA newspaper from several years ago about the California Civil Liberties Public Education Act." He searched on his phone. "I think it was Section 13000. They added language into the code so that people would remember how we unfairly kept all those Japanese out of schools, and so no group of California children would ever be excluded from school again – discrimination – over a fear that they were dangerous to society – prejudice. Find the exact wording for the story."

Peter jumped back in. "But we also need to examine circumstances *today* in which a majority of the misinformed public ignorantly develops a prejudice, then discriminates against that minority because they wrongly think they are somehow dangerous to the majority. So, what minorities? LGBTQs? Blacks? We need something original."

"We'll put our heads together and come up with a few," said Janet.

"Ok, next, Jim and Jerry, you two will take bullying," continued the chief. "Let's not just do the same old cyber or school bullying though. Let's think of something new. Any ideas?"

Jerry took the lead. "I like Peter's idea of presenting the definition, because many people make some wrong assumptions about a term.

Webster says bullying is abuse and mistreatment of someone vulnerable by someone stronger, more powerful, etc. But it doesn't have to be physical. It could be emotional, ideological, or even financial."

"Ideological – I like that," applauded the chief. "Like using one's position of power to bully others into accepting your ideas, or of convincing the public that another person is wrong or bad. It almost ties into discrimination and prejudice."

"We could use examples of big corporations or entities that do this," added Jim. "Say they don't like someone's beliefs or ideas. They would then use their influence to bully that person into submission – to shut them up. Public shaming works wonders, too. Take them out of the fight. And they would stop at nothing to achieve that goal. They'd lie and cheat in any way to get their point across and the opponent's ideas quashed. We see corporations use the media as a weapon in that battle too, don't we? The unscrupulous media, that is. Politicians do too."

"Well, that happens in science, in business, everywhere. I like the ideas, and you two will have to decide what arena to focus on. OK, finally, vaccines and unvaccinated people. Thom and Harry, it's your turn for this topic. What are your thoughts?"

Thom Johnson had covered this before for this East-Coast-based online news magazine, and he already had a pretty good idea where he wanted to take it. He could almost write a new piece in his sleep.

"Well, I'd like to explore what's happening out in California with the new vaccine law, and try to draw parallels to what's going on here in our own state. First I want to really hit the parents of unvaccinated kids pretty hard. They are ignoring basic science. I don't care if it's religious or what, parents who don't believe vaccines are safe and effective, like the rest of us do, are just plain stupid. Too many of these kids are still being allowed in schools, when in reality *none* of them should be there. Apparently, California messed up when they passed their mandatory vaccine law: they grandfathered in a lot of these unvaccinated kids until 7th grade. They should have just forced them all to stay at home as soon as the law went into effect. There isn't anything we can do about that, but if we can help get this same law passed here in our state, we'll have to help make sure it's done right. Next, kids in California who have had 'bad vaccine reactions' are being given medical excuses, which they also wrote an allowance for in the law. So, if we can't get these kids out of schools once our own law is passed, we can try using public pressure to paint them as dangerous, unfit, unclean. And I have just the way to do it. We have access to public health department data that show the percentage of unvaccinated kindergarteners in every school statewide. How about we list the top ten schools with the highest percentage of unvaccinated kids? We out them. Maybe those school administrators will be ashamed that so many of *those kids* are at their school. And the cooperative families at those schools who got in line with the law can start nosing around to figure out who those kids are. Put some pressure on them. We don't even need to wait until our state passes this law – we'll do this now to get the pressure started."

"Brilliant Thom. I knew you'd come up with something edgy. It's our job as the media to make these kinds of things public for the good of our society. When a minority of people don't agree on something because they are stupid, or maybe because they just look at something differently, but wrongly, it's our job to convince the majority around them that they shouldn't be treated as equals."

"Exactly," beamed Thom, glad that his boss was on the same page. "We also have to tear into why these people believe the way they do and show why it is so unreasonable. Stir up the mob against them. I mean, we as a country shouldn't tolerate such people."

"Harry, what are your thoughts?"

Harry Little jumped in. "There's a new interesting study that fits in well with this idea too. It looked at the risk of recurrence of adverse events following immunization. They evaluated whether or not it was safe to re-immunize kids after they had a bad reaction. That's why some school kids are getting a medical excuse, right? Well, this study showed that less than 1% of kids with a moderate vaccine reaction had that reaction again the next time. On the other hand, 20% of those who had an *allergic* reaction had another such reaction with the next dose, and 80% who had extensive limb swelling after a vaccine suffered it again, so those may be legit claims – maybe. The researchers in the study also stated that they couldn't really tell for sure what the rate of repeat reactions would be because most patients who had a very severe reaction wouldn't agree to do any more doses. The 1% recurrent reaction rate was only in those who had reactions mild enough that they agreed to more doses. But these additional findings kind of complicate the issue, so we wouldn't have to go into all that. And I already have a quote about the new study from a doctor: 'A child who has a serious adverse reaction after an immunization has a very low risk of repeating that reaction again after the next dose.' I'll leave out the fact that this only applies to mild or moderate reactions, not severe ones.

"Then, we also need to put some heat on doctors here in our state who agree with these patients who have had 'bad reactions' and give them excuses to not do any more shots. I've heard that some California doctors are literally selling vaccine exemptions over the phone and over the internet."

"Where'd you hear that? Is it a reliable source?" The Chief always wanted to make sure they didn't print anything that was legally libel.

"An investigator from the California medical board is a friend of mine. He told me that a patient complained to them because he suspects his ex-wife bought his kids' medical exemption online from this one doctor so she could keep her kids in school."

"Suspects? He doesn't know for sure?"

"Well, apparently that dad didn't really know, because he isn't involved in the kids' lives much. He's just assuming. They are still investigating it."

"Well, what's happening with this here in our own state?"

"I found an on-line list of doctors who accept non-vaccinating patients and called them, posing as a patient who needed a medical exemption. They said all I have to do is bring in medical records that show my kids have had bad reactions to vaccines and I'd get an exemption. Or, rather, the doctor would consider it after looking at my evidence. So with the next call I posed as someone who'd never given the kids any vaccines. They said I'd need to bring in detailed descriptions of several other relatives who have had severe reactions, and they'd consider it. Apparently that's how they do it out in California. There's some sort of family history clause in the vaccine law that allows a doctor to consider how other family members have handled vaccines."

"That sounds totally bogus," said the Chief. "Let's name names in the article – out these doctors. A little public shaming, when it's for a good cause, goes a long way."

"I like that too. Good investigative work, Harry," chimed in Thom. "If we can pass this same law here, even parents whose religion doesn't follow vaccination practices will no longer be able to enroll their kids anymore, not even in that religion's own school. There are some things that are more important in this country than religious freedom. But there is one thing that I'm not sure of though: our state constitution entitles a public education to each and every child. If that's true, then that might be an obstacle to our legislators passing the law here."

"Well, the California constitution says the same thing, and they still passed the law," added the Chief. "They probably felt that since there was a war going on – a war against measles, a war that affects the whole world – the right thing to do would be to force all those people to stay home, regardless of the constitution. Hey, wait a minute, we can tie in the Japanese thing into this story, too. It's almost the same thing: the Japanese-American children posed a danger to our society, so we were justified in excluding them from California schools during the war. Now it's the same for the unvaccinated. I love it."

"Wait, don't people now feel that what we did to the Japanese-Americans here in California during the war was unjustified? Like, they really weren't a danger to anyone, especially the children?"

"That depends on who you are talking to, Harry. Ha-ha! Ask a Japanese person and you'll get one answer. Ask a World War II veteran and you get another. When prejudice is justified, it isn't really prejudice, right? Hey, that could be a phrase we coin: 'justifiable discrimination.' That describes excluding the unvaccinated kids perfectly."

"Ok," conceded Harry. "And for the grand finale, we finish with pointing out that the only two other states – West Virginia and Mississippi – with mandatory vaccination laws have the highest vaccination compliance in the nation."

"And I bet they have the healthiest kids in the nation too, right?" asked the chief editor. "Double check on that – you can find children's health ratings by state online. Add that to the story, if it's in say … the top ten or so. That would really look bad if those two states were at the very bottom of our nation's health ratings, right?"

Laughter from around the table concluded the meeting.

Chapter 14

Crossing the Line

"So, explain something to me. If your kids are vaccinated, what are you afraid of from my kids who are not?"

"Your kids are dirty and dangerous, and shouldn't be allowed in public."

The two women faced each other, arms crossed. Behind one of them was a crowd of hundreds, holding signs with various slogans: No Mandatory Vaccines – My Child My Choice – My Child Was ONE MORE *Victim* (with a picture) – No More Pharma Lies – and more. Behind the other were about a dozen people, with "I Love Immunity" badges. The State Capitol building loomed tall and white behind them, embracing both crowds in its protective shade so they wouldn't have to endure the afternoon sun.

"But your kids are protected. If my kids have a disease, which they don't right now, and your kids have the vaccine, what's the worry?"

"Well what if my kid's vaccine doesn't work?"

Pause ...

"You have a valid point there. What *if* your kid's vaccine didn't work, and my child got your child sick. You would have a right to be angry at both me and at the vaccine for not working."

Silence ...

"But, what if *your* vaccinated child's vaccine didn't work, and your child got sick first, and then got *my* child sick? Whose fault is that?"

"It would be the vaccine's fault for not working. And you certainly couldn't blame *me* because I did what I was supposed to do."

"And I didn't, right?"

"Well, my vaccinated child wouldn't get your unvaccinated child sick in the first place because I wouldn't let *your* child near mine."

"What if you didn't know my child wasn't vaccinated? Is there some way to tell? When you are at the playground, or drop your kid off at school, can you point out the unvaccinated kids to your child so you can warn him? Or her?"

"Her. And, well, no."

"Don't they have dirty faces, or torn clothing? You know, something to indicate they aren't well taken care of at home?"

Silence.

"Mine's a boy, by the way."

Silence.

"What if your girl met my boy, and she liked him?"

Eye roll.

"What if they were sixteen and fell in love? And *then* you found out mine wasn't vaccinated."

"Now you're just being silly. She'd be practically a grownup. I'm sure she'll have made all kinds of bad choices by then."

"I don't have any vaccines, you know. Never have, never will."

Silence.

"You are talking to *me.*"

More silence.

"I'll admit something. I'm impressed. You didn't even take a step back when I said I'm not vaccinated."

Silence, and surprise.

"Most people do, you know."

"Do what?"

"Step back."

Silence.

"I'm pretty healthy, you know. I'm also a pretty decent person. I'm nice. I'm also fun. At least my husband and my child think so. And my friends."

More silence.

"I have a question."

"Yes?"

"Most of your childhood vaccines have worn off. So you are now in the same boat as I am."

"That wasn't a question."

"Why are you standing so close to me? I'm not vaccinated. Am I not dangerous?"

Silence.

"Here's another question. If my child was vaccinated, but the vaccines wore off before your child's vaccines wore off, would you let them play together?"

"You are being silly again. There's no way to tell … and, I would at least feel better about them playing knowing that you did your civic duty."

"Ahhhh, duty. If I did my duty, and my child was permanently injured by a vaccine, would you still be my friend? *If* we were friends at the time, that is."

"Of course … I would like to think so. I'm a pretty decent person myself. I wouldn't turn my back on a friend."

"But my child wouldn't finish that vaccine series. Not after the injury. So, my child could catch that disease and give it to your child. If we were still friends."

"Well, you would have tried to do your civic duty and …"

"And what?"

Silence.

"And he paid the price? And he became a victim? Like a wounded soldier, sacrificing himself for the greater good? I would be so proud of him – doing his duty like that."

"Now you are just being mean. That would be just … awful."

"Yes, it would."

Silence.

"You see that sign over there?" Pointing. A girl in a wheelchair.

"Yes."

"I know her. It's very sad."

"I don't believe it happens."

"That's the problem, you know."

"What. I'm the problem?"

"Oh no, that's not what I meant. I meant that nobody believes it really happens … until it happens to their own child. But then nobody around that person believes it was from the vaccine."

"Well, sometimes it's not from a vaccine. Some people just develop neurological problems for no reason."

"Yes, that's probably true. But I know that mom and child. I was their friend when it happened. She was a happy, playful, talking and walking toddler. And then 3 days later she wasn't."

"Wasn't what?"

"Any of those things. Ever. She's five now, and that picture is pretty much what she is."

"That sounds awful. Three days? Well, they do admit that very rarely that can happen I guess. They do disclose that in the vaccine info, you know. Just so people can be warned. It's just so rare."

"It wasn't rare for her though."

Silence.

"Are you still friends?"

"Yes. We try to go over at least once a week. My child doesn't really know what to make of her though. He doesn't remember when they were one, of course. But I do it for the mom. I couldn't bear not being there for her."

"You would make a good friend, it sounds like."

"I'd like to think so."

Silence.

"I'm the only one though. Of all her friends. I'm the only one who stayed."

Longer glance at the sign. "She looks angry. The mom, holding the sign."

"Oh, she is."

"She's angry at me … I can tell. For not believing her."

"Yes. That's probably the hardest part of all. Knowing that your child was injured that way, but having no one believe you. No one at all."

Silence.

"How come there are no signs of kids on your side of the line?"

"Well, our kids are all healthy I guess."

"That's good. Mine is too. It's a blessing to have healthy kids."

"Yes."

Silence.

"You know that Monsanto thing? Where that guy got 289 million because glyphosate supposedly caused his cancer?"

"Yes."

"It's in vaccines too."

Eye roll.

"No, it really is. A company sent a bunch of vaccines to an independent laboratory and they found glyphosate in five types of vaccines: MMR, DTaP, Hep B, Flu shots, and Pneumococcal vaccine."

"I don't believe you."

"Don't take my word for it. Read about it. So, technically, by promoting mandatory vaccination, you are trying to get glyphosate injected into my kid. That's just one of many reasons why I'm on this side of the line."

Silence again. No more eye rolls.

"We have signs of kids too – back at the office."

"You have an office?"

"Yes. We get some funding from a non-profit organization. They fund any group who supports immunity."

"That must be nice."

"Oh, well, it's not a lot of money. And we are all volunteers. I wouldn't feel comfortable getting paid to do this."

"Where does their money come from? The non-profit who supports you. Do you know?"

"Yeah – I looked it up. Some sort of a foundation. I forget the name."

"A lot of those foundations are started by, and funded by, pharmaceutical companies to help promote health ideas and policies."

"Hmmmm."

"Not saying that's a bad thing … but, what if your particular benefactor was a pharmaceutical company? And you are essentially fighting against people who refuse to use their products. If that was true, what would you think?"

"I think I'd be sick to my stomach." A brief swallow.

Silence.

"What signs?"

"What signs for what?"

"What signs do you have? At the office?"

"Oh. We have signs of kids with cancer. And kids who have been injured by a disease. You know, that's a pretty important issue – immunocompromised kids. That's who we are fighting for. We want them to be protected. Unvaccinated kids put them at risk."

"So do vaccinated kids."

"What? Why?"

"Unless a vaccine is 100% effective, and none are, then even a vaccinated child could catch the disease and pass it to an immunocompromised child."

"Yes, but it's less likely."

"Yes, I agree. For some vaccines, it's probably less likely."

Pause.

"The live germs in vaccines can make them sick too though."

"Make who sick?"

"The immunocompromised kids. They aren't supposed to be around anyone who's had a live vaccine. For a few weeks."

"I didn't know that."

"So, who stays home?"

"Who stays home when? And who? You ask confusing questions."

"I don't mean to. What I meant was, when the class gets live vaccines, like they do when they are five, and there's an immunocompromised kid in the class, who stays home? The sick kid, or all the ones who just got the vaccine?"

"I don't know … I've never been in that situation."

Silence.

"Do you know any?"

"Any what? Unvaccinated kids?"

"No. Immunocompromised kids."

"No."

"Are there any at your kid's school?"

"I don't think so. Not that I know of."

"So, you want my child to not go to your school, so that an immunocompromised child who isn't even there can be protected?"

"But we could get one."

"Yes, you could. But you might not. There aren't that many, you know. Which is good. I wouldn't wish that on anybody."

"Neither would I."

"You know what there are a lot of though?"

"What."

"Vaccine-compromised kids. Like my child's friend on the sign."

"You think there are a lot of them? I don't ever really see any."

"How would you know? Do you look? Do you ask? If you see any child in a wheelchair, or any child acting different or crazy, do you go up and ask the parent what happened?"

"No. That would be rude."

"They don't mind, you know."

"Mind what?"

"If you ask. In fact, they welcome it. They welcome any chance to tell their story, to see if they can find that one person who will believe them and maybe become their friend. You should ask the next one you see. And it might not even have anything to do with vaccines. Like you said, sometimes those things just happen. But, sometimes it *is* because of a vaccine. And they have rights too, you know."

"Well, yes. Of course they do."

"They have just as much right to be in school, and to be there with no more vaccines, as the immunocompromised child does."

"I suppose so."

"But the immunocompromised make better poster children. Let's save the kids with cancer. Let's make all schools germ free in case one comes along. But let's forget about the vaccine-compromised. Let's leave them at home. They just don't have equal rights."

"No one really thinks that way."

"God, I hope not. But that's how what you and your group are doing makes them *feel*."

Silence.

"But, you know, most vaccines don't work that way."

"Don't work what way?"

"Don't prevent someone from catching the germ, carrying it, and spreading it to others."

"Really? I don't believe that."

"It's true."

"Which ones?"

"Which ones what?"

"Which ones don't prevent the spread of a disease?"

"Well, whooping cough vaccine, for starters. Tetanus. Diphtheria. Meningococcal or however you say it …"

"I know, right?"

"What?"

"That name of that disease, and vaccine. It's so hard-to-pronounce."

"Yeah, it's a tongue-twister. Polio vaccine too, by the way. At least the one we use now. And the flu shot."

"I thought all vaccines prevented the spread of the disease."

"Nope."

"I'm pretty sure *some* vaccines do prevent the spread though. Measles. Chickenpox. Hepatitis B."

"Yes, I think you are right about that. I know measles can be bad. Thank God it's so rare. But come on, chickenpox?"

"Well, yeah. I guess chickenpox doesn't matter. But measles does. So maybe I'd let your child play with mine if you at least got *some* shots."

"But not all?"

"I guess not."

"And hepatitis B though? Really? You know how that's passed, right?"

"Yeah, I guess you're right. They wouldn't need hep B either."

"But the schools now say they do. What exactly do the schools think our five-year-olds are doing there that would pass hep B?"

Thoughtful silence.

"And I guess by the time they *did* need Hep B vaccine, I don't think they'd tell *us* that they needed it, right?"

"Oh my God, I don't even want to think about that."

"I know, right? These kids are going to grow up someday."

"I know. They say it happens fast. Right now it seems very slow."

"I have an idea. How about I'll teach my kid how to use a condom, and you teach your kid how to not share IV drug needles, and we'll let them play together."

Laughter. A half step forward. Even a hand on a shoulder.

Then a step back, glance around behind at their respective crowds, and a return to arms crossed.

"I think I get something now that I didn't used to."

"What's that?"

"You, and the dozen or so behind you, don't want your kids to get sick, and you think our kids are more likely to get them sick because we don't vaccinate. Since I know that's not true, I've always just blown off your fear as irrational, and taken offense over it. But just because it's not rational doesn't take it away. I don't want you to be afraid of my kids, but I guess I can't just blow it off either – if I want us to get along, that is."

"Well, yeah, I don't think that anyone wants anyone's kids to get their kids sick, right? I'm sure you don't want my kid to get your kid sick either."

"I think that if my people started acknowledging your people's fears a little more, we might get along better."

"How would you do that?"

"Maybe my people could be a little more responsible when our kids are sick. Well, we all should be, right? But especially us. If we have a bad cough, get it checked out. Got a fever and a rash? Don't go to school until the doctor has checked it out."

"Feel like you have the flu? Stay the F home, right? For both sides."

"Yeah. Guilty, I'll admit."

"Here's another one: take a long family vacation to Europe, maybe stay home for several days after you get back to make sure your child didn't pick up measles while you were there."

"That seems a bit unnecessary."

"But that's exactly how measles happens, and that's what we fear. You said you wanted to listen."

"You are right. About how measles happens. And that's technically not an irrational fear."

Silence …

"I'm going to admit something too."

"Ok. What."

"The real reason I'm mad at you for not vaccinating."

"You mean it's not for the immunocompromised kids?"

"Oh, well, yes it is. But they aren't why I'm mad about it."

Silence.

"I'm mad at you for not agreeing to take the chance with vaccines for *your* child that I felt compelled to take with my own child."

Long silence.

"I think it's subconscious though. Like, I don't think most of the moms on my side of the line realize that's what they are really mad about. But I think it is."

"That's … interesting."

"I mean, you chose to not vaccinate because of the risk. You read all the risks, and you weren't comfortable taking those risks. So you didn't vaccinate. I wasn't given that choice."

"You were, you know."

"Theoretically, yes. But in reality, no one ever offered me a choice. I didn't even know there *was* a choice. My doctor just did them without any mention of risk. I figured, 'Oh, I better get my baby her shots because that's what people do.' When the nurse brought in five syringe-fulls, my jaw dropped. But I didn't say anything, because that's what you just did. Society expects it of us. Those who came before us did it, and now it's our turn. My child is now five, and just got her boosters. And still, no discussion from the doctor. I never thought to ask. I never thought to read. I never thought anything about it. And you did. And that pisses me off."

"That makes a strange kind of sense. However, those who came before you only risked about 24 doses. I'm talking the 80s. Now it's 70 doses. If it triples again it will be 200. Would you wish 200 doses on your grandchildren?"

"No. Not on anyone's children."

Silence.

"I'm still mad though. My child had to risk all of that – about 50 doses so far – and *your* child doesn't? It's not fair. You should be forced to take the same risks my child did."

"Really?"

Silence.

"No. I guess not. It sounds ridiculous now that I say it out loud. I'm just venting, you know."

More silence.

"I just realized why we fight so hard against you and all your crazy - sorry, I guess not so crazy - friends who don't vaccinate. We pretend it's all about the science, but seriously, there's rarely a real scientist among us."

"Yeah, that slogan 'The Science Is Settled' is pretty catchy. But if you aren't defending the science, what are you defending?"

"My motherhood. I'm defending my very motherhood, dammit!"

Silence.

"I feel like when you try to tell me how dangerous vaccines are, and parade your injured children in front of me, you are saying that I'm a bad mom for deciding to vaccinate."

"Oh dear, I never …"

"Oh, I know. I know that now. I know that's not what you are really saying, but that's how I *feel* when someone tries to argue against vaccines. So, I really can't do anything else besides stand up for vaccines and the CDC and proclaim that it's all good. Otherwise, I'm a … a …"

"A bad mom?"

A nod.

"For deciding to fully vaccinate?"

Another nod, and a tear.

"No. Not a bad mom. I can tell you are a really great mom. Other good moms can tell that sort of thing. Because you thought you really were doing the right thing. And who knows, maybe you were, especially if your kids handled all the shots. We aren't saying it's wrong to vaccinate. Some of the vaccines are probably pretty good. We just don't want them to be forced. We want choice, and we want equality. And we want people to know what the science really says, and doesn't say. There's risk, and you should have been told that. You should be joining us, not fighting us, because it's not pure science you are defending, and it's not *your* science. It's *their* science – science that they bought and paid for. But I appreciate you telling me how we've made you feel though, because no mom should ever have to feel like her motherhood is being called into question."

"I'm just throwing that idea out there, because I think if you really could look into the minds of each of these moms in my side, you'd find the same thing. Not that any of them would admit it."

"That is the most intelligent, most insightful thing I think I have ever heard."

A smile. And another tear.

"But you know who you are really mad at, right? Because I don't think it's me."

"Yes. Self-loathing really sucks."

"You and I could be friends, you know. I like you."

"I like you too. But …"

"But what?"

A half step forward again.

Chapter 15

Doctors, Am I Right?

"Wait. What? My child has strep? I thought you said she has pneumonia."

Karen didn't understand a word the doctor was saying. All she knew was that her Candice had been sick – very sick – for over a week, and she'd spent the last two days and nights in this hospital and no one could tell her what exactly was wrong with her child. *And now this dipwad is trying to tell me my child only has strep throat? She doesn't even have a sore throat. She's coughing and has a high fever and ...*

"No, Mrs. Anderson. Sorry for not being clear. Candice does have pneumonia. And a bloodstream infection. But the blood tests have shown that both infections are being caused by a bacteria called Streptococcus pneumonia. We call it pneumococcus for short. I know it sounds like strep throat, but it's really a totally different bacteria from the one that causes strep throat."

"How the he ... heck did she catch a blood stream infection? How does that even happen?"

"Well," explained the too-young looking doctor. "These bacteria are very common. Most people who catch pneumococcal disease just feel minor cold and cough symptoms, and most will get better without even knowing they ever caught it. But some people, and we don't know exactly why, will have the bacteria move down into the lungs and grow into pneumonia. That's why Candice has such a bad cough and started to have labored breathing a few days ago."

"But then we saw the doctor and started antibiotics. Shouldn't that have worked?" Karen wasn't stupid. She knew antibiotics were supposed to work.

"Well, yes, they usually do work. But we discovered why they didn't work in Candice. The bacteria moved into her bloodstream from the lungs, and we were able to find the bacteria in the blood work we did when she was admitted here 2 days ago. It always takes the lab a day or two to find these infections, but they did identify exactly what it is just an hour ago. And the reason Candice isn't feeling better is that it's a particularly serious strain of pneumococcus called strain 19A, which is resistant to many antibiotics, unfortunately. So the antibiotics she started last week from the doctor didn't work. And the antibiotic we've been giving her through her IV isn't working either. With most strains of pneumococcus, she would have felt better within a day or two of what your doctor prescribed. But not with 19A. We will have to give her a very strong IV antibiotic to get ahead of this infection. I know this is a lot to take in, but she'll have to stay here for several more days at least."

"So, my stupid doctor totally messed up? He should have given us a better antibiotic?" Karen was pissed now.

"No, no Mrs. Anderson. That's not it at all. Like I said, most cases of pneumonia are just caused by regular bacteria, and respond well to antibiotics. In fact, some pneumonias will even get better without antibiotics. Your doctor made the right call to start a regular antibiotic when he first suspected pneumonia, back when Candice didn't look too sick. That would work in most cases. But there's no way to predict who might have strain 19A, and it would be wrong to just start every child with pneumonia on the strongest of antibiotics. Then those antibiotics would someday stop working."

Whatever, Karen thought, having tuned him out halfway through whatever-the-hell he was saying. *This doctor sounds as dumb as Candice's pediatrician. He should have known this could happen. I should call my sister, Allison. She's a nurse for that big pediatrician group where she lives. She can ask one of her doctors about it. Maybe that Dr. Jones she's always bragging about ... Wait! Pneumococcus sounds so familiar. Why? ...*

The doctor's pager went off and he excused himself, promising to come back in a little while, but Karen didn't even notice. She was busy rummaging through her purse for Candice's ... *Yes, here it is!* She unfolded her child's yellow vaccine card and scanned down the confusing rows of letters, dates, and stamps. She didn't see what she was looking for, but then turned the card over and *yes – there it is. I knew she'd been vaccinated against what this doctor is trying to tell me she has. Four doses of pneumococcal vaccine, back when Candice was a baby and toddler.*

She can't have this disease. She was immunized against it four times. She looked up and around for her doctor, but he'd apparently left the room. *How rude.*

Karen walked over to the door to Candice's private hospital room and opened it. She glanced back at her seven-year-old daughter, but she was engrossed on her own cell phone playing whatever the latest game was, not letting the IV or the nasal oxygen get her down. Karen didn't see her doctor anywhere, just a bunch of nurses looking very busy. She thought about asking one of them for more information, but then thought better of it. *If the doctor is stupid, then the nurses will be even stupider.*

Karen sat back down and started searching for what she wanted to know online. It took her over an hour, but find it she did.

Candice Anderson was fully vaccinated, just like most children. And she handled the vaccines pretty well, just like many seem to. And Karen made sure to get them all done right on time. Candice got all the recommended doses of pneumococcal vaccine – pneumococcal 7 that is. This vaccine protected against the 7 most common strains of pneumococcus that were going around at the time. And that seemed like a good thing.

But Karen discovered numerous research articles that discussed the emergence of other strains of pneumococcus – strains not in the vaccine. As the vaccine reduced the 7 most common strains in the population, other strains increased to take their place. The result was that there wasn't much of an overall decrease in pneumococcal disease, just a shift in which of the more than 90 strains were prevalent. And one such strain that increased was strain 19A, which was resistant to most antibiotics.

Back before pneumococcal 7 was introduced, strain 19A was almost unheard of. But now it was making itself known, and it had struck her own child.

Then Karen discovered that in 2010 they came out with a new version called pneumococcal 13, which protected against the original 7 strains, plus 6 more that had increased over the years - including 19A. But Candice hadn't been given that updated version. All babies got it now, of course. They don't make pneumococcal 7 in the U.S. anymore. And some kids were offered one booster dose of pneumococcal 13 to at least give some immunity to the new strains, but apparently Candice hadn't. *Again, because my stupid doctor probably never offered it.*

There was also a pneumococcal 23 vaccine that protected against 23 strains. But it didn't give much lasting immunity, and it didn't work well in babies, so it was only used for short-term protection in certain susceptible older people. *Maybe Candice can have that version while she's here in the hospital,* Karen thought. *But I doubt this young doctor even knows about it. I'll have to tell him.*

But then Karen got a little confused as a new thought dawned on her. *Wait, if this strain 19A didn't used to be a problem, but then it increased because of the use of the old vaccine, then isn't it actually the vaccine's fault that my child is now sick?*

Karen's head started to hurt. She looked up at her daughter, now asleep in her bed, but thankfully breathing comfortably.

This is all so confusing. Just how deadly is pneumococcal disease anyway? And how many strains are there? If we keep making vaccines with more and more strains, are we going to eventually eliminate pneumococcal disease like we did with polio and measles? Or are we just going to keep triggering an increase in any strains not covered by whatever the current vaccine is? Will there be a pneumococcal 2000 someday? Would that even be healthy? Have we started a war against a complicated and intelligent germ that will keep trying to outsmart us? Would it have been better to just leave well enough alone?

Karen wondered what "well enough" had really been like. That is, what was pneumococcal disease like before we started vaccinating against it? That didn't take long to find. Before the first pneumococcal 7 vaccine came out in 2001, the CDC estimated that there were about 60,000 cases of something called Invasive Pneumococcal Disease each year in the U.S., mostly in old people, some in adults, and about 25% in children under 5 years old. This invasive thing meant that a routine infection – a mild case, like what this hospital doctor had told her most kids get with pneumococcal – gets more serious. The bacteria invades into the lungs, like with Candice, or into the bloodstream – again, like Candice – or even worse, into the brain. *So there are probably millions of mild harmless cases of this every year that we don't even know about,* she thought.

I can't believe that many kids get that sick from this every year. How come we never hear about it? She then read two things that made her wonder. First, the 60,000 cases each year was just an estimate. And apparently the CDC likes to over-estimate things just to scare people. Like they seem to do with the flu, warning people that over 36,000 Americans die every year of the flu, but only about 1500 such deaths are actually reported. She read about that on one site. She then discovered that no one really had any idea how common both mild or invasive pneumococcal disease ever was because it was never a reportable disease. Meaning, whenever hospitals or doctors had a case, they didn't report it to the CDC. *So, they are just guessing that it's all over the place and threatening people left and right. I mean, obviously it does threaten people – look at what it did to Candice. But I feel like I should have heard tons about this disease if it was so common and so bad. We hear about measles all the time, but that's only like 100 or 200 cases a year, and no one dies.*

Having been the victim of a vaccine that ended up not working for her child made Karen angry. She put down her phone and looked out the hospital window. *No wonder I read so much online about people complaining about vaccines. They all talk about bad side effects, and then everyone who loves vaccines, like I do – did – says there's nothing to worry about and they all work just fine. But they don't all work fine. And sometimes they make things worse, like causing resistant strains. Sure, this vaccine probably helps some people, especially now that it has 19A in it. But the whole thing's starting to sound like a sales pitch. If vaccines were so perfect and safe, everyone would get them, and no one would get sick. Then there would be no debate. And they wouldn't have to try so hard to sell them. Why can't it just be like that?*

Feeling tired, Karen put down her phone and turned on the TV. She decided she better take a nap while her child was still asleep. What she saw on the screen shocked her. The coincidence. The irony.

"Ask your doctor if pneumococcal 13 is right for you, because pneumococcal disease can be very serious ..."

Karen threw the remote at the TV ... and missed.

Chapter 16

An Ironic Blanket

Jackson Jones was usually very certain about most decisions placed in front of him. But the idea of subjecting Dr. Donaldson to a semi-public debate on mandatory vaccination troubled him. A colleague at the American Pediatric Association had called him with the proposal this morning, and he'd tentatively agreed. The debate would be featured at the upcoming APA National Convention. The colleague had proposed the title *The Physician's Responsibility in Supporting Mandatory Vaccination Laws.* Jones had already shot that stupid title down. *You can't just blatantly tell the public you are trying to mandate anything on them.* But he agreed to the idea, as long as they shifted the title to focus on non-medical exemptions to vaccination. Essentially, should any children anywhere in the country be allowed to attend school at all if they don't have all vaccines, unless they have a medical excuse? Do those who are members of a religion that doesn't support vaccination still have the right to attend public school, or even their own religious school? And do those who decline vaccines due to their personal or medical beliefs have the right to attend school? That was the gist he agreed to, tentatively.

But he couldn't get it out of his mind and move on to his myriad other tasks for the day. And that fact alone, he realized, is a good sign that it is a bad idea.

I'm just not certain that Donaldson could hold her own in a live debate against another physician who is really opposed to mandatory vaccination.

He checked out the doctor who was slated to go up against her – a Dr. Gibson. *A bio-ethicist.* Jones hated ethics. It, or they, always seemed to get in the way of his plans, and the plans of his benefactors.

There's no way I'm going to let Donaldson publicly speak in front of thousands of pediatricians. I'm just not sure she'll be able to get my points across clearly and accurately enough. But he liked the idea of taking this opportunity to sell his agenda to the pediatricians of the nation.

If I can get Dr. Gibson to agree to a scripted "debate," carefully crafted, with both sides working together on the questions and answers, so that Jane isn't surprised by anything, and I can get her to stick to the script and not try to formulate any of her own ad-lib ideas, because that never goes well, then maybe this would work. We'll have all those card-carrying young pediatricians believing that it is good to mandate medicine to a public that is hesitant to accept what's good for them freely.

Ha! Putting on a fake debate with a bioethicist. Now that's ironic.

But irony is one of the things that kept Jackson Jones warm at night.

Chapter 17

Sage Advice

Sophia finally found what she was looking for - on social media. A guide to writing the report she so desperately wanted to write for so long, posted by someone who sounded a lot like herself, but with a way cuter screen name: SavingSages. After a few PMs, Sophia discovered that Sage was the name of the woman's child, and she'd had a severe vaccine reaction similar to Sophia's own daughter, Arabella.

The Guide, as they called it, provided 'step-by-step instructions on how to submit a complaint to your state medical board if you believe your doctor was negligent in his or her treatment of your child regarding the administration of vaccinations and/or the handling of vaccine reactions' – a quote from the intro to the Guide.

Sophia's daughter was now four years old, and she was a brilliant, outgoing, and happy child in so many ways … now, anyway. But she hadn't always been that way.

Sophia had vaccinated her daughter more carefully than most, spreading the shots out a bit because she thought that would be safer. After the two-month shots – two shots only instead of the usual six – she had suffered hours of inconsolable screaming on and off for days, her arms and legs started spasming and shaking in a way that looked like seizures, and she had staring spells that seemed like the kind of seizures where you blank out for several seconds.

Like a "good" mom, Sophia called the doctor's office to report these concerns, and was reassured that all this was a normal response to vaccination. And, also like a good mom, she listened to her doctor's advice nurse.

At three months, Arabella got two more vaccines – different ones this time. At that appointment she even told the doctor she thought her baby had seizures and other problems after the first shots, and still wasn't quite herself, and the doctor reassured her that the baby was fine. Arabella didn't seem to have any immediately severe reactions this time, or after any of the other shots during her first year of life. But she had a host of behavioral and intestinal problems all that first year, all of which had started 3 days after those first shots.

After her two vaccines at 12 months of age – again, spread out so she didn't get them all – she changed dramatically: she started spinning in circles, banging her head on things, biting herself, and became very hyper. Her GI system went crazy again, with terrible diarrhea that smelled awful starting the day after those shots. Again, her doctor reassured her this was all normal, and when Sophia told him she didn't want any more shots, he kicked her out of his practice.

Sophia was thankful that Arabella's reactions weren't extreme – not as bad as Sage's, who had to be rushed to the ER, twice – and she felt like she'd dodged a bullet by skipping some of the vaccines (especially the MMR) and spreading out the ones she did do. But what had always bothered her over these years is that her doctor wouldn't listen. Her baby had a moderately severe neurological, behavioral, and intestinal reaction – twice – and he never wrote a single thing about it down in Arabella's chart. Nothing. Well, he had written that mom was concerned about seizures, and that mom was concerned about vaccines in general. And he'd written that he warned her about the risk of diseases if she didn't continue vaccines. Sophia learned all of this when she finally got a copy of Arabella's medical records and saw all that was, and wasn't, written down.

Sage's case was so much worse, as Sophia learned in her online conversations with Sage's mom (whose name she still didn't know). But the negligence was similar. And Sophia had always felt helpless that she couldn't do anything about how negligently she felt she'd been treated. She spent some of her free time talking to legislators and speaking in public to try to prevent the mandatory vaccination law in her state, but she'd never found any way to make peace with the harm her own child had personally suffered, until she saw a story in a newspaper.

It was from San Diego, and it was about an immunocompromised child who had been used as a poster child to help pass the state's mandatory vaccination law. The dad, according to the story, had testified before the senators that he was afraid his child, who had had leukemia and had recovered, was put in danger from other kids around him who weren't vaccinated. Then a doctor, who apparently was on the other side of the fight, spoke up and said yes, these kids should be protected, but that in reality unvaccinated kids are healthy and don't pose a significant risk to immunocompromised kids. Well, the San Diego story was all about how the dad was now angry that the doctor had spoken about his kid's medical condition in public, and he was going to complain to the California Medical Board about it. A spokeswoman for the medical board was quoted as saying that this isn't the type of thing that one can complain about; but, if anyone in the public does have any complaints about how a doctor is providing improper care or advice about vaccines, they *should* report this to the medical board.

When Sophia read that, a light went off in her head. Finally, she could do something. She knew she couldn't sue anyone, because pharmaceutical companies are shielded from being sued for vaccine injuries (although not for medication injuries, which she couldn't understand). She went to the medical board's website and found that their main function is consumer protection – protection from negligent medical care. They also had information on patient abandonment. So she'd gotten Arabella's medical records and started to write out her complaint.

But something was missing. There was no authority to it. No documents to back up her complaint. She just sounded like a whinny mom who had her feelings hurt. She needed more. She needed medical documents and research papers to back up her case. And that's when she found SavingSages and the Guide.

The Guide had two parts. The first was about the failure of a doctor to give proper informed consent for vaccinations, and provided details about how the vaccine Package Inserts instruct doctors to explain the risks of vaccination prior to administering their products and how the United Nations and the American Medical Association mandate informed consent. It provided quotes to this effect from the Package Inserts and links to where these PIs can be found online. It also showed how the CDC's Vaccine Information Statements are mandated by federal law to be given to patients before vaccines.

The second part dealt with improper care *after* a vaccine reaction occurred. It discussed a doctor's responsibility to write down such reactions in the chart and report them to VAERS, even if he doesn't think the vaccine was responsible. The events should be documented in the chart, just like any other health problem a patient comes in for. The doctor also has a responsibility to listen when babies have neurological reactions to vaccines, examine them to make sure they aren't neurologically injured, and then warn a patient about further injury if the vaccine is repeated.

When Sophia realized that *none* of this had been done before her doctor gave her baby the first vaccines, and all the subsequent ones, she felt … betrayed. Like, who would do surgery without getting consent? Who would give any medical treatment without warning about the risks? And then when something bad *does* happen, and there are very clear guidelines and warnings the doctor is supposed to follow and advise the patient on when a bad reaction occurs, and the doctor doesn't do any of that … betrayal is too nice a word. More like criminal negligence. There are rules and laws in place that mandate informed consent for vaccines and procedures to follow after a bad reaction, but no one follows those rules. And no one gets in trouble for not following the rules because no one reports it. At least, as a minimum, write down the symptoms of the reaction so that there's a medical record of what happened.

And that's why SavingSages put out this Guide, and happily

emailed it from her gmail account to anyone who needed it – to help more parents report vaccine negligence in the hope that the medical boards would encourage change in how doctors give informed consent and handle reactions when they happen. Maybe they'd mandate some sort of training on how to recognize reactions, how to write them down, and how to report them. And how to warn patients about repeated reactions.

But Sophia realized that if all this occurred, it was possible that vaccination rates would go down a bit. Because everyone who had a bad reaction would think twice about repeating that vaccine. And the one thing that Sophia had learned that no medical organization would do is create a policy that would *reduce* vaccination rates. It just went too much against their nature.

But what if they were legally obligated to do so? The medical board doesn't make medical policy, it just enforces it. It's there for consumer protection, not doctor protection. So they should *want to do something about this negligence. And maybe they are even legally obligated to investigate it.*

Sophia wasn't sure, but all she knew is that reporting what happened to her would be one tiny contribution among many, if everyone this happened to put in a report. And the statute of limitations on submitting a report, at least in her state, was 28 years of age, or ten years after the child reached adulthood. Hundreds of thousands of parents could potentially file such reports. And maybe, just maybe, there would be change – 10 or 20 years down the road. And maybe there would be fewer "Sages" and "Arabellas" out there who are harmed or nearly harmed. She knew her doctor probably wouldn't get in trouble, and she wasn't even sure if she wanted him to. A slap on the wrist, maybe. But she knew her doctor was probably doing the same thing most do, and that he was probably trained to not recognize, document, and warn about vaccine reactions. It was the *system* that needed change, and submitting a complaint at least gave Sophia a sense that she was doing something to help bring about this change. And that felt good.

Chapter 18

A Rose Isn't Always a Rose

"Seriously? You are going to start having sex now?"

"Yeah, now that it's totally safe."

"I don't know. I feel like I'm too young."

"Well, you have to start sometime, right?"

"Actually, I started already …"

That got the girls' attention, and they all turned to look at Samantha.

"Seriously?"

"With who?"

"Where? When?"

"What was it like?"

The five junior highers were enjoying their monthly slumber party (at least that's what all their moms called it). And the conversation was different this time. They were eighth-graders – kings, or rather, queens, of the school. And their bodies had all gone through quite a transformation into adulthood (as they saw it) over the past year. Well, all except Julie.

"Yeah, my doctor said it's safe now cuz I got the first shot. I won't get cervical cancer from having sex. She told me a few other things, like how to use a condom – yuck, right? – and … well, I won't say. You'll all find out, soon I hope."

"What kind of pediatrician do you have, girl? Mine certainly doesn't talk to me about sex. But he's a man, and that would be awkward. It was bad enough hearing my mom and him discuss my periods."

"My doctor is a woman," explained Samantha. "She's very open and up front about things. She even asks if I want to have any private conversations without my mom there. Confidential conversations. She's really cool. At my last visit I got my first shot, and she said I'd be protected from cervical cancer now. Well, she really said I should wait until after the second dose next month, but … last weekend I let Thomas … well, you know." The teen now blushed, despite her earlier bravery. But this was a safe place to talk, among her best friends. They could talk about anything. And they had, over the years.

"Did it hurt?"

"What was it like?"

"Did you like it?"

"Yes, it hurt. And it was fast. It definitely wasn't the big huge amazing deal that they make it out to be. Thomas was so eager – it was his first time too. Geeze, I didn't even ask him if he had his shots. But I guess that doesn't matter, since it was the first time for both of us. You should have seen the look on his face though! That was worth the whole thing. He is so in love with me, it's not even funny."

"They say it gets better with practice," chimed in Rose. "Although I wouldn't know yet. I'm not really in a hurry. I'm thinking of waiting until Prom night or something like that. Junior Prom, that is, not Senior."

The girls chuckled.

"Well, I got the shot."

"Me too. I've had all three."

"I just got the second."

"I haven't had any doses of the HPV shot yet," admitted Julie quietly.

"What?"

"Seriously?"

"Wait, can you even do that? Not get the shot?"

"How are you even in school?"

"Ha-ha. Wait, are you four serious? Of course I'm still in school.

It's not an actual requirement, you know. I know they say it is, but that's a stretch of the truth. It's not required for school, and my mom didn't want me to get the shot."

"She probably doesn't want you to have sex yet," said Samantha. "But you've seen the commercials. I'm going to be 'one less' girl with cervical cancer. You don't want to catch cervical cancer, do you? Wait, are you thinking of not having sex yet? Like, waiting until marriage?"

"What if I was? No, I'm not totally thinking that. But yes, I am going to wait. Plus look at me – I don't even have boobs yet. But listen, I'm not just automatically going to get cervical cancer if I don't get the shot. When the time comes, I am going to use condoms. Unless I wait until marriage, and I marry a guy who's also been careful. But if I don't wait, I still want to prevent HIV, chlamydia, gonorrhea, syphilis, and all. There's a pretty long list of things we don't have a vaccine for that I don't want. So I can wait, and be careful when I'm old enough to be responsible about it. No offense, Sammy. With it being both of your first times, I guess it makes sense not to use a condom."

"But you don't want to get pregnant either, right?" This from Rose.

"Well, no. But I've started my period again, so ..."

"Wait Julie. Why don't your parents want you to get the shot besides to encourage your prolonged virginity?"

"I don't think it has anything to do with that. My mom says there are all kinds of bad side effects. Like, really bad things can happen. Nerve damage, immune system problems, psychiatric conditions. They say teen girls are being seriously harmed all over the world by this vaccine. Yeah, it's probably pretty rare, but it has been documented and is really happening. And I think I agree with her. I mean, maybe if this was a disease I couldn't protect myself against. But I can. And I could have all the sex I wanted if I'm safe about it ... well, when I get something for the guys to hold onto I guess. I don't think getting this shot, or not, has to play into these decisions."

"Ok, Samantha." Rose again. "Tell us more. What was it really like?"

———◦———

Slumber party night again.

"So what are we going to do tonight?"

"We definitely have to stay up all night again like we did last month."

"Think we can sneak out without getting caught this time?"

"Maybe we should go over to Thomas's house and see if he's got anything going on. What do you think, Sam?"

"Oh … I don't know … I feel like I'm still trying to recover from last month," Samantha answered tiredly.

"OMG, are you pregnant?!?!" Rose.

"No. I don't think so. Truthfully, I haven't really felt like fooling around lately. I think Tommy is getting a little annoyed."

"You *have* seemed off, girl. Tired. You don't even answer texts after 10 anymore."

"Yeah, I've been going to bed early. I've been having a lot of head-aches. And other stuff."

"Well, we can just hang out here and make it a quiet evening, don't you all think?" suggested Julie.

"Sounds good to me," added Rose.

"Samantha, what are you doing?"

The tired girl had turned toward her backpack and had tried to inconspicuously take a pill out of a prescription bottle, but not much could be hidden from this crowd.

"Are those birth control pills?"

"Are you on the pill?"

"No, dummies. Those come in a round disk … I think." From Rose.

"My mom would kill me."

Sigh. "No. I'm not on the pill. These are for something else … I … I've been having these terrible migraines."

"What?"

"Seriously?"

"Where? When?"

"Are you OK?"

"Yeah. It's only happened three times. All here at home within the last month. I've been to my doctor, and a headache doctor, and they can't find anything wrong – any reason for the migraines. I have to take this medicine now to prevent them. Maybe that's why I've been so tired."

Slumber party weekend coming up again. Julie's house this time. Julie's mom answered her cell phone half way through that Friday afternoon.

"Hey Tamara. What's up? Is Samantha excited about tonight?"

"Well, that's why I'm calling. I don't think Sammy's going to make it."

"Oh no. Really? For the first time in how many years? What's wrong?"

"She's just not herself. She's really sick. Not like contagious sick. Just, she's had all kinds of problems over the past two months. You know about the migraines. But she's also having seizures now. And terrible arm pain. At first it was her left arm, and now it's both arms. She has numbness in her toes, and she sometimes has difficulty walking. Last night her right hand started twitching – she couldn't even do her homework. It's … it's just terrible."

"Oh my gosh, Tamara. That's awful. Do they know what's wrong with her? What's causing it?"

"No. The doctors are stumped. We've been to two neurologists, a rheumatologist, and our own doctor of course. They ran all kinds of tests, but no one has any answers yet. What the hell is going on with her? They tested her for drugs. They ruled out pregnancy – they insisted on doing a test before doing an MRI, although I told them it was totally not necessary. And this is way beyond pregnancy symptoms anyway. I just don't know what to do. She used to be so healthy, and lively, and energetic. She had to quit the soccer team. And some days she can't even get out of bed."

"When exactly did all this start again?"

"About two months ago or so. We even had gone to her pediatrician right before that and she was totally fine. A clean bill of health. Then within a week the headaches started, and other symptoms. And then the seizures … and …"

Julie's mom didn't hear any more of what Tamara said. She was suddenly overcome by dread, and she sat down on the floor – right in the middle of her kitchen – staring numbly at her phone.

"Leslie? Leslie, are you still there?"

Julie's mom couldn't speak. Tamara was her best friend. Samantha was one of Julie's. They'd had many discussions about vaccines over the years, but Tamara hadn't really been open to any of Leslie's concerns. They'd agreed to disagree, and not let it come between them. But now this involved her friend's precious little daughter, and Leslie was as heartbroken as if her own child had become a victim of …

Julie had told her mom about the conversation the girls had at the last slumber party. No, two parties ago. The discussion about HPV, and the vaccine, and even about Samantha's comment about the TV commercial. *And now, poor Sammy is not going to be "one less" … she's going to be one* more. And Leslie thought about the timing of the symptoms – the terrible headaches had started within 3 days after the first dose, which should have been a warning sign to think twice about continuing. But she knew her friend wouldn't have thought of that. Neither would her doctor. Most wouldn't. Because they just don't know to look. And then things got much worse – seizures – after the second dose, given just one month later.

"Leslie, why don't I come over right now. I have some ideas, and I want to show you some information. I think I might know what's going on with Sam."

Tamara would need to be shown some convincing proof about HPV vaccine side effects. Fortunately, there was already a lot of good published information on this, about side effects, about lawsuits against the manufacturers in other countries, about corners being cut in the safety research protocols. All kinds of information was out there, if you just took the time to look.

Leslie wiped the tears from her eyes, got up, and got to work.

———◄◌►———

"I just don't believe it. I mean, I believe it, now that you've shown me all this information. What I don't believe is why nobody else believes this can happen … until it does."

Rose's mom was covering the sleepover back at the house so that Leslie could spend the evening with Tamara. They knew she'd need some serious support.

The coffee table was littered with printed-out research articles, magazine stories, and internet blogs, along with a half-eaten package of Oreos and a now-empty bottle of wine. Serious support.

"The truth is, I wanted to protect her from my own mistakes. Did you know that I had a positive PAP smear about 10 years ago? Pre-cancerous cervical changes. HPV. We didn't know you guys yet. But it was easily treated – a simple cone excision or something like that. I've been clean ever since. But the weeks I spent in fear while waiting for the all-clear from my doctor were tough. And getting re-checked every year since then, and the few days it takes for me to get the phone call about my negative results, is torture. I mean, I sit here and stare at the phone waiting for the doctor to call. When it rings, I get chest pains and actually have to lie down on the floor while the doctor reassures me that all is well. They I cry after I hang up. Then I'm good again for another year. I know it's stupid. Early pre-cancerous cervical changes are pretty much 100% cured with the cone procedure. So it's an irrational fear. But I didn't want Samantha to have to go through any of that. I thought this vaccine was amazing; she'd never have to worry about HPV. Did you know that there are about 10,000 cases of cervical cancer each year in the U.S.? And about 3000 or so women die? I was so scared I'd be one of them. And I didn't want Sam to be one as well. Cervical cancer is awful, but I was lucky. What if I hadn't caught it early? But now that you've told me all this," gesturing to the coffee table, "I just feel sick. Betrayed. Stupid. The vaccine only prevents some strains of HPV. You still have to use condoms to prevent all the other strains and all the other diseases. So it doesn't really make sex any safer. And they never even proved for sure that the vaccine really prevents cancer from those strains before they released it. They skipped most of the safety and efficacy research. Even the doctor who did that research for one of the vaccine makers has spoken out about that. What was it? The four-year clinical trial was stopped after just 15 months? I mean, let's say the vaccine actually *does* work – that it *is* useful in reducing HPV. Is it worth it to take this risk? Certainly wasn't for Sam. But what about everybody in general? Is it worth the risk just so you might not get the nine strains of the disease that are in the vaccine? Or is it better for people to simply make good choices: use condoms, choose abstinence, wait until you are older and seriously monogamous. Whatever. Then get your yearly PAP smears. That's what that one doctor says in that article. That OB/GYN. Just be smart and get your PAP smears, and this vaccine may not even be needed. But just give people a *real* choice, right? Inform them about the benefits and the risks of a vaccine. Let them choose. Don't just hide the facts, and then hide behind the law when things go wrong for some people.

"And this is happening to young women all over the world. That documentary about all those girls in Denmark? What's it called? Sick and Betrayed? And our own documentary here in the U.S.. The Greater Good. Those stories are about Sam! And there are the lawsuits in other countries. Sixty-three young women in Japan who reacted just like Samantha did are suing the vaccine maker over this! And the Japanese government took the vaccine off of their recommended schedule way back in 2013! Why didn't we hear about that? Sure, they left it on as optional, but added warnings about how to watch for severe reactions written right there in the footnotes of their schedule. Imagine that! A government actually being up front about the danger! And that doctor in Columbia who wrote about his 62 patients who suffered the same thing? And here we are, in the most advanced country in the world, and I can't do a damned thing about it?

"And finally, to find out that our own government VAERS system has received over 40,000 complaints about reactions to this vaccine? Yeah, they're not all severe – what, only about 4000 serious reactions causing a permanent disability or hospitalization? But over 225 fatal reactions reported? Why is all this just ignored?

"Then there's this new Cochrane Review published last year. That's a mainstream group, with doctors and researchers who have been publishing rave reviews about vaccines for years. Even *they* now have concerns. What's that title again?" Tamara leafed through the articles strewn across the table. "Here. 'Aluminum adjuvants used in vaccines versus placebo or no intervention (Protocol).' Right here, on page two, they tear apart the safety research on this vaccine. Even *they* admit there are serious potential flaws in the safety research that got this vaccine approved. They describe five published articles that discuss how all the adverse events that have been reported from this vaccine – the same symptoms that Samantha is suffering – were so bizarre that no one knew how to categorize them in the reaction reports. They didn't fit any known syndrome, so they were just ignored. How did they put it? 'The observational studies, which based their results on registered diagnoses, may have excluded an important fraction of eligible participants with unclear adverse symptoms … most girls that claim to suffer … receive no clinical diagnosis, and are therefore unlikely to appear in medical registers. Moreover, the randomized clinical trials on HPV vaccines … have been blamed for not using true placebo … as the control.' They used aluminum injections as the placebo. Makes me so angry!" The stack of loose papers scattered like leaves as she flung them across the room. They were still floating down when she picked up another study.

"But not as angry as the other Cochrane study that just came out. And I quote: 'None of the [26] studies have followed participants for long enough to detect an effect on cervical cancer.' That's supposed to be the whole point of the vaccine, and they don't even know if it protects against cervical cancer? Sure, preliminary studies show it lowers the risk of precancer, but that's all they know. How can they get away with marketing it as cancer prevention, and mass-vaccinate an entire world, without knowing if it actually works?

"And here's another doozy: 'All but one of the [26] trials was funded by the vaccine manufacturers.' Twenty-five safety and efficacy trials paid for by the vaccine makers, and only one study that wasn't? How is that even ethical? Are we all really that blind and stupid?"

Leslie hadn't said much over the past few hours while her friend had read, and cried, and screamed, and cried. She'd asked a lot of questions, and Julie kept it simple. She wasn't there to try to talk her friend into believing something. She wanted her friend to come to her own conclusions. It was better that way – for people to really understand and believe something, not to simply just be talked into it.

"You tried to warn me, you know. Many times. But I wouldn't listen, would I? Was that hard for you? You certainly put up with a lot of shaming from me over this, right? I mean, I really thought you were nuts, Leslie."

"I regret not trying harder – making you listen," Leslie teared up. "If I had gotten through to you … maybe Sam wouldn't be …"

"Now you stop that. You know how stubborn I am. I won't listen to anything unless I decide to open my mind. Looking back now, I think you tried to reach me way more than most friends would have. I appreciate that. And now I am royally pissed. Especially because the pediatrician, who we saw 4 days after that first HPV dose because of her sudden migraines, completely ignored the possibility that this was related to the vaccine. 'Oh, migraines just happen and we don't know why.' Ugh!!! I am so angry I could … It's so obvious now, in hindsight. No one in the family has migraines. When those hit, and she started to complain of feeling weak, and other symptoms, my doctor should have thought of the shot. That's not *my* job. How would I even know? But these side effects are listed on the doctor's prescribing information right here!" Again, the table. "She should know this stuff. She should have said, 'Your child may be having a known neurological reaction to a vaccine. We should hold off on the next dose until things settle down.' But she didn't. So we got the next dose a month later and wham – the seizures and everything else. She's falling apart. If only we had realized the connection and stopped after that first shot! I'd give anything for Sam to 'only' have migraines. And you know what scares me the most? Suicide. You might think I'm crazy, but we both saw that kid on social media who was severely injured by the HPV vaccine. He became a quadriplegic or something. He killed himself because he didn't want to be a burden to his family anymore. What if Sam ..." Tamara couldn't even finish for the tears.

Leslie had no answers. She wondered if she should tell Tamara about that online Guide on how to report your doctor to the medical board for failing to recognize a vaccine reaction. *Maybe I'll email her that SavingSages gmail address in a few days, after she's calmed down a bit.*

"And you want to know what Sam said to Jim and me just this morning?" Tamara continued after composing herself. "After her usual remorse over 'Why did this happen to me,' she turned and looked at us, and asked, 'Did you know, Dad, Mom? Did you know this could happen when you let the doctor do this to me?'"

The tears flowed freely again from the broken hearts of both women long into the night.

Monday at school. Lunchtime. Julie sat alone with Samantha.

"Why me? Why did this happen? Why didn't anyone warn me? Why?"

There wasn't any good answer that Julie could give; none that would make any difference.

"Now look at me. I'm tired, weak, and getting fat from having to take steroids. Thomas has totally bailed on me. Who would want to fool around with this mess anyway? At least my seizures seem to have stopped, with two meds now. I just wish ... I wish I could go back and ..."

Julie hugged her best friend, and knew there wasn't a thing she could do. She looked across the lunch yard at all the other kids – all the healthy, smiling, laughing kids. *Why Sam? Why not any of them? Why do only a small percentage react this way? And why won't anybody listen? And ...*

She saw Thomas sitting a few tables away, his arm around a new girl, whose face Julie couldn't see. But even from behind, the hair looked familiar.

Rose.

News Alert:

October 2016: In an unprecedented move, health officials have announced they are eliminating the second dose of the HPV vaccine in the three-dose series. Since its introduction in 2007, the vaccine had been recommended for all kids at age 12 years, with a second dose a month later, and a third dose 6 months after the first. New research shows that two doses – given 6 to 12 months apart – work just as well if both are given prior to turning 15. Officials state the reason for the change is to improve acceptance and completion of the series: only 42% of teen girls and 28% of boys now complete the three-dose series. This new move, with a longer interval between the two doses, is hoped to improve consumer compliance.

Critics of the vaccine are questioning the publicized reasons for the change, citing reports that serious adverse events following that second dose, given so close to the first, might be the true reason officials are reducing and prolonging the doses. They point to the abandoned safety and efficacy testing when the vaccine was first approved by the FDA as a possible factor, testing which was supposed to take four years but was stopped after just 15 months, a process called fast-tracking. Vaccine safety advocates are calling for officials to admit that improved safety is the real reason for the change and to come clean with consumers. Health officials have so far declined to comment.

Chapter 19

Correlation and Causation

"I'm not saying it absolutely can't happen," pointed out Jim Garderson, one of the spokespersons for the NFL. "We take the possibility of CTE very seriously. And we are doing everything we can to make sure football is safe."

The sports commentator, himself an ex-football player, seemed to be on Jim's, and the NFL's, side in this matter. But he also had a job to do. *I respect his objectivity on this, thought Jim. He's at least being neutral and fair ... so far.*

"But this new study about the risks of long-term neurological problems in kids who start tackle football before the age of 12 is concerning," continued the TV host. "Yes, we know that the NFL spends a great deal of time and money each year to reassure worried parents that playing football at the youth level is safe. What I want to know is this: Is the NFL also spending the same amount of money, or even *more* money, on actual research to improve the safety of football, both in children and adults, now that we know there are some risks involved?"

"I can assure you, Bob, that yes, the NFL is committed to ensuring the sport is safe for children and adults alike. But every time a story like the Hernandez one comes out, and the media jump all over it, it ratchets up the fear and makes parents wonder if they should keep letting their kids play. We would ask you and all reporters to just stick to the science we know: there's no definitive link between football and

Chronic Traumatic Encephalopathy. There are a host of factors, both environmental and genetic, that play a role in …"

"Yes, but repeated concussions are one of those factors, you must admit. The science seems pretty clear on that. Is the NFL going to take responsibility for this, and figure out how to make it safer? Or are you going to keep dancing around the issue? Because that's what worried parents think you are doing."

Well, that was a bit of a curveball, Bob. "Well, in regard to what actually causes CTE, there are still a number of questions that are unanswered about the incidence and prevalence of head trauma in all areas of life."

"But the numbers are really starting to pile up, Jim. First there were 20 identified cases of CTE. Then 50. And now we have over 100 confirmed cases in which NFL players have developed CTE. And it's not just 40 years later. Seau and Duerson were in their 40s and 50s. And now a 27-year-old, Jim. At what point is this just no longer a coincidence?"

"At the point that we can prove it scientifically, Bob." *Geeze, I probably shouldn't have put it that way, but these questions are way out of line.* "There is a lot of doubt in the validity of the research that's been done, and …"

"Sounds like the NFL is stalling until they can figure out a way to keep this game alive."

Silence. *You f-ing practiced that, didn't you Bob.* Jim could feel his smile starting to strain.

"And we'll be right back with more questions for Jim Garderson, spokesperson for the National Football League, after these messages."

Like hell we will, Bob.

Oh my God, that was painful. ESPN, Fox, and ABC wouldn't have done that to me … to us. I wonder if this is payback for this network losing out on this year's coverage rights. I should have anticipated …

Jim's phone rang. "Hello, Sir. You saw it? I've no idea where that came from," Jim tried to explain to his boss. "I had this all worked out with the producer. She assured me we'd focus on the fact that football is safe and effective in growing confident and successful young men in our community." *Damn, I forgot to mention the 'effective' line, didn't I?*

"Look, Jim. We rely on you to be on top of these things. I have my own plate full putting together a new idea for Congress. Todd likes it, but doesn't think we have the votes yet. We are trying to figure out how much money we'd need to donate to what campaigns in order to move forward."

"You mean trying to push through a federal law about CTE and football? The Board thinks that will work? Because I have my doubts."

"That's why you are in Kansas right now and I'm in DC. But what can go wrong? Clearly America wants football. America needs football. Where would we be without it? And although there's no real evidence that CTE is real, and most people who play football are just fine, people are beginning to suspect there are risks involved. So if we can get Congress to put this into law, federal law, then the players *can't* sue us. Seriously, if we lose a few more of these CTE lawsuits, we'll be bankrupt."

"Really, Sir?"

"No. We can probably weather a few hundred of them and we'd still be fine. But why should we have to? With this new law, the NFL would no longer be liable for CTE. Players report their injuries to the Football Adverse Events Reporting System, or FAERS, so we can keep track of all injuries, including CTE. We add a surcharge to ticket sales that goes into a fund. We're thinking of calling it the Football Injury Compensation Program. FICP has a nice ring to it. Players who really do get injured plead their case, they get a bunch of money – that they rightly deserve – and it doesn't cost us anything. The fans ultimately are paying for it, and that's how it should be, right?"

"Well, good luck Sir. I think it's a brilliant plan. I'll check in with you when I get in tomorrow."

Jim clicked off the call, but his phone rang again. It was his daughter calling. *Ahhhh. I wonder how little Julie is? What is she now, six months? Nine?*

"Hello Eileen. How is the Samson clan doing?"

"We are all doing well, Dad. In fact, we are on our way to Julie's nine month appointment now. Which is why I am calling. I wanted to ask the doctor what he thought about Jimmy Junior upgrading to *tackle* football next year. He'll be 10, you know. We're trying to get him started early, because you said that would be a good idea."

"Uh, yeah honey. I remember that conversation. He's playing flag now, right?"

"Yup. You should see him play, you really should."

"Yeah, I know I should get out there. Work has been crazy busy though, and ..." *Should I tell her? I don't want to worry her ...*

"Ask your doctor about it and let me know what he says. If anyone would know about what's safe for kids, it will be your doctor."

"I will Dad. Thanks. Love you!"

Love you too, Daughter.

Chapter 20

A Carefully Crafted Response

"A nd now I'd be happy to answer any questions."

"Director, what is the first thing you plan to do about Zika virus?"

Oh my God, Toby rolled his eyes from his seat in the third row. *What is it with Zika?*

"Well, I can assure the American public that …" Toby tuned the newly-appointed health official out. She'd spend the next 30 seconds or so saying nothing important, and Toby wanted to time his own hand-raising perfectly so he could get in a question that actually mattered. He liked covering the White House during the 'here are all my new picks' week. And the new President's choice for this particular position was an interesting one. A decade ago, a former health director had left under some unusual circumstances: the whole $4 million in Pharma stock fiasco that wasn't, meaning not a single mainstream press outlet covered the story. But this new one didn't have any direct financial ties to Pharma, as far as anyone could tell. *Not like the new FDA Director. That was a surprise! To appoint someone to head the FDA, the federal organization that oversees Pharma, whose career has largely been in Pharma, was a shock, even for Washington. Oh the Director sounded like she was wrapping up … and … now!*

"Yes, the gentleman in the third row. I'm sorry, I don't know many of your names yet."

"Toby Turner with the Post. Director, with all the controversy

267

surrounding childhood immunizations, what steps do you plan to take to increase the public's confidence in the CDC immunization schedule?"

"As you know, vaccines are safe and effective, and I will assist the CDC in continuing to demonstrate this scientific fact to the public through ongoing research and as new vaccines are developed."

"A follow up: are your kids vaccinated?"

"I am a mother. I am fully vaccinated. I urge everyone to follow the full CDC schedule for their babies and themselves. Yes?" pointing to the first row again for the next question.

Toby relaxed. He knew it was a softball anyway, with an easy response, one that his boss wanted to make sure the American public would hear. Especially the part about her vaccinating her own kids – fully ... Wait. She *didn't* specifically say that. Toby replayed the exchange in his mind:

Are your kids vaccinated?

I am a mother. That wasn't really an answer.

I am fully vaccinated. Neither was that.

I urge everyone to follow the full schedule ... Still didn't answer what was asked – just some platitudes.

Did she dodge the question? But why? It was a softball. She must have had something prepared already. Her press chief must have prepped her. Why not just say 'Yes, my kids are fully vaccinated?'

Toby was pretty sure no one would notice the slip. *They'll just see the 'vaccines are safe and effective reassurance' and move on. Won't they?*

Chapter 21

Blacklisted

"Well, that's it then. No more MEPP program."

"Yeah, but we did get some good information out of it."

The two government employees were enjoying coffee just across the main road from the beach at the local breakfast hot spot.

The Medical Exemption Pilot Project was a joint effort between schools and the public health department to review vaccine medical exemptions from doctors to make sure they were being written properly. Several school districts had implemented the pilot program across the state, but there had been some snags along the way.

"Stupid public notice laws. That's what almost got us in trouble from the start," grumbled Terry. As an employee at the county health department office, he had been the one tasked by his boss to get the job done. "If we hadn't been required by law to put out a notice we were having the first MEPP meeting with the attorney general's office, our public health department, and school district officials, the meeting you and I were at, then we might have been able to get a lot more information. But apparently getting the state's legal team involved in a local health and education issue violated some sort of anti-collusion law that I still don't understand, and the health freedom activists called us out on it."

"Yeah," agreed Carlos, an employee in the local school district.

"But we went ahead with it anyway, just without the attorney general's office."

Sips of coffee. Bites of donut.

"So how many did we end up catching?" asked the school employee.

"How many what? Doctors? None, at least not directly through the MEPP program. Turns out they were all following the new law. All their medical exemptions were done properly."

"No, I mean how many parents did we end up catching? Parents trying to get around the new law? I never really thought we'd catch any doctors. Pediatricians are probably the most ethical of all the medical specialties."

"Oh. No parents either. Hard to believe, but they were all legitimate exemptions. As you know, the MEPP directed all daycares and schools in our county to send all vaccine medical exemption letters to the county Department of Public Health so they could be scrutinized. Now, technically, these letters are confidential medical information. Like any medical record, it is illegal for any daycare or school to share these letters with anyone else. But we thought that if we told the school nurses and daycare directors to be sure to cross off any personally identifiable information, or PII, on the letters – you know, the children's names and addresses, things like that – so that anyone who saw the letters wouldn't be infringing on the childrens' right to medical privacy, and the daycare directors and school nurses wouldn't be breaking HIPAA laws, we'd be ok. Turns out we were wrong.

"In order to legally make a medical record completely free of all PII, you have to cross off the child's date of birth, the date of the medical visit, the doctor's name, all address and phone number information, and any medical diagnosis. It takes a bit of training for someone to know how to do this properly. And the first vaccine exemption letters from doctors that the school nurses sent into the health department violated HIPAA in a big way. Some quick phone calls soon got people onto the right track, and eventually we got a total of 153 medical exemption letters for us to review. We found 17 that didn't have all four required items to make it a proper medical exemption. I'm not talking about actual medical reasons for exemption, because that's up to the doctor, not us. For now, anyway. Plus, that type of info was, or should have been, crossed off. What we officially were reviewing was whether or not the letter listed the vaccines which were being exempted, an expiration date on the exemption, a statement that says the vaccines are considered to be unsafe for that child, and that it came from an M.D. or D.O., not a chiropractor or naturopath. Just real doctors."

"What is a D.O. anyway?"

"It's like a chiropractor, I think, but they can prescribe meds. Anyway, we found 17 letters that didn't have all the criteria, mostly not listing which vaccines they were opting out of and some without an expiration date. We sent these back to the schools, the schools contacted the parents, and 15 of the parents got a corrected letter from their doctors. All this was done by myself and my boss at the health department. You probably weren't directly involved with any of this, right?"

"Well, I was the contact point at the school district for all the nurses to send their reports in to. And I'll tell you what, some of the nurses faxed me some of those original exemption letters. With all the PII there for anyone to see. I'm glad you got on that quickly. But with all the PII removed, what good did the letters ultimately do you? I mean, I figured that the real reason for the MEPP program was to find out which doctors were writing exemptions so we could sic the medical board on them. Maybe get their licenses to practice medicine revoked. I don't even know for sure if that was the ultimate motive. It's a shame the AG's office couldn't join us for our MEPP meetings. After all, it's the attorney general's office that would have been in charge of prosecuting any doctors we found who were trying to skirt the law. Anyway, once they removed the doctors' PII, did the letters even do you any good?"

"Well, yes. The first letters we got had all the information we'd need to track these doctors down. And each doctor's letter had a unique formatting and layout. So, as later letters came in without all the PII, we could still tell what doctor wrote it by matching it with what we already knew."

"So what ended up going wrong? Sounds like you guys did things at least by the letter of the law, after you straightened out the HIPAA problem."

"Well, it may have something to do with the medical board, I suspect. Some school nurses, in addition to sending exemption letters to the public health department for the MEPP program, also started reporting doctors to the state medical board for writing exemptions. And they'd send in the exemption letters to the medical board with all the PII on them."

"Well, there doesn't seem to be anything wrong with that. I mean, as far as the nurses reporting the doctors."

"No, but the school nurses sharing the students' PII with the medical board may have violated HIPAA. In reality, they really only had the right to identify the doctor in their complaints. They shouldn't have shared the students' personal info without the parents' permission. They violated HIPAA the same way they did with the MEPP program."

"But is it really illegal? I mean, yeah, maybe it was illegal for the school nurse to share the PII, but was it illegal for the medical board investigator to *accept* the PII, and act on it and go after the doctors?"

"I think you are right. My boss had me check into that so we would know whether or not the public health department had any liability in this for what the school nurses did. We don't care about what the medical board investigator did. First, the school nurse may have broken State Health and Safety Code Section 120440, which highlights the school's responsibility for confidentiality of medical records and their civil and *criminal* liability if they break it. The law states that schools may share info with health departments in the event of a declared state of emergency, but does not include the medical board as one of the departments they are allowed to share it with. And there are a bunch of grey areas, such as needing a parent's permission before the school shares this info with anybody. Then there's the federal FERPA law. The Family Educational Rights and Privacy

Act. This states that schools can share information with certain other educational programs without parent's consent, but not outside the educational system without their consent, and that school medical records are also under this restriction. Then there is HIPAA, which states that sharing these full exemption letters, with the PII on them, with the health department is only allowed in a declared state of emergency. I'm no lawyer, but sharing them with the medical board seems like a big nope."

"Wow. So what happened to the school nurse?"

"Nothing, so far. Parents can sue over this type of thing and get monetary compensation, but I don't know if they have, or if the school nurses were ever punished. I think this whole thing is still pending. But that's not all the school nurses are doing. Some are now actually denying exemption letters turned in by parents."

"Wait, can they do that?"

"No. I've no idea why these nurses think they have the authority to countermand a letter from a patient's personal physician. I think the nurses are getting such orders from higher up, but I don't know for sure. They are telling parents, 'I'm sorry, your letter is missing a few words that are required to be on an exemption letter,' or 'I'm sorry, we don't accept exemptions based on family history of vaccine problems, just exemptions when your particular child has already suffered a severe reaction.' But that totally goes against what the vaccine law actually says. It says it in plain English, right there in the law: 'circumstances including family history for which the physician does not recommend immunization, that child shall be exempt.' Plus, our own state's medical board wrote a blurb in their newsletter about the new vaccine law, instructing doctors that, and I quote, 'when issuing a medical exemption, a physician *must* consider the family medical history of the child.' Not *can*, must. So I don't know how these nurses can justify what they are doing."

"So, they just don't let the kid into school, even though the child has a legit medical exemption letter?"

"Oh no, they eventually have to, because that's the law. After the parent comes back into school to argue about it for the fifth time and gets the principle, and maybe a lawyer, involved, and maybe after the first few days of school have gone by. *Then* the nurse says, 'Oh, I'm sorry. This was all a misunderstanding. I misread your letter. Of course your child can come to school. I am just sooooo sorry. My mistake.'"

"Are school nurses really like that? I hope that's the exception and not the rule. You'd think parents would sue over this. Maybe some will. Anyway, let's go back to the doctors who are the objects of these nurse's complaints to the medial board. What's happening to them?"

"Well, I'm sure the medical board will likely investigate the doctors. That could take years though. As for the MEPP program, now that the public health department has ended it and reported that they found virtually all exemption letters were up to standard, and got the substandard ones up to par, they're calling it a successful pilot project that is no longer needed. And they're probably hoping no one will actually call them out on the HIPAA violations. But I think the real reason they shut down the program is that they don't want all these violations to come back and haunt them. They may be hoping parents just forget it happened."

"And the medical board? How hard are they going to be on these doctors?"

"That remains to be seen. One of the legislators who wrote the new mandatory vaccine law has appeared on the news saying that he is working with the medical board to make sure doctors are evaluating medical exemptions properly, and that any who are not deserve to be punished. And he's been very critical of doctors who write medical exemptions using criteria he doesn't agree with. However, his partner, the other legislator who co-wrote the law, seems to be trying to keep things on the up-and-up. He's been quoted as saying he does not support any attempt by the medical board to try to intimidate doctors."

"Wow. Sounds like a decent guy. But why would the medical board try to intimidate doctors? Isn't the board supposed to protect doctors?"

"Really? No. Medical boards are there for *consumer* protection – the patients. They crack down on negligent doctors."

"But writing medical exemptions isn't negligence, especially if a family has suffered severe reactions to vaccines."

"I agree. But the medical board is already investigating a number of doctors for doing just that. I know of another school district who gave a stack of exemptions from one doctor in their area to the medical board, and the board investigator – a different one than my prior example – has been submitting repeated accusations against that doctor. Poor girl is spending tens of thousands of dollars she doesn't have to defend herself, dollars she can't afford, as pediatricians are probably the lowest-paid doctors there are. I've seen some of her exemption letters. They seem pretty thorough to me. I think someone is really trying to put a stop to all exemptions, but I don't really know for sure."

"So, whose bright idea was the MEPP, anyway?"

"I think this came all the way from the state capitol. Like I said, someone up there doesn't want any children to be excused from vaccines, except, I assume, kids who have suffered serious and permanent harm. And the MEPP program was a first attempt to find doctors who excuse patients who've had less severe reactions, like seizures, moderate allergic reactions, developmental regression, or temporary injuries. And now it's up to the medical board to scare doctors away from excusing these patients."

"I'll tell you what, Terry. If my kid had a bad reaction to a vaccine, like that one student you told me about last week – anaphylactic shock – I sure as hell wouldn't want to give *any* vaccines again. Even if it was just a seizure reaction or a moderate allergic reaction, or some sort of temporary but serious reaction, I wouldn't want to keep shooting up my kid. And I probably wouldn't give my next kid the vaccines either. But I'd want my kids to be able to stay in school."

"I hear you, Carlos. I hear you. But eventually, the way things are going, only kids who have near-death experiences from the most severe reactions will be allowed a medical excuse."

Chapter 22

Should Have Let It Go To Voicemail

"So, how do we decide who's exempt from vaccines for medical reasons and who is not?"

Four heads turned toward the senator expectantly, but she had dozed off. Jackson Jones couldn't blame her. The leather couch chairs in this Four Seasons suite would have put anyone to sleep. And the scotch probably didn't help either. Jackson elbowed her respectfully. "Doctor. Pardon me, there's a question for you."

Dr. Donaldson sat up in her chair and smiled. "Sorry, guys. It's been a very long week. You'd think, as a surgeon, that I'd be used to these long hours. Maybe I'm getting too old for this."

Polite chuckles all around from the other leather couch chairs and scotch glasses.

"We do appreciate you coming out here to Minnesota, Senator. We know you are selflessly giving up your time to help more states follow your state's, and California's, lead. You have our thanks. So, what we are wondering is how you figured out what kids can be exempt from vaccines for medical reasons. If we are going to make vaccines mandatory for school and daycare here too, we want to know how we figure out which kids can opt out for medical reasons, and what those reasons might be."

"Well," began the surgeon, "We followed California's lead on this, and it went down pretty much the same way for us. Our bill started out saying that kids could only opt out if they had a contraindication.

Essentially, they would need to have had a near-death experience from a previous vaccine in order to opt out of future doses. And only future doses of that vaccine. They'd still have to get all the rest. That's what I wanted, anyway. But I had to compromise because, in reality, very few people meet contraindication criteria."

"That can happen? Near-death? Or even death?"

"Oh no. Of course it can't. But sometimes children coincidentally suffer a catastrophic life-threatening medical emergency on the day of vaccination that is likely unrelated, but because it's related *in timing* to the vaccination, more doses of that shot are contraindicated."

"Like a seizure, or an allergic reaction like hives all over the body. Things like that?"

"Well, no. Not exactly. Those are just moderate reactions, and ultimately harmless."

Looks were exchanged by the Minnesotans, which went unnoticed by the doctor but not by Jones, who came to the rescue, like he always had to when someone asked an off-script question.

"What the doctor means is that the medical community has a very strict definition of what's considered a contraindication. It's a short list of life-threatening reactions that make that vaccine off-limits for that person. No exceptions. Even if a patient wanted that vaccine again, the doctor couldn't give it. It's not a judgment call, it's a federal law. And there are some temporary contraindications like pregnancy and recent blood transfusions, or steroid therapy. And that's the guideline we wanted to follow in California because that's the standard of care nationwide. But ..." Jackson's cell phone rang. He looked at the screen and said, "I need to take this. Why don't you five take a break from this for a few minutes. I don't want to miss the discussion." *And I don't want this idiot to put her foot in her mouth ... again.* He stepped out of the room.

But Donaldson liked eating feet. "Anyway, my fellow senators insisted that children with even moderate reactions be able to opt out," she continued. "Things like seizures, moderate allergic reactions, temporary nerve injuries, temporary shock, things that people recover from and are ultimately harmless, but seem scary at the time."

"Shock? Shock would be considered a harmless reaction?"

"Well, yes, by most doctors. But most legislators aren't doctors … uh, no offense … so they don't really know medicine like I do. But they wouldn't listen to me on this. So, we had to take 'contraindications' out of the bill and make medical exemptions based on 'circumstances for which the physician does not recommend immunization.' That's the exact language we used, same as California."

"Sounds like the other legislators wanted medical exemptions to be left up to the discretion of each person's individual physician, doesn't it? Instead of a list somewhere?"

"Yes. I didn't like it, but I had no choice. You see, some of the legislators had family members who had moderately bad vaccine reactions, and they wanted this bill to not impinge on schooling for people who had reactions like they did. One of the assemblymen whined that he had a nephew with autism, and that family didn't want to vaccinate their next baby."

"What does autism have to do with vaccines?"

"I know, right? But his sister – the mom of the autistic child – insisted that the autism signs started within 2 days of the kid's one-year shots. As if that can even happen." Again, oblivious to the questioning glances between her guests. "But this Assemblyman was on the Health Committee, and I needed his vote. The bill wouldn't have passed the committee without it. So, I had to insert a family history clause into the bill. Essentially, doctors can consider an exemption if the child's family has severe vaccine reactions or medical conditions they think are related to vaccines.

"Personally, I'd encourage you to start with contraindication language. Actually, don't even have any medical exemptions in your bill at the start. Let the opposition bring it up, and you can act like you are meeting them half way with it. Then try to keep exemptions limited to contraindications. Maybe none of them will think of diluting it down like we, and California, had to.

"Oh, and speaking of diluting your bill, I'll tell you something else we learned from California: allow the opposition to dilute the bill *for* you. If California had gotten their bill passed as originally written, over 200,000 kids could have been denied school entrance in the upcoming school year. Some of those kids were only missing one or two shots, but many were from families who don't vaccinate at all. But can you imagine the crap-storm if that many kids had been denied school all at once? All together? The march on Sacramento would have been ground-breaking – literally. In fact, I wonder if the bill would even have passed if that many parents were simultaneously pissed off. And public schools would have lost a ton of funding. Private schools might have even chosen to ignore the new law because it would have put them out of business overnight, or they might have sued for unnecessary governmental interference in their business. The mass exodus of schoolchildren would have been quite a spectacle. So, an amendment was allowed into the bill that grandfathered kids in until 7th grade. Meaning the unvaccinated kids were allowed to stay in school until 7th, then they were kicked out or had to start vaccinating. We did the same thing in our state. Although I didn't like it at first, in hindsight I'd say it was brilliant. It divided and conquered the opposition. Instead of 200,000 pissed off parents with kids kicked out simultaneously, there were only about 20,000 or so affected right away. Everyone whose kids were allowed to stay in school had no reason to fight, and by the time the next wave of kids were kicked out the following year it was too late to do anything about the new law. So each year there will be a smaller number of angry parents, which is much easier to handle politically. If your opposition proposes something similar, I'd take it, and feign reluctance. And if they *don't* offer it, maybe hold it out as an olive branch."

One of the Minnesotan senators leaned into his neighbor and muttered several words. The neighbor answered back quietly, both nodding their heads.

"So, back to the doctors. How are your doctors handling this? And what are they doing in California? How many kids are getting medical exemptions?"

"Well, that's the good news. First of all, over 99% of California doctors won't even evaluate kids for medical exemptions from vaccines. Same with my state. They are all too scared."

"Scared of what?"

"Oh, of being ostracized by their colleagues. Losing patients who don't want to be around other non-vaccinating families. Losing their medical licenses."

"Why would they lose their medical licenses?"

"For writing bogus medical exemptions, of course," said Donaldson, looking a little confused that that wasn't obvious. But then again, these four weren't doctors like her.

"I thought you said it was up to the discretion of the child's personal physician. Wouldn't that doctor know the child best?"

"That's the beauty of it. It ultimately doesn't matter what the individual physicians think, because to grant medical exemptions from vaccination for reasons outside of the list of contraindications goes against the standard of care. So ..."

"Wait, you lost us there. You took contraindication out of the law, but now you say that's what exemptions should be based on?"

"Right. Considering family history and moderate reactions in a medical exemption case isn't how most other physicians would look at it. That's how the standard of care is determined: how would most doctors in your area handle a case. And nationwide, contraindication is the standard of care for exemptions."

"Wait, let's go back to what most physicians do. You said that 99% of physicians don't even take these cases. So, how could they be setting the standard of care if they aren't even doing it? It would seem to me that the physicians who *are* evaluating these kids are setting that standard."

"But they aren't going to be around for long, because I have the medical board harassing them. They'll either lose their licenses or stop writing exemptions for reasons of family history and severe reactions that aren't contraindications. So, if you need to compromise on your bill even to the extent that I had to, it's OK. You'll get what you want in the end – 100% vaccination statewide in every school.

"Meanwhile, I have also instructed our state director of school nurses to tell all her underlings statewide to challenge parents who try to turn in a medical exemption from a doctor. You could tell your school nurses to do the same. First, don't accept their medical exemption letter when they first try to register for school. Tell the parents the letter doesn't have all the correct wording on it and they can't accept it. The parents have to spend a week or more getting their doctor to rewrite the letter. Then the nurses tell the parents that they can't accept an exemption letter that's based only on family history of medical problems or vaccine reactions. So then the parents start to freak out, and as the first day of school approaches some will just go ahead and get the shots their kids are missing. Some will push back against the nurse and go to the school principle, or maybe even lawyer-up, and eventually the nurse will have to accept the letter. But this approach gets at least some of these parents to cave; parents seriously start to panic at the thought that little Johnny or Sally won't be able to attend the first day of school. And for those parents who stand their ground and eventually get around the nurse, at least their unvaccinated kids are kept out of our schools for another week or two. Either way, our schools are made safer."

More hushed conversations between all four of the Minnesotans this time, then "Well, Doctor, this has been very enlightening. You've given us a lot to think about. Let's call it a day. What are your plans after this?"

"Oh, Mr. Jones is working on that. We are trying to hit every state in the North Midwest before heading back home again. Got to spread the gospel, right?"

The four Senators didn't shake her hand as they left. Donaldson didn't even notice.

Jackson clicked off his call and stood numbly for a minute. *Nobody? Not a single co-sponsor? No one at all?* He couldn't believe it. After all the momentum he and Jane had gained from their mandatory vaccination law, Jackson, and his superiors, had assumed that Jane's next bill – the children's rights bill – would be a walk in the park. *Who the hell doesn't want children's rights?*

Apparently everybody ... at least right now.

The children's rights bill would have allowed their state to intervene on behalf of all children if the State deemed that the parents weren't making the right medical or educational decisions for their kids. Protect children from stupid parents. Who wouldn't want that?

Just about every parent, it would seem.

Even though a similar bill fell dead in California, Jackson had thought he could get it to fly in his own state. *I mean Donaldson's state*, he self-corrected. He'd approached every legislator who co-sponsored the vaccine bill, and they'd all turned him down. The phone call he just received was his last "no thank you." And Jackson now just realized why. Jane had become *persona non grata*. Poison. No one wanted to touch her. All the legislators who had lined up to support the vaccine bill had received so much backlash from their constituents that none of them wanted to sign up for round two.

And her latest idea, again stemming from California, which she had dropped on him yesterday, was even worse. Donaldson was sick and tired of people posting bogus vaccine information online and on social media. Some of these posts attacked her personally for her role in passing her vaccine law. So, her "brilliant" solution was to put forward a bill that would prevent people from writing and posting whatever they wanted to online. And not just about vaccines – about *everything*. No more written ideas anywhere unless it was fact-checked, verified true, and backed up by research. Well, Jones had read *1984* along with every other person on the planet, and the idea of having real-life *thought police* worried even *him*. Plus, there was that tiny little matter of the 1st Amendment and all. *Is Donaldson losing it, or does she really and truly think this is a good idea?* Jones wasn't sure which of those two choices was worse.

Oh well. I guess we'll have to find a new legislator. But Jackson had no idea who that might be.

"Do you think she's serious? Like, she actually believes what she is saying?"

"That's what's so scary ... yes."

Senator Longfellow swirled his glass and watched the half-melted ice make a circle around his drink. An echoing soft clink told him that Senator Waterman was doing the same.

Now this *is scotch,* he thought. *Not that crap that guy Jones poured us.*

"I mean, I'm in favor of vaccines just like you are. Hell, we all are, right? But what she's talking about? Midwest folk would never stand for that, don't you know?"

"Yeah. Heck, no American should. I don't know what they're doing out there in her state, or in California, but it sure as hell isn't democracy."

"And she's a Democrat too, just like us."

"Not like us though."

The two old friends sat in silence for a while, letting the ambiance of the bar soak in.

"Messing with how a man makes a living? Especially a doctor?"

"Yeah. No senator belongs in a doctor's office, telling doctors what to do. Doctoring should be left up to the doctor ... and the patient."

"And what was that about working with the medical board in her state? Can she even do that? I thought we had constitutional separation of powers for a reason. We legislators make the laws, and the executive branch enforces those laws. They don't work together because that's a huge conflict of interest. But I see what she's doing. She had to compromise with a watered-down version of her law in order to make it through committee. Without that compromise, it wouldn't have passed. And now she's using her state medical board to harass doctors who are simply following that law as written. In effect, she's making sure the law is based on contraindications after all. I gotta hand it to her. It's pretty brilliant."

"Yeah, I'm positive it wasn't her. No way she'd think three steps ahead like that. Someone smarter than she is pulled them strings."

"I wonder if anyone will call her out on it."

"Would serve her right. Plus, she's messing with a system that's working just fine already. I betcha she'll have even more people in her state refusing vaccines now that she's trying to force them, don't you know?"

"The way I see it, if someone has a seizure after vaccines, they don't need to get anymore. And what did she call it? A harmless reaction? Not in my book."

"My niece has been trying to tell me for years that something like that happened to her kid. A seizure the day of his vaccines, then he stopped talking, and now he has special needs. I thought she was crazy. But under this type of law, her kid wouldn't be able to go to school anymore. Keeping kids out of school makes no sense."

"I can see re-vaccinating if something really bad is going around. Like polio or something. But that doesn't even happen nowadays."

"What about those Africans over in Hennepin County that all had measles? It was also in Ramsey and Le Sueur. I hear they weren't vaccinated."

"Well, that was their choice, right? And it didn't spread around. I remember there were state-wide warnings to be on the lookout, but it never really amounted to much. It was easily contained. Plus, it was measles. You and I both had measles when we were kids."

"Yup."

"You know what that Jones guy said to me this morning when I asked him if the Disneyland measles outbreak played a role in California getting this law passed? He said it sure did. It was timed perfectly, like he was glad it happened. And I actually think he *was*. So I asked him if we missed the measles boat with our own outbreak, meaning that since it died down before we even finished with the first draft of our bill, it will probably be long forgotten by the time our bill starts heating up."

"And what did he say?"

"He said don't worry about it. They got themselves a new study that shows what could happen if measles vaccination rates drop too low. Kind of a doomsday scenario. A mathematical model that shows how dangerous it could be. They are holding its publication until someone needs it. Or until several states need it to push their agendas forward, he hopes. So we should just proceed as planned and he'll make sure the study drops when it will be most useful. And, he said, who knows? Maybe we'll get lucky and have a real measles outbreak again."

More silence. And scotch.

"I'm glad we met with Donaldson. Geeze, we all thought this law would be a great idea right? On the surface. But underneath? There's a lot we wouldn't have thought about. Nice of them to drop by."

Chapter 23

Simple Math

J udy Carlson thought the verdict would bring some sort of relief. Some sort of escape from the pain. Vindication. But no. Her heart was still empty – a void that no amount of money could fill.

Judy had liked the pediatrician for the first 20 minutes of her baby's 2-month checkup, now so long ago. He had taken his time answering her simple questions. He had talked at length about several health and safety issues for two-month-olds, including making sure baby is properly secured in the car seat, nurses enough to grow well, gets his tummy-time exercise, and even several important tips on SIDS prevention, including making sure he sleeps on his back, no one who smokes sleeps in the same room as the baby, and a fan is used to keep fresh air circulating. He had seemed to be in no hurry at all, not like other doctors her friends had complained about. He'd then stood up, as if the appointment was coming to an end, and said, "The nurse will come in with the baby's vaccines. And we'll see you at 4 months for another checkup."

"I do have a few questions about the vaccines though," Judy had tried to explain. "I do want them, of course, but I have a few concerns."

"The nurse will give you some paperwork to read. That should address any of your concerns." And with that, the doctor had been out of there.

Judy Carlson had planned to get baby James vaccinated, but she'd wanted to ask the doctor about spreading the shots out a bit: get

286

some this visit, then finish off with the rest at three months. She was planning to do the same at 4 and 5 months, and so on. She'd thought this would be safer, and had wanted to ask the doctor about side effects from the two shots she was planning for that day – DTaP and Rotavirus.

The nurse had come in with some paperwork – two-page handouts about six different vaccines. "I'd like to only do a couple vaccines today, if that's ok," Judy had said timidly. "DTaP and Rotavirus."

"Oh dearie, there's nothing to worry about. It's only a few shots. It's easier to just get them all done with," the nurse had tried to persuade her.

But Judy had stood her ground, for all the good that it had done her baby in the end, and after reading the two-page information sheets about the two vaccines, the nurse had administered the one injection and the one oral vaccine.

And he'd died that night. SIDS was the diagnosis: Sudden Infant Death Syndrome. Her husband, Jim, had been the one to find him early morning, lying on his back in the crib, just as she'd left him hours earlier after a middle-of-the-night feeding. He wasn't breathing. He was limp, lifeless, and blue. 911, the ambulance, CPR, and the Emergency Room staff's best efforts had been in vain.

And now, just a few hours ago, five years after the death of their baby, after years of gut-wrenching research, preparation, and testimony, they'd gotten a verdict from the vaccine court Special Master:

"In this case, I have determined, after reviewing all the data, that the vaccines played a significant role in the death of J.C.; he likely would not have died without the effects of the vaccines. The role of inflammatory cytokines as neuro-modulators in the infant brain has been thoroughly researched and published and is likely one of several reasons for a number of SIDS deaths occurring when babies catch mild infections. It is my conclusion that it is likely the vaccine-stimulated cytokines found in the brain of J.C. had a similar effect and more likely than not contributed to his death."

Their lawyer congratulated them, warned them not to reveal the amount of compensation the court had awarded, and walked them out of the courthouse through a side door to avoid the media. But it really didn't matter how many millions of dollars they'd be getting. It would never be enough – no amount would.

Judy now sat in the extra bedroom that they still hadn't filled with another life, and continued to re-live that day, trying to find something, anything, she could have done differently. *I could have decided to just wait on the vaccines, that's what.* But that thought had echoed through her mind thousands of times ever since, to no avail.

What made her angry still, after all these years, is how the doctor that day had spent so much time lecturing her on stuff she already knew, including SIDS prevention, and never even once asked her what *she* wanted to take about. And when *her* concern happened to be about vaccines, he had no more time. *I just don't get it. Vaccines are a complicated intervention with dramatic effects on the immune system and the whole body. Yes, they may provide some immunity, but they do a whole lot more. So why is it that the doctor, and every doctor for that matter, won't give any patient the time of day to discuss the single most significant medical intervention their baby will ever have? We can talk for hours about eating, sleeping, diaper rash, and behavior. But try to talk about the 70 doses of vaccines a baby is supposed to get throughout their childhood? Nope. There's no time, and it isn't necessary. It's like, vaccines are just automatic. People think they are so simple. They are not.*

She and her husband had learned a lot during their court preparation. Most of it came from their lawyer, who'd done this many times before, like the fact that the vaccine Package Insert, or PI, for the brand of DTaP their doctor used actually had SIDS listed as a reported adverse event following the release of the vaccine into the general population. But it had been Jim who noticed something on their baby's autopsy that gelled with some of the SIDS research: inflammatory cytokines. These were chemicals released by the immune system in response to infection or vaccination. And the autopsy had found extremely elevated levels in the medulla part of James's brain. The lawyers for the Department of Health and Human Services couldn't explain that. There was no evidence of any recent illness or infection. All those tests came up negative. The only known recent event that would raise cytokines was vaccination. Most parents with SIDS right after vaccines lost their case in years past because numerous universities and medical centers had published research showing there was no link between the two. But this was new information, and the Special Master listened to it because there already was research that showed vaccines triggered inflammatory cytokine production as the immune system reacted to the vaccines.

Judy had no illusions that the medical community would suddenly admit there's a connection. They'd find a way to explain away the cytokines. And mainstream medicine was already taking steps to hide any connection between SIDS and vaccines by changing its name to Sudden Unexplained Infant Death. She suspected they thought that by losing a catchy acronym it wouldn't be as easy to talk about. And by spinning it as 'unexplained' instead of a 'syndrome' people would buy the lie that there couldn't be a cause. It just happens, for no reason at all. Just like when they changed ITP – a potentially-severe bleeding disorder that can be triggered by some vaccines and will, in some cases, lead to stroke – to BTP: Benign Thrombocytopenic Purpura. That way, even when it *does* happen after vaccines, that's okay because it's "benign."

But Judy would forever know that her baby died of SIDS caused by a vaccine. *And maybe our case will help others think twice before they agree to vaccination – even partial vaccination. I thought giving just one shot would be safe. But this just goes to show that you never know, until it's too late.*

They wouldn't use the money for themselves. But they'd find a way to use it for good and warn others what can happen.

If only I had known. If only someone had told me, *"Judy, don't do it. It's just not safe for a small minority of babies, and there's no way to know if your baby will be one of those who react." She'd make sure each and every parent who faces vaccination for their baby would be informed about the possible reactions. Everyone has the right to know the risk.*

The fact that her doctor had spent so much time warning her how to prevent SIDS – or SUID – then demanded that she accept the very thing that ended up causing it, was something that Judy wasn't sure she could ever get over.

Judy had done the math: there were about 1600 annual SIDS deaths in recent years, down a bit from the 2000 it had been every year before that.

And how many young babies died of vaccine-preventable diseases in the first year of life? She'd done the math on that too:

Pertussis – about 20

Flu – about 20

HIB meningitis – 1 or 2

Pneumococcal disease (pneumonia, meningitis) – unknown, because it wasn't a reportable disease; but not more than 300

Rotavirus – about 5

All the other vaccine-preventable diseases? Either none, or occasionally 1.

This thought hurt more than any other – that a baby is statistically about three times as likely to die of SIDS than of a vaccine-preventable disease. At least that's how she looked at it. *So, if there is a connection, why would anyone ever choose vaccination? And that's why the government, and the mainstream medical community, won't ever admit it's possible. Because that knowledge would just be too dangerous ... and costly. And that's why we'll continue to see a study published every few years that reassures people vaccines don't cause SIDS. And the warning that they* can *will forever stay hidden in the small print of a vaccine warning label no one ever reads.*

Chapter 24

A Bathroom Too Far

Half way through the day, right before lunchtime, Jaelen saw the last patient she would ever see as a nurse. It was time to move on, and she came to terms with that. But it was still sad. Ever since she'd had to watch her grandmother wither away to nothing from cancer, she'd wanted to be a nurse. That's all she ever wanted to be. To help the sick. To serve people when they were at their most vulnerable.

Nursing school was actually the easy part. She was a top-notch student academically. It was a lot of work, but she was good at work. Jaelen was also an open-minded person. She was easy-going and flexible. She could brush quite a bit off her shoulder before something got to her. So she'd thought nursing would be perfect for her. And at first it was.

But one can only take so much, and the years of know-it-all doctors, you-are-just-a-nurse doctors, and I-am-God doctors had finally taken their toll, and this morning was the last straw. She knew that if she didn't quit, she'd be fired anyway. And she also knew that she wasn't going to try nursing anywhere else. She was done. Yeah, there might be a doctor or two out there somewhere who was kind, open-minded, flexible, and there to serve his patients, but she hadn't been able to find one to work for yet, and she was done trying.

This morning the Samson family had come in for their one-year. Little Julie was such a cutie. Jaelen had placed them in their room, tried, unsuccessfully, to do all the measurements, chatted with mom for a little while, and had observed the toddler as she walked around the room exploring. She wanted to get into everything, and wouldn't spend more than two seconds on any one part of the room. Except the drawers in the desk. She was quite fascinated with how they opened and closed, opened and closed, again and again … and again. Jaelen realized that the toddler hadn't even looked at her. *She should either be scared of me, or in love with me. But it's like I'm not even here.* And any attempt to weigh, measure, or approach her in any way was met with an impressive display of resistance. She kept a smile on her face, told Mrs. Samson that the doctor would be right in, and closed the door.

Not another one, she groaned. The groan wasn't for herself; it was for the mom. Because Jaelen knew what Mom was in for if Julie's development didn't turn back around and start going in the right direction again. Jaelen remembered seeing them at nine months. *Julie was just fine then. Now she's changed.* Jaelen had seen three other Samson children grow up healthy, without a single developmental concern. One of the boys was very large, like his daddy. Eileen Samson said they were hoping to make a football player out of him someday. *Her dad was some bigwig high up in the NFL.* Things like this were even more heart-breaking to see happen to a family she already knew and loved. And she was determined to make sure this little child didn't regress any more.

Jaelen knew that most doctors believed the research that showed vaccines are not connected to autism. But she also knew that the research had some serious limitations. First, no one has studied the complete vaccine schedule to see if it increases the risk of autism. All the mainstream research was focused on only two aspects of vaccination: 1. Is the MMR vaccine connected to autism? and 2. Is the mercury in vaccines connected to autism? That's all that mainstream medicine can claim that their research has looked at. No one can claim that vaccines in general, especially the entire vaccine schedule, are not connected to autism. *It's almost as if they've purposely avoided that research. Like they picked two narrow areas that they knew they could prove were unrelated, and no one realizes it.*

These thoughts ran through Jaelen's head as she stood outside the Samson's room wondering what to do. Then she noticed Dr. Alice Choi walking toward her, head down, looking at her phone.

"Dr. Choi, the Samsons are ready for you," Jaelen said as the doctor stopped in front of her. "And I'd like to mention something I observed about ..."

"Hold on a sec," pausing long enough from her two-handed texting to hold one of her fingers up in the air at her. "Ok. What is it?"

"I noticed some red flags in Julie. She's ..."

"Lemme look at her developmental questionnaire," cutting Jaelen off and taking the paper chart out of her hands. "Mom answered all the 12-month questions perfectly. I don't see any reason for concern."

"But you haven't even seen them yet. Watch how she ..."

"Thanks for your concern, nurse. I will take a look. Really, I will." And through the door she went.

"Jaelen, you have an order up," Wendy stuck her head into the lunch room to let Jaelen know.

What? What possible orders could Dr. Choi have for me on a one-year-old who is showing obvious signs of autism? Surely she isn't planning on ... Jaelen stepped out into the hallway, took Julie's chart out of the rack, and there it was. MMR, Varicella, and Hepatitis A vaccines. *Is she serious?*

She saw the doctor heading into her office for her own lunch and walked quickly to catch her before she closed her door. Because you don't interrupt Alice Choi during her lunch hour.

"Dr. Choi, can I ask what you thought of Julie Samson?" she asked, standing in her doorway. "Her development?"

"She seemed fine to me, Jaelen." *So she does know my name.* "She's not banging her head against the wall, flapping her hands, toe-walking, or anything like that. Ok, so she doesn't have any real words yet, I'll give you that, but neither do most one-year-olds these days. I know what you're thinking. But I can assure you, Julie Samson does not have autism." And with that, she closed the door.

I can't do it, Jaelen thought. *I just can't. Not again. I've seen too many of these borderline-developing kids get suddenly worse after their one-year vaccines. Yeah, I still don't know if vaccines actually cause autism, and all the scientists say they don't, but I've seen it be a trigger too many times. Like, the final straw. The factor that tips them over the edge. Maybe some would have developed autism anyway even without vaccines, but maybe some wouldn't if they hadn't vaccinated. Maybe vaccines might make the autistic problems much more severe for some kids.* Jaelen didn't know. She just knew what she'd seen happen over and over again to too many families.

If Peter was still here, or even Dr. Jameson, they would understand, she thought. *They know.*

She saw Dr. Goldstein come out of a room.

"Alan," she got his attention, glad that the main boss didn't mind first names when they weren't around patients. "I have a patient ... well, one of Dr. Choi's patients ... who is showing some early signs of autism. I spoke to Dr. Choi about holding the vaccines for a while and ..."

"Let me guess, she said no?"

"Yes. I mean, correct. I know there's no evidence of a vaccine/autism connection in most studies, but ..."

"Listen, Jaelen. We've talked about this. You are right, there is no connection. Even if this child *was* showing some signs, I'd still do the vaccines."

"But I was just reading last night, and I wanted to run this by you. One of the vaccine PIs says that you should hold vaccines if there is an unstable neurological disorder, and autism is very unstable in its early stages."

"I've read that too, Jaelen. I've read all the PIs, at Peter's insistence back when he was here. That section of the PI doesn't apply to autism. It's for extremely severe neurological disorders. Besides, it's Alice's patient. You know I'm not going to over-ride her."

His pat on her shoulder wasn't any consolation as he walked away. *Well, at least he's human enough to have a conversation with me about it,* Jaelen mused as she walked slowly back down the hallway to the nurse's station, chart in hand. And that was when she realized that this chart, the chart of this precious little girl, one of several charts for a family that she'd grown very close to over the past several years, was the last medical chart of a patient of hers that she would ever hold. Because she knew this was the last one. There would never be another, and that broke her heart.

She pulled three vials out of the vaccine fridge: MMR, Varicella, and Hepatitis A. Three syringes and two vials of vaccine diluent came out of the drawer in front of her. She uncapped the two vials of diluent in order to draw them up and mix them with the two live virus vaccines. But her hands shook too much for her to even get the needle into the first vial. She took a deep breath. *You can do this, girl. It's the last one. It's just one more. Then you're done.*

Jaelen tried again, but the shaking was worse. She re-capped the needle and set everything down.

"What's wrong, J?" Allison walked up and put her arm around her co-worker.

"Oh, I'm just frustrated. My hands are shaking and I can't draw up these vaccines."

She tried to smile at her friend. Probably the only true friend she'd made here at this office. The nickname Allison assigned to her was endearing, too.

"Maybe your blood sugar is low. Have you eaten anything yet?"

"Yes. I've had half my sandwich. I don't think it's blood sugar. It's ... it's just ..." Then the tears flowed freely, and Jaelen started sobbing uncontrollably.

"Oh my poor dear. Come on into the lunch room and sit down." Allison guided her into the lounge and sat her on the couch.

"What's going on girls?" This from Melinda Stephenson, the office manager, who was trying to enjoy her lunch break.

It took another two minutes for Jaelen to compose herself enough to explain. She told them everything. Julie Samson's development, her own concerns about giving these vaccines right now, Dr. Choi. She saw the look she expected to see on Melinda's face: annoyance. Turning to Allison, she saw concern. Not agreement, and not concern for the patient, but concern for a friend who might be losing it.

"Not this, again," chided Melinda. "We've talked about this before, Jaelen. We do what the doctor orders. We don't think. We don't question. We just do our jobs. And you have to get over this vaccines and autism thing. They aren't related. Yes, autism sucks. But it's not vaccines. Now, get in there and give that baby her damn shots." With that, the office manager left the lounge. She had spoken.

Jaelen sat in shock. Even Allison was surprised at the stern direction. "Oh dear, don't you worry. I'll do the shots. You just sit here and collect yourself."

"No. Don't do it, Allison. Listen to me. That child already has signs of delay. We give her these vaccines, and she'll be back in here within three days a completely different child. I've seen it too many times now. And you have too, although you don't really *see* it. The DTaP and MMR VIS forms even state clearly under the 'What if there is a serious reaction' section to beware of behavior changes or unusual behavior after the vaccines. It's right *there,* although I doubt the CDC will keep those phrases there for long: they've been altering the VIS forms lately to remove some of the side-effect information. But it's there now. Why won't anyone pay attention to the CDC's own warnings?"

"It will be fine, J. Trust me. You are over-thinking this. Sure, some kids have bad reactions. But we can't help that. I saw Julie this morning too, when they came in. She's a totally healthy little toddler. She's going to be fine. We don't want to leave little Julie susceptible to diseases, right? I told you about my niece who just got out of the hospital for pneumonia? Pneumococcal pneumonia and bacteremia. Bad diseases happen, and vaccines prevent them. I'll do the shots, but keep it quiet. If Melinda finds out that I did this, you might get fired."

"I'm leaving anyway, Allison. I just can't do this anymore. It's too heartbreaking."

"I didn't know you were thinking of leaving, Girl." Allison got a tear in her eye now too.

"I didn't know, either. Until today." Deep breath. "Thanks, but I can do these last shots. I think."

"Nope. I got it. You finish your lunch, collect yourself, then go home. I'll take you out for drinks after work and we can commiserate together then, ok?"

"Ok. Thanks Allison. I owe you one."

Jaelen watched her friend go through blurry eyes. *Should I try to stop her? Should I go warn Mrs. Samson? Will Julie's mom even listen to what must look like a raving lunatic by now?* Jaelen was numb. She couldn't move. She just sat there for a few minutes in silence.

A muted cry came from down the hallway a few minutes later.

Jaelen gathered her things, and left.

"Allison, there's a call for you. I think this was Jaelen's patient, but you inherited them the other day when she left."

"Thanks Melinda. Send it to extension 13 and I'll grab it in the hallway." Allison picked up the beeping phone next to the nurse's station. "This is Allison."

"Umm, hi Allison. This is Eileen Samson. I was there with Julie the other day. You gave her her shots because, I think, Jaelen had to leave or something."

"Yes Mrs. Samson, I remember you. How's Julie doing?"

"Well, that's why I'm calling. She's acting weird."

"Oh?" A sinking feeling started in Allison's stomach.

"She won't look me in the eye. She's banging her head against the wall. I mean, she's had fevers like this before, but this time it's different."

Allison's knees felt weak, and she let herself sink to the floor as she listened. "Well, kids just do that sometimes. She probably has a headache from the fever, and …"

"She's also tiptoeing all over the place, and flapping her hands.

She wasn't doing any of this a few days ago. I don't get it. My neighbor, who is an EMT, came over, and he said kids who have autism do all those things. But I know she doesn't have autism. Dr. Choi said her development was fine. Should I bring her back in so she can check her? Maybe she just has an ear infection again, like she did after her six-month shots."

"Yes, Mrs. Samson. You'd better bring Julie in right now and we'll see."

Allison hung up the phone, and managed to make it almost all the way to the staff bathroom before she threw up.

Chapter 25

The Silent Whistleblower

Bob couldn't believe he was having this conversation again, for the umpteenth time, and he already knew how it was going to end. He'd gotten used to seeing the signs. First came the unbelief. His colleagues simply thought it was all a hoax. Then came the concern when they realized it might actually be true. Then came a different concern when they realized who exactly they would be going up against if they chose to believe it. After that came the fear that each tried, unsuccessfully, to conceal. Fear of losing support, fear of not getting re-elected, and fear of being labeled as anti-establishment. And finally came the resolve – resolve to stick with the status quo, to not stir things up, to just let life go on as normal, to maintain the certainty that it must all be a hoax, stirred up by a crazy disgruntled scientist who obviously should have retired years ago. Because *that* belief was way easier than entertaining the possibility that what Bob Stanley had to say might be the truth.

What is wrong with people? he fumed silently. *Why won't anybody in Congress stand up for what is right anymore?* Well, he knew that wasn't quite true. Many of his colleagues were happy to stand up for what was right. But only when it wouldn't cost them their seat. And he knew as well as the next guy that you don't stand up to Big Pharma. That was almost as suicidal as standing up to Big Oil. *So why did I do it?* he asked himself, also for the umpteenth time.

Congressman Bob Stanley had been approached by the lawyers

representing Dr. Laura Johnson three years ago and had dropped the bombshell: Dr. Johnson claimed she had participated in research fraud, and she was now coming forward to fess up and make things right. She'd been granted official whistleblower status by the President, and had turned over all her research documents to the Congressman. Bob Stanley and his team had read through the boxes of data and confirmed that Dr. Johnson was telling the truth, at least as she saw it. Dr. Johnson, along with four other scientists, had allegedly published a falsified study that "proved" vaccines do not increase the risk of autism. The fraud occurred when, according to Johnson, the team discovered that vaccines, and the MMR vaccine in particular, did seem to increase the risk of autism in African-American boys. So the team of five gathered together and burned some of their data – literally. Burned it in a trash can. But Johnson, realizing what was about to happen, copied all of the data and kept it safe before joining the bonfire. And it was these documents that she turned over to Bob Stanley's office.

The research team had then changed the parameters of the research study, eliminated some of the test subjects who'd come down with autism in the study, allegedly, and published a squeaky clean version that gave them the results they wanted. And ten years later, Johnson's conscience caught up with her and she came forward.

When the story broke, the public was outraged, of course. For about an hour. Then everybody moved on to the next news item and forgot all about it. Except for the approximately 1 in 36 American families with autism, especially the black families. And except those fighting for more openness and honesty in vaccine safety research.

In order for Dr. Laura Johnson to be able to legally come forward with her story and remain protected by whistleblower laws, she had to be subpoenaed by Congress and be called to testify in an official hearing. Bob had tried to stir up support in his House of Representatives during a 5-minute summary presentation to the House, but his words had, so far, fallen on deaf ears. And since then he'd set up meeting after meeting with fellow Congressmen to try to get enough members to call for a hearing. He'd gotten some support from state governments, but no one on the federal level had the balls to join his crusade yet.

Numerous public organizations had also called for a hearing, and a few doctors and lawyers had published books and research articles discussing the alleged research fraud and what the raw data really showed. And tens of thousands of activists had dutifully called their senators and congressmen asking them to support a Johnson subpoena.

One state legislature – Rhode Island – just passed Resolution S2670 that called for the U.S. House of Representatives to subpoena Johnson and launch a full investigation into the research on vaccines and autism. The state also called for better informed consent for patients and more thorough safety research testing. And RI wasn't the only state to do so. Hawaii's house concurrent resolution 157 disclosed a number of vaccine safety concerns and severe reactions and called for the federal government and CDC to do better safety research, improve medical education and public awareness of vaccine side effects, and enforce better informed consent practices.

The only problem with state resolutions is that they have no power. The federal government, and the CDC, can just thumb their noses at them.

But at least it's a start, Bob mused. *What amazes me about the Johnson scandal is that everybody probably does believe those research-ers lied just to help keep vaccine safety ideals intact. But as long as Congress just looks the other way, this issue will eventually just go away. Oh, the CDC has taken quite a hit over this. And the SPIDER coming out of the closet has added fuel to the fire. Just not enough fuel.*

SPIDER was the acronym for Scientists Preserving Integrity, Diligence, and Ethics in Research. This was a group of over a dozen senior scientists at the CDC who lodged a formal written complaint in 2016 that the CDC is compromised by corporate and government interests and has lost its mission to objectively safeguard the health of our country.

SPIDER had been smart; they had steered clear of the V word. Their complaint focused more on fraud, corruption, and conflicts of interest in drug safety testing and approval, which is a politically safe position, even when it goes against Pharma. *Because it's ok to speak out against one medication that is killing people. Pharmaceutical companies can take those small hits. Seriously, if a drug starts killing old people, the public cries foul, and Pharma pays their fine (after raking in ten times more in the preceding years) and everybody moves on. But if a* vaccine *kills babies, no one cares because it's just coincidence.*

All these thoughts took about 5 seconds to run through Bob Stanley's mind before he realized Congressman Temple had asked him a question.

"I'm sorry, Thomas. What did you say?"

"Tell me more about this CDC SPIDER, Bob. I mean, if there really are over a dozen *senior* CDC scientists willing to come forward and confirm there's a problem at the CDC, that's a whole new ballgame. So, how exactly would that go down if we decided to listen to these SPIDER people?"

"That's a good question," Bob Stanley hid his surprise that the congressman showed some interest. "The challenge is this: the CDC is funded by the government, and its directors are appointed by the government – us. And all of the scientists and employees who work there are government employees. So they aren't there for the money, they are there for the science and the service to humanity. But, as with all large altruistic organizations, there will always inevitably be some who feel like they do want to make more money. And that's where Pharma comes in. Pharma gives grant money to many of these doctors so they can run research programs back at their universities. And Pharma also allows some of these scientists to own stock in their companies. It's perfectly legal, but it puts objectivity at risk. Now you have doctors doing safety studies on the drugs and vaccines made by the very companies these doctors have stock in or have received funding from, or are hoping to land a job with someday when they're done serving humanity. They all like to pretend they're objective despite this money. I wonder if they really can be.

"Then there are the doctors who sit on various approval boards at the CDC and the FDA. I mean, you know this already – Congress published two reports on this very problem, in 2000 and again in 2007. Heath and Human Services found in 2007 that 64% of the doctors serving on the ACIP – the committee that approves vaccines – had conflicts of interest that were either not disclosed or not acted upon. Meaning, some of these doctors were allowed to vote in vaccine-approval meetings on their *own* vaccines."

"Actually, no. I hadn't heard that." Thomas looked even more interested.

"But here's the problem. Who is going to enforce these rules, and who is going to bring down the hammer on this corruption? That would be us – the government. Congress. But, and I say this with all due respect to you, Thomas, because I know you have a good heart, we are bought off too. Pharma has donated so much money to most of our campaigns, that to listen to people like SPIDER and Dr. Johnson is political suicide. The only way it could happen would be for everybody in Congress to suddenly decide they are willing to give up all their Pharma money, and their seats in Congress, to do the right thing. But again, and I'll admit I've done this for other issues in the past, we convince ourselves that we have to stay because there is so much other good we can do."

"So, we accept a little bit of bad so we can do a lot of good. I know, Bob. I've told myself that many times."

"It sometimes seems like an impossible situation, with no reasonable fix," continued Congressman Stanley. "And I'm not expecting you to stick your neck out with me ... unless you really want to. I guess I'm just here so you know what's going on. So you know the truth. And see if you have any bright ideas, because I sure as hell am fresh out."

"It seems like all we would have to do is stop allowing doctors with Pharma stock to participate in policy meetings. And to be heads of departments. Crack down on that. At least that would be a start."

"But we already have that rule, Thomas. We just aren't making the CDC stick to it. It's like, they are sticking their tongues out at us to mind our own business. Like, they know we wouldn't dare enforce the rules. And, by the way, please tell me you do know that one of the former heads of the CDC allegedly held Pharma stock? $4.5 million dollars worth, supposedly. I've never been able to confirm it's true, but please tell me you've at least heard the rumor?"

Thomas looked guilty. "I just don't pay attention to that stuff. There's always just too much to do. But seriously? 4.5 mil? Holy Mary, I'd probably take that kind of money if it was offered to me. Who wouldn't?"

I wouldn't, Bob Stanley didn't say. *Would I?*

"Hey, that reminds me, Bob. I just heard the new CDC director stepped down. Apparently she, too, owns stock in pharmaceutical companies and even tobacco companies. A news outlet called her out on it and she resigned. How do people with such blatant conflicts of interest even get considered to head the CDC? No wonder it seems the public doesn't trust them anymore. Maybe now some of us in government will start taking our oversight role more seriously."

"I doubt it, Thomas. There's a new House Resolution that makes me think our own house is going to be even *less* likely to enforce the CDC's vaccine oversight rules, not *more*. It's Resolution 327. It's a very pro-vaccine resolution, which isn't necessarily a bad idea. But it has some very concerning language that goes way too far. It states that 'there is no credible evidence to show that vaccines cause life-threatening or disabling diseases in healthy children or adults.' This statement completely discounts the findings of our own federal Vaccine Adverse Events Reporting System, in which we receive about 2000 reports of life-threatening or disabling vaccine reactions every single year. Not to mention the hundreds of published research studies about severe side effects. 'No credible evidence?' Seriously? The fact that 20 Congressmen have co-sponsored this Resolution so far gives me no faith whatsoever that our government is ever going to fix the conflicts of interest at the CDC."

"Seems like an insurmountable problem, Bob."

"I could go on and on, but I'll just tell you one more way that Congress - us .... you and I - are ignoring vaccine safety. You know the 1986 Vaccine Injury Act, right? The one in which we let Pharma off the hook for any liability when someone has a severe vaccine reaction?"

The blank look on the Congressman's face said it all.

"Yeah, I didn't either until I looked. Well, part of that law demands that our own Department of Health and Human Services submits a report to Congress *every two years* that outlines what steps HHS is taking to improve vaccine safety."

"Well, that sounds like a good idea."

"That's all it turned out to be - an idea. Because in the 30 years since then, not a single such report can be found. That Kennedy lawyer just took HHS to court to demand they release these safety update reports, of which there should be, what, 15 or so by now? And HHS came up empty, according to Kennedy. They can't find a single safety report. Think about this: vaccines are killing and maiming a small minority of people, but are apparently helping the majority; the public demands something be done, so Congress creates the Vaccine Injury Compensation Fund so injured people can be paid off; Pharma gets shielded from all liability, and HHS promises they'll look into vaccine safety and update Congress every two years. That was 30 years ago, and HHS hasn't once reported to us that they are doing anything to improve safety. What does that tell you, Thomas?"

"That we don't care?"

"It's probably more like we don't *know*. It's my belief ... perhaps naïvely, but I hope not ... that if more of us knew, we'd band together and do something. Is that too much to ask of us elected officials? To actually band together to right a wrong?"

"It shouldn't be. As long as it doesn't cost us our seats."

"And that's the catch, right? As I already said, you don't stand up to Pharma if you want to stay in the game."

"But why does Pharma care so much about this one issue? Don't they make enough money off of selling medications? Aren't vaccines just a tiny part of all that?"

"I thought so, but I asked a pediatrician friend to do the math for me. Here's what Monty came up with: it would cost him about $2700 per patient if he was to buy every vaccine for that child to be given over the 18 years of his or her childhood. Some are cheap, like $20 per dose. Some are expensive: $200 or more per dose. The $2700 is what he would actually pay to pharmaceutical companies if he was to buy every vaccine for a patient. He doesn't ... buy every vaccine, that is. He gives some, but not all. Anyway, there are about 4 million kids born each year in our country. 4 million times 2700 is over 10 *billion* dollars. That's how much Pharma can make on vaccines every year - just from the kids. This doesn't include adults. If 10% of people don't vaccinate, that's a billion dollar loss to an industry. That's not pocket change. So yes, Thomas. They care. They care big time."

"You've sold me, Bob. Or bought me."

A hearty chuckle between the two friends.

"Well, I've been working on a separate issue that I'd also like to run by you. It's HR 3615, and it calls for the National Institutes of Health to take on a large study of the long-term health of unvaccinated children and see how it compares to that of vaccinated children. This gets the ball rolling on what HHS and the CDC are failing to do."

"Haven't they already done that? I mean, they'd have to, right? To make sure vaccines are safe?"

Perceptive he is, but just as naïve as most. "You'd think so, but no they haven't. In my opinion it's one of the biggest scientific oversights of this generation. We've embarked on an enormous vaccination campaign without studying long-term outcomes. And without studying a control group of kids who don't get them. I want to change that."

"Now *that* sounds like something I could get behind. But tell me, why the NIH? Why not ask the CDC to do the ... oh. Wow, *now* I see your point. You wouldn't *want* the CDC to do the study."

"Plus, we asked them five years ago, and they refused."

"They what? Can they do that?"

"Yes, they can and they did."

"What are they afraid they'll find if they do the study?"

"Exactly. At this point it would be better if an entity who is completely separate from making vaccine policy did the study. That's why I picked the NIH. Yeah, I'm sure there's some conflict of interest there too, but not nearly as much. And I will personally oversee this project to make sure it's done right. And I'm looking for some co-sponsors."

"Well Bob, send the draft over to my office and I'll take a look."

"Thanks Thomas."

Chapter 26

Always Tell Your Momma

Franklin never told his mom about the gash. He'd gotten all types of wounds and injuries over the years, and they always healed just fine without her kissing them all better. He wasn't three anymore.

But a week later when he couldn't eat his breakfast, he knew he needed his mommy.

"Come on, Franklin Junior. Finish your breakfast. The school bus'll be here any minute."

"But mom, I can't chew my food. My mouth won't work."

"Well then, finish your juice and get. I can see the bus comin' down the lane."

Backpack on, lunch box in hand, Franklin was ushered out the door and down the front porch steps, then made his own way down the dirt driveway to the country lane where the bus would stop. Amy Walker stood on the porch watching her son as the morning sun reflected off his white-blond hair. *First day of second grade. He looks so big. He'll be as tall as his daddy someday – maybe taller.*

She saw him stumble and fall. *What the …?*

"Franklin Junior! You better not scuff those brand new patches on them pants of yours!" She watched her son get up, dust off his knees, pick up his lunch box, and make it to the opened doors of the bus that only needed to wait for about 30 seconds.

That boy. Just like his daddy. Never a clean piece of clothing on him. If he comes home with ...

She saw the brake lights on the back of the bus as it came to a halt less than a minute later. The door opened, and the bus driver – *that looks like Tom Mason's boy* – waved his arms in her direction, all S.O.S. like.

What in blazes? The number of reasons why the bus would stop flashed through her mind as she made the two-minute jog down the drive, then diagonally across a corner of the field, straight in a B-line to the little crowd of children and one adult gathered around the open door. *Did that boy forget his lunch? No. Did he finally decide to stand up to that Jones bully? No, sadly. Did he have another fit? One of them seizures again? God, I hope not – he ain't had one for years. Did the bus driver have some sort of heat attack? No, there he is, standin' right there, still waving at me. I'm commin' dammit!*

The little crowd parted as Amy approached, and Joe Mason reported:

"He don't look real good, Ms. Walker. Says he can't feel his legs or somethin'."

Franklin Junior sat leaning up against the large front tire of the bus, a mixture of guilt and worry on his face. "My legs won't work right, Momma," he said, through clenched teeth. "And look at my arm?"

That was when Amy Walker knew something was seriously wrong. She stood up and turned toward the house, and called out in her shrill voice that was known across the county: "Franklin Senior!!! Get the truck started up and get it over here. Now!"

"Mrs. Walker ... Mr. Walker. I'm not 100% certain yet, but I'm pretty sure that little Franklin has tetanus."

Dr. Tom Jameson, now a grandfather himself, had heard the stories from *his* grandpa about tetanus during the War. The first War. He'd shared all kinds of stories with him and his little brother, Mike, and that's why they'd both gone into medicine. Their grandpa had been a field medic, and when he heard both his grandsons were going to be doctors, real bonafide doctors, he pulled every story he could think of out of his hat. And one particular lesson that had stuck with Dr. Jameson was about tetanus. "*See, back then all we had was horses. None of them jeeps or tanks. It was horses what got us around fast. All that horse manure and all that dirt – it was a hay day for tetanus. So listen, if you ever have a patient come in complainin' that they can't move their jaw, and their face, arms or legs don't work right, and their muscles are twitchin', you pay attention now, you hear?*"

Fifty years later, working all those long hours as an ER doc out here in the middle of nowhere, even with all these farms and horses around, Dr. Jameson had managed to never see a single case of tetanus. Not a one. Until now.

I bet Mike's never seen it either, up there in the North West. Although, maybe he has, with all those logging accidents. Wait, he's a pediatrician, so probably not. I wish he'd stayed here in Texas, though. Maybe he wouldn't be so close to early retirement like he'd told me the other day. Something about all his partners making some business decisions he didn't like, but he didn't want to get into it over the phone.

"Tetanus? Lock jaw? But he ain't injured."

"Can we see him Doc?"

"Yes, come on. He's resting. He's feeling ok. Just a little weak. And scared. See, he showed me the wound on his leg. Said he got it about a week back, but thought he knew how to clean it out. It's healing ok. But that may be where the tetanus got in."

They passed a few other patients and nurses on their way over to the corner of the room, where Franklin Junior lay on an exam table, an IV going into his arm, and a heart monitor displaying his vital signs. He was asleep.

"We have him sedated because the muscle twitching was getting a little painful. I already have antibiotics and the anti-toxin going into him through the IV. I'm not sure if it will make a difference at this point, but we're doing everything we can for him."

"So, it was this wound that did this, you think?" asked Mr. Walker.

"Probably. Although, tetanus can happen from a whole variety of reasons: surgery, burns, crush wounds, dental infections, animal bites, piercings, and tattoos. It isn't always from a deep, dirty wound. Some cases don't even have an obviously identifiable cause."

"Why's his arm so stiff?" asked Mrs. Walker, holding her son's hand.

"That's the tetanus toxin affecting his nerves. See, tetanus is a bacteria – clostridium tetani. But the bacteria don't really do much harm. It's the toxin they secrete that does the damage. A little bit of tetanus would be harmless, but if enough of the germs are allowed to fester and multiply in a deep wound that isn't cleaned out well, or introduced in one of those other ways I mentioned, then the toxin secreted by all those germs finds its way through the bloodstream into nerve cells. It binds to the nerves and paralyzes them. For some reason, the nerves that control the jaw muscles are often the first to be affected. But the toxin can spread to other nerves and paralyze any part of the body."

"That's why you are giving him anti-toxin? But you said you're not sure if it will work?"

"Well, the anti-toxin is actually antibodies taken from donated blood units. They filter out any antibodies that healthy people have against tetanus toxin – antibodies they generated from getting the vaccine. These batches of antibodies are pooled together from several donors until there's enough to use in a patient. We infuse the antibodies, and these antibodies will go through his bloodstream and find any toxin floating around and neutralize it. The problem is, it won't neutralize any toxin that has already bound to his nerves. So any nerves already affected might stay paralyzed for weeks."

"We should have given him his shots, Frank. We shouldn't have been so afraid of doctors."

Franklin Senior nodded.

"Well, if he'd cleaned out the wound or, even better, told you about the wound so you could thoroughly clean it, this likely wouldn't have happened. Tetanus doesn't just infect every wound it gets into; thorough cleaning usually flushes out enough of the tetanus germs so that they don't take hold. But allow the germs to sit in there and fester for days, and you get tetanus. But, yes. If he'd had his tetanus shots – they give it mixed with pertussis and diphtheria as five or six doses throughout childhood – he would have his own antibodies against the tetanus toxin, and those would likely have neutralized the toxins on their own. Also, and I'm sorry to say it, if he'd come to you sooner and fessed up that he hadn't cleaned out his wound, we could have given him the anti-toxin – called TIG, or Tetanus Immune Globulin – at any time before these symptoms began and he'd likely not have gotten sick. Most minor wounds and punctures we wouldn't even worry about. But his looks like it was fairly deep. But, he wouldn't have known, and I know how these boys are, not wanting to go crying to Momma for everything."

"Wait. You said you've never seen tetanus before. So how do you know this is it?"

"Well, the timing fits. It usually takes about a week for tetanus symptoms to start after an injury. And he told me he got this wound last Monday. But there aren't any special tests we can do to confirm it. We just have to go based on his symptoms, and I'm fairly certain I'm right. There are two types of tetanus: local and generalized. Local tetanus is when the toxin only affects the nerves and muscles near the wound. Those muscles contract and stiffen up for several weeks, then gradually relax and return to normal. The second type is generalized tetanus, and that's what I think Franklin has. The toxin spreads to the spinal cord and brain and starts to affect other parts of the body.

"But yes, tetanus is now so rare, most docs won't ever see it in their lifetime. In fact, in the entire U.S., there's only about 1 case in young kids each year. If you include older kids and teens there are roughly five cases a year. In adults, there are between 20 and 50 each year – in the whole country. Some are in people who don't get their shots, but some happen in people who got their shots but then didn't get a tetanus booster. And it's not just rare because many people are vaccinated. We are simply better at cleaning wounds and using sterile equipment for procedures. Many folks around here don't get all their shots, and they'll go their whole lives without tetanus – in most cases. So, I wouldn't blame yourself over this. Honestly, the statistical chance that any one child is going to get tetanus is tens of millions to one."

"We shoulda taught that boy how to clean his wounds better. We shoulda told him to always ask us for help. We shoulda ..." his daddy trailed off, probably thinking of too many shouldas that had come to mind.

"We shoulda got him his damn shots, that's what we shoulda done," declared his momma.

"Well now, Mrs. Walker, maybe yes, but there's risk in getting the shots too. Kids can have seizures, something that Franklin Junior already had a risk of. There are even paralyzing syndromes people can get from strange immune reactions to the shots. In fact, with tetanus being so rare, you're probably more likely to have something bad happen from the shot than you are to get tetanus. So don't knock yourself about this."

"I know you're just tryin' to be nice, Doc. And we appreciate that. But if we were gonna skip the shots, we shoulda taught him better how to take proper care of his wounds, livin' on a farm and all. And to speak up. We could have prevented this by havin' him seen for his wound. We could have gotten him the ... what, TICK shot?"

"TIG shot."

"We could have gotten him that, and he would have been fine. And it would have been ok that we'd skipped his shots. We shoulda been better prepared if we were gonna skip the shots."

"So what's the plan? We just watch and wait?"

"We are going to need to transfer him by ambulance into the City. He'll need to stay in the hospital there until there's no sign that the nerves and muscles that control his breathing and other vital functions are being affected. Honestly, because a whole week has gone by, and some nerve symptoms have already set in, the toxin is likely already bound to other vital nerves. He may continue to decline, even after starting the antibiotics and the TIG. There is about an 11% fatality rate. So we need to be prepared in an ICU to support his breathing and anything else we need to do, and that's better done in a full hospital, not out here. But it is possible that we got to him in time for none of that to happen. The next few days will tell us."

Chapter 27

Code Club

Shray and Adah Bhatia were so happy to finally feel the excitement of bringing their baby home. Born 2 1/2 months early, they had watched and waited as their tiny Prisha fought for her life in the early weeks, endured countless interventions, weaned off the ventilator, learned to feed, and overcame every obstacle in order to arrive at this day: discharge day.

The doctors and nurses continuously commented on how their "beloved gift of God" passed every challenge with flying colors. They reassured the two young parents that, despite what looked to them like countless problems and invasive medical care, their particular little preemie did better than most born at her age. She avoided any eye complications and brain bleeds, she required less respiratory support than most, her gastrointestinal system tolerated feedings without any problems, and she grew faster than expected. She even managed to not have any apneas. And today was the day they'd finally get to bring her home.

The couple arrived right at the start of visiting hours, washed their hands, gowned up, and entered the NICU like they had every day, but they immediately sensed something different in the unit on this early Saturday morning. There were more staff than usual, and as they navigated their way through the rows of incubators they could tell that most of the night shift were still there, which they found odd because the haggard nurses and on-call doctors were usually finished with their sign-outs and were long gone before visiting hours started.

They caught snatches of conversation between nursing pairs as they crossed the unit:

"As and Bs last night …"

"Re-intubated around 2 a.m …"

"Had to up the O2 back up to 50% …"

"Probably GERD-induced again, but we'll know after the sleep study …"

These had all become familiar terms to the Indian couple as they got to know some of the other families around Prisha. They felt fortunate that their baby had never taken a single step backwards during her stay. But as they neared the two familiar nurses sitting next to Prisha's incubabor – *What? Why's she back in an incubator?* – they heard the words "Apneas and bradycardias last night, so we had to hook her back up to …"

"Good morning Janelle, Lisa," Shray greeted the two nurses politely (as always). "What happened to Prisha? Why is she not in her crib?"

"And why is she back on a cardiac monitor?" inquired Adah, noticing the wires going from her baby's chest to the quietly beeping device which she thought she'd never have to listen to again.

Janelle stood up and hugged Adah. "Good morning. It was a rough night. But little Prisha did much better than most."

"I'll fill the two of you in," added Lisa. "Let's let Janelle take off. She's beat."

Janelle glance at Lisa gratefully, nodded to the couple, and walked toward the exit to the nurses's lounge.

"What happened last night?" Shray asked again.

"Prisha had some A's and B's last night – some stop-breathing spells, and her heart rate slowed down several times. It's nothing really to worry about, and it's fairly common, even at this late stage. But it does mean she'll have to stay a few more days. I'm so sorry, you two. I know today was supposed to the The Day."

Adah looked around, noticing that two other "feeders and

growers," babies who had been at the same stage as Prisha and were ready to be discharged, were also now hooked up to monitors again and one was also back in an incubator. Their parents hadn't arrived yet.

Lisa noticed Adah's inquiring gaze. "Yes, several others took a step back last night as well. I can't, of course, share anyone else's private details with you. But everyone's pretty much ok … except …"

The nurse's explanation was cut short by some commotion from the other side of the unit. Adah and Shray could see the Rawlings parents standing next to their baby over in the acute care section, talking to Dr. James. Their neighbor baby had been right next to Prisha just yesterday and was also slated for discharge today. But they could see the ventilator and tubing even from this distance, and knew their little one had taken a drastic turn last night.

"Janelle said it was a very rough night last night for some," Lisa admitted. "I'm sure the Rawlings' will fill you in once things have settled down again. If they want to."

"But why?" Shray asked for the third time. "How does everyone just happen to have all these problems all of a sudden, and all on the same night?" He looked around the unit, up at the ceiling, and around on the floor. "What? Is there some sort of gas leak or did the power go out last night? This can't just be some sort of coincidence."

Lisa knew it wasn't just a coincidence. She knew exactly why. And she knew she'd have to eventually tell the young couple, whom she'd grown very fond of over these many weeks as they were always so patient and kind. But that conversation was always a long one, with lots of questions. And Lisa wanted to at least get the rest of her patients settled before she sat down with them for that.

Janelle slumped down next to Todd on the leather couch in the nurse's lounge.

"*That* was way more rough than the usual Code Night," she groaned.

"Yeah it was," the male nurse sighed. "I hate Code Night."

"I'm surprised you were actually here. You usually manage to wheedle your way out of it."

"I know. I was doing Mai a favor. She begged me to switch with her, and you know I can't say no to her."

"Ha, yeah I do. How come you never take *my* Code Nights?" Janelle asked rhetorically.

Todd had the grace to blush a little.

"I thought so," she laughed, hitting him on the shoulder. "I had a feeling about you two."

"Keep it on the D.L. though, would you? We want to avoid all the gossip until we are really sure."

"Oh please, dude. Everybody knows. We all knew even before you two did. You guys were made for each other."

"That obvious? Well, that's actually a relief."

They sat quietly for a minute, trying to get up enough energy to gather their things and head home. The door opened and two more nurses walked in.

"How'd the Rawlings take the news?" asked Todd.

"Oh, about what you'd expect," offered Maria, who looked more worn out than the other three nurses combined. "I managed to sneak away before Dr. James got to telling them *why* they had to re-intubate little Tommy last night. I hate Code Night."

The fourth nurse, who had followed Maria in, looked at the other three in confusion. "What's Code Night?"

"You don't know about Code Night?" asked Todd.

"I mean, I know what codes are, of course. I just transferred down from Peds, but we don't have codes very often. I had to lead a code just last week because the floor doctor was down in CT with a patient. We brought the little guy back to life, thank God. I would have lost it if I'd failed my first code. But you three talk about it as if you expected it. Like, it's an actual thing."

The three veteran NICU nurses looked at each other. Janelle volunteered to not explain. "Welcome to Code Night, girl. But the first rule about Code Night is that you do not talk about Code Night."

"Huh?" The young nurse looked confused.

"Kids these days," Todd chuckled as he shook his head. "They never get the classic movie quotes."

"The second rule about Code Night is you *do not* talk about Code Night."

Maria shook her head, clearly not as amused as the two on the couch. "I'm outta here. See you all tomorrow. And let me know if junior here gets it."

"What the heck are you three old people talking about?"

Todd patted Janelle on the leg as he got up to leave too. "Well, that's just it, Sara. We're not talking about it. That's part of the Code."

Despite the fun they always had with the new NICU nurses, Janelle never found anything about Code Night to be fun. It sucked. But she knew it was necessary. *I mean, we can't just send these little ex-preemies out into the world unprotected,* she reflected as she guided her car toward the parking structure exit. *Gotta feel bad for little Prisha though. She was just about out of there. But she's way luckier than little Joe Rawlings. He just bought himself another two weeks at least.*

She rolled down her window and swiped her ID through the slot at the exit gate. *But what's the alternative? Not vaccinating? Letting these preemies go home and be exposed to whooping cough, polio, meningitis, and countless other deadly diseases? No.*

The policy was to give every NICU baby who turns two months old their first round of shots before they go home: Hep B, DTaP, HIB, PC, Polio, Rotavirus, and Flu in season. And they coordinated them to be given to all eligible babies on the same night if they could, so they could be prepared with the extra staff they always needed. Not to just give all the shots, but to help with the inevitable consequences. And they didn't just give the shots to the ones who were almost ready for discharge. They gave them to everyone who turned 8 weeks old that month. So, it wasn't as big a deal for those who still had weeks of NICU care to go. *And at least we are giving the shots here in the NICU, where they can be monitored so that alarms go off when their heart stops or they stop breathing. If we waited until they went home, they'd die of these reactions.*

Janelle had seen the research. Dorothy, her old NICU supervisor, who had retired early because she couldn't handle this issue anymore, had shown her study after study that warned how preemie babies suffered severe vaccine reactions way more often than full-term babies: apnea and bradycardia seemed to be the least of these problems. Some babies' hearts just stopped beating completely. Or they stopped breathing and didn't start again. That's when they would call a Code, and everyone gathered around to bring the baby back to life. And that's why they called it Code Night, because there was always at least one. The unlucky ones went into respiratory distress and had to be re-intubated, like little Rawlings. Prisha simply suffered some apneas and slow heart rates, but didn't need anything other than to have her IV restarted with a little caffeine added to prevent further As and Bs. Janelle didn't know the baby who fully coded and needed CPR last night, but they'd brought him back quickly and he was surprisingly stable this morning.

Thank God there were no intraventricular hemorrhages last night. Janelle had also seen the research on IVH after vaccination (from Dorothy, of course). But that was less common. She'd only seen it twice, and those could have just been coincidences. *I'm using that word too often now,* she admitted.

And that's why they called it Code Night. Sure, codes happened on other nights too, but they were always unpredictable. But at least on Code Night they were prepared. They always did the shots on the night shift, so the parents wouldn't be around. *I can't even imagine subjecting all the parents to that much trauma.*

There was one thing that Dorothy tried to achieve in their NICU before she left, but failed. She tried to get the NICU director to spread out the shots. Give them in two or three different rounds, spread out over the NICU stay. She thought that would reduce the sudden, life-threatening events, although she admitted there wasn't any research that showed doing that was safer. *Preemies could even react poorly to just one shot,* Janelle mused. And Dorothy had also tried to get the director to only give the shots that were really necessary, but delay ones like polio and Hep B for the pediatrician's office. But the director said no. This is the way it's done all over the United States, and this is what the CDC recommends, and this is what we are going to do, he said. And that was when Dorothy announced her retirement, after being the head nurse for 20 years.

Janelle didn't agree with Dorothy, at least not on those points. And she didn't agree when Dorothy tried to institute a separate Informed Consent form just for vaccinations. The director had shut down that idea right away too. You just can't tell parents that their ready-to-go-home baby, or their still-sick baby, might react poorly to vaccinations tonight and may have to stay a few more days … or weeks. Better to have vaccinations grouped into the general NICU consent form all parents sign when their baby first comes in.

Since Dorothy left, no one has really talked about it. They just all accept it as a necessary evil, or necessary good. It was at her retirement party that Todd had come up with his stupid Fight Club analogy for the new nurses. *Maybe that's his way of dealing with it.*

But Todd is still right. There's an unspoken rule about Code Night. We are not allowed to talk about it.

Chapter 28

Good Mom/Bad Mom

"**M**on Dieu! If I have to change *another* diaper today, I'm going to just quit."

Mrs. Dubois knew it was an idle threat. No mom every quit on her own baby for real. And she said it in French, so if anyone overheard her they wouldn't accuse her of being an even worse parent. *But after the 10th messy, runny, smelly dirty diaper for that day, they should at least let me take a break.*

Adeline Dubois felt like the nurses and the doctors blamed her for being here. Like, it was her fault her baby caught rotavirus, got dehydrated, and needed IV fluids to get him through the dehydration. She didn't want the vaccine, so she could do the diaper duty, one nurse said, turning her nose up like a … like a French woman would.

Americains et leurs vaccins, she thought. *Always so eager to get so many vaccines, and blame anyone who doesn't want all of them.*

The French people do vaccines right. They vaccinate against the important stuff: polio, diphtheria, tetanus, and measles. No one wants to die of those. Many Frenchmen also do a few other shots: HIB, mumps and rubella, pertussis. But these are optional, although there were rumors that even these may soon be mandated in her home country.

But les Americains, they do every shot they can do, not just the ones they should do. If Pharma can make it, they will come and get it. Not so in France, and in much of Europe. For now. But Adeline saw most of the American vaccines making their way inexorably onto the European schedules, and she didn't like it. Nor did most citizens. So she had baby Madeleine only partly vaccinated against the main diseases before starting her in daycare, and her doctor supported her decision since she was at least doing the important ones. She now wished she hadn't had to get a full-time job outside the home to make ends meet in this country of foreigners, where everything is so expensive. Because after only a week of daycare, her five-month-old baby came down with rotavirus. Despite her still breastfeeding, Madeleine got too dry, and her doctor sent her here to the ER for rehydration. But after several hours, Madeleine was still unable to keep anything down, so they admitted her for an overnight stay in the hospital.

Some of the nurses were sympathetic, like nurses should be. But some felt it was their ethical duty to inform a mother when she was a bad parent ... over and over again. Well, she didn't want the likes of them touching her baby anyway, so diaper duty it was ... again.

Adeline had opted out of the three doses of the oral rotavirus vaccine at 2, 4, and the upcoming 6 months for three reasons: 1. The original version of this vaccine was taken off the U.S. market in 1999 because it was found to cause an unacceptable (even by American standards) number of severe intestinal reactions. The live-virus germs in the vaccine are intended to multiply in the intestines, create a mild version of the infection, and generate immunity so that when a baby is later exposed to the real infection she might not get sick. *And need to be admitted to hospital for IV fluids,* she thought. But the vaccine version of the infection occasionally triggered a severe form of intestinal blockage called intussusception. This was found to happen in about 1 in 10,000 doses of the vaccine. So when the Americans gave it to their 4 million babies every year, and about 400 required emergency care and sometimes surgery to relieve the blockage, the American health authorities decided the vaccine wasn't a good idea after all. The disease killed about 40 babies every year, which was tragic. But the vaccine was worse. So it was recalled.

The second reason Adeline Dubois didn't trust the new version of the vaccine was that it was also suspected to increase the risk of intussusception - in about 1 in 20,000 babies, according to the American CDC. Well, they say it is somewhere between 1 in 20,000 and 1 in 100,000. Regardless, there's a risk. And she wouldn't accept that risk for her baby.

The third reason was that Adeline was still breastfeeding Madeleine, and she planned to continue for at least two years. Breastfed babies were less likely to catch rotavirus, but if they did it was less likely to be severe compared to if a baby was not breast-feeding. In fact, Adeline knew that Madeleine *would* catch rotavirus if she put her in daycare. Every baby, or toddler, or preschooler did. It wasn't a matter of *if*, but *when*. She didn't expect it right away, but here it was. And Madeleine's dehydration from the disease was an anomaly. For every baby who needs an IV, there are thousands who don't. Virtually every breastfed baby with rotavirus wouldn't need hospital care. But Madeleine did. *C'est la vie.*

The Frenchwoman's reverie was interrupted by a new arrival. A mom, about Adeline's age, with a baby, about Madeleine's age, in a crib. With an IV. But this baby didn't look well. Not well at all. He, or she, was limp, not moving. But breathing calmly. Pink/white face, not pale, not blue. Seeming to just be resting. A nurse was tending to the little one, and the mom stood a few paces away from the crib, staring. Then the baby suddenly let out a blood-curdling wail, pulled its legs up to its tummy, tensed the arms, and screamed. This went on for several minutes, and more than one nurse came in to help, followed by a doctor, who examined the baby, spoke with the mom for several minutes, then gave an "I'll be right back" gesture and walked out quickly. Then the baby was suddenly quiet again, as if a switch had been turned on then off. The heart monitor returned to a steady, calm heart rate and oxygen level, and the mom seemed to be able to breathe again.

Adeline walked over to her. "Excusez-moi ... Pardon me, my name is Adeline ... my baby is Madeleine. What's your baby's name?"

The woman stared blankly at her for a moment, confused. She looked at the sleeping Madeleine, then back at Adeline. The French woman recognized the "why is this crazy stranger with the accent talking to me" look on her face, a look common to Americans when confronted with civility and humanity. Then the look disappeared, and was replaced by a look of thanks. Thank you for caring. Adeline got that look a lot, too.

"Jerome."

"Ahhhh, Jerome. A lovely name. That means 'Holy' I think."

"It does? Oh, I don't know. We aren't religious. It was his grand-father's name."

"He looks peaceful now, no? But that crying. That is why you are here? Do they know what is wrong?"

"No. He's been vomiting a lot. But now he won't eat. And he alternates between being completely lethargic and this screaming. There's no in-between. I don't get it. We were just at the pediatrician yesterday. His 4-month appointment. He also got sick after his two-month appointment – got pretty bad diarrhea and spat up a lot. Then the doctor said he had reflux. Antacid meds took care of that. So yesterday the doctor said we could stop the med. Oh my God, could this be his reflux coming back?"

"What is this … this reflux?"

"Oh. It's spitting up. From too much stomach acid."

"Ahhhhh. Brule d'estomac. Yes, I have heard of this. But why would he get this reflux at two months? Why not since he was born? Did you change something at two months? Give him formula? Something like that?"

"No. I've been breastfeeding this whole time. It just came out of nowhere after his two-month checkup. And now this! Right after his four-month checkup."

The doctor came back in. "I am going to look at the baby again, while he's calm." He poked around for a minute: the soft spot, the neck, the heart, the abdomen. The abdomen again. "Hmmm." He gently pushed into both sides of the belly, up high, down low. "His belly is very firm. Distended. Even when he's quiet." The doctor turned toward Jerome's mom. "When is the last time he went poop?"

"Umm. This morning, I think. No wait. Last night. He hasn't

pooped today. Could that be …" More sudden, high-pitched scream-ing startled all three of them.

The doctor suddenly looked very concerned. He stepped over to the wall, pulled a rubber glove out of a box, squirted some gel onto his gloved little finger, undid the baby's diaper, and gently but pur-posefully inserted his finger into the baby's bottom.

"What on earth are you doing?" the mother asked, grabbing the doctor's other arm. "A rectal exam? On a baby? What does that have to do with …" She trailed off in a gasp as what looked like jelly came oozing out of the baby's bottom when the doctor withdrew his finger. Black-red jelly.

"Page Peds Surgery. Now!" the doctor commanded, sending one of the nurses running out of the room toward the nurse's station.

Jerome's mother fainted … into the arms of a French woman whom she barely knew, but would get to know much better in the days to come.

"Intussusception. Can you believe it? Right here on our floor. I've never seen it before. I was a labor-and-delivery nurse for these last few years and I'm new to Peds. They call it 'black-currant jelly sign,' Dr. Jacobson said. It's pretty much diagnostic of intussusception."

"That poor mother. She's lucky she brought him in here when she did. She's a good mom. But that baby spent how many hours in the ER before coming up here to the floor? And no one thought of it down there? He could have died. It's bad enough that he lost part of his bowel. They had to do a partial resection and colostomy – on a baby! But at least he's alive."

"I know. I mean, who thinks of doing a rectal exam on a tiny baby, right? Well, Dr. Jacobson, that's who."

"He's single, you know." Sigh. "And he's quite the tall glass, don't you think? I'm actually glad I got married early. He would be quite the distraction otherwise. Wait, are you blushing? Oh my God, are you two dating? You lucky girl. What's he like? Is he as awesome as I'm trying not to imagine he is?"

"Yes, he is seriously amazing. A total gentleman when we go out, and not-so-gentlemanly when I don't want him to be. I mean, you know how good of a doctor he is, right? We saw that this morning. And he's so good with the kids. Well, times that by about ten when he's outside of the hospital, and ..."

Adeline Dubois didn't mean to eavesdrop. She approached the nurse's station simply to ask about when her discharge was going to go through and didn't want to interrupt what she thought was a medical discussion. She stood back for a minute, and by the time she realized what they were really talking about she couldn't help but blush. But she hadn't missed the beginning of the conversation. *Ahhhh. Intussusception! That makes sense. And right after getting the 4-month dose of rotavirus vaccine, along with the other 7 vaccines they give in America at every baby checkup. Plus, her mom had told me Jerome reacted after the two-month vaccines as well. A warning sign, ignored?*

Adeline recognized one of the two nurses as the one who felt it was her ethical and medical responsibility yesterday to belittle her as a mother for not vaccinating Madeleine against rotavirus. The nurse who was obviously a very bad choice for someone like this Dr. Jacobson. Or maybe a very good temporary choice for someone like him, but not a permanent one.

Adeline decided her discharge needs could wait. "Pardon me, Nurses. Do you provide vaccines here in the hospital, for anyone who wants or needs them while they are here?"

They both looked up, and both said yes. "We keep them in a special refrigerator behind the nurse's station," said the married-of-the-two. "Why do you ask? I thought that you didn't ..." She trailed off, glancing sideways at the other nurse who was the real target of Adeline's inquiry.

"Well, I am now re-thinking my decision, in light of what has happened. I would like to read some information ... starting with this rotavirus vaccine, since that's what my baby caught."

"Oh, yes. We have a folder of information on all the vaccines," said the single-but-now-dating nurse. "Let me get it for you." Even a foreigner could detect the smug righteousness on the American's face.

Thirty seconds later the nurse returned, laid the folder in front of the Frenchwoman, opened it up and flipped through various different-colored laminated pages, and stopped on a rather unattractive orange color, with "Rotavirus Vaccine: What You Need To Know" printed at the top.

Adeline made a show of reading through the CDC VIS form. She'd already read it – twice. And she knew where to find what she was looking for. There, on the back side of the form. Risks of a vaccine reaction. Serious problems. Intussusception. And below that, a description of intussusception that matched Baby Jerome as a textbook case.

"Can you explain this part to me, Nurse ... Julianna Vitelli?" glancing at the nurse's name tag. "What is this 'intussusception' this CDC warns about? They say it is a possible, but rare, reaction to this rotavirus vaccine?"

"What? Oh, don't be silly. That can't happen after a vaccine." All-knowing righteousness again. "Let me see that ..."

Adeline waited patiently as both nurses read the CDC warning, but she didn't really feel any satisfaction. It was more like sadness. Sadness in how they fail to train the very people who give these vaccines. *You wouldn't see this in my France. They at least learn what the reactions might be.*

"Oh, well, they don't really mean that it can happen, you know. It's more of just a legal thing. Like, maybe since it happened once, they have to legally warn you about it. But it's not like it ever really happens."

The married nurse kept reading the information Adeline had pointed to.

"Do you know how old is Baby Jerome?" asked Adeline.

"Oh, we can't discuss another patient, dear. That's confidential."

"You misunderstand me. I know how old he is. I spoke with, hugged, and held his mother. For a long time. Right before his surgery.

I know how old he is. He is four months and two days old. You see, his mother is a very precise woman. She took him in for his four-month checkup exactly as instructed - at four months to the day. She got him his vaccines, like a good mother, including this rotavirus vaccine. A day later he has symptoms of intussusception. He almost dies. His life is saved. And he has this colostomy you speak of.

"I, on the other hand, took my Madeleine to her four-month checkup a few weeks ago. I got her two vaccines, but I decided to skip this rotavirus vaccine. My Madeleine got rotavirus, got an IV, and is now going home – with a healthy colon. And she didn't almost die."

The married nurse looked a little confused, but listened with interest. *Ahhh. She must have little babies of her own. I can tell.*

Nurse Julianna, on the other hand, looked pale, like she would rather be any place on the planet right now other than standing here, in front of this Frenchwoman.

"You called Jerome's mom a 'good mother.' And I agree. She is a good mother and a wonderful person. You had a different assessment of me yesterday, Nurse Julianna. Is there something you would like to say to me now?"

Chapter 29

The Long Bus

"I just don't see how we are going to get away with this without massive lawsuits ... lawsuits in Federal Court."

It was warmer than usual for a summer evening in Santa Barbara, which suited the eight gentlemen and eleven ladies just fine. The sunset-over-the-ocean view from the hotel's rooftop lounge topped off a long day of discussion and debate, and the cocktails and hors d'oeuvres were a nice reward for their hard work.

"Oh, you worry too much, Jimmy. It's not like they can sue *us*. They'd be suing our school districts."

"As if any of them had any money for a lawsuit."

"Yeah ... as if!"

The group of four middle-aged men who all grew up watching Wayne's World on SNL chuckled at Arnold's impression of the 80s iconic male figure.

"No, I'm serious guys. We all know we will be directing our schools to break federal law by doing this, right? I'm not just imagining that?"

"Yes ... you are right," admitted Arnold. "And our legal council has advised us of that already. But he assures us that playing the 'keeping the kids safe' card will at least protect us in the public eye. And, officially, it will be the school districts that are breaking the law. He's confident the few parents that this vaccine law applies to won't have the money or energy to sue the schools over this."

The four men, and the 15 other members of the gathering, all worked for the same department in their school districts – Special Education. They had all flown in from a variety of other states to enjoy the warm California weather and to meet with one of the Californians to learn how to deal with the special kids in their own states. It was their sworn duty to ensure that all special needs kids in their state received a decent education, and any speech, occupational therapy, and educational services that were required to achieve that. But the new mandatory vaccination laws were making that problematic.

Jim Ratzenberger - no relation to the actor - had been at this job in the Midwest for going on 20 years now, and he loved it. But the one thing that bothered him was how the number of children with special needs in his state continued to rise. He checked the California numbers on the flight out here, which were now up to 734,000 kids; up almost 20 thousand from last year, and up from about 550,000 twenty years ago. And much of that increase was due to autism. Some of the other disabilities, like dyslexia, had decreased slightly. But autism continued to rise, and that bothered him. *How is it that we, as a modern nation, which should have the healthiest and smartest kids in the world, are continuing to fail so miserably when it comes to raising mentally and intellectually-healthy kids? What the hell is going on in the parenting and pediatric world that we are missing?*

He'd asked himself that many times, and he'd asked his colleagues. But no one had an answer. Almost 10% of public school-children were now enrolled in special education in his state; and that number was 12% in California. Jim remembered his own years in elementary school back in the 70s. *Back then, we only had one ret – oops, not supposed to call them that anymore – one special kiddo in the class. Every school only had 4 or 5 total – large schools, that is. We used to tease them about having to ride the short bus to school. Now we don't even* have *short buses anymore.*

The laughter around Jim shook him out of his reverie. He'd missed a joke, he knew, but smiled to play along anyway.

"So let me just lay this out one last time, guys, and then I promise

I'll shut up," Jim jumped back in. "I know, I know. This is supposed to be a party ... but hear me out. We know that the Federal IDEA law – Individuals with Disabilities Education Act – requires that all kids with disabilities have access to an education. An *equal* education. We can't keep them out of school, no matter how disproportionate the cost per child that is involved. And none of us want to keep them out, of course.

"Knowing that fact, Senators Pan and Allen here in California caved to allowing an amendment into the new mandatory vaccine law SB 277 that states, and I quote from Section 2 (h): 'This section does not prohibit a pupil who qualifies for an IEP – an Individualized Education Program – pursuant to federal law and section 56206 of the Education Code, from accessing special education and related services required by his or her IEP.' Plus, IDEA doesn't just guarantee special services to these kids; it guarantees a *full* and equal education.

"Now, we all know that when Pan and Allen first submitted their vaccine bill, there was no mention of IEP kids. They hadn't even thought of that. They were just going to force vaccination on all those kids or kick them out of school and their IEP services. They'd just sit at home to rot. I'm told by a friend in the legislature that when someone pointed that out to them, Pan was like, "So?" I can't imagine Pan reacting that way – he's a pretty decent guy. But that's what my friend told me. Anyway, Allen got upset, supposedly. He said not only would that hurt him politically, kicking these kids out of school, but it was also wrong. So he convinced Pan to compromise and allow the amendment. Allen even clarified this during the hearing in the California Assembly – that the federal IDEA law was important, and the amendment to the vaccine law covered this issue. Allen's a lawyer, I think, so sticking to the federal law was important to him.

"But Pan made the language of the amendment too confusing. It's open to interpretation. I think it's very clear what it meant, and what they intended by it, but some of you don't agree. Anyway, during the Assembly hearing when they were arguing in public against the opposition to this bill, Assembly-member Waldron – she related this to me later, she and I go way back – was handed a question from one of the doctors in the audience who opposed this bill asking her to challenge Pan and Allen on the wording of this amendment. So Waldron actually called Fred – Fred Balcom, the head of special education for the entire State of California – up to the stand and asked him if the amendment meant that kids with IEPs would be allowed to not only get their special services, but also participate in normal classroom activities with all other kids? Essentially, would they be able to attend school like normal kids? And Fred said yes. She asked again, 'And that's just with that amendment that allows that?' And again, Fred said 'Yes.'

"And now we are all going back on that. We are all here this weekend from all corners of the country to decide how we are all going to interpret that amendment when this law comes to our states; to decide if we are going to follow IDEA and allow unvaccinated IEP kids in school or make them stay home.

"Furthermore, Allen has put the word out confirming that kids with IEPs should be allowed in school and not have to submit to the new vaccine law. His office has been fielding calls from parents asking for help. He's even spoken with a few school districts. But he has no power, no authority to influence what schools do now. It's like, he opened Pandora's Box with this law of his, thinking it seemed like a good idea, without really thinking through all the implications. Now he's trying to save some of the kids he's kicked out of school, but he can't. California schools don't have to listen to anything he says.

"And what's also ironic to me is that some – yeah, not many, but some – of these kids have IEPs because of severe vaccine reactions: those rare reactions where a kid has a seizure the night of vaccines and is never the same again. Their brain is fried. The parents complied with vaccination, their kid got gorked, and now they want to keep coming to school without completing vaccination, and you all want to deny them what semblance of a normal life they might have? Even if they didn't get their special needs because of vaccines - like, maybe it was genetic, or maybe they had meningitis, or maybe they just developed problems for no reason - the brains of these kids are already fragile enough. Aren't they now even *more* susceptible to chemicals and anything that can irritate their system, like vaccines? Isn't that a valid argument?"

Jim paused, and looked around at his three friends – all decent guys, whom he'd known for many years. What he saw reflected in their eyes wasn't annoyance or disagreement, like he'd seen on many of the faces when he'd made the same plea to the whole group earlier that day. It was something else. Resignation? Helplessness? He glanced into his empty glass. "F. How many of these have I had?"

"Listen, Jimmy," Arnold sympathized, again with the hand on his shoulder, the earlier joviality gone from his voice. "You know I … we … agree with you. But we also want to keep our jobs. This plan is going to be forced on all of us. We either play nice or get out of the bathtub. And I don't even think it was up to Fred here in California either. Someone way up at the very top, and I don't know who, has decided that all school children – each and every single one, without exception – must be fully vaccinated. It's going to happen in my state, and in each of yours. Most of the IEP parents don't want to finish the vaccines. And a growing number of all parents are questioning vaccines, especially vaccines that their kids don't need. So, now the powers that be have a chance to at least force the special needs kids to get vaccinated or get out, and they are using us to get it done. It sucks. But I don't see any alternative."

"But the way they want us to go about this is just … I don't know … criminal?"

"I think that it's the only way," jumped in Todd. "And it puts the onus back on the parents. We don't technically kick them out of their Special Ed services. We offer to provide them at home. We tell the parents we have to follow the part of the law that says they can no longer set foot onto the school campus, but yes, they are entitled to their Special Ed services. So, we send the services to them, at home. Yeah, it will cost us more money to do that in the short term for every parent that elects to keep their child home instead of vaccinate. But the number of families who will choose that is small, in my opinion. And our lawyers already told us that even though this violates IDEA, they will deal with the federal lawsuits. We won't have to.

"I spoke with Sally from one of the California school districts. She said this approach is going well. They only had three takers in the whole county. Three moms who said OK, bring the services to my child at home. Sally did, and the kids spent the first week of school at home getting their half hour of speech therapy that week and their one hour of daily tutoring. What they did the other 7 hours of every day I don't know. Then they went and got medical excuses from a doctor who agreed that their kids had severe reactions to vaccines earlier in life, so they shouldn't get any more. Two of these kids are currently back in school ... for now. The director of the county public health department disqualified one of the medical excuses. I don't know how or why he would be able to overrule the child's own doctor. But all other special needs kids in the entire county are finishing their vaccines, or had already done so because the parents didn't think vaccines were a problem. Vaccination rates are way up in her county overall. These parents need their kids to be in school full-time so both parents can work. They can't afford to not send their kids to school. And seriously, for some of these kids who are totally gorked out, it doesn't matter where they are – at home or at school. They ain't learning nothing, as my English teacher used to joke. And the parents know it. They just need us to babysit their kids all day so they can either work or get a break. A much-needed break, I'll admit. But bottom line is that it's working. And so now the higher-ups want all the public school districts nationwide in every vaccine-mandatory state to follow the same approach: abide by the law by giving the special kids all their IEP services at home. And those who do manage to get medical excuses to not vaccinate, well, we've been assured that that's going to go away soon as well. We'll have our 100% vaccination rate, no matter what. But hey, don't shoot the messenger. I'm just telling it like it is."

"Well then the California Public Health Department better get off its fat ass and change their website," said Jim. "Because right now, on ShotsForSchool.org under FAQ #3 it clearly states 'Students who have an IEP should continue to receive all necessary services identified in their IEP regardless of their vaccination status.'"

"But that's just it," said Arnold. "We will be doing that, but at their homes. We are going to have to stop writing "7 hours of mainstream classroom time every day" into their IEPs. You are correct, Jimmy, that legally right now we are required to give all these kids everything that is written in their IEPs regardless of whether or not they are finishing vaccines. And many of these kids have their normal classroom time – sorry, 'mainstream' classroom time; we're not supposed to use the "N" word around these kids anymore – written into their IEPs … *this* year. But next year that will change too. We'll only write in their Special Ed services. So, that's all they will be entitled to."

"And that," countered Jimmy, "is where all the lawsuits will come into play. Because we will be completely ignoring the 'equal education' part of IDEA. We aren't just required to provide special services. *All* aspects of these special kids' education need to be equal. And at-home ain't equal. We already have enough of these parents suing the school districts because we don't provide enough services. Now they'll be taking us to Federal Court. They already spend $12 billion a year here in California alone on Special Ed. My state spends about half that. And the federal government only provides about 10% of that. How are we going to afford these lawsuits?"

"Who exactly do you think is going to sue us? The parents? They don't have any money for that. They are all tapped out. Yeah, there'll be a few, but that's it. Our lawyer in my state is very confident of this. The ACLU won't touch this. They already made that clear back when the California mandatory vaccine law was being debated. Sure, there are some public watchdog groups who may file. But our lawyers are ready for that."

"But won't parents start suing us when some of their special needs kids start reacting poorly to their vaccines?" threw out Jim, his last argument.

"Seriously, Jimmy?" Todd again. "Who would even be able to tell if more vaccines made them worse? How are they even going to prove that? Their kids are already damaged. What's a little more going to hurt?"

Chapter 30

Who Doesn't Like Chipmunks?

*N*ot another F-ing mumps story, Francine grumbled as she read the email from Jim Remington. *Jim knows what to do. Why does he keep asking me for approval?*

Francine hated mumps. She'd never had them, of course. But she hated them nonetheless. Which was ironic, because Francine loved most vaccine-targeted diseases.

But mumps was different. Because the vaccine didn't work. Well, that wasn't completely true. It worked a little bit. But not like the rubella vaccine and the measles vaccine. *Virtually every case of mumps we've had in the past few years has been in vaccinated people,* she sulked. And *that* didn't do her any good at all. Her job was to *sell* vaccines, not publicize the ones that don't work. Thank God the public is stupid. *Every time we announce a mumps outbreak, and quietly admit the fact that it's going around in fully-vaccinated young adults, and we conclude with the reminder to make sure you are up to date on your mumps vaccine, we still get an uptake on extra MMR boosters in teens and young adults. Like people are just that stupid:*

"Hey! Go get this vaccine because the two doses you already had didn't work."

"Uh, ok."

And the warnings about sterility don't hurt either. For some reason, even though sterility from mumps virtually never ever happens, people panic as if it's totally going to happen to them if they even think about getting mumps.

Francine liked that part of mumps outbreaks: the fear. And the fact that there is no individual mumps vaccine anymore, so everyone who panicked and ran to their doctor to get a mumps booster was actually getting the full MMR, and they probably didn't even know it. This helped keep measles away. There used to be a separate mumps vaccine, but it was taken off the market because there wasn't enough demand. *Plus, it encouraged people to listen to the quacks who said it's better to get individual live-virus vaccines one-at-a-time. 'Get measles vaccine, mumps vaccine, rubella vaccine, and chicken pox vaccine each in their own separate years, which better mimics how the natural diseases used to be contracted.' Stupid.*

But what she didn't like the most is that every mumps outbreak gave the anti-vaxxers the opportunity to publicize the mumps vaccine fraud case still pending in federal court. According to the plaintiffs, back when the MMR vaccine was formulated in the 70s, the researchers who were responsible for creating the mumps component, Drs. Krahling and Wlochowksi, claim they were having difficulties. They couldn't get it to work. Getting a vaccine to "work" was measured by its ability to generate protective antibodies against that disease in test subjects. But everyone they tested the mumps vaccine on would only generate a partial antibody response. No matter what they tried, they couldn't trigger a high enough antibody response to get the vaccine approved as being effective.

So their supervisor, allegedly, ordered them to infect a group of rabbits with mumps, filter the mumps antibodies out of the rabbits' blood, and add those antibodies to the blood samples of the vaccinated human subjects so that the results would show high mumps antibodies. Genius. Only, the two scientists then got a conscience – what? 20? 30 years later? – and decided to blow the whistle. Of course, they couldn't prove anything, and no one even knew about the blown whistle, until their stupid lawyer decided to bring the case to federal court.

And that, Francine admitted, was a stroke of genius. By allegedly faking the research to get their MMR vaccine approved, combined with being the only MMR vaccine on the U.S. market, the company was guilty of defrauding the U.S. government with a monopoly. Apparently the government doesn't mind if you trick them, but if you do it with a monopoly, that's bad.

Fortunately for the vaccine maker, the federal judge assigned to the case keeps allowing a continuation. The two scientists and their lawyer keep showing up every year to try the case, and the Pharma lawyers keep asking the judge for a continuance, and the judge allows it – for 7 years running now. Allegedly, that is.

So Francine was sick and tired of hearing about mumps again, but Jim was just doing his job. She did have to sign off on every story. She skimmed it quickly making sure the "sterility" and "make sure you are up to date on both doses of the vaccine" points where there, and replied back to him with an A-OK.

Would someone please just die already! She complained. *No one dies of these diseases anymore.*

Oh wait! Now would be the perfect time to release that new mumps study – the one from the University of Iowa that showed getting a third dose of MMR vaccine reduced the risk of catching mumps by about half. The University had an outbreak of about 260 cases in 2015, and gave 5000 students the MMR vaccine to try to reduce the spread of the disease. Plus, the CDC did just officially approve this 3rd MMR dose for everybody at risk during a mumps outbreak. *I wonder if the CDC was worried about the possibility of worsened side effects when you give the MMR to adults? But what was worse, more MMR side effects or more mumps?*

She sent a second email to Jim with instructions to add the new study, then closed her laptop. Francine was getting bored. Even Jim no longer excited her. That was why she assigned him to the night shift at the Center. *Thank God it's almost flu season. We'll soon have about 30 or so dead babies we can use, if this season goes as well as most.*

Chapter 31

The Scarlet Nametag

Evangeline sat by her baby's bedside, watching the monitors blink and beep their reassurance that her daughter was stable. Feeling herself starting to nod off, she decided to slip out of the room and stretch. *Maybe there's coffee in the nurse's lounge,* she hoped. She saw a young woman, about her age, sitting in a chair against the wall next to the closed door to the ICU room across from hers, quietly crying. The woman looked up at the sound of her door clicking shut, and Evangeline knew instantly that this must be a young mom, just like her, with a child on the other side of that closed door. *You can always tell by the look on their faces,* she thought. *If it's a husband, there's more worry than sorrow. If it's a relative, there's concern. But if it's a child ...*

She knew her own face must have looked just like that when her little Angela was admitted several days ago and had needed a ventilator to keep her alive. But now her baby was extubated – not needing a machine to breathe for her anymore – and was doing well. Evangeline glanced down the hallway, longing for the coffee, but her altruistic side asserted itself and she pulled up a chair next to the woman.

"I know. I know, Dear. It's hard." She put an arm around the woman's shoulder.

The woman glanced up at her with a mixed look of confusion and annoyance. "How can you possibly know what it's like to ..." Then she saw Evangeline's eyes, and saw the anguish – saw her own feelings reflected in this stranger's face. She looked at the closed door across the hallway from where they sat and continued, "You too?"

"Yes. Me too. Her name is Angela."

"I have little David," said the woman, her head nodding toward her own door, through which sounds of activity could be heard – life-saving activity. Evangeline had sat in this same chair outside Angela's door just a week ago, listening to the same sounds. But alone.

The two sat for a few minutes, the newbie taking comfort from the veteran. Both knew that to try to explain more right now would just end in a torrent of sobbing tears. So they just sat.

Anna sat at the nurse's station with her freshly-poured cup of coffee, just brewed for the night shift. She was charting her care notes from her first rounds on her two patients. She pulled her face mask down past her mouth and sipped her coffee, then slid it back into place.

Thank God Angela is finally doing well, she thought. *It was touch and go there for a bit. But she pulled through and should be out of here in another day or two. It's so hard to see the flu hit a baby that way.*

Anna still felt some guilt over her decision to avoid the flu shot again this year. As an ICU nurse, she saw first-hand how bad the flu could be. But, also as an ICU nurse, she'd seen just how bad the rare but severe side effects from the flu shot can be. She'd seen Guillain-Barre Syndrome not only in her own grandma, but had cared for two patients with it here in this very unit. All three had occurred within days of getting the flu shot. Anna was only 12 when it struck her grandma, but she could still remember the weeks in an ICU when her whole body had been paralyzed by the autoimmune reaction to the vaccine. Anna had visited her every day, and it was that experience that had prompted her to go into nursing. And the months of physical and occupational therapy her grandma had to suffer through to learn to eat and walk again had convinced Anna she did not want to be a rehab nurse.

Anna learned more about Guillain-Barre Syndrome, or GBS, in

nursing school, and had been angry when many of her instructors had laughed at the very idea that it could be caused by a vaccine. She still felt guilty for having pretended to laugh along with her classmates whenever Ms. Johnson, the worst of them, made fun of "parents who didn't believe in science." But Anna knew that the research was very clear on GBS; not only the flu vaccine, but other vaccines as well, were now medically-accepted causes of GBS. She even showed Ms. Johnson this research one day, and she'd just laughed it off. But two of her nursing instructors had listened to her, and her story about her grandma, and looked at the studies on GBS, and conceded that yes, GBS could be a severe autoimmune reaction to a flu shot. As the immune system created antibodies against the flu viruses in the shot, it also created abnormal antibodies which attacked part of a person's own nervous system, damaging the nerves in the spinal cord and brain.

So Anna never got flu shots, and the mask she had to wear at her job for 6 months out of every year was her punishment. Because those who didn't get flu shots posed a danger to their patients, the hospital board ruled when she and 10 other nurses protested the policy. When they asked the board to produce a research study that demonstrated they posed a risk to their patients, they were waved off. They didn't have time to show them the research that was obviously out there in numerous studies: "Why else would every hospital in the country have a mandatory flu shot policy? It's because we know it prevents the flu, and prevents you from passing the flu to your patients."

But Anna and her friends knew there wasn't any such research. Oh, there was research that showed the vaccine reduced the severity of the flu – by a little bit. Not by much though. And there definitely wasn't any research that proved that healthcare workers who were vaccinated were less likely to carry the flu viruses in their respiratory tract and pass it to patients. Anna's review of the data concluded that the flu shot might make you feel less sick when you are exposed to the flu, and it might reduce the chance of having complications from the flu by a little, but you'll still carry the virus and shed it to others regardless of vaccination. No study had ever proven otherwise.

And it only helped reduce symptoms from the strains covered by that year's flu shot. Every year, flu shot makers tried to guess which strains would go around next year and make flu shots with the three most likely strains. No, it was *four* strains now, since they've added the swine flu strain every year now. Sometimes they got it right, but they often got it wrong, and in many years the flu shot was determined to only be 20% effective.

Geeze, last year it was only 10% effective. No thanks, Anna reminded herself. *I'm not risking GBS each and every year for the rest of my life for something that may or may not even help me. And you know what? I would do it for my patients, if there was any evidence that it would prevent me from carrying and passing the virus. So, again, no thanks.*

When the first GBS case came to the Unit a few years ago, and it became known that the patient had gotten the flu shot a week prior, the staff started to look at Anna's masked face with more curiosity. Like, maybe she wasn't so psycho after all. But that patient soon left, and so had the reminder. So when it happened again just last year, Anna wasn't surprised to see two other nurses now wearing masks for this flu season. The message was starting to get around. *I just wish Tim would listen to me on this.* Her brother, Tim, was a pediatrician for Prestley-Churchill. He'd called just the other day to complain about another change in their vaccine policy. But he still got the flu shot every year. *He watched what happened to Grammy just like I did. But as a Ped, I guess the GBS risk is so much smaller in kids, he wouldn't have seen it since.*

Plus, there was even new research that showed getting flu shots several years in a row may make people *more* vulnerable to the flu in later years. Anna played with the edge of her mask as her mind re-ran this litany, like she did every time someone came in with severe flu complications. It was annoying to have to wear it, but she knew she could just never bring herself to get the shot. Not unless they could find a way to eliminate the GBS risk.

Anna's hand wandered down to her ID badge clipped to her chest. Now *that* really annoyed her – the red sticker she had to put on her badge that also indicated her refusal to get the flu shot. That way other hospital employees could remind her to wear her mask if she forgot, and hospital supervisors could make sure each of their underlings were being compliant with mask-wearing.

I don't know how this is not considered a HIPAA violation, she mused for the umpteenth time. *My badge, and this mask, openly disclose my confidential medical information to everyone around me. How is that even legal?*

Anna was happy to read a story about a Canadian judge who ruled against a hospital with the same policy – ruled for that very reason. Mask-wearing and badge-labeling violated the HIPAA rights of hospital employees, and because there was no evidence that the flu shot reduces person-to-person transmission of the virus, the hospital's policy was illegal. *Those nurses were brave enough to take the hospital to court over this, and they won. I wish I was that brave.*

But what really hurt her, what really stung, were the patient-warning posters all over the hospital that went up this year for the first time. Anna could see two of them from where she sat: "Why Is My Health Care Provider Wearing a Mask and a Red Dot on the Badge?" All you could see of the girl in the picture were her eyes, but she was obviously a beautiful model. Then below her were listed all the reasons as to why the hospital's mandatory flu vaccine policy is there to keep patients safe, and a reassurance that anyone wearing a mask and with a red dot on their badge isn't necessarily sick, so patients don't need to worry about being near them.

Anna felt like she would be less humiliated if she came to work naked.

And in order to avoid as many misunderstandings as possible, Anna was usually not assigned to care for any patients admitted for flu complications, because her supervisor worried that if such families found out that Anna didn't vaccinate against the very disease that had landed their family member in the hospital, there would be a lot of extra anger to deal with, and they didn't need that here in the ICU. Anna's supervisor actually agreed with Anna's opinion on the science – that the mask made no difference – but there was no easy way to get a scared family to listen to reason, especially when the reasoning went against all the flu vaccine propaganda they would have already seen.

But then little baby Angela was admitted, and Anna was assigned to her case every night since then. Because Angela's mom had declined the flu shot at her six-month checkup, the intake nurse had discovered. And Anna was happy to take on the job. She had many conversations with Evangeline since then, and found that they were kindred spirits. And when the actual strain of flu that was cultured from Angela's nasal passage turned out to not be a strain that was even covered in the flu shot this year, Evangeline and Anna had hugged for quite a while, both glad that the young mom wouldn't need to forever question what might have happened if she'd just gotten the shot at her baby's check-up.

"Good morning, Anna."

Anna was startled out of her reverie by the arrival of Dr. Saul. "Oh, hello Abe." She knew he liked to go with first names when not around patients. "What are you reading?"

Dr. Saul looked up from his phone. "Oh, well … I'm a little embarrassed to say, actually. And it seems I may owe you an apology."

"Really? How often does *that* happen? A doctor apologizing to a nurse?" She smiled.

"Well, I'm reading the latest Cochrane Community blog about the flu shot. And it seems that you were right all along. According to Cochrane, yearly flu deaths are, and I quote, 'little more than 1000 yearly.' They describe how the CDC grossly over-estimates them at about 36,000, and how that's because they group all pneumonia deaths in with flu deaths in that number, just like you've told me for years. And the three latest flu vaccine updates from Cochrane are very telling: the shot has surprisingly low efficacy, and there's very little actual research evidence to back up most of the claims that are made about the shot. I'm beginning to think that all the marketing hype behind the shot may really be simply because all those hundreds of millions of doses they scramble to make every year expire in June. They have to sell most of them or they lose big time."

"Now who's sounding crazy?" Anna teased.

"But that's not all. I was reading more about the Cochrane author of these flu studies. The Vancouver Sun published two Op-Eds of his a few years ago about mandatory flu vaccine policies in hospitals. His insights were really quite intelligent. First, he said 'It is not my place to judge the policies currently underway in British Columbia, but coercion and forcing public ridicule on human beings (for example by forcing them to wear distinctive badges or clothing) is usually the practice of tyrants.' In another piece about the flu shot, he said 'The inactivated [flu] vaccines should work in theory, just like many things work in theory, but real evidence suggests they are not having the desired effect. So far we have distortion of research findings, evidence-free statements and evidence-free policies supporting coercion of human beings. What next?'"

Anna didn't know what to say. She fingered her badge without even realizing it.

"Anyway, I'm going to start rounds. I'll see you later."

"Oh, where can I find that blog? In case I want to show it around?" Anna asked.

"It's called 'Why have three long-running Cochrane Reviews on influenza vaccines been stabilized?' And you can't get more objective than Cochrane." He showed her his phone. "It looks like you may not have cooties after all, I guess." He winked and headed down the hallway.

Anna's gaze lingered on his retreating form for several seconds, then she stood up and headed down the hallway to check how things were going with the new admission. Another flu case, this one vaccinated, so Anna knew she wouldn't be assigned to it. But it didn't sound like things were going very well in that room, and she wanted to lend a hand if needed.

Tammy raised her head off the woman's shoulder as a masked nurse walked by and entered David's room. For the ten seconds it took for the door to swing closed, she heard numerous voices saying all kinds of things that made no sense to her, and an incessant alarm beeping again and again. Then it all died back down again to muted murmurs. She wiped her face on her sleeves and looked over at the woman who had sat down next to her. "Tammy," she managed to get out. "Tammy Stone."

"Evangeline. And my little Angela is in the room across from yours. She's almost nine months old."

"How is she doing? And why is she here, if I may ask?"

"She got a really bad case of the flu and was admitted here 7 days ago. It was touch and go at the start, and she needed full life support and everything. But she's doing much better now, I'm happy to say. It wasn't easy. It never is. But listen, your little David is in very good hands. I'm sure he will be fine too."

"What an unusual coincidence," Tammy breathed. "David is here because of the flu as well. It just came out of nowhere. One hour he was fine, and the next he was burning up, then vomiting, then coughing. Twenty-four hours later we were at the doctor, and he sent us right here to the ER. By the time we got here he was pale and even a little blue. They snatched us right out of the ER waiting room and got to work on him right away."

"What have they had to do so far?" Evangeline prompted, knowing sometimes it made it easier to talk through the medical side of things.

"They have him on a breathing machine and IV fluids. They said they had to sedate him as well so he wouldn't fight the machine. And now his blood pressure keeps going down and they have him on a medication to try to keep it up."

Evangeline took a deep breath. "Angela went through all those same things. Now all she has is just an IV and she's looking very well again. Wanna see her?"

The woman nodded and they both stood up and stepped into the quiet room.

"She is beautiful. You are lucky." Looking back toward the doorway, Tammy managed, "I just hope …" Then the sobbing started up again, and the two sat back down on the more comfortable couch this time to ride it out.

"Really? You didn't give her a flu shot?"

It was three days later, and Evangeline had come into David's room to say goodbye to Tammy. David was off the ventilator and doing better, having responded well to the IV anti-viral medication. They'd gotten to talking, and Evangeline had shared a few things.

"Now, of course, I wonder if maybe I should have," answered Evangeline. "But given that Angela's flu strain wasn't even in the vaccine, it wouldn't have made any difference. But you did. You gave David a flu shot, and he still got very sick from one of the strains the shot was supposed to cover."

"Well, I don't even remember getting him a flu shot," Tammy explained. "I mean, I know he got a few shots at his six-month appointment, but no one asked me if I wanted him to have a flu shot."

"They usually just group them all in together, and might not have specified all that he was getting. The regular vaccine schedule actually calls for 9 vaccines at six months of age, if you include the flu shot."

"Wait, nine? Nine vaccines? He certainly didn't get that many. I only remember there being about three shots – oh, and one liquid by mouth."

"All the doses can be grouped into about 4 injections." Evangeline knew this well, because she had looked more deeply into it when she started investigating the flu shot. "DTaP, which is three shots in one, can also come mixed with Hep B and Polio – so that's 5 in 1. Then HIB and PC each come individually. The flu shot makes 4 total injections of 8 vaccines. The oral one is Rotavirus."

"Geeze, I don't even know what most of that is," cringed Tammy. "Why didn't my doctor explain any of that to me, or even go over the pros and cons of the flu shot?"

"I think most doctors just follow the routine, and they expect parents to read up on it themselves. They don't really have the time to explain all that anyway, at least not the really busy doctors."

"I don't think I could live with myself if all this happened and I'd said no to the flu shot. I'm glad Angela's strain wasn't in the vaccine because I know you now, and I know that would have been even harder on you. But what are you going to do next flu season? And what am I going to do? If the flu shot barely even works, why bother? But if there's a chance it would prevent *this* from happening again, then I'd be crazy to not get it, right?"

"Well, Tammy, here is how I look at it. First, is the shot likely to work? Second, how dangerous is the flu likely to be in most cases? And third, what are the risks of the shot? What are the side effects? You should talk to my nurse about this – Anna. She is wonderful. And she knows a lot about the flu shot and its side effects.

"So, to answer the first question, the flu shot is actually the least effective vaccine they make. Most shots work pretty well, right? Not the flu shot. Researchers have attempted to prove that the shot even provides any benefit to infants and toddlers, and the consensus is no – they have not been able to even show it's protective in our young ones except that it may reduce the chance of flu complications. Maybe. But the jury's still out on that. Now, they do have some research showing it works in older kids and adults, but that efficacy varies. Some years it's as low as 10% effective. A few years have had high efficacy, but only up to about 60%. Even that is lower than the supposed efficacy of any other vaccine. But then there's the elderly. Research shows it's actually less effective in the elderly than in younger adults. And it's the elderly who need it the most. That's why they made the vaccine in the first place, and it barely even works in that population. And they figured out the nasal flu spray doesn't seem to work in children at all lately, so they stopped advising it for kids – the nasal one, that is."

"But they push it so hard. Advertisements, discounts at the drug store if you get your shot. They sell it as if it's totally going to protect you."

"Well, they are in the business to sell things – they being the companies who make the flu shots, the stores that give them, and the doctors that provide them. My thought is that they advertise flu shots more than any other because every year all the product they make has a very short shelf life. It's only good for that one season. Whatever they don't sell they have to throw away. And you know what I've also read? About half the flu shots have mercury, so they have to dispose of them as hazardous waste. Isn't that ironic? It's perfectly safe if they inject it into your baby, but try to throw it away and suddenly it's a hazardous material."

"That's crazy. That really makes me a little angry. Mercury? They put that into my baby?"

"Maybe, maybe not," reassured Evangeline. "The bottom line on this one vaccine is that it just doesn't do your baby or toddler much good. But the next question is, just how dangerous is the flu? Despite what happened to your baby and mine, we are anomalies. For most people, the flu is harmless. Tragically, about 20 babies die in the U.S. every year. And about 20 toddlers/preschoolers. In total, about 100 children ages 0 to 18 die from the flu each year. When it comes to adults and the elderly, there are about 1500 confirmed deaths each year."

"Wait, but I've heard that the flu kills about 36,000 Americans every year. You're saying it's what, only about 1600?"

"For some strange reason, the CDC groups all flu deaths and pneumonia deaths into the same category. The two together add up to about 36,000. But most of that is bacterial pneumonia. Other databases that only tabulate flu data show about 1000 to 1600 deaths annually. That's still tragic, but many of those deaths are in people who got a flu vaccine.

"But then you have to compare all those disease risks against the risk of getting the shot. The CDC collects data on all severe vaccine reactions in their system called VAERS. This system has received over 1000 reports of fatal reactions to the flu shot. There have also been over 9000 hospitalizations, 1800 disabilities, and 1700 cases of nerve injury or paralysis. Ask nurse Anna about her grandmother. She'll tell you all about it. I'm not saying people should or shouldn't get the shot. I'm just saying give people a choice, and inform them when they are trying to choose. And don't look at them funny or punish them when they say no, because there are good arguments both for and against it.

"But there's another danger from the flu vaccine if you are allergic to eggs. Flu viruses for the shots are grown in eggs, and they extract all the flu viruses from the eggs and process them into the vaccine solution. But they can't filter out all the egg proteins. So if you are allergic to eggs, you could go into anaphylactic shock and literally die right there on the spot. Or you could just have a slight allergic reaction, like hives."

"Hey, wait a minute … David had hives once. It was around 6 months. It was two days after his shots, and his flu shot. He got a rash on his face and chest and seemed itchy. I remember the timing now because the doctor joked about us being back so soon. He said it was hives, but nothing to worry about and to give him Benadryl. We did, and the hives went away. We never did find out what caused the hives. The doctor didn't mention anything about this being an allergic reaction to the shots, or to the flu shot."

"Plus," added Evangeline. "Most babies haven't even tried eggs yet when they are old enough for their first flu shot at 6 months, so you wouldn't even know if your baby is allergic yet. But they push the shot on every baby regardless. All for very little gain.

"But it gets worse. Even though the manufacturers who make flu shots advise against giving it to anyone who is allergic to eggs, health experts advise that all egg-allergic patients should get a flu shot anyway. Just make sure it's in a doctor's office so if you go into shock they can revive you."

"That's stupid," said Tammy loudly. "For a shot that barely works? 'Hey, get this shot. It may kill you, and it probably won't work, but here's $5.00 off on your next purchase here at our drug store.' Are people just that dumb?"

Evangeline didn't answer. She just waited.

Tammy turned and looked into the mirror over the sink in the hospital room. "I guess we are."

Anna waved goodbye to Evangeline and baby Angela as the double doors to the ICU swung closed, happy to see her patient finally get discharged. It was nice to serve patients who were kindred spirits. With a sigh, she entered another room where her second new admission for the day had just arrived. A post-op case in a seven-year-old girl who had had some complications.

"Hello Mrs. Jenkins. I'm ..."

Anna stopped as the mother of the little girl stepped in front of her, blocking her path to the little girl's bed.

"Stop. Don't come any closer to my daughter, please."

Startled, Anna complied, then reached her hand out to touch the woman's shoulder and started to ask what her concern was. But her hand never reached its target because the woman shrank back from it. Anna heard the door open behind her, and assumed it was Dr. Saul.

"Doctor, can I please speak with you, now?" demanded Mrs. Jenkins.

"Why, of course, Mrs ... Jenkins," he finished, glancing quickly down at the chart in his hands. "I'm Dr. Saul, by the way." He reached out his hand in greeting.

Anna was about to say something to warn him that this mom, for some reason – maybe religious? – didn't seem to like physical touch, when Mrs. Jenkins reached out and clasped the doctor's hand with *both* of hers.

"Can I have a different nurse, please? One who isn't ... you know ..."

Anna froze as understanding dawned on her. *The posters.*

"Mrs. Jenkins, I can assure you that Anna is literally our best nurse. Your daughter is in very good ..." Anna could see understanding dawn on Dr. Saul's face as well when he glanced at her and his eyes shifted downward almost imperceptibly to her mask, then her badge. "Oh. Umm ..."

"And I also insist that my daughter's nurse not have HIV either. Or hepatitis B. Or anything else that could possibly be spread through touch. Oh my gosh, if you give my child herpes, I'm going to sue!"

"Mrs. Jenkins, even if one of our nurses or any other staff is HIV positive, or anything else like that, you can't catch it from …"

"Like hell I can't," the mom interrupted. "This surgery almost killed my daughter. I don't want some … hussy infecting her with something else. I demand that she get a nurse who doesn't have AIDS or anything."

"Now Mrs. Jenkins, there is no danger from any of our staff. That type of information is confidential anyway. Even I don't know which nurses or doctors have …"

"But the posters are kind enough to warn me who has the flu? I want to know what color mask the HIV people wear, and what color sticker those people have on. I mean, compared to those, who even cares about the flu, right? Please. This is my daughter we are talking about. I don't want anyone, or anything, to put her in danger."

Anna could tell that Dr. Saul was at a loss for words. As was she. Then the doctor did something that ordinarily would have resulted in an HR report, but that Anna would remember gratefully for the rest of her life. Dr. Saul – Abraham, as he became to her later – stepped over to Anna, pulled her mask down, and kissed her. Not just on one cheek, but on both, to show that there's nothing dangerous about an unvaccinated person.

"We'll find you a new nurse, Mrs. Jenkins," he said as he guided Anna out of the room.

Chapter 32

The Seven

"Ok, so we are all in agreement then? We are reversing our previous stance against the nasal flu vaccine, and advising that people can resume using it for the upcoming season. For the last few years we cautioned against it because it didn't seem to protect against the swine flu strain. Now that they've re-formulated it with a different version of the swine flu, there is some evidence it works. So, this year we will recommend that it's a viable option again. Just so we are all clear."

The six other faces around the table all nodded agreement. One of the six decided to throw in a final word.

"Well, recommending against it was an easy decision, and a safe one. We had the data that showed it didn't work nearly as well as the shot, so we recommended against it. And there was only one company that made it, so we weren't pissing off a cohort of supporters. And the dozen or more makers of the flu *shots* liked that decision."

"None of us care about that, Frank," admonished Dr. Baker. "At least, we shouldn't."

"OK, OK. I know. Just saying."

"But now the maker of the nasal spray has new data showing it does work, so we are back to a show of support again," continued Dr. Davidson, the Chairman. "The next decision is what to do with the combined MMRV shot."

Groans from the group.

"We've already hashed out all the arguments for and against, and I'm not going to make us go through it all again. But we are voting on this right now so we can move on to the more important issue we've tabled three times already."

Even more groans.

"So, do we continue to remain neutral regarding MMRV, which is the MMR and Varicella vaccines combined into one shot? Just let doctors make their own decisions about which to use – the combined MMRV or the separate MMR and Varicella shots. Or do we finally come out in favor of the separated shots – recommend people get an MMR and a Varicella separately? By doing so we don't actually have to recommend against MMRV. That would be a step to take in later years. It would simply be a show of preference that people get them separately in order to reduce seizure reactions."

"I'll say that I think the recommendation in favor of separation is a good move," contributed Dr. Adams. "We all know that the MMRV combo reportedly triggers seizures in 1 in 1250 doses, compared to the 1 in 3000 rate of seizures when kids get them separately. It's because the combo has ten times the amount of varicella germs in it. That's what they need to make it work after being mixed in with measles, mumps and rubella viruses. And by making the policy, we demonstrate to the public that we are concerned about vaccine safety and taking steps to improve it."

Nods from some around the table.

"And you are sure the vaccine manufacturer doesn't care, Darren? We don't want to piss them off." This from Dr. Frank Fitzhugh, again.

"Well, I thought they wouldn't care. They make both versions of the vaccines, and no other company makes these in the States. So they don't really care if people get the combo or the separated ones domestically. But internationally it's a different story. They are pushing their combo hard, and they have some competition with foreign makers of MMR. Offering the combo in some of the emerging markets has an advantage. If word gets out that the U.S. isn't advising the combo anymore because of the seizures, acceptance of the combo may wane internationally. So, although we aren't supposed to care about that," glance at Frank, "I think good relations with Industry should factor into this equation."

Thoughtful looks from all around.

"Something else to consider," offered Dr. Fitzhugh, "is that this decision has to do with safety issues. The nasal flu vaccine issue had to do with efficacy. By bringing a safety concern out into the open in a policy, we bring attention to it." A glance at Dr. Adams, who had made the opposite observation earlier.

"OK," Dr. Davidson took control again. "I guess we aren't going to reach a consensus on this today. All in favor of tabling this decision to a later date, say aye."

A chorus of "ayes."

"On a similar note, speaking of international vaccines, Francine called me this morning to ask if we can delay our condemnation of thimerosal for at least three more years. She says too many foreign companies need more time to change over their production to single dose vials of the flu shot. She agrees that we eventually need to be done with multi-dose flu vials containing mercury, but if we come out with an admission now that mercury is dangerous, and that it should no longer be used, that will force all the American flu shot makers to only make mercury-free flu shots next year. They are ready to do that, as soon as we and the CDC give them the go-ahead. But internationally, most pharmaceutical companies are not ready. If we admit that mercury is dangerous now, we'll scare the international community. If, instead, we keep using it here in the U.S. for another three years, as a demonstration that we believe it's safe, especially for babies and pregnant women, then international acceptance of the growing vaccine schedule will continue unabated. If, on the other hand, we stop using it, then they are all going to want to stop using it, and they'll stop accepting all mercury-containing vaccines. So, to do this when everyone is ready is better for all of us in the long run. Since we all had already discussed this last month, and agreed, I told her yes. We'd keep a lid on it."

Unanimous nods.

"I also got a call from Elizabeth at the CDC to give me a heads-up on another idea they are considering. This is something I've suspected was coming for a long time too: the DTP vaccine."

Davidson paused to see their reactions.

"What about the DTaP?" asked Dr. Baker when no one else took the bait.

"No. Not the DTaP. The plain old DTP. The whole-cell version we stopped using in the 90s."

More silence.

"Wait. You mean using it? Like, on people? Children? Babies? That's ... preposterous," Baker objected. "We already have enough adverse events after the DTaP. They want to go back to all that encephalitis? Hypotensive hyporesponsive episodes? Seizures? The public won't stand for it."

"Well, some at the CDC think they finally have enough research to pull it off. First, there are the data that show all those thousands of babies who we'd thought were brain damaged from the DTP vaccine back in the 70s and 80s really turned out to just have Dravet Syndrome – a genetic mutation in the SCN1A gene that made them prone to reacting to the vaccine. They would have developed seizures and intellectual decline anyway, as all kids with the Dravet mutation eventually do. The vaccine just brought on the problems earlier, an average of two months earlier. But it was their genetics that made them react that way, not the actual vaccine."

"That's bull, and you know it Darren. The Dravet studies on DTP were done decades after these kids reacted. They were retrospective. And they only included a tiny fraction of all the kids who developed encephalopathy – brain damage – from the DTP. They cherry-picked some of them with the mutation and tried to show that they *all* had Dravet's. It was totally bogus, in my opinion. There were thousands of kids without Dravet's who were damaged. Even the titles of the new studies are biased. 'Alleged encephalopathy.' Aaron, Chris, and I were there, Darren. We saw this happen every single month in our offices back in the 80s. You four didn't."

"Well, as you put it, we have to go with the science. The new study out of Boston University gives the CDC the data they would need, *we* would need, to secure acceptance of the old vaccine again. The BU data, and dozens of other studies in the last five years, have all demonstrated how the acellular vaccine is failing. We all know the old whole-cell vaccine works better. We stopped using it because of the *appearance* of brain injury. But these data now tell us that the kids who suffered encephalopathy would have done so anyway – the vaccine just triggered it sooner. In fact, one of the Dravet studies shows that you can even continue giving the vaccine after the onset of encephalopathy because it doesn't worsen their intellectual outcome."

"Please tell me that even *you* don't believe that!" Dr. Chris Charleston finally contributed. "What, someone's brain that is totally fried doesn't seem to get any worse after more doses? There is no worse? Fried is fried?"

"I'm with Chris on this, Darren," jumped in Adams. "Bringing back DTP may reduce pertussis again, but it's going to destroy confidence in vaccines – confidence that's already precarious. Does the CDC really want to risk this?"

"Liz said they aren't sure. She wanted to know what I thought, so I'm bringing this before all of you. The old DTP vaccine is already being accepted internationally. Many of the Asian and Pacific Island nations have started using the whole-cell vaccine again. And it's working there. Officially, the CDC doesn't need our blessing to move forward with this. And they aren't quite sure if or how they are going to do it. They may start by just making one of the DTaP doses be the whole-cell version at first. Then expand it from there. So, we don't need to vote on this today. I'm just giving you all a heads-up. I get why you two – three? – don't like it. You lived through it with your patients. But the ACIP at the CDC runs the show on this. Liz does want our opinion, but she's not beholden to it. I'll let her know how you three feel, and keep you all updated.

"Moving on then to the main issue, and I'd like to hear what you have all come up with since our last meeting. Do we advise policymakers to stick with the old-school approach and just continue to promote vaccination as they always have, or do we take the leap into advising a policy which states vaccines should be mandatory – for everyone."

The seven colleagues were all tired. It had been a long day, and they all wanted it to be over. But, they also wanted consensus on this particular vote. They wanted every member to agree on the course of action. Right now it seemed like it was 3 votes to 4. But the four members of the committee who wanted to move forward didn't want to do so without the three old-timers. The three were the history of the group. They helped get the field of pediatrics to where it was today, they were smart, and they knew the science. But they were also stubborn. And maybe it was time they stepped aside in favor of progress. Although the group of seven weren't part of any official organization and didn't have any official power, most of the policy-making organizations that *did* listened to them.

"And I'm not referring to mandatory vaccination just for school. That ship is already sailing, partly because we were able to steer clear of using the very word 'mandatory.' Very few Americans want any medicine to be mandatory. So, by framing the new school vaccine laws as 'removal of non-medical and religious exemptions to vaccines' in our policy, we were able to keep any impression of coercion and mandate out of the policy. It's become popular to turn against religious ideas now anyway, and even the term 'non-medical exemptions' puts those families into the 'crazy' category – 'those' parents who shun medicine. It was brilliant, and it worked.

"So, no. I'm not talking about just mandates for school. I'm talking about straight-up mandates. Mandatory vaccination for all. All the big medical organizations want it, and this may be the time to go for it."

Several moments of silence.

Dr. Adams was the first to pick up the baton. "I doubt we have the science we need to determine if that would be a good long-term move, and we probably won't have that science for decades, if ever. You're probably thinking we have to act now, before vaccination rates get too low. But I'm telling you, Darren, and Eli, Frank, and Greg, that I don't think it's our job to *make* people vaccinate, to actually force medicine on anyone. We present it, we advise it, we promote it, and we encourage it. But force it? That just crosses a line, unless we have sound scientific reasons as to why we should. American medical organizations put science first. They, and we, always have. It's our foundation. To stray from that now could really cost us in the long run. We make a policy like this without science, people will find out. They always do. And they'll lose trust in us and our leadership. And not only the public, but organizations will lose trust in us as well. The whole-cell DTP was bad enough decades ago, and re-opening that box is going to create a lot of problems. But you also weren't around during the hepatitis B vaccine mistake."

"Now Aaron, that was a long time ago too. Most people have forgotten about that as well."

"Have they? I don't think so. We advised adding a vaccine to the infant schedule in the 90s that we had no scientific basis for adding. The 'science' that was presented was bull. But Bill and I were the only two on the committee who saw it that way, and we were overruled. And you know what? We lost the trust of many doctors. Not some, many. They were like, 'What? Hep B vaccine? Really? Why?' I still hear it at conventions. That's the one and only vaccine they complain about. Yeah, they give it anyway because 'it's on the schedule' and 'you can't vary from the schedule.' But they don't like it. And you know what I overheard a group of physicians laughing about at last year's convention? That it was 'a vaccine without an audience,' meaning that it was created for prostitutes and drug users; but when none of them would show up for their shots, the companies that had invested hundreds of millions in development were pissed and they needed *someone* to give their vaccine to. So we handed them our babies – all of them. Yeah, I actually heard these pediatricians laughing about that. And I think they half believed it. And then last year the CDC adds that it must be given within the first 24 hours of life. Why? Why not day 2, or day 7? What's the hurry? I suspect the real reason they put the 24-hour time clock on it is that too many people had relatives come to visit on day 2 and 3 who'd say, 'Oh, be sure you don't let them give your baby the hep B shot. It's for an STD, so it's not necessary until they are older.' But if it's already done, it's done. Get it in there before the parents have any chance to think about it. Sure, it's an effective policy, but most pediatricians realize how unnecessary it is. So, if we put out a policy that now officially mandates all vaccines for every single child without having the science to prove that's better than our system now, and all kids will be better off because of it, we risk losing a lot of trust from the general medical community."

"How can kids *not* be better off fully vaccinated? Vaccinating kids has always been the number one goal of pediatric medicine because a vaccinated kid is a healthy kid. So any policy that increases that will obviously be better for their long-term health."

"No, Frank. We only *think* vaccinated kids are healthier. But the only science-based statement we can really make about vaccinated kids is that they are vaccinated. Oh, and they are less likely to die of that disease. That's not synonymous with being overall healthier in every other aspect of their well-being. In pediatrics, every time we discuss a policy that improves vaccine rates we all assume that's a good thing. Like, for example, the new hep B shot within 24 hours of birth. That policy will obviously increase vaccination rates. But that's all it does. We don't have any evidence that it will be better for kids' health in the long run. Everyone assumes increasing hep B vaccine rates will somehow magically create some sort of better long-term outcome, so we need a policy to make sure it happens. But do we actually *know* we are gaining anything by it? Scientifically, we don't. We've all sat around on a number of vaccine-approval committees, and that's the one thing that's always bugged me. Every policy decision is made with one goal, and one goal only: to increase the rate of a vaccine. Everyone nods their head in approval with the assumption that anything, and I mean *anything*, we can do to get that vaccine into more people is automatically good. We never bother to take it a step further and make our policies based on whether or not something additionally beneficial will come out of *that*. Like, prove that all babies who get hep B vaccine at birth are healthier than babies who don't *before* we make a policy on it. Do you get what I'm saying?"

A nod from Bill and Chris, but confused looks from the rest.

The "science" these gentlemen were discussing, or rather were not discussing, because it didn't exist, was the science that would show *vaccinated* children are healthier than *unvaccinated* ones. The three old-school members had always insisted that if they were going to issue a policy statement that came right out and said all vaccines should be mandatory for all children, they had to be able to show that this move was scientifically beneficial to the long-term health of all children, or at least virtually all children. They wanted this decision to be driven by science – proof that getting the complete vaccine schedule was so good for kids that it *should* be mandated. In order to have science on their side, they'd need to demonstrate that children who get the entire vaccine schedule live longer, better lives than children who don't. The only thing anyone had been able to prove so far, and only for some vaccines, is that children are less likely to die from that infectious disease if they were vaccinated against it. That's all. But that wasn't the same thing as saying they live longer and better.

In fact, one of the concerns holding the three back was that there were now data that showed *unvaccinated* kids live healthier lives: they have less allergies and asthma and less autoimmune disease. And they didn't have any data to counter that. That was scientifically problematic.

Plus, there was that new study out of Jackson State University that was the first published study to really take a good look at this issue, and the results didn't look good. Data were collected on the health of 405 vaccinated and 262 unvaccinated elementary age kids from four different states, and the vaccinated kids were 30 times more likely to suffer from allergies and about 5 times more likely to suffer ear infections and pneumonia. Vaccines were actually supposed to protect from those things. But it didn't end there. ADHD and learning disorders were also 5 times more common, and autism 4 times more common, in vaccinated kids. And the findings also held up in kids who were only partially vaccinated – same numbers whether they had some or all the shots. The unvaccinated kids were healthier. Especially the preemies: 32% of the preemies in the study who were vaccinated had a neurodevelopmental disorder, whereas none of the unvaccinated preemies grew up to have such a disorder. That was probably just a fluke, a finding because the study was so small. What their committee needed was a better, larger study that showed the opposite.

Their organization had a long and proud history of only supporting policies based on things they could prove. Like, kids lived longer, better lives if they weren't exposed to lead. Kids lived longer, better lives if they ate healthy foods and were less obese. You know, Science.

"Lemme tell you guys how I look at this," chimed in Chris, who'd been pensive for a while. "Are we here to serve all children and help ensure the highest health of all children? Or are we here to ensure the highest vaccination rates we possibly can? Let me try to re-phrase what Aaron is saying, because I agree it's critical to understand why those two statements are mutually exclusive. But before I do, here's a related thought that's been on my mind. I keep thinking about all the families who chose to only get some vaccines, or even most vaccines. And the few who chose no vaccines. It's bad enough, in my opinion, but I know I'm in the minority here, that pediatricians kick these patients out of their offices if they don't comply with the entire schedule on time. Many of the large twenty-pediatrician groups have gone that way. But those kids need pediatricians too. If we condone that, and join the mandate crowd, we force those families into even further hiding. They get no pediatric care at all. Keeping vaccines optional allows all families to have a pediatrician. All children get served, not just compliant ones. We can then use our skills and our relationship to influence them gradually. And really, if some still don't vaccinate, that's ok. That's their choice."

Silence for a bit as they absorbed this idea.

"But let me go back to my earlier thought. What is our purpose? Why is our committee here? What is our ultimate goal? If it's simply to maximize vaccination, then mandating them is a no-brainer. If we, instead, are here at the service of all children and families to provide care to all, then I think mandating vaccines is incompatible with that mission. We can't do both."

"But we know that all vaccines are good for all children. We *know* it."

"No, we *think* we know it, Darren. But you can't show me a study that proves vaccinating is healthier than not vaccinating in the long run. Look at what the Institute of Medicine said four years ago, and they haven't found any research to update their statement. They came right out and said we don't have long-term safety research on our complete vaccine schedule. We really have no idea whether or not it's safe. We all think is, but again we don't *know* it is. Until we do, I personally think it's unethical to force the schedule."

"Well, it's possible the NIH is going to undertake such a study. You've heard about Stanley's bill, right? He wants to force the NIH into doing the vaxxed/unvaxxed study. Long-term health outcomes. So, we might have the data we need someday."

"Or, we might see data that we don't like."

"That's why I wish this study would be done under the supervision of the CDC." This from Dr. Fitzhugh.

The room was silent for quite a while as the group mulled these ideas over in their individual minds.

"I've never really heard it put the way you just did, Chris," offered Dr. Davidson. "I mean, what you say makes sense. But look at what's happening right now. Acceptance of the full CDC schedule is steadily declining. More people are opting out than ever before. It's inevitable that we will see a rise in disease. Are we just going to let that happen?"

"If – no, *when* – diseases return, many such people will start vaccinating again. Opinions shift depending on disease trends. So it's not like we would go back to the Dark Ages. Not in a modern country like ours. Vaccines aren't the only reason these diseases are low. And the one disease that isn't low – whooping cough – is partly because our vaccine is failing. Listen: diseases happen. We can't change that. They will always happen. Five hundred years from now there will be diseases. We will keep them low, and we may eliminate some. When they come back, vaccines go up. When we get complacent because we are doing too good a job and there's little to no disease, vaccines go down. Up and down. That's how it will always be. But we'll always stay ahead of the diseases. That's what a modern society does, using a whole variety of measures. Nutrition, sanitation, quality healthcare, education, and for most, vaccination."

"I'll tell you my opinion on this in one short sentence," Dr. Gordon this time. "Although I agree with Darren's proposition, I also feel that vaccines should be so good, and so safe, and so right, that people *want* them. That *everybody* wants them. Something *that* good shouldn't have to be forced. So, we focus on how good they are, how safe they are, and almost everybody will get them. That's good enough for me. Forcing them automatically makes them bad. People will start to think, 'Why are you forcing these on me and my kids? Aren't they good? Wait, I want to know why they need to be forced. I'm not going to get them yet until I figure out what someone thought was wrong with them that they had to become mandatory. Just hold up!' That's what people are going to do. I think mandatory vaccines will actually reduce vaccination rates because people will rebel – even people who like vaccines. Even if we do eventually get the science that you three are asking for, I'm not sure that would make me want to mandate them even *then*."

"Greg has a good point, Darren," continued Dr. Aaron Adams. "What the state senators are doing, making vaccines mandatory for school, could end up backfiring. Yes, it will increase vaccine rates in school, and maybe overall for a time, but that move is forcing all the families who don't fully vaccinate to speak out against vaccines even louder than before. They've been pretty quiet for many decades be-cause no one was bothering them. Well, now more and more families are having their kids kicked out of school in the nicest place in the country to live and being forced into homeschooling, and they are pissed. So they are getting loud and proud. None of these anti-vaccine groups even existed before the California law, and before it passed in that other state as well. Or they were very quiet. Our Kids Our Choice, A Voice For Choice, Learn The Risk, Immunity Education Group, Vial, Vaxxed, Children's Health Defense, Citizen's Committee on Immunization Practices, Parents Questioning Vaccines, First Freedoms, and a host of state medical freedom groups, like California

Coalition for Health Choice and Health Freedom fill-in-the-blank state. They've all risen up in just the past few years to raise awareness of vaccine risk. And there are also physician-based groups as well, including that new Physicians for Informed Consent bunch. Before the new laws, these groups were silent or non-existent. NVIC was the only one we had to contend with. And these groups aren't crazy zealots. They are intelligent, organized, calm demonstrators. And what happens when some of the in-school families start to listen? And start to think about what could be wrong with vaccines that they need to be forced? And start to think that their neighbors and friends are equal citizens who shouldn't be quarantined for their beliefs. Could this first step backfire? And if we proceed with making them mandatory period – mandatory not just for school but for ... life – how is the public going to react? It's a very astute observation, and it's one that I think we all need to consider."

More silence.

"Well, I can see that we won't reach any consensus on this issue. But I like what you are saying, Aaron. The state legislators are doing this for us now. Vaccines will become mandatory for school entry in every state eventually. And the people will let it happen. They'll think, 'Oh, we'll just go to private school.' They won't realize until it's too late that these laws will apply to *all* schools. So, we let this play out for now, and let the legislators be the bad guys.

"As for a full mandate, policymakers will want an opinion from us at some point. It doesn't have to be now. Maybe we do remain neutral on it for the time being, as a committee. Whoever wants to can individually continue to help get the school laws passed in all states. Hey, they didn't even need our help in California. And they didn't need our involvement in the state where it was just passed either. That state's medical academy took care of it all."

"Yeah, and now more people think that these state medical academies aren't real medical organizations, but just political lobbying platforms for Pharma." This, uncharacteristically, from Dr. Fitzhugh.

"Well, at least we Seven are off the public grid. And you three, once again, have made us all examine this from angles we wouldn't have considered. I think we all need more time to think this over. For now, we'll stay silent on this. But eventually we will have to decide. Do we help support mandatory laws for school, or do we take it further and help make them mandatory for … mandatory to be a parent of a child?"

Concerned, and some scared, expressions all around.

Chapter 33

If You Could Read My Mind

"So, what are our options, Doctor?"

"Well, you can move to a different state. You can't go to West Virginia or Mississippi – they've always had mandatory vaccination laws there. Ironically, they also have just about the worst child health ratings in the country too. And after many decades of freedom from Pharma, California and one other state just fell. All the other states are free for the most part, for now. Your other choice is homeschooling."

"Oh my gosh, we could never homeschool. We want our kids to be normal."

Dr. Ward didn't outwardly roll his eyes. "Well, I tell you, my grown-up kids – two are already through college – tell me that the best, most social, intellectual, and well-rounded kids they met in college, and are still friends with now, were homeschooled. One of my kids even married one."

"Well, I just couldn't do it. I'm not nearly smart enough."

You're not smarter than your kindergartener? Dr. Ward didn't say. "I know it's frustrating, but that's the law."

"I can't believe we have to do this. I didn't even know they were passing this law. When was it again? In 2015? We weren't planning to vaccinate, and we don't really watch the news, so we had no idea this was going on. We would have stopped it if we'd known."

Seriously? How could anyone living here not *have known this was happening?* It annoyed Dr. Ward when people who didn't lift a finger to try to prevent the new law complained about it. *Not that they shouldn't complain about it. More should. We all need to speak up.*

"I almost wish we did have a bunch of vaccine injuries in our family that we could use to get a medical excuse to not vaccinate our kids. But John's side of the family grew up natural, and none of them vaccinated. My family did, but none of us had any bad reactions that I know of."

"Hey Doc, what if one of us got just one vaccine now, and had a really bad reaction? Would that opt our kids out of them?"

"Interesting thought. Maybe, but it would have to be a serious reaction like a seizure, or nerve damage, or sudden onset of a severe autoimmune disease like diabetes or rheumatoid arthritis, or a neurological disorder. But that's really unlikely. I mean, I've seen those reactions happen, and there are a lot of published research articles that describe all kinds of severe, chronic allergic, autoimmune, and neurological disorders being triggered by vaccination, both in children and adults. I've seen tic disorders, severe psoriasis, all kinds of stuff happen to healthy people. Even psychiatric illness – that's published too. I've had two families in my practice begin vaccinations in their child because of this law and their kids both developed severe facial tics – that very evening of their first vaccine. Or sudden, severe allergies, with no prior history of them. I'm seen toddlers suffer developmental regression. Yeah, those kids were then exempt from having to get any more vaccines. It happens, but the chance of it happening is very low. I don't know how low, or high, but it's uncommon. So, the chance that one of you is going to have such a reaction that is severe enough to then opt your children out of having to start them is unlikely."

"Plus, John, if you were injured like that and couldn't work ..."

"Yeah, I just wish we didn't have to vaccinate."

Again, no one's forcing you to, technically, he again didn't say.

Dr. Ward didn't say a lot of things to his patients. Not that he wasn't a compassionate and understanding doctor. He dealt with this issue so much, and it frustrated him as much as it did his patients.

He understood their plight. Most of his patients were low-income or middle-class families, and for such to live in California required two incomes, or at least one decent one. Many couldn't homeschool for that reason. So, essentially they were being forced to vaccinate or move. To force families to move out of a state or deny them access to education over a medical decision was unethical and unconstitutional in his book; but the legislators had ignored that minor inconvenience, and now he, as a doctor, was no longer in the position to independently advise families about their health care decisions. It was as if a certain senator/doctor was also sitting in his exam room next to him offering his or her own opinion about the efficacy and importance of vaccination. *This, and all medical decisions, should be made by these parents and these parents alone, with their own in-person doctor - me - to advise them, not a panel of law-makers sitting 400 miles away.*

Dr. Ward remembered several years earlier when a different California senator had introduced a bill that mandated ADHD meds for all schoolchildren with a diagnosis. But that bill hadn't gone anywhere; it had been thrown out right away. The theory behind the law was that making ADHD meds mandatory would make life better for teachers. Keep all those kids calm and quiet and focused, and the teachers could then spend equal time with all the students in the class. Plus, treating ADHD with meds is better for the kids, and parents who deny them these meds are putting their kids at risk of failure. That's how that law had been introduced. But then the obvious arguments had shot it down: you can't force parents to give their kids a medical treatment. It's unethical and unconstitutional. Parents are the ones who get to decide. And kids with ADHD have the same right to go to school as all other kids. And they aren't a danger to anyone. They may make life a little inconvenient for their teachers and other students, but that's life. Plus, the meds don't work on everyone. And if you force all kids to take them, and some kids die from the cardiac side effects, would that make it all worth it? And who would then be liable, the California government for passing the law, or the pharmaceutical company who made the drug? The parents would sue, and win. So, the legislators said no thank you and moved on.

The parallels between that and the new vaccine law were so obvious, but this time around the right mix of legislators were in office to make sure enough of them conveniently didn't draw the same parallels. *It amazes me that parents don't mind letting their legislators take away their rights to make medical decisions. Sure, most parents get their kids vaccinated, but don't they at least want to decide? Don't they want it to be a free choice? And don't they realize that once they give the government the power to make one medical decision for them, they'll seize on any other such opportunity they can because now they know the public will just sit back and let it happen? What's next, mandatory antibiotics or antivirals for every single infection? Mandatory birth control for everybody? You, the parents, don't get to decide – the State does. Mandatory psych meds for all kids with 'problems?' Get your problem child drugged up or keep him home please. He's bothering my child.* Sadly, he *could* see parents of 'normal' kids ganging up on the challenging ones, jumping on the bandwagon, and making them all stay home or get their damn meds.

Not that he was against psych meds. Sometimes they did some good. Some kids needed them. But again, who decides? A doctor and parent, or a legislator? Again, it came back to letting the government have even one arena of control over this, and they'll look for more. *We'll see if the public keeps re-electing these politicians. If they do, then I guess we know the answer.*

Dr. Ward's mind had wandered through all these thoughts so often that he could now ponder through it all in about a second and a half, and he came back to the patients in front of him.

"So, if you are going to vaccinate, let's discuss how you can go about doing it in a gradual way. There's really no guarantee that this will be safer. A child can have a severe reaction to even one vaccine, and no one has researched the cumulative safety of any vaccine schedule, whether it's the full schedule or an alternative one. But I know you both know all this already, because we've talked about it before.

John Phillip Ryan

"Here's what we can do with your three-year-old. He hasn't had any vaccines yet. In order to start preschool, he'll need to at least have the first round of every shot. Then you can complete them all after your child has started school. Some schools, especially private ones, will let you go slowly. But technically, the CDC advises kids to finish all necessary vaccines in as quickly as 6 months, again with no safety research on *that* accelerated schedule. Public schools, and some private ones, may make you do them that fast. Now, your child is three. If you aren't planning to start preschool until age 4, we have a year to get some in, spread out as much as we can, and then perhaps another six months to a year to finish them while in school. Here's what your child will need for preschool and to move on to kindergarten: 5 DTaP, 4 Polio, 3 Hep B, 2 MMR, 2 CPox, and 1 HIB. That's 17 injections of 31 vaccines, because some are three-in-one. Plus the Tdap booster for 7th grade, but that's a long way off.

"But we can whittle this down a bit to 22 doses, and here's how: you only need 4 DTaP and 3 polio if we time them right so that the final doses occur when he's 4 or older. Kids usually get 4 DTaP and 3 Polio as babies, and then the 5th DTaP and 4th Polio at age 5. But if you start them later, like you are, then the whole series works just as well with one less dose. This in the CDC catch-up schedule online.

"The next vaccine you can go without, *if* you are willing to put off school until he's 5, that is, is HIB. This vaccine is only approved for use through age 4. Once a child turns 5 it's not approved. Babies normally get 4 doses when younger, but when you delay it and don't give any until 15 months or older, one dose works just as well as if you'd had all 4. That's in the CDC catch-up schedule as well. So, going into preschool at 3 or 4 you'd need just the one dose. If you wait until 5, you don't need any.

"Next are the MMR and chickenpox vaccines. They require two of each, but if you get a blood test about two or more months after you've had the first doses, and the test confirms that the first doses worked, you don't have to get the second doses. This only works with these two live-virus vaccines. Schools won't usually accept immunity testing to get out of more doses of all the other vaccines.

372

"As for the Hep B series, you need all three doses for preschool and kindergarten no matter what age you start.

"So, you really could end up just needing 4 DTaP, 3 Polio, 3 Hep B, 1 MMR, and 1 Chickenpox. That's 12 injections of 22 vaccines. Again, I know it's 22 more than you want, but that's the law now. We can be glad they didn't make all the vaccines on the CDC schedule mandatory, like HPV, Pneumococcal, Hep A, Flu, Meningococcal, and Rotavirus. They might try to add those on someday, but they took such hell from passing this first law that maybe they won't try.

"Another option to consider, if you want, is that the DTaP vaccine is only approved for use through age 6. You can't get those 4 doses once you've turned seven. So, if you homeschool until then, you can cut the DTaPs out of the plan. At seven, you'd need one dose of Tdap, which he'd need for 7th grade anyway. You'd just be doing it 5 years earlier, and wouldn't need it at 7th grade because only one dose is allowed, unless you are pregnant – you can get one dose with each pregnancy. Sorry, that's a little off topic. Anyway, some schools may also make you get two doses of Td – that's just the tetanus and diphtheria vaccine – to complete the immunity for those two diseases. I say 'some schools' because the Td vaccine is now very hard to find. There's a shortage. I haven't had any for a couple years now. It's stupid, though, because tetanus isn't contagious, so a school shouldn't care if your child has full tetanus immunity. And the diphtheria vaccine does prevent the spread of the disease, not that we even have diphtheria here anyway. But the legislators, in their wisdom, seem to know best. The benefit of doing this is that you avoid 4 doses of the 'P' component - pertussis. This is the most reactive part of the vaccine. The D and the T are usually better tolerated.

"So, the 7-year-old plan would be 1 Tdap, maybe 2 Td, 3 Polio, 3 Hep B, and 1 MMR and Chickenpox with a blood test.

"And finally, another way to get out of some of these but go to school later is to home school until 7th grade because the Hep B vaccine, according to the new law, is not a requirement for 7th grade and beyond. So, a 7th-grader would need 1 Tdap, 3 Polio, 1 MMR, and 1 Chickenpox. And maybe 2 Td. However, I just read that California schools are going to mandate hep B vaccine anyway, even though current law allows people to opt out from 7th grade and up. I don't know how the schools think that *they* can make a vaccine mandatory that the state already declared not mandatory, but they are doing it. So, hep B may be needed for unvaccinated teens in the years to come. So, there are all your options. And I want to make one thing clear. I'm not actually saying you should do, or not do, all these. I'm simply saying what will be required by law if you enroll your child in school.

"You can still consider homeschooling. You have to decide what's a better and safer decision for your child – vaccinate and go to school, or don't. In my opinion, the safest option, and one that fits the natural lifestyle ideals of parents who want to raise their kids more naturally, is to accept the homeschooling lifestyle for the early years through all of elementary school. Of course, there are many opportunities for group homeschooling, co-opting with other families to school your kids together, and enjoy field trips and social events together. Homeschooling is what you make it to be. Give the 8 shots very slowly, one at a time, spread out between ages 8 and 12 or so, and your child will then be ready to enroll in school for 7th grade. That's what I see a lot of my patients choosing. Or, some don't ever begin the shots and remain as homeschoolers, especially if they've found a 'village' of other families whom they've grown close to. And since homeschooling tends to be a better education anyway, and unvaccinated kids are often smarter and healthier, at least according to some research, who knows? Maybe these unvaccinated kids will grow up someday, become our leaders in government and industry, and get rid of mandatory vaccination. Anyway, I digress. What do you think?"

"Well, we want to start school when he's four. So, I guess we should get started now that he's three to give us time to spread them out."

Well, I tried, Dr. Ward, again, didn't roll his eyes. "Now, let's talk about the baby. She's two months old now, and that's when the regular schedule starts. But I assume you'd want to wait?"

"Yes. We aren't starting this young."

"Ok. So, you probably want to delay things as long as you have for your first?"

"Yes. And maybe they'll have changed this law by then."

"I wish, but not likely." *Not if parents like you keep expecting* them *to change it for you. It's* you *that have to jump into the fight and get this done, get out there and convince pro-vaccine people that laws like this are unnecessary, unethical, and just the first step toward everyone's medical freedom being taken away.* He, again, didn't say out loud.

But maybe he should start.

Chapter 34

Vaccines Are the New Black

Trina looked at herself in the metal mirror for what she hoped was the last time. Her black eye had faded to a dull yellow-brown, and she hoped it would cover up nicely before she saw her kid again – *if* she got to see him, that is. Her lawyer had managed to get a hearing for later that afternoon to try to get visitation rights. She was optimistic. *Maybe the black eye I got here in jail, the jail that judge sent me to, will get me some sympathy. I'll leave off the make-up.*

Trina still couldn't believe it. That in America, a parent could be put in jail for not vaccinating her child. She'd heard stories from other people, but always thought there's just no way. *Look at me now.*

Trina looked back on the last 5 years of her life, and tried to think of what she could have done differently. *I could have chosen a husband who didn't turn out to be so ill-suited for me, I suppose.* The divorce had been easy, as they'd only been married a few months. But then her periods stopped, and the realization that a child would forever tie her to her "ex" was a hard pill to swallow. *But Jack is such an amazing boy. I can't imagine life without him.*

The back and forth shared custody wasn't easy, but at least Jim didn't push Trina to vaccinate their child, something that she was strongly opposed to. Until this year. Jim had a change of heart and took the matter to family court. The judge ordered her to begin vaccinating Jack, but she refused. So the judge held her in contempt, awarded full custody to Jim, and tossed her in jail where she'd spent the past week.

Her lawyer tried to tell her that she wasn't in jail for not vaccinating, she was in jail for contempt of court – for not obeying a judge's order. But as far as she was concerned, it was the same thing. What scared her more than being thrown in jail for contempt over not complying with vaccines was that a judge, which ultimately was the government, could force any non-emergency medical treatment at all. If a judge can force a child to get 70 doses of vaccination against the will of a parent, what other types of invasive medical treatments can a judge force?

And why now? Courts had historically ruled that one divorced parent could not give a child any type of non-emergency preventive medical care without the consent of both custodial parents. Such family custody circumstances had always ended in a stale-mate. One parent wanted to vaccinate, the other didn't. So no action was allowed. What had changed? Why now? There was no increase in diseases. There were no threatening outbreaks. What would prompt *this* judge to change decades of precedence? Her lawyer had no answers for her.

Trina didn't know exactly what shots were given to her child the next day – 6 days ago now. All she knew was what her lawyer was able to tell her: that Jim took Jack in to the doctor the very next day and got him vaccinated; that night Jack suffered a severe asthma attack – his first ever – and was rushed to the hospital and admitted to the ICU; after 5 days in the hospital he was just now being sent home. And Trina hadn't been able to see her child through any of it. *What must he think of me?* she wondered.

Trina knew there was plenty of medical research that linked vaccines to asthma attacks. But she also had a sinking feeling that the judge wouldn't see it that way. The word "coincidence" was already ringing in her ears. She knew she wouldn't get custody, and wouldn't be able to stop the next round of vaccines either. *If Jack dies, who is held responsible? The judge? The state? Or the Vaccine Injury Compensation Fund?* Trina knew all about the fund, but it was for those who voluntarily vaccinated. What about someone who is forced? She was afraid that no one would be considered liable because it didn't fall under any known precedents. And she knew she didn't have any money to fight this. *Do I just give up on Jack? Let Jim have him and his asthma, and move on? No, of course not. Maybe this would be his only asthma attack. Or maybe Jim would see reason.*

But Trina didn't think Jim was a very reasonable person, and she was starting to toy with the idea of trying reverse psychology on him, and the judge. *What if I start pushing for ongoing vaccinations? Jim is likely to automatically want to do the opposite of what I want, no matter what it is. What if I have a 'change of heart,' and 'demand' that he continues vaccines as soon as possible? Would Jim reverse his position, and tell the judge that given this possible bad reaction, maybe he shouldn't keep vaccinating? Would that give the judge a way out as well? To let him save face, and get over any guilt he may have that his ruling landed my child in the ICU?*

Trina felt like this might be her only chance. Play the broken con-ciliatory mom role. It sickened her to even think about it. But she'd do anything for Jack. She always had.

Jail though. Seriously? Going to jail for refusing a voluntary pre-ventive medicine? In America? Who would ever have thought?

Chapter 35

Dirty Children

"And our fourth public comment will be from ... Mrs. Mancini," announced the deep voice of the chair of the school board for the local public school district.

Rhianna Samuels watched from her seat in the back of the multipurpose room as a tall, dark-haired woman stood up in the front row and confidently stepped up to the podium. The first two public comments had been just OK, focusing on vaccine reactions and the unfair exclusion of kids because many vaccines don't prevent disease spread. Then there'd been questions put to the board as to why they were now mandating hep B vaccine for teens, when existing law allowed teens to opt out. And Rhianna had been surprised to see the chair of the school board actually respond. *They usually just sat there in silence and let the public have their say.* Although she, and most in the room, didn't like their answer. The department of education interpreted the new mandatory vaccine law as now requiring hep B vaccine for *all* kids, even though an additional statute excludes that vaccine for teens. The *new* law wins. Rhianna hoped someone would sue the state over this.

So that's *Sophia Mancini,* Rhianna thought to herself, coming back to the present. *Pretty. Well-dressed. A good spokesperson for our movement. No wonder people like her.* She had never personally heard Sophia speak before, but several of her friends had and said she knew her stuff. Rhianna knew it would be her own turn next, and was realizing now that this woman might be a tough act to follow.

"Ladies and gentlemen of the board," began Mrs. Mancini. "Thank you for opening up the floor to comments. I am speaking today on behalf of the approximately 20 students in our school who will no longer be able to attend this school, or any school for that matter, because of the new mandatory vaccination law. This type of discrimination is …"

But that's as far as Mrs. Mancini got. And Rhianna felt a knot in her stomach as she, and the rest of the room, saw the source of the interruption stand up from her chair among the other school board members and unleash what she'd been obviously holding back for a while now.

"EXCUSE ME, Mrs. Mancini!" Board-member Smith nearly shouted, and Rhianna saw Sophia Mancini flinch at the podium and turn uncertainly toward the board member. "I will not have *you*, of all people, come into this room and accuse us, or our state government, of discriminating against anybody! How dare you have the nerve to compare your petty little white-people problems to actual discrimination! You have no idea what discrimination is!"

"Order, please. Order!" the chair of the school board called out, using an actual gavel that usually rested undisturbed in front of him. "Board-member Smith, please restrain yourself. This is not the …"

But Alyssa Smith would have none of it. "No, I won't sit down and be quiet, Thomas! You should be on *my* side on this. *Our* side. Discrimination? I don't see any of us forcing any of these children or their parents to do anything. I'm tired of these people parading through here claiming discrimination? How dare they accuse us?" Turing her glare back to the victim of her pent-up feelings. "How dare you accuse *me* of discriminating against *you*?"

Silence permeated the room as the two women both stood there, staring at each other. The seconds ticked by …

Oh dear Lord, thought Rhianna. *This is not good.*

Rhianna didn't even realize she had stood up until she was already halfway down the center aisle, her own speech forgotten back at her seat. She saw Sophia turn toward her, a stricken look on her face mixed with uncertainty. Rhianna put one hand on Sophia's shoulder and used her other to gently move the frozen woman a few inches to the side so she could access the microphone herself.

"Mr. Chair, Mrs. Smith, and all the members of the board. My name is Rhianna Samuels, and I believe you will find my name on your list as next in line to speak." Rhianna knew that this board, like all boards, thrived on rules and procedure, and if her name was next on their list, she knew they couldn't object to her interrupting the interruption.

"Umm … Yes, Ms. Samuels. You are correct. If Mrs. Mancini does not object, you may have the floor."

"Stay here, Sophia," Rhianna whispered. "You aren't finished yet." She watched the woman exhale, clasp her shaking hands in front of her, and relax her shoulders a bit.

Rhianna knew every eye in the room was now on her, and she had to represent not only her own people, but her *new* people as well – people whom she agreed were now being discriminated against for a brand new reason.

Deep breath …

"Mrs. Smith, I would like to ask you, with all due respect to you and your position on the board, what on earth does the color of someone's skin have to do with their right to talk about discrimination? What, do we black people have some sort of monopoly on discrimination? Like we are the only group that can be discriminated against? If there is a group of people here who feel discriminated against, wouldn't you like to know why they feel that way? Who cares what their skin color is? I am against discrimination in all its forms, as I know you are too. We all are. Shouldn't we pause and listen?

"I know there are centuries of hurt behind us, and I know we still have a long way to go until the color of our skin is no longer used against us. I know this as well as you do, Mrs. Smith. But I also know that one reason racial prejudice and discrimination have lasted for so long is that no one is ever willing to listen. How long did our ancestors plead for the 'white folk' to listen? How long did they beg to be heard? How many centuries went by before Mrs. Mancini's ancestors finally listened to *our* ancestors? And what good came when they finally did listen?

"I was scheduled to speak tonight about how unnecessary this new mandatory vaccination law is based on the fact that our unvaccinated kids are healthy and pose no threat to anybody. But now I'm curious to hear more about the discriminatory aspects of this new law. Because you know what? All the things that white people used to say about 'us black folk,' that we were somehow contagious and needed to have separate bathrooms, separate drinking fountains, separate seating sections, and even separate schools, and all of these things were never even close to being equal. All those things they used to say about us? Well, now our state government is saying those very same things about my unvaccinated child, about Mrs. Mancini's unvaccinated child, and about almost 2 dozen more unvaccinated children in our school. In *your* school, Mrs. Smith. Our kids are contagious, dirty, infected, and dangerous. Too dangerous even for separate bathrooms and drinking fountains. It's better that they just don't come to school at all. If that isn't the very definition of discrimination, Mrs. Smith, then I don't know what is.

"Mrs. Mancini, here, might not have centuries of history behind her right to claim that her child is being treated wrongly, but if she feels that her child is the target of discrimination now, I, for one, want to hear why. Mrs. Mancini?"

She turned toward the woman standing next to her and was surprised to see tears streaming down her face.

Hold it together, Soph. Hold yourself together.

But Sophia could not, and she started sobbing as this stranger put her arm around her shoulders and gave her a gentle squeeze.

Fortunately, Sophia was a fast crier, especially when there was business to be done. Once the flood gates opened, they ran dry quickly and she composed herself after about 15 seconds. A gentleman in the front row handed her a handkerchief, which helped break the tension as the school board Chair said something about old-fashioned manners. Alyssa Smith had the decency to appear mildly chagrinned.

"Board members … and Mrs. Smith in particular … and Mrs. Samuels here," Sophia resumed, a grateful smile briefly directed to the woman on her right. "I would never, ever, in a million years, pretend that what my child and myself are being subjected to today even begins to approach the atrocities perpetrated upon the members of your family who came before you. There is no comparison … there never could be. And I hope and pray there never will be again. And that's why I am here speaking on behalf of these 20 families today, and the tens of thousands of like-minded families across our state.

"Technically, although it matters very little, my family came here from Italy about 60 years ago. So although I am light-skinned, my family are relatively new to the United States in regards to the aforementioned historical atrocities. And even though I personally have never experienced prejudice for who I am, my grandparents sure did. Simply for being Italian, and daring to immigrate to this country. They couldn't find jobs, and couldn't find housing. For no reason other than they were Italian. It still doesn't even come close to what *your* grandparents suffered, but if you are willing to feel some remorse for unfairly grouping me among those who did your ancestors wrong, I am willing to acknowledge that I can never fully understand the gap that still exists between the black and white communities of this nation and how that still impacts you and your family every day."

Ooooo, thought Rhianna, glancing over at Alyssa Smith to see her reaction. *Sophia can cry, but she can also humbly hold onto her pride.* She saw board member Smith tense momentarily, then nod her head in acceptance of the offered truce. Rhianna glanced sideways at Sophia again. *When she gets knocked down, she gets right back and up again. Good.*

"Discrimination and prejudice, in all forms, is wrong. And what I want you, the board members, to listen to and hear is how this new vaccine law discriminates against a group of us for having beliefs different than yours, and how the fear that we are dangerous is unfairly prejudicial. Prejudice is defined as unreasonable feelings, opinions, or attitudes, especially of a hostile nature, regarding an ethnic, racial, social, or religious group. Discrimination is the unjust or prejudicial treatment of different categories of people.

"Families who opt out of vaccination are a 'social group,' and some even opt out for religious reasons. We are a 'different category' of people with different medical beliefs. And the reason that our exclusion from society is 'unreasonable' and 'unjust' is that our children are healthy, clean, and not contagious to anybody. Diseases happen to vaccinated and unvaccinated alike, since most vaccines don't prevent a child from acquiring germs and becoming contagiously symptomatic. There is no scientific evidence that demonstrates unvaccinated children pose a danger to others. And even though an unvaccinated child will occasionally pass a vaccine-preventable illness to another child, so will vaccinated kids. In order for our total exclusion to be 'just' and 'reasonable,' there would have to be clear and convincing evidence of danger. From children. From innocent, healthy, and equal children.

"Our own state's Department of Justice Civil Rights Handbook says that 'the right to a public education is a fundamental right *fully* guaranteed and protected by the state constitution. The Legislature has enacted numerous laws designed to promote equality in educational opportunities and to safeguard students against discriminatory practices in public schools.' Your very own Code of Education prohibits any school activities which reflect adversely upon any person because of creed, color, or national origin. Creed is 'an idea or set of beliefs that guides the actions of a person or group.' The Code also prohibits a public school from requiring a student to attend a particular school because of race, creed, or color.

"Mrs. Smith, the children in your family who came decades before you were forced to attend different schools because of their color. Now, *our* children are being forced to attend a different school – school at home – because of our creed. I would like you to tell my child – my Arabella (Sophia reached into her shirt pocket and held up a picture of her daughter) – what it is about her that she can't attend this school anymore.

"Listen. This one law that begins the discrimination against people is just the start. That's often how prejudice begins: an idea that a certain group deserves fewer rights. For now, all they are doing is making us stay home. But you know what bill came next, right after this one? A bill that would take decisions about medical care out of the hands of parents and put such decisions into the hands of the State. That's right. If we parents don't cooperate with vaccination, the State could come in and do it for us. Thankfully, our legislature saw reason and that bill is dead. But this is what scares me: the fact that such a bill could even be thought of. That someone in power decided that our society needed such a law. That's how prejudice and discrimination move forward.

"As Mrs. Samuels put it, her own ancestors' children, and the children of many of you here in this room, were called dirty, contagious, and dangerous because the people who ruled this nation were afraid of their differences. The injustice of this ignorance ... no, stupidity ... has haunted our society for decades. We are trying to become *one* people, and this law only divides us further. I would ask you, members of the board, to accept our children as equal to your own, with equal rights and privileges, and see this new law for what it really is."

The room was silent for several moments. The gentleman in the front row stood and walked his second handkerchief over to board-member Smith, who suddenly seemed to need one too.

Thomas and Alyssa still sat in their chairs a half hour after the meeting had adjourned and the public had filed out. Both were trying to process what had just happened. Samantha Yamamoto, one of the other Board members was still there too, and seemed to be busy trying to find something on her phone.

"Here it is," Samantha exclaimed. "Thomas, Alyssa, there is something that really struck me about what that woman said about historical examples of excluding kids from school. This happened to my very own grandmother 70 years ago. She's told me stories of her family's internment during World War II, and how she was kicked out of the public school for two years. Later, our own California Department of Education added Section 13000 – the California Civil Liberties Public Education Act – that says this: 'Ensures that the events surrounding the exclusion, forced removal, and internment of civilians and permanent resident aliens of Japanese ancestry during World War II will be remembered, so that the causes and circumstances of this and similar events may be illuminated and understood.' This wording was added to our Code so that schools would never kick a group or class of children out of school ever again, for any reason. I remember thinking as a child, 'How awful that they did that to my Grandma. I'm glad we would never do anything like that now.' And here we are. We are doing it. Sure, it's not because of race or ethnicity. But it is because of creed. And religion too. This seems both illegal and unethical to me. I've a mind to recommend that we, as a school, disregard this new law."

"We can't do that, Samantha," said Alyssa. "We are a public school. Maybe small private schools could get away with it, but we can't."

"But what we *can* do is make this as easy as possible for those people. Damn, did I just call them 'those people?' Thomas smiled. Even Alyssa laughed, a rare occurrence in these meetings. "And that will start with us removing the hep B vaccine requirement for 7th graders. That one speaker tonight was correct. I checked. Section 2 (c) of the new vaccine law states very clearly, 'full immunization against hepatitis B shall not be a condition by which the governing authority shall admit or advance any pupil to the 7th grade level.' I know that our district nursing coordinator has told us that we do need to start mandating hep B, and all the school nurses have been given that instruction. But I don't know where these nurses are getting their orders, because it's certainly not from the new vaccine law. Someone in Sacramento is actually instructing our nurses to ignore the hep B part of the law and force it on our junior highers. And *that* pisses me off!"

"And nothing ever pisses *you* off Thomas. That's why you are the Chairman."

"But what kind of person would even come up with a vaccine law like this anyway?" asked Samantha, to no one in particular. "Denying a class of children the right to attend school. How is that even constitutional? Probably a white person came up with it. I mean, no Asian or African-American or Latino would dare, right?"

Chapter 36

School in the 80s

"So, the next item on the agenda is new enrollment for next year. Our numbers are down. Way down. We're talking about a 20% decrease in our student body next year. 20%! Nothing like this has even happened before. Sure, we've had our ups and downs, but never like this. Tricia and I spent the last week trying to figure out why, and it finally hit us last night. It's the new vaccine law. I'll let Tricia explain what we found."

The six school board members of the small, private, Christian school turned their bored eyes from the Head of Schools to his administrative assistant.

"Chris and I went through every file for every child who is leaving and we found one common denominator: each one is either partly or fully *unvaccinated*. I called each family – I've known some of these parents and kids for years now – and they all said they want to keep coming, but they also don't want to give all the newly-required vaccines. Especially hepatitis B and chicken pox. They'd rather choose home-schooling."

"Can't we handle a drop like this?" asked one of the board members. "We'll work harder on new enrollments for next year."

"But that's just it," continued Tricia. "This 20% drop is all from our preschoolers going into kindergarten and sixth-graders going into seventh. That's when the new vaccine law requires these kids to catch up on vaccines or get out. I've looked at the files of all our students who will be hitting this checkpoint *next* year too, and we're going to lose another 20% next year. And the year after that."

"I did a little research on which families tend to vaccinate less," Chris jumped back in. "Surprisingly it's the wealthier and more educated parents – the families who tend to enroll in private schools, like ours. We can't financially handle a drop in tuition revenue like that, not for more than two years in a row. We might be looking at having to close down. We are already so small, and losing that many children might just do us in. And we are the last Christian school in this tri-city area."

The discussion continued for a while. The board members chimed in about vaccines, diseases, outbreaks, parental rights, and every other aspect of this issue. But Steve sat quietly, mulling over an idea. He was a lawyer, *and* his kids were among the unvaccinated ones who would be leaving after 6th grade. He already knew the ins and outs of what his friends were ranting about around him. He knew the vaccine law was unnecessary and unfair. He knew unvaccinated children belonged in schools just like every other child. And something about what the Head of Schools had just said sparked an idea in his mind, and he thought that maybe, just maybe it might work.

"Let's sue."

Steve was a soft-spoken man – unusual for a lawyer – and no one heard him.

"Let's sue the bastards!" he said loudly, standing up.

This brought all the discussions to a halt.

"Excuse me?" asked Chris. "Sue who, Steve? The parents?"

"No. The State of California. For wrongful infringement on our private business. Especially given the fact that unvaccinated kids pose no danger to our school and that there is no current disease crisis that should grant the State emergency powers to exclude some of our students. They are interfering with our right to conduct business for no good reason. But an even stronger case – a constitutional case – rests in the fact that the State is taking away the rights that our Christian students have to fellowship with one another and learn in a religious environment. *That's* where I think we could win this."

"But we're just one small Christian school. We have no money for a lawsuit," chimed in one board member.

"I can guarantee we should be able to find a legal organization who would take the case pro-bono. And if not, we can't be the only religious school this is happening to. And this isn't just about Christian schools. All faiths could be facing this type of discrimination. Jewish schools, Catholic schools, Muslim schools. And especially Jehovah's Witnesses – they don't even go to mainstream doctors. The State is now denying these children's constitutional right to engage in religious fellowship and learn in a religious environment. If we all got together on this, we would be quite a force to reckon with."

"But none of this helps us in the meantime," lamented Tricia. "By the time this goes anywhere, our school will be closed."

"Not if we peacefully resist the new law *now*," answered Steve. "Conscientious objection. Or religious. Or both. We continue to operate as we are now. We admit all students, regardless of their medical choices. If we do it, and are open about it, other schools may follow."

"But isn't it illegal to openly encourage other schools to break the law?"

"Well, we'd have to do it right. With legal, and religious, counsel. But I think we could do this. Because I, for one, want my kids to keep going here three years from now."

"Wait, your kids too?" asked another board member, one whom Steve knew fully vaccinated her kids. "But you've always seemed so …" She trailed off.

"Intelligent? Educated? I know. But that's who tends to not vaccinate – those of us who actually get educated about it. But that's not the issue here. It's about choice and religious freedom. And medical freedom."

"But if we publicize it, the State will be knocking on our door the very next day."

"Well, we know the State is already auditing all small private schools to make sure we are complying with the new vaccine law. They'll be here in the next year or two anyway. This just speeds up the process. And that might actually help us."

"Help us how?" asked Chris. "By shutting us down right away?"

"I don't think they have the authority to do that. I don't know for sure – I'll have to look into this. But if we play it right, having them try to shut us down may help us more than it hurts us. Listen, here's how I see this playing out. First of all, who is actually inspecting us and our vaccine records? The public health department. They don't have the authority to take any action against us, I don't think. But then they'll report us to the Department of Education. Education steps in and does what? We are a private school, not a public one. What can they do? They can revoke our credentials as a school, perhaps. But that's not an easy process. And they can't force us to close our doors, can they? Not without an actual disease outbreak. We go on operating, business as usual … religion as usual … and the State harasses us for a while. But hey, my legal time would be free, and if I can get a legal organization to lead the way, and get other schools to join us, we could win this legally. But forget the legalities for a minute. Think about the public pressure. If we play this right, we make the State look like either a fascist group of dictators from the 1940s or the Thought Police from Orwellian 1984.

"Picture it: news footage of authorities coming in, blocking the school entrance, riffling through our school records, finding that some children 'don't have their papers,' escorting children off campus. Escorting school administrators out in handcuffs. Arresting parents because their kids are truant because they are attending an unlicensed school. Arresting you, Chris, for overseeing all of this. Ha, arresting me, of course. I'd probably go *first*. Would the State want all of this on the evening news? How would that make them look? My guess is that either they back down and hope not too many schools hear about what we've done, or they step in and try to make an example of us. Then we fight it out in court, if we are willing to take it that far."

Steve paused in his rant, and that's when everyone noticed Tricia's quiet sniffling and tears.

"What's the matter," asked Chris, a hand on her shoulder.

"I'm just thinking about my grandfather. The stories he told me of his escape from Eastern Europe. What you are describing is … is the exact same thing he told me happened every day where he lived. Soldiers, authorities, inspectors. All looking for papers. All ensuring full compliance with the law. But, it wasn't really about the papers, or the law. It was about the *people*. They were doing it looking for people who were different, or came from a different place. They didn't care if you didn't have your papers - they cared if you were the wrong type of person. If we do this, Chris, Steve, you have to promise me I won't be having to tell my own grandchildren the same stories some-day. Promise me that our legal battle will prevail, and it won't come down to people actually being arrested and thrown into jail over this. Promise me none of the children will get hurt. Because, ultimately, that's who we are all here for. The children. We all signed up to be teachers and school administrators to help the children. If anything should happen to them …"

"Well, that's just it," Chris said, sitting up straighter in his chair and looking at Steve. "That's who we would be doing this for. The children. And I can't think of any more noble cause than that."

Chapter 37

Two Legs Are Better Than One

"So, they say I have to take antibiotics now, before I even feel sick, because I am her roommate and might have shared some water or food or something. They say that will prevent me from getting sick."

"And you are sure you feel ok? Right now? No fever? Did you check you whole body for that rash, whatever you called it? Petichio rash?"

"Yes Mom! Geeze, I feel fine. I *am* an adult now, you know."

"Do you need your dad and me to come down there? We can be there in just a few hours, you know."

"No Mom! I'm fine. I gotta get to class now. Love you, bye."

Giselle did feel fine. No fever, no flu symptoms. No headache. Her neck wasn't stiff. She didn't think she had a rash. The student health nurse asked her all those questions already. And more, like had she kissed her roommate lately? Giselle had pretended that would be gross and said no. Although she and Tanya *had* tried that at a party a few months ago … once … but they both decided it wasn't for them. Then the doctor had given her the bottle of antibiotics and told her to let them know if she felt sick. *Why, so they can lock me up too? Miss that much class? I don't think so.* But she really did feel fine. Plus, Giselle had read about meningococcal disease on the internet so she already knew everything she needed to know, including two

393

facts that made her wonder why the health nurse … and her mom, apparently … seemed so worried.

First, the disease doesn't pass easily from person to person. It's not like a cold or the flu. You don't catch it just from being in the same room with someone. You have to either share saliva or live with them. They call it lengthy contact, like being a roommate or boyfriend. The internet said you have to come into contact with their oral secretions. Like with mono. Even though they were roommates, they didn't share saliva – not on purpose anyway.

Second, 10% of people already have the germs living in their nasal passage anyway. *So why doesn't everyone get sick from it?* she wondered. They called it being an asymptomatic carrier. And they – the internet – didn't know the answer. Something about host susceptibility or some such term. *So, you could carry the germs for years, and suddenly they turn on you and make you sick out of nowhere? So, many people who get sick might not have even caught it from someone else. It can be their own germs.*

Apparently, this was one of the shots she was supposed to have gotten when she was a teenager – well, she still was a teen, technically. But her mom had decided somewhere along the way to stop getting her her shots. She'd said there were just too many nowadays and she didn't trust them all anymore. *Whatever.*

I wonder if I should get the shot now? I'll have to ask the health nurse.

She opened the bottle and took her dose of antibiotics, just in case. *Since I am the roommate.* And Giselle stripped down in front of her full-length mirror to make sure she didn't have whatever rash her mom and the nurse had been talking about.

"I'm telling you, John. It's not a big deal. These things happen on many college campuses. It's not going to hurt enrollment."

The Director of Admissions didn't sound convinced. "You keep saying that, Dr. Rangel. But you know how the press is. They'll blow this way out of proportion, like they did with mumps two years ago. They'll scare everyone into thinking their grownup kids are dying left and right. You know how they are. They can't just give accurate, level-headed information. They play out the worst-case scenario every chance they get."

"Well, you and I know the truth. I told you the numbers already. There are only about 50 cases of meningococcal disease nationwide every year among high school and college-age students. That's not very many, considering the large population of all such students. And there are about 10 fatalities each year in this age group. These are all tragic, but it's fortunately a very tiny number. The disease also infects about 100 infants and toddlers annually, with about 5 deaths. Interestingly, the disease seems less dangerous in the younger kids. This may be because most infant/toddler cases are caused by the B strain of the disease. But they don't have an infant vaccine that's approved for routine use yet. They do have a B strain vaccine, but it doesn't work very well and so it's only reserved for immunocompromised children.

"Anyway, looking at the 2015 disease numbers nationwide for all age groups, there were only about 360 total cases. 50 deaths. Most of these cases and deaths were in adults and the elderly. But we don't routinely vaccinate them because they haven't gotten around to studying that yet. For the teens and adults, the ages that you and I work with, we don't see much type B like they do in babies. It's mostly one of the other 4 strains of the disease: A, C, W, and Y. Those are the four strains covered in the teen vaccine, the vaccine that you and the Board are considering making mandatory for all incoming freshmen. But the total number of annual cases nationwide is so small that it's really not much of a risk to each individual if you think about it. Fifty cases out of every high school and college-age child in the nation. Eight deaths in 2015. Plus, the disease is barely contagious. Not like measles, or even the flu. Only close, intimate contacts are at risk. In fact, the CDC even says only about 3% of cases are related to outbreaks. Meaning, when one college student gets sick, he or she may only infect one or two other students before it's contained. Or possibly none at all. Most cases have nothing to do with outbreaks. So when it does hit a college campus, it really shouldn't even make the news."

"But it does. And parents start panicking. Not the kids though, they still think they're invincible. But the parent calls we get. You are lucky we don't patch them all through to your health center. Hey, wait. That's a good idea. What do you think?"

The doctor knew his friend well enough to know when he was kidding. He thought. "Personally, even I, a doctor, don't think there's a reason to make it mandatory. There isn't any actual evidence that the vaccine prevents the spread of the disease."

"Yes, you've told me that before, Doctor. Ten percent of people carry the germ. Most cases are people's own germs deciding to suddenly invade. Getting the vaccine may reduce the chance that a person's own germs might invade and make them sick – individually. And the vaccine may give the non-carriers some immunity when they *are* exposed to someone who is sick. But we don't know if this vaccine prevents someone from becoming a germ carrier and passing it along to others. So, it shouldn't be mandated for admission. And that's why we haven't made it so, unlike some of the other universities. But making it mandatory would have all the parents feel better when we do have a case. And that may be reason enough to mandate it, just for the PR advantage."

"Well, that's your department, not mine. The public health department is bringing over more Cipro to use as prophylaxis in case we get any more cases and close contacts. We do have plenty of vaccine in stock at the health center, and older teens only need one dose of the vaccine to be protected for several years; we don't give the usual two doses at this later age, just one. Interesting story on that …"

The Director rolled his eyes, knowing the doctor couldn't see him over the phone. Steven and his stories could go on for quite a while, although he admitted that they were always informative. "Yes. I have time for a story."

"When the teen vaccine came out in 2005, they only gave one dose to 12-year-old kids. But then they found a problem: it wore off after about five years, so by the time they got to college, when they needed the protection the most, the immunity was gone. So they added a booster dose at age 16 to carry them through the college years."

"That's not very 'story worthy' compared to some of your past offerings. They've probably done that with all the vaccines over the years – added more doses to boost immunity."

"Yeah, that's not the story part. This is: the addition of the booster dose was hotly debated by the ACIP – that's the CDC board that approves the vaccine schedule. It's made up of doctors, researchers, and representatives from vaccine manufacturers. They were trying to decide whether to move the single dose to age 16, or keep the 12 year dose and add a booster. Well, you can guess what the Pharma reps voted for, but a surprising number of the doctors didn't want to add the second dose. They felt two doses weren't necessary when one, given at the right time, would work. They said there was a lack of data to make a scientific decision at that point. They wanted more data to know exactly how two doses would work, and proof that it would work better than one at age 16. They also considered cost, because, like all brand new vaccines, it's very expensive.

"The vaccine costs about $120 dollars per dose for doctors to buy from the two companies that make them. So, you figure every year there are about 4 million 12-year-olds to vaccinate in our country. So Pharma already could make half a billion dollars each year on the 1 dose. Given the chance to double that, they actually had to bring in towels to mop all the drool off of the Pharma Reps' end of the conference table when the meeting was over."

John had a good laugh. Doc always managed to make his stories entertaining despite their dry content.

"But the doctors and health policy makers where concerned about adding another half billion to annual medical expenditures. Insurance companies, which means ultimately the patients, have to fund these policy changes. In the end, the vote was close: six in favor of adding the booster, five opposed, and three abstained. It was very surprising that the CDC would even allow a change in vaccine policy without a clear majority from the ACIP. If something makes sense scientifically, most scientists are going to agree with it. If they don't, then to me that means the science isn't clear yet and they should wait. But all the ACIP needs is one more yes than no. Some doctors, especially those who understand the vaccine better, do just give the one dose at age 16 or even 18 right before college.

"Plus, this vaccine has had some reported neurologic side effects. They are rare, but they have been reported. And as a doctor, I'm not for any type of forced medicine. Or coerced medicine. Medicine should be so safe and good that all people want it. When there's a risk, even a bit of a risk, we shouldn't shame or shun people for refusing that risk, especially when it doesn't endanger anyone else. California public universities made the move last year to make this vaccine, and a few others, mandatory. Someone out there is pulling their strings, because they know they don't have legitimate *medical* reasons for mandating these. Same with the Tdap. Remember when a couple of our board members wanted to mandate Tdap vaccine for all incoming freshmen last year? And I fought them on it because that vaccine doesn't reduce the spread of any of its diseases. The two board members were pissed, and it turned out that they had stock in a company that makes the vaccine. Makes me wonder if that's what is driving many universities nationwide to mandate Tdap now."

"Well Doc, next time the board meets, I'll have you come by and give us the five minute version of why you think the college doesn't need to mandate this vaccine next year either. Because even if there is only one case right now, they'll be looking at doing everything they can to ensure there are no cases next year."

Giselle nodded to the nurse sitting at the visitor's station on her way to Tanya's room. The nurse was wearing a mask. *Should I have a mask?* She wondered. But then, none of the other nurses had one on … *No wait, there was another over there.* She pulled one out of the box hanging on the wall outside Tanya's room anyway and slipped it on before quietly opening the door.

"Hey girlfriend!" Tanya's always-cheerful voice warmed Giselle's heart. She'd missed it over these past several days. "Good news! I get to keep my foot!"

Giselle breathed a sigh of relief. Ever since she'd first heard that her roomie's rash on her left leg had been so severe at first that the doctors thought they might end up having to amputate her foot due to the loss of blood flow, Giselle had been sick with worry for her best friend. And she'd also stripped down naked to check every inch of her own body two, sometimes three, times a day.

"I want to give you a big squishy hug, but I guess I probably shouldn't," Giselle said through the mask.

"I bet you are glad you and I haven't gotten too drunk at any parties lately too, huh?"

Giselle blushed, which made Tanya smile even wider. "Ha! It's so funny how you can't just shrug that off like it was no big deal. Anyway, the doctors said that the antibiotics finally kicked in and that I'm out of the woods. They said most cases do well like me – about 80%. But about 10% die, and about 10% of survivors suffer some sort of permanent damage, like deafness, nerve damage, or … having to hop around the rest of your life. I can't even imagine the rest of college – the rest of life even – without a foot. Did you know there's a vaccine for this? My mom told me so. Oh, you just missed her, by the way. She's grabbing lunch in the caf. Anyway, we didn't have medical insurance for the last few years, so I never got that vaccine. They said that the key for me was recognizing the rash and acting quickly. My mom had warned me about this, since she knew I wasn't vaccinated. So that's what saved me, the doctors say. I made sure my mom knew that, so she doesn't feel guilty about me not getting the vaccine. You should ask your mom if you had it."

"I already asked her. She said I'm all good." Not totally a lie. She'd discussed the shot with her mom yesterday during one of the five daily calls her mom made to her since this started. Her mom had reminded her why they'd skipped the shot: one of their neighbors had suffered a very severe reaction; she'd become temporarily paralyzed two weeks after the shot. Something called Guillain-Barre Syndrome, a known, but rare, reaction to that vaccine and a few others, like the flu shot. Giselle's mom had even texted her the warning in the vaccine prescribing information that states there is 'a potential for an increased risk of GBS following meningogoccal vaccination.' *She's afraid I'll panic and go get the shot.* "Plus, they gave me antibiotics to take, which will prevent me from getting sick even if I did pick up the germ from you. So, when do you think you'll be outta here?"

The ringtone interrupted a very good dream, so Francine was already annoyed when she discovered that some bonehead at the Center had decided meningococcal disease was worth waking her up for. Then her annoyance rose when she realized the caller was a newbie, someone who had just transferred in and didn't really know the protocols yet. Although, his voice sounded very deep over the phone … and deep voices usually meant …

She glanced at the still-sleeping form in bed next to her. It *was* time to move on again, and maybe she could mentor this new guy in the ways of the world … if his face matched his voice, that is. Anyway, back to business.

"Listen here, Mr. … what's your name?"

"Umm, Johnson sir. I mean, ma'am. Chris Johnson. I … I'm new here. But I thought you'd want to know about a case of meningitis at a college on the east coast."

"Mr. Johnson. I'm only going to say this once. Meningococcal disease is never, ever … ever … a reason to wake me up in the middle of the night. Got it? *Maybe* if someone dies. But we usually only get one or two cases in any one place at any one time, and that doesn't make people panic. So it doesn't do *me* any good. Got it?"

Francine realized she'd better compose herself before she said anything more to this newbie.

"Listen, Mr. Johnson. Since most deaths are in adults and the elderly, it's not a scare for parents. Remember, our target is all the little mommies and daddies with little babies. But this is a teenage vaccine, for a disease that doesn't cause epidemics in this country. So, it's only good for the slow news at the bottom of the hour. Got it? Oh, and come see me in my office before you leave in the morning."

She hung up the phone, then, nudged her partner awake. She'd need some help getting back to sleep.

Jim Remington watched Chris hang up the phone, look around, and realize that everyone in the Center was smiling at him.

"Told you so," Jim said from the desk next to him.

"Yeah, but …" Chris looked chagrined. "She's gonna take my head off for this, isn't she? I've heard the stories."

That, and a whole lot more Jim didn't say out loud. "Naw, she's all bark and no bite … or is it all bite and no bark? I forget. But you'll find out in about 5 hours."

The night shift gang always loved to let the newbies find out the hard way what their boss liked and didn't like, Jim reflected. New hires were always so eager to make a good first impression on Francine – Ms. Donahue to them – and they always thought that if they could be the first to notify her of a serious disease somewhere they'd get bonus points. It was the lucky few who were able to figure out what really made her tick, which was why Jim had been promoted to night shift supervisor. But recently Jim had begun to realize that there was a darker side to his lover. Francine didn't just enjoy keeping vaccination rates high. There was more to it, something else about these disease outbreaks that really got her off, but he couldn't quite put his finger on it. Whatever it was, he was almost glad that his promotion had necessitated a schedule change to the night shift. And that had resulted in a change in his job "perks." And he'd been mostly OK with that.

I wonder who's helping her get back to sleep right now? he only slightly lamented, remembering when it used to be him.

Chapter 38

The Three

Alot of clandestine meetings happened at Starbucks, even if there really was no special reason for cloaks and daggers. It was the perfect cover – you just saunter in, grab a cup, find a quiet table to sit at that's a respectful distance from any other tables, and ears, and you could talk about anything you wanted to.

Charlton had ordered his coffee on his app when he parked, so he wouldn't have to stand in the long line, something that always made him feel as if everyone was staring at him. So he was the first one to the table. He saw Madeline waiting in line, trying to blend in. But not very many 60-something women went to Starbucks - at least not many who dressed like she did. Her outfit probably cost more than all the money people spent on coffee here in a day. Well, maybe not.

He read his newspaper as he sipped. Actually read, not just pretending like they did in the movies. But, like in the movies, he occasionally glanced up and around, and on his third such peek he saw the third member of The Three pull up in his Tesla.

That's a good choice in cars, thought Charlton, himself a driver of one. *It's nice, but there are enough of them around now that it doesn't stand out.* He felt his cell phone vibrate in his pocket and pulled it out. It was from F. All his dozen or so contacts in his special phone were first name abbreviations only, for security. Some needed two letters to tell them apart, but there was only one "F" that would call him on *this* phone. He let it go to voicemail; he didn't want any distractions from this particular meeting.

Charlton chuckled as he watched James skip the line and walk up to the counter for his app-ordered coffee as well. Cream, sugar, then he joined Charlton at the table with no words. Just a brief hand shake. No reason to start business until Madeline was there too.

The two gentlemen stood as she approached, and James politely pulled out her chair, something she appreciated in their mutual generation.

"Let's skip the pleasantries, gentlemen, and get right down to it," suggested their last arrival.

"You know, Madeline, you really need to figure out how to use an app one of these days. It saves a lot of time, and you don't have to queue up with the peasants." Charlton just couldn't let an opportunity pass without teasing the oldest of the three about her fear of digital technology.

"Honestly Charles, I still don't understand why we can't just meet in one of our board rooms like civilized people," she shot back pleasantly. "But yes, my grandson did promise he would show me how to use these new-fangled phones one of these days."

James entered the conversation. "Ok, enough small talk you two. We really need to make the right call on this, and I'd like it to be unanimous. Over a dozen companies rely on our expertise to provide them with the data they need to keep immunization rates high. That's our ultimate goal, because we, and they, know that a fully-immunized nation is a healthy nation. The five companies I consult with are waiting on our decision, but I'll be honest. I'm still torn."

"As am I," agreed Madeline. "And I know you are as well, Charles."

Charlton nodded his head. "I honestly don't know which way to go either, because this is largely uncharted territory. I'll lay out what I've been thinking, then I want to hear from each of you.

"First, let's discuss the status quo – how things are now. Almost everyone is happy with our country's voluntary vaccine program. Most people get them, and the few that don't really have little to no real impact on disease rates, yet. And yes, vaccines are very profitable for the companies that make them, which, this being America and all, they have every right to make as much money as they can.

"Second, we know that vaccination acceptance in this country *is* declining. But it's declining slowly. The CDC still says that the percentage of Americans who completely avoid all vaccines is still less than 1% ..."

"Oh that's crap, Charlie, and you know it," James jumped in, then held up his hands with a sideways glance at the lady of the group. "My apologies, Madeline. I don't mean to turn this into a locker room, but we all know that the number of non-immunizing families is way more than the 0.7% the CDC claims. You saw that new Research America and ASM study about waning confidence in our vaccines: only 77% of Americans are still confident in our vaccine system, down 8% from 10 years ago, and only 59% believe they have personally benefitted from vaccines – a 16% drop. But even worse, now only 90% of parents think vaccines are important for their kids; 10 years ago it was 96%."

"Ok," Charlton acquiesced. "Sorry. I'm so used to spouting that 1% number to the media, I almost believe it myself. I agree. The number of people who completely avoid vaccines is probably as high as 5%, and more and more people are opting out of *some*. But we don't want anyone to talk about that, because if too many vaccinators find out just how many people are *not* vaccinating, they'll start wondering why. And because we don't have any real increases in vaccine-preventable diseases to keep them worried, people are losing respect for the diseases."

"Yes, but you know we can make the public believe anything we want them to believe," added Madeline. "The only good finding in that new study is that the number of people who still think non-vaccinating families are putting their kids and the community at risk has risen to 61%. Our measles-outbreak messaging is working, and ..."

"Media messaging is only a small part of this whole issue, Madeline," Charlton laid a hand gently on her wrist to soften his interruption. "I'm trying to figure out the bigger picture here – figure out what is actually *right*."

The silence was filled with the soothing background sounds of busy baristas and quiet conversation.

"Can you expand on that Charles? I'm not sure what you mean."

The old man took a deep breath. "I'm trying to figure out which choice will improve public acceptance of vaccines and increase vaccination rates because that goal is simply the right goal for our nation. Not through trickery. Not through fudging the numbers and slick media sound bites. And forget about how much money is involved for the people we give our opinions to. What I want to figure out is which of the three paths set before us will result in 100% immunization rates? Or hell, you know we'd all also settle for the 95-something percent rates we have now. We just have to stop this decline … because it's the right thing to do."

Charlton sat back in his chair and Madeline picked up the baton. "Ok, I like where you are going with this. Almost as if the question is not what path we can choose, and certainly not what path is going to make our clients the most money. Rather, what path will get us there based on its own merits. Because it's right, as you put it. Because the public sees and accepts it as *right*. So, just for the sake of discussion, I'll lay out our choices:

"Number one, we advise that everyone simply continue what they are doing now, leave vaccination as a voluntary choice, and see how things play out in California and Donaldson's state. Let things settle down. Don't push for more states to follow suit. Re-build trust in vaccines with the current on-going safety research programs – hopefully. Essentially, do nothing and continue the status quo.

"Number two, we push for more states to pass mandatory vaccination laws now, encourage more companies to make vaccines mandatory for employment, and deal with the challenges of making this hot topic even hotter.

"Number three, we advise medical organizations, and our pharmaceutical clients, to 'come to the peace talks,' so to speak, and openly agree that yes, vaccines can cause some serious side effects, and we want to start looking into why, and how we can make them safer for everybody so that almost everybody will keep getting them. Does that about sum it up?"

Two heads nodded agreement with the lady in the group, who, the two men knew, was the most skilled at laying things out logically.

"Can I add an addendum to these," added Charlton, "which could be tacked on to either numbers 1 or 3? Transparency. It's getting more play recently, and Doshi – an editor for the British Medical Journal no less – just published a piece in November last year that questions the ethics of how some non-profit organizations who are funded by vaccine manufacturers are openly calling for mandated vaccination. The article discusses how the CDC, AAP, and vaccine-advocacy groups receive Pharma money, and how much money, and discloses the roles these organizations play in promoting mandated vaccines. Except the CDC. The CDC can't, and doesn't, openly support mandates, just information. But the CDC does provide grant funding, according to the article, to groups that do promote mandates. I want to read you two a quote from this piece, because it's brilliant, and it plays right into what we are talking about: ' ... these groups are so strongly pro-vaccination that the public is getting a one-sided message that all vaccines are created equal and vaccination is an important public health strategy, regardless of the circumstances. That is as unhelpful as an 'anti-vaxxer' approach that assumes all vaccinations are harmful. Reality is a little different: some vaccines are enormously important to public health; others are marginal at best and likely best avoided.' If the BMJ is brave enough to start talking about transparency like that, others are going to start discussing it. If more and more people start *demanding* it, we are screwed. That could set us back decades."

"I read the piece too, Charlie. It's bogus. It suggests that people may start questioning all the mainstream sources of vaccine information because, in some cases anyway, it is Pharma-funded and one-sided. People just aren't that smart. Well, the smart people are, but the majority are not. They read something official-looking, attached to a medical-sounding organization, and it's gospel. What Doshi is suggesting may be true for the intelligent consumer, but not for the general public. I don't see that we need to make transparency a part of any plan. In fact, I noticed that the CDC just removed the statistical risks of certain adverse events from their MMR Vaccine Information Statement, as we advised they should. The VIS form used to say that the risk of seizure was 1 in 3000, the risk of an arthritis-like reaction was 1 in 4, and the risk of bleeding from low platelets was 1 in 30,000. But statistics like that scare parents, so they took out the numbers and just state that 'a person might experience' these. That's less transparency, not more. If the CDC wanted to shed more light on vaccine issues, they would add *more* information to the VIS forms, not take it away. I would expect them to eventually take the stats off of *all* the VIS forms completely, like they finally did with that 1 in a thousand chance of encephalitis from the DTaP vaccine; that number alone was killing compliance. They finally removed the 'behavior changes' phrase from the 'What if there is a serious reaction' section of the DTaP VIS, and I'm still trying to get them to take 'unusual behavior' off of the MMR and the Chickenpox VIS forms."

"I agree with James, Charles," continued Madeline, receiving a conciliatory shrug from her colleague. "Transparency won't help us. Moving on. I think we can all agree that choice number one is the easiest. It's the status quo. Most people get all vaccines, and most people never even investigate them. That's the key – to make this as non-controversial as we can. We continue to encourage trust in vaccine safety and efficacy. And we could add a little bit of transparency to this if we needed to … eventually.

"The worry that some in the industry have with the status quo is that we are gradually losing ground. We know that the higher the level of education that people have, the less they vaccinate. That would suggest that the more people read about vaccines, and investigate the controversies, the less they like them. The obvious counter to that would be to make vaccines less controversial, not more. And I think choices one and three achieve that. And what saves us is that if vaccination gets too low for a particular disease for which the vaccine actually helps prevent it's spread, like measles, and we do see more outbreaks, vaccination increases again and problem solved. The system balances itself. So, in my opinion, those who push for mandatory vaccination – option two – are wrong about their fears of diseases returning to kill us all, and I feel myself mostly drawn to keeping them voluntary."

Thoughtful looks on the two male faces, then James cleared his throat. "So let me lay out option two, and what we've learned so far from California and from Donaldson's state. Those who are against vaccines have come out of the woodwork, and they are turning more people away from vaccines by focusing on the risks. I'm not just talking about those who are actually anti-vaccine, anti meaning they think that *no one* should get them. The anti-vaxxers are mainly people who claim to have a child injured by vaccines. They find it their civic duty to make sure everyone else is warned about the dangers. But they aren't the ones I'm worried about. It's the moderates, who are now speaking out loudly against any type of mandated medicine, that concern me. They are a much larger group. They've always been quiet, letting everyone go about their business. Now that vaccines are mandated in California, and with Donaldson on the loose after getting them mandated in her state too, the middle-ground majority is starting to speak out *against* vaccines. These are people who are pro vaccine, but against mandated medicine. They partially or mostly vaccinate, and maybe even fully vaccinate, but they demand it be their choice, not the government's. So they are speaking out against vaccines now because the government is trying to force them. They are openly publicizing the dangers of vaccines in order to convince people that they shouldn't be mandated, at least not in a free country anyway. It's the middle-ground majority who I'm really worried about.

"So the risk with option two is that a push to pass mandatory vaccination laws in every state may backfire in the long run. Sure, it may temporarily increase vaccination rates, as we've seen in California. But you know how people are: offer them something good, and they willingly accept it. *Force* them to take something, and force them to give it to their children, even if it is good, and they run the other way.

If people feel forced into it, and the more that vaccines become a hot topic in the news, the more people investigate them. And you know as well as I do what happens when people investigate vaccines. They stop getting them, because there's nothing good to read on vaccines. It's all negative press. Yeah, most of it is bull ... stuff, but educated people love to read and investigate until they are certain they have an answer. And all it takes to steer any reasonable person away from vaccines is to read about the side effects. It's less education and less attention that we want, not more. Option two opens Pandora's box, in my opinion."

A few seconds of thoughtful silence.

"I don't think either of us disagree with you, Jim," concluded Charlton. "So let me lay out option three: admit that there are some risks with vaccines and openly work to make them safer. Figure out why some people suffer severe reactions, but most don't. Begin research on the full CDC vaccine schedule to demonstrate it *is* safe. Research long-term health outcomes in vaccinated versus unvaccinated children to show that vaccinated kids are healthier in the long run, or at least that the unvaccinated are not – healthier, that is. Do the work and the research that it takes to demonstrate to the doubters that their fears are unfounded. Do any of us really think this path is a good idea?"

No takers.

"Neither do I. It admits too much, and what if the research shows something we don't want it to show?"

"Well, we can control that."

"Only to some extent, Jim. Research like this will have to be objective and unbiased. No conflicts of interest. The other side will make sure of that. Anything short of that and we're back to where we are now."

"But the CDC already looked at the feasibility of researching vaccinated versus unvaccinated kids and determined it wasn't feasible."

"I, personally, don't agree with them on that, Madeline. The research could be done. It wouldn't be easy, but it can be done. And that's why Stanley's bill calls for the NIH to do the study, not the

CDC. I worry that the CDC is losing too much credibility. Granted, that's only among the educated. For the general public, the CDC is still an ivory tower. Anyway, I'm not arguing for option three, I'm just saying that if we ever decide we should go down that long and hard road, there is, indeed, a road there."

More thoughtful silence.

"Do either of you two really think we could even get our clients, and the government, to consider option three?" Madeline broke the reverie. "Neither do I. Even if we decided it was the best choice, would they listen to us? We'd probably be out of our jobs. So it's really down to options one and two. And when I try to imagine option two moving forward, I get a bad feeling about it. James?"

"I keep thinking about the liability with two. Right now, if anyone suffers a vaccine injury, no one is held liable. They are compensated by a federal fund built by a tax on all vaccines. If the state governments force, or coerce, people into getting vaccines, and *when* the injuries begin, not *if*, but *when* - because we know there are thousands of severe reactions being reported each year now - people are going to start suing at the state level. States don't have any such compensation fund."

"They won't win, Jim. The law is …"

"The law applies to voluntary vaccination, Charlie, at least in spirit if not in letter. These cases will likely lose at first, but eventually they'll get to the state supreme courts, and I can see enough justices deciding that a government-mandated medical treatment with known risks makes the government liable when someone suffers."

"So, that really just leaves option one, gentlemen. But I can't escape the feeling that doing nothing is just delaying the inevitable. We can't keep pretending that vaccines have no risk forever. Sooner or later the CDC is going to have to research its schedule, and manufacturers are going to have to figure out what it is about vaccines that makes some people react. Clearing up those two questions would go a long way."

"You are suggesting option one, with a gradual roll-out of some aspects of option three? A very slow and controlled roll-out? That sounds tricky. And complicated," James sat back.

Silence again.

"Think we can pull back on the reigns of the legislators who are trying to follow California's lead? And Donaldson? She's working hard to help other states follow suit. Could we really reign her in?"

"You know we can, Charles. Ironically, it may end up costing our clients *less* money. Ha, giving legislators *no* agenda is free, at least as long as no one else comes along with the opposite agenda. But circling back to your original point about what is right, and what will likely preserve the highest vaccination rates in the long run. Status quo, forced vaccination, or back-peddling? Do any of us feel that any of these three choices is absolutely the best one? Because we have to make a decision and go with it."

"What do The Seven think?" James asked, looking at Charlton.

"Honestly, they are as stumped as we are. They definitely do not advise option 3 – no concessions, no going backward. But they are torn between options 1 and 2. And they are even discussing an option 2.1: help push to make vaccines mandatory period. Not just for school, but period. They know that's a long way off though. But they just aren't sure what choice is going to end up achieving the highest vaccination rates in the long run. Freedom to choose, or coercion and mandates? They are stumped, just like we are."

"So, that kind of leads us back to option one, right? That's the default choice. But remember, we are slowly losing ground if we don't do something."

"Well, there already are many 'option two' mechanisms in play that will help preserve vaccination rates, and they have nothing to do with allowing people to choose. First, all school nurses are trained to tell incoming families that vaccines are mandatory for school enrollment. And in the 47 states in which they are really optional for school, the nurses conveniently leave that fact out. So many uneducated parents already think that 'no shots, no school' applies to them. And now we not only have the new school law in California and Donaldson's state, California is trying to pass what I like to call, only to myself, of course, the 'no shots, no food' law." A soft chuckle. "Poor families who don't get their shots lose their state financial aid. Since these are pretty much all poor, undereducated minorities, I assume they will all line up for their shots so they can feed their kids. Such families aren't supposed to investigate vaccines anyway, if the research is correct. This new law will test that theory. But besides new laws, more and more insurance plans nationwide are now adding rules that penalize doctors for not sticking to the CDC vaccine schedule. Before, they were just rewarding those who do. Now they've started adding penalties to those who don't. And patients are being penalized too, with some insurance plans refusing to cover their vaccines unless they are done per the CDC schedule. Not to mention all the hospitals with mandatory vaccination policies for employees and colleges with mandatory shots for students. We've got such a large proportion of industry believing that full vaccination makes people healthier in the long run that such policies will help preserve our rates, even if more of the public decides otherwise."

"But is that really true, Madeline? Will it preserve rates? Or will more and more people decide to live their lives outside of the mainstream medical and educational systems? That thought really scares me, and those I advise."

James, who liked to use humor to mask his uncertainty, broke the silence. "Or there's option four: just sit back and let more and more people opt out of vaccines and see what happens. If Pharma is right, they'll all die off – from polio, measles, tetanus, and so on. But if the people are right, and they all grow up way smarter and healthier than the rest of us, they'll take over medicine and the government and fix things for us. Either way, problem solved."

Genuine laughter from the three earned some looks from nearby tables.

Then silence once again, as each of the three gradually stopped laughing, then stopped smiling. None of the three said out loud what all of the three were thinking: *What if?*

Chapter 39

A Probable Answer

"So, there's got to be a right answer."

"A right answer for what?"

"A right answer for all the millions of parents out there who are trying to figure out what to do. They read books, they research online, they ask their doctor and their friends. Some tell them not to vaccinate. Most tell them to vaccinate, or at least partially vaccinate. Most doctors tell them to fully vaccinate or 'get the hell out of my office.' But nobody actually tells them what the 'right' answer is for their individual child."

"Well, I think the 'right' answer is going to be different for everybody," said the one pediatrician. "Basically, those who feel that vaccines are safe enough can vaccinate. I'm personally not a fan of the full CDC schedule, but people can have the option to follow it if they feel it's the right choice for them. Because, in my experience, most kids seem to handle their vaccines just fine. Not all do, but most seem to. So, I don't think vaccines are too risky to use. There is some risk we know about, like immediate side effects. Admittedly we don't know if there are any hidden risks, like changes to the immune system or subtle damage to the nervous system that causes trouble in the long run. But many parents would rather their kids have the disease protection."

"But parents who are anti-vaccine ... truly *anti*-vaccine ... would disagree with 'I don't think vaccines are too risky to use,'" said the other pediatrician. "They think vaccines should be abolished. Like, no one should get them."

"That's because most who are completely anti-vaccine have a vaccine-injured child. So can you blame them? They feel like they have to warn others that it can happen to them too. I think people can opt in, but they shouldn't do it blindly. They should be told the risks up front. Like, there should be some sort of mandatory informed consent that every parent has to read."

"Yeah, ironically in some states there is mandatory reading or informational video-watching for parents to be able to opt *out*. So why not have the same for everyone who opts *in*? Do you think the anti-vaccine people would settle for that?"

"I don't know. If informed consent was mandated, and everyone was given a free choice, maybe. And I hate calling them 'anti-vaccine.' They are really pro-health, or pro-natural lifestyle, or pro-whatever. But they don't have a catchy label, so they're anti-vaccine for now. Anyway, in my opinion, people should be allowed to choose. Like, what if we abolish vaccines, and then your kid is the one kid who dies in the U.S. this year from tetanus. Wouldn't you have wanted the choice to get the tetanus shot? Sure, that shot has risk, like seizures and nerve injury, but you could still choose to accept that risk for the disease protection."

"I would settle for better informed consent. Like, patients have to proactively be shown information about the pros and cons. No one should just go ahead and be offered vaccines without any investigation or understanding on their part. But that would be in a perfect world. As things are now, vaccines are 'so good' and 'so perfectly safe' that most people vaccinate without knowing or asking anything. They don't even *know* there is even anything to 'consent' to. Most of these parents simply accept all forms of medicine without question, because they assume it's completely safe. They have no idea there is risk. So, isn't it a doctor's responsibility to tell them that it isn't 100% safe? Shouldn't doctors take better steps to inform them?"

"Yes. But, legally speaking, doctors don't have to. And it takes so much time. So, unless a doctor feels it's important, they are not going to volunteer to give informed consent. Because doctors have the backing of the medical policy-makers who have guaranteed vaccines are safe. Those families fully vaccinate by default. And they go on believing vaccines are the next best thing since ... the new Star Wars Trilogy, or even sliced bread ... until their own kid has a bad reaction. *Then* they start investigating and see that there are all kinds of informed consent materials out there that they should have been given, or should have thought to ask for but didn't; materials that do warn about such reactions. They are seriously pissed, and rightly so. They feel betrayed. Then they start warning others. But, fortunately, the percentage of kids who react so severely is probably small, so the number of parents who are truly against vaccines is small. The number of kids who suffer a moderate reaction, something bad enough to cause the parents to halt vaccines, but that doesn't cause permanent injury, is probably much larger. But these parents don't turn against the system, they just push for better informed consent and choice."

"So that's the vaccinating group, and the used-to-vaccinate group. For most, vaccinating was the 'right' choice, and for some it was clearly the 'wrong' choice."

"And you know what's totally messed up? Most doctors would sit down with the parents of a vaccine-injured child, hold their hand, look them in the eye, and tell them they still made the right choice. For two reasons: 1. It was for the good of society, which we know is mostly bull, and 2. The vaccine probably didn't cause the injury anyway. Your baby's brain just coincidentally got fried the night he was vaccinated because, well, that just happens to some kids. Which is also bull. Then the doctors have the nerve to recommend they continue vaccines, because the single most important consideration is not long-term health and well-being, but disease protection. That's primary. That's how they honestly see it. Vaccinate or die."

"I know you make it sound so extreme, the way you put it, but I agree. That's really the way many doctors look at it. And until *that* changes, we are unlikely to see reform come from within the system. It's going to have to come from outside the system."

"That reminds me of one patient I just saw. She got the MMR

vaccine at age one, like usual. Got a fever and was fussy, like usual, and four days after the shot, boom! Both her eyes went crossed. Not just a little crossed, but both eyes completely deviated inward. They call it ocular palsy."

"That can happen?"

"Yes. Even *you* didn't know that?"

"Never seen it. But given all the other severe neurological reactions listed in the MMR Package Insert, I'm not surprised. So how did you end up getting involved?"

"The mom called my office asking for help. Her own pediatrician said it wasn't the vaccine – these things just happen. Same thing with the ophthalmologist she saw. And they said there is nothing to do about it, and it should just go away. But you and I know that one-year-old babies, with no history of strabismus at all, don't just suddenly develop severe bilateral strabismus, or ocular palsy, for no reason. There's always a cause. And it wasn't just mild. By the time I saw her, a week after it started, I was shocked. Honestly, I thought the mom was exaggerating over the phone. But one eye was completely turned inward, and the other eye was about half way turned inward. The kid would look at me with the better eye, but not straight on. She had to turn her head a little away from me so her eye would point at me, just so she could see who was talking to her. And it didn't come and go; they were solidly stuck that way. Knowing that high dose vitamin A can treat live measles infections, I recommended she give it to her baby as per the CDC two-day dosing protocol."

"I've seen literally several hundred patients with severe reactions whose doctors tell them 'no way, vaccines can't do that.' But the reactions are listed right there in the vaccine PIs."

"You know what? Ocular palsy is listed in the MMR PI – right under reported reactions."

"Seriously?"

"Yeah, no. It is. You'd think one of her doctors would have paused just for a second to look that up. But no, they are trained in medical school and residency that these things just don't happen. But get this. The mom took her baby to a neurologist who told her that there is a known cause of ocular palsy: live viral infections. And he confirmed that yes, the live viruses in the MMR vaccine can and did cause her child's ocular palsy. He said there's nothing to do about it, and it should resolve over time. But, he advised her to never give her child any live-virus vaccines, like MMR and chicken pox, ever again. At least she got that little bit of satisfaction. No, that's not the right word. I don't know what is. She's pissed. She feels betrayed by a system she trusted. She even thought she was being careful by only getting an MMR that day, instead of the chicken pox and hep A vaccines that were also due. She read a book about vaccines that had warned her about all the severe possible neurological side effects, but she'd read through that long list and just assumed it wouldn't happen to her own child. And the book advised her that if she decided to give the MMR vaccine at age one, at least don't do any other simultaneous vaccines. It might be safer that way. Yeah, it wasn't."

"That's why I stopped giving the MMR to infants. I wait until they are at least several years old. Although, reactions like that could happen at any age, I suppose."

"And the way her two other doctors just ignored the possibility pisses me off. Her doctor would have given her the second MMR dose at age five without a second thought. If she believed her doctor that it wasn't the vaccine, because 'doctors know best' you know, who knows what would happen? I told her to report her doctor to the medical board."

"Wow, really? I thought doctors weren't supposed to turn on other doctors."

"When you see such gross negligence, you do. How else would her doctor learn that ocular palsy is listed in the MMR PI, and when that or any of the other severe reactions occur, you aren't supposed to repeat the vaccine. A warning letter from the medical board just might make him think. And if more patients informed their state medical board when these things happen, the boards might institute some sort of educational process so that doctors know what to watch out for."

"Yeah, it would take a whole lot of such reports for any state medical boards to even lift a finger about something like this."

"I agree. But given enough reports, legally the boards would have to take action. After all, their mission is consumer protection against negligent medical care. I'm surprised there isn't some sort of organized effort to Guide parents on how to submit medical board reports. Maybe there is, but I haven't seen it."

"I guess you're right. But why won't most doctors admit these reactions can happen? Do you think they know they can happen, but are trying to hide it? Or do you think they simply just don't know?"

"I'd say for the vast majority of practicing physicians it's the latter. And it's not really their fault. They are trained that way. The mantra 'vaccines are safe and effective' is grilled into them, especially the pediatricians. And they are taught straight up that vaccines *can't* cause these bad reactions. They literally can't. Then they see one baby die of a vaccine-preventable disease during their training years and they become converts for life. And a mere parent who says they've read all the possible side effects and are worried isn't going to change their mind."

"But the data are right in front of them. The side effect data are available in hundreds, maybe even thousands, of research articles."

"But only if they look for it. Listen, you know how busy we Peds are. We don't have time to re-invent the wheel unless something prompts us to. You and I got interested in this, so we've spent decades reading everything about it. Most Peds don't. Once they learn what they think they need to know in med school, some may not even read a single thing about vaccines ever again. And if they do, it's the Kool-Aid that their policy-makers pour them."

"So why are all those side effects listed in the vaccine PIs and warned about on the CDC VIS forms if nobody is supposed to admit, or even know, that those things can happen?"

"It's so the CDC and Pharma can say, when anyone does get injured, that there *were* warnings available for the patients to read. Maybe it takes the liability away, I guess, or makes them feel better."

"It's like, all the people who make and approve vaccines write down in the fine print all the bad things that *can* happen, then they teach all the doctors those things *don't* happen, and they *don't warn* the parents that anything bad can happen, then they pull out the fine print in court when something bad *does* happen and say, 'We warned you.'"

"*Caveat emptor.*"

"What?"

"You know, 'buyer beware.' I wonder what the Latin is for 'patient beware?'"

"Yeah, they don't teach Latin to us anymore, do they?"

"But you know how the dictionary actually translates *caveat emptor*? 'The principle that the buyer *alone* is responsible for checking the quality and suitability of goods before a purchase is made.'"

"Ha-ha. Kind of lets the doctors off the hook then, right?"

"Yeah, no. Because with every other single medical treatment and procedure on the planet, a doctor would lose his or her license for simply telling a patient '*caveat emptor*.' It's the doctor's responsibility to provide informed consent – to provide any necessary warnings up front. I wonder why vaccines are the only medical treatment for which doctors are allowed to put the '*emptor*' on the parents."

"I think it's the '*caveat*' they are putting on the parents. I guess. I don't know any more Latin than you do. But yeah, good point. Why are vaccines the only thing doctors don't have to give any warnings about? Especially when they are literally the single most comprehensive and invasive medical interventions their child will ever receive. Ever! Unless they need chemo or something someday. When else in a person's life are they ever going to receive 70 doses of an immune modulating and inflammatory treatment? If anything, vaccines deserve *more* proactive informed consent than pretty much anything else any doctors do. So why are vaccines exempt?"

"I think it's the Iron Triangle concept."

"I know there's a triangle in Bermuda, but what's an Iron Triangle?"

"It's the principle that three entities work together to keep a certain process going, and no one else has any authority to intervene.

With vaccines, the three points of the triangle are the companies that make the vaccines, Congress who makes the laws regarding vaccines, and the CDC who promotes the vaccine schedule."

"Well, what's wrong with that?"

"The lines that travel back and forth between those three points, that's what. Pharma donates millions of dollars every year to Congress and to the CDC, or to individuals in Congress and the CDC. Pharma employs doctors, donates millions for research, and offers jobs to ex-CDC employees. The CDC, presenting itself as an independent and objective organization, promotes Pharma's products. The CDC educates the doctors. Congress provides oversight to make sure the CDC and Pharma are doing the right thing and not breaking any rules. So, if something is actually going wrong inside that triangle, who is going to say anything? Iron Triangles are unbreakable. Until that changes, until a 100% independent group is created to oversee vaccine policy in the U.S., a group that is outside of this triangle, more and more people are going to lose trust in vaccines."

"It seems like triangles can be broken if enough of the public speaks up."

"Yes, and that's what many people are now trying to make happen. But there are other financial factors that play into why most doctors kick patients out if they don't accept the complete CDC vaccine schedule. Like the ocular palsy patient I saw – her doctor kicked her out of the practice. More and more medical insurances are starting to give doctors year-end bonuses based on their patient vaccine compliance rate. And not a small bonus either. I'm talking 5 to 10% of their annual revenue in some cases."

"Well, that puts some pressure on doctors, I'm sure, but they can still say no to the bonus and allow patients a free choice, right?"

"Wrong. Think about it. Insurance pays so little to doctors nowadays that they barely break even. In order to survive and make a middle-class income, doctors have to band together into large group practices that are business machines. With good management, those practices can do ok. But not if insurance takes away 5 to 10% of their income. Without that, these large practices go bankrupt. Or the doctors in that practice accept a low middle-class income. So, I'm thinking they literally have no choice but to kick these patients out, which is sad because many of the patients who say no to vaccines are really just opting out of the stupid ones, like hepatitis B. But by keeping those patients, big-business practices go bankrupt."

"So, it's the insurance's fault?"

"Only in part. The insurances think they are actually doing a good thing by helping force all their clients to vaccinate using the complete CDC schedule. But here's what they don't know: the full CDC schedule has not been safety tested to make sure it is safe in the long run. They are forcing their pediatric clients to accept the single most invasive and comprehensive treatment they will ever receive, and forcing their doctors to demand that treatment or else, without knowing it is safe. And the doctors aren't warning their patients, and when a patient does suffer a reaction, the doctor denies that's even possible. Then the patient gets kicked out of the practice so the doctor forgets it ever happened."

"That's the most F-d up thing I've ever heard you say. So, both the insurance companies and the doctors are to blame?"

"No."

"What? Seriously?"

"Yeah, no. Think about it. Most doctors, in my opinion, aren't knowingly being nefarious. And neither are the insurance companies. They actually think what they are doing is right and good. I would say the blame goes higher up than that. It's the policy-makers and institutions that teach doctors and direct health care policy."

"I get what you are saying, and I'm going to guess what you are going to say next: they aren't necessarily nefarious either, right? It's not like one big conspiracy where those in power *know* vaccines have risk. It's that everybody simply assumes they are perfectly safe, even those at the very top of power. But without proving it with research. They must be good for everyone, so it's okay to force them. Is that about right?"

"Yes, I couldn't have said it better. Except you left out one thing – the real factor that allows the denial of harm to exist in the first place.

Money. When those who have the power to make policy decisions and force a medical treatment stand to make large sums of money, denial for the good of society comes naturally."

"But doctors *could* stand up to this system, right? They don't have to accept the insurance bonuses. They don't have to let insurance companies dictate how they care for their patients."

"Yes, but then they can't earn a decent living, either. Now *that* would be a doctor I'd take my kids to."

"Ha-ha. You already do. Thank you for your patronage."

"And thank *you* for yours."

"Anyway. Back to our earlier discussion about choice. We've covered people who decide to vaccinate, or opt out when something bad happens. What other 'right choices' are out there for parents?"

"Well, another 'right' choice is those who believe that vaccines just aren't safe enough from the start, or haven't been adequately proven to be safe, and are really OK not vaccinating. The chance that their kid is going to catch something dangerous is so low that it's not an unreasonable path to take. And the chance they will be responsible for a disease outbreak is extremely remote. They really don't pose a danger to others. They just have to accept the very tiny risk that their kid may catch something bad, and probably worry for their child's first year or two. These parents feel that is the right choice for their child, and an OK choice for society. They eventually stop worrying as their baby grows up into a healthy child and they realize their kid is going to be fine."

"Probably."

"Yes, almost definitely probably. No 100% guarantee. You just have to be OK with 'probably.' And you know what? That probably also applies to those who vaccinate. Your child 'probably' won't suffer a severe reaction."

"'Probably' can also apply to mild vaccine reactions, of course. Your child 'probably will' have a mild reaction. I'd categorize moderate reactions as a 'maybe.' Thank God the severe reactions are … what? 'Probably not?'"

"Ha-ha. I like that. And if you don't feel comfortable with letting your baby risk the rare but potentially dangerous diseases, you vaccinate against just those ones. Vaccinate against the things that have the potential to kill or severely harm your baby: whooping cough, HIB, pneumococcal. Pretty much just those three. And either do them at their regularly-scheduled age – infancy and toddlerhood – and maybe spread them out a bit from each other if you want, or delay them until the baby is a bit older and needs fewer doses: 6 months, 1 year, 2 years, whatever."

"Yeah, for those who just aren't ready to give any of these things to their tiny, vulnerable little babies, as they see it, but want to eventually get the protection."

"Right. Meaning, not that that's the right answer for everyone, but yeah, that's how some parents see it."

"Maybe do some of the less important vaccines as the kid gets older, like age 5, 8, or 10? Less important meaning those diseases that are mostly eliminated but can occasionally hit as a small outbreak or could cause trouble as an adult."

"Right. Like measles, mumps, and rubella. Tetanus. Polio if you are really paranoid. Meningococcal for college. Maybe chickenpox, although even that disease is mostly harmless for adults too. But honestly, most of my patients who start out delaying vaccines at first, thinking they'll start them later, realize their child is so healthy that they end up never even starting them. They just let their kid grow up into an adult without those immunities because the diseases are now rare enough that the danger really is low enough to live with."

"Probably."

"Yeah, probably."

"Are there any that just really aren't worth doing at all, ever? Like the disease isn't something to fear at all?"

"In my opinion, yes. Just because there is a vaccine doesn't automatically make it a good idea. In my book, hepatitis A and B and rotavirus fit that bill the best. Maybe the flu shot. Maybe chicken pox, too. Then there would be the vaccines that may not be a good idea based on potential side effects. Like yeah, the disease could be bad, but the vaccine may not be worth the risk. HPV comes to mind.

Maybe MMR, but not as much. Definitely the old DTP that caused so much brain damage. You know they took that vaccine off the U.S. market in the 90s, and stopped using it in most countries, but then actually started using it again in many Asian and Pacific Island nations? And they are considering bringing it back to the U.S.? Because the current DTaP doesn't work very well, they may want to bring the old one back? They don't seem to care that it's frying brains – literally, not figuratively. Disease prevention is number one, at any cost. So, yeah. That vaccine is definitely not worth doing."

"But you're not saying people shouldn't vaccinate, right? Like, vaccines aren't outright plain dangerous for everybody."

"Right. No vaccine is so dangerous that nobody should get it, the old DTP excluded. Meaning, if you think a vaccine is the right choice, chances are good your child will tolerate it well enough. Probably."

"Geeze, I'm beginning to hate that word. Some parents don't feel that 'probably' is enough reassurance, whether it's 'your child will probably be ok if you don't vaccinate,' or 'your child will probably not have a severe reaction to the vaccine you are about to give'."

"But 'probably' is all anyone can scientifically give them."

"What about all those supposedly safer alternative vaccine schedules you see out there? Those make the vaccines probably safer, right? Ocular palsy excluded."

"Actually, we don't really know, do we? There's no thorough research that compares them. Theoretically they could be safer, but they could not be. I once heard someone say 'one bullet to the brain will kill you just as dead as ten.' Meaning, getting one shot may cause that bad reaction you fear just as easily as getting ten shots together. Personally, I feel that spreading them out probably is safer. I don't know that it is though, and I have seen babies do poorly even from one shot."

"So, we don't know that alternative vaccine schedules are necessarily safer."

"Right. But it's not just alternative schedules. We don't know that any vaccine schedules are safe, because none of them have been studied. So, you can't just say 'screw the alternative schedules, I'm going with the full schedule because at least we know that's safe.' We don't. No one can claim safety with any schedule."

"So why did some doctors come up with alternatives?"

"I've spoken with some who have, and you know what they told me? They weren't intending to advise that parents actually go ahead and vaccinate. They don't really recommend that everyone follow their schedules. They don't recommend people do or don't do anything specific. Their alternative schedules are there for people to follow if they themselves decide to vaccinate. Like, *first* decide whether you want any vaccines at all, *then* if you do, give them in a way that slows them down and spreads them out. But don't just blindly follow the schedule because it's there. And they make no safety claims. They aren't claiming that even their schedule is going to give those parents that 'probably' they are looking for. The schedules are there for people who otherwise would have followed the full schedule, but instead want all the vaccines spread out a bit. One of the doctors found that many people were following his alternative schedule suggestions without reading all the warnings and precautions. They were just blindly doing the schedule because they heard it was safe, or they had the misconception that he actually recommended that people should do it, but they weren't studying all the pros and cons of vaccines. He wasn't happy about that because, in reality, he doesn't actually recommend any vaccines. He doesn't advise *against* any of them, but he doesn't advocate *for* any either. And having a schedule in writing was viewed by some as a guarantee that it would be safe."

"There are just too many options. Some parents want a printed plan to tell them what to do. Maybe that's who alternative schedules are for."

"As long as those parents read all the warnings and potential dangers of even the alternative schedules, and they feel safe about doing the vaccines, then sure. Go for it."

"So, again, what's the *right* answer, for these parents who are trying to figure out what to do?"

"Well, by 'right,' do you mean safer? Technically, it's safer to just not do *any* vaccines. Statistically speaking, the chance of having a moderate to severe adverse event after vaccination is much higher than the risk of catching a severe case of one of the diseases you are trying to prevent. Like, the chance of suffering a symptom of encephalitis after DTaP vaccine is 1 in 1000, but the chance that your baby is going to catch whooping cough and die from it is about 1 in 200,000. The chance of having a seizure after MMR vaccine is about 1 in 3000 and the risk of a potentially severe bleeding disorder is 1 in 30,000; but the risk of catching and then dying from measles, mumps, or rubella is less than 1 in a million. Rotavirus? Chance of intussusception is about 1 in 20,000; chance of dying from the disease is about 1 in 400,000. Not vaccinating is often a safer choice, statistically speaking. I'm not at all saying it's the *right* choice. 'Safe' and 'right' are two different words."

"So, for those who are looking for the safest choice, you're saying don't vaccinate?"

"Yes, as long as they are willing to accept the tiny disease risk."

"It pisses me off that the CDC took the numerical stats off some of the VIS forms so people wouldn't realize exactly what the vaccine risks are. Why do you think they did that?"

"My guess is that they think the numbers scare parents too much. Knowing an exact number makes it too real. Hiding the numbers takes the reality out of the risk. But you know what else they just took out of the DTaP VIS? In the section called 'What if there is a serious reaction' they used to list 'behavior changes' as a reason to be concerned and call your doctor. I was surprised that the CDC would admit that 'behavior changes' could be a serious reaction. And you know what? They just took it out. The updated DTaP VIS as of last month only lists severe allergic reaction in that section now. But it's still in the MMR and Varicella VIS forms, although it's listed as 'unusual behavior' as a serious problem that warrants a call to your doctor. I expect they'll take that out any day now too, because what do 'behavior changes' or 'unusual behavior' after a vaccination sound like to you?"

"Oh my God. That was in the VIS, and they took it out?"

"Yup. I have the old DTaP VIS in a file to prove it. Anyway, continuing with our discussion about what's right and safe, here's another angle that adds to this equation: the theory that unvaccinated kids have healthier immune systems because they haven't been subject to all the artificial influences of vaccines."

"That's so ironic."

"I know. Vaccines may give you some level of protection from specific diseases for 10 or 15 years. But there's a trade-off in that they lower the health of your general immune system. So you'll have a lot more ear infections, colds, flus, sore throats, and all the other ailments of childhood - things that vaccines don't prevent. The unvaccinated kids rarely suffer these because they have better immune systems. Twenty years down the road, when all your vaccines have worn off, you are in the same boat as the kids who didn't get vaccines in that none of you have any vaccine-preventable disease protection. Only now, you have to live the rest of your life with a crappy immune system. More allergies, more heart disease, more cancer, and more autoimmune disease. And now you may be more likely to catch those vaccine-preventable diseases as an adult because now your immune system sucks. Kids who grow up unvaccinated have more functional immune systems to see them through the rest of their lives. Sure, you have to go through childhood with the tiny risk that you may catch a serious vaccine-preventable disease, a risk which is very, very small; but then you're healthier for the rest of your life. Most people don't consider this angle. Yeah, I don't have conclusive proof that it's true, but it's a sound theory that has some research behind it already. And because I believe it, I now have a hard time actively recommending that any of my patients vaccinate. Again, I'm not against them. But I'm not *for* them either. I try to give my patients objective guidance to help them choose what they feel is the right choice for their kids."

"That's so profound, but you know what? I believe it."

"A parent surprised me the other day with another interesting perspective I hadn't considered before."

"This just keeps getting better and better."

"Yeah, well, any pediatrician worth his metal knows to listen to, and learn from, smart patients. Anyway, he told me the reason he and his wife chose to raise their baby without vaccines is that they were more comfortable accepting a passive risk than taking an active one. Actively engaging in vaccination presents a statistically higher risk than passively accepting the much smaller risks of the diseases. Actively vaccinating creates risk, but doing nothing passively presents a lesser risk. He said he felt more comfortable letting the normal course of life play out than he did actively taking a risk that could endanger his baby, as he saw it. He felt better about passive inaction than he did about active risk-taking."

"Interesting perspective. Never thought of it that way, but I can see why some parents would look at it like that. I'm just not sure that most parents are smart enough to sort all this out."

"I disagree. I think they *are* smart enough. It just takes time and effort, and looking at resources other than the CDC."

"So, do tons of reading and research, then ask your doctor for help?"

"Yes, and when the doctor won't help, which is the case for many people nowadays, you turn to other parents who are smarter than you. They'll help you figure it out."

"Probably."

"Ha-ha. Yeah. Probably."

"So, nutshell it for me. Are unvaccinated kids really healthier?"

"Honestly? Yes. In my 30 years of pediatrics, I'd have to say yes. They grow up with healthier immune systems, and will probably live longer, healthier lives. Which is so ironic. And the fact that most vaccines don't prevent disease spread means these kids have little to no impact on herd immunity, despite what the Pharma-controlled media tries to claim. I think that more and more parents, and a growing number of doctors, are beginning to realize that the whole Pharma program of complete and total vaccination may not be in everyone's best interest."

Chapter 40

The Project

The home looked like any other home, in a suburb that looked
like any other suburb, and was filled with about 20 people
who looked like any other people: white, black, Asian, Latino,
Middle Eastern. People from all over the world were represented, although each one of these families lived within about a ten-mile radius
of this neighborhood. Most of them had a baby on a lap. Some still
had babies *inside* their laps. A few were standing in the back of the
living room tending to a little one. And all were listening intently to
the speaker.

"And so, to conclude, you've heard a lot of information tonight.
You should now have a pretty clear understanding of each of the
diseases that vaccines are designed to prevent, and the risk that these
diseases pose, or don't pose, to your little ones. We discussed the
known risks of vaccination, the risks that the CDC has determined
are real and valid. We've also looked a bit outside the CDC at other
published research to get a broader understanding of vaccine risk.
You also have a basic knowledge of the vaccine schedule and how
your doctor will be presenting it to you. I've explained what the vaccine law is here in this state now, and how that law will apply to your
child. And I've briefly shown you what factors doctors might consider
in granting your child an exemption to this law. Then there's my
own experience with vaccines in my family, which I've shared with
you. Please understand that my personal stories and beliefs are not

necessarily the same as The Organization's. I've been very careful to separate the two, so you would know what is their official information that has been very carefully vetted, and what is simply my own opinion. So now we have some time for questions, if there are any."

Twenty hands went up, as Donald knew they would. They always did.

"Let me ask you to keep your hand up if you are wanting me to try to help you make your own personal decision about vaccines. Yup. Ha-ha. That's what I thought. Most of you. Well, let's get the few other questions out of the way first, then we'll see if we can tackle the general uncertainty that I know you all share. I was uncertain at some point as well. So … let's start with you, in the front."

"Well, I want to know why my doctor won't explain all this to me. You've given me more information about vaccines in one evening than my doctor ever has in the three years I've been going to his office. I think you know more about vaccines and the diseases than he does."

"My pediatrician won't even have this conversation with me. I've tried – twice. And he just said that I have to vaccinate or get out."

"Mine too."

"Yeah. Mine actually did give me a two-minute talk on how rare it is to see bad reactions, and seizures and high fever are about the only things to be aware of."

"Really? Mine too. Who is your pediatrician?"

"It's Doctor …"

"Hold up, folks. This is a good question. And let's not name names here. These doctors do deserve our respect … at least if they have shown *you* respect, which most of them do."

"Not mine."

"Yeah, mine neither."

"I know. I know. I hear all the stories. But let's focus on what you all want to learn tonight. You want to know what you should do, and why your doctors won't discuss it with you. First, doctors don't have a lot of time. If you've tried to ask a lot of vaccine questions at a checkup, and the doctor felt pressed for time, then that's more your fault than his, or hers. Schedule a separate time for a Q and A session;

that way your doctor has time to discuss it. Now, your doctor may still not agree with your concerns, but at least you'll have time to voice them. But realize that your doctor can't spend hours with you like I just did, so you can't expect your doctor to educate you. You have to educate you, then run your questions by your doctor. Second, you really have to go to a doctor who is at least open to spreading out the shots or delaying some you don't want - a doctor who won't kick you out if you don't want to follow the CDC schedule. Because any doctor who won't keep you as a patient if you don't comply simply won't give you an objective conversation. You want a doctor who will serve you and your child no matter what you decide. That's the kind of doctor whom you can have this conversation with. The Organization has a network of such doctors. These are physicians who take informed consent for vaccination more seriously. They will go over all the pros and cons of vaccination, or give you objective materials to read so you can make a fully educated decision.

"The third reason it's so hard to have this conversation with most doctors is that many just flat out believe that vaccines are so good, and so safe, that there isn't, or shouldn't be, a choice. So they honestly don't think there is anything to discuss, and they are annoyed that you want to talk about it. They aren't out to get you, or deceive you, in my opinion. They just see vaccines as so good and necessary, that there's only one right choice. Most of their patients seem to handle vaccines well, and the ones that don't often end up leaving so the doctor doesn't remember them. To them, vaccines are safe, and they are entitled to that belief. And you are entitled to find another doctor."

"But why do they get so angry?" one mom asked. "I mean, seriously, red-in-the-face angry."

"I hear that a lot. I suspect that, in addition to the fact that they truly think that all vaccines are equally safe and effective, and that they will save your baby's life, the reason for the extreme anger is that they mistakenly believe you are being misinformed about vaccine risk. That someone is lying to you. That you are getting all your information from an actress/playboy model or heretic doctors who have lost their licenses to practice medicine. It's like, they think you've joined a cult. They get so angry that you are buying a lie perpetrated by non-medical people. They are angry that you are believing people outside of medicine over and above their own well-trained expert opinion. And, honestly, if all that were true, I'd be mad at you too. But I know the truth about where you've gotten your information. You've all read CDC information, and vaccine warning labels from the manufacturers themselves, and published medical research. *These* are your sources, and that's why you are worried. Sure, you'll also get input from 'heretics,' (a little laugh from the room) but most of what you've read before coming here is basic medical information. That's a tactic many doctors and the media use to discredit people who speak out about vaccine risk; they attack them as people so that the public will discount their opinions. But can't a former playboy model turned actress be an intelligent woman with a valid opinion and a real story to tell? Are all doctors who lose their licenses automatically heretics? The way I see it, every person who researches vaccines is entitled to hold an educated opinion. And that's why we, as an organization, are so careful to only educate you with solid medical data, and disclose when something we say is more just an opinion.

"But this type of closed mindset from doctors is what really gave rise to this Project. The doctor who started this is himself a pediatrician. He and a few others realized that there was a nationwide, and even a worldwide, need for people to be able to openly have this conversation with educated, trained, experienced people who have a thorough understanding of vaccines and infectious diseases. I know, I know. This should be a conversation you can have with your doctor. But most of you can't. And honestly, can you really spend two hours with your doctor asking questions? No. So, we provide a safe place where you can. Realize that I can't, and won't, give any of you specific medical advice, because that would be inappropriate. But I will give you general advice that is specific enough so you can reason out this decision on your own, or even in groups as you discuss this with each other in the weeks to come. Even at the next meeting, which you are all welcome to bring another friend to. That's how we grow. And if you want to learn more about becoming an educator yourself, let me know. And I definitely encourage you to continue asking your doctor questions until you feel satisfied with the decision you make.

"OK. So, should you vaccinate or not? I already told you that I can't officially tell you that. But I can walk you through the decision-making process and help you find a decision you are comfortable with, whether it's all vaccines, some vaccines, or no vaccines. And I anticipate that some of you will still be unsure what you should do after we've talked through all the options. That's why this group isn't just one meeting. Keep coming back until you are comfortable making a decision, then help others make their decision too. Sadly, since most people can no longer get this help from a doctor, we're the ones who will help you. And we are well-trained to do it.

"I know a lot of you like the concept of vaccination, but you're not necessarily comfortable with the risks. Otherwise you wouldn't be here. Consider this idea as your first exercise: what is the default position, or the status quo, so-to-speak? If you can't decide, what should you do by default? Do you just go ahead and vaccinate because that's the norm, and you can't find enough reasons *not* to do it? Or should you, instead, only proceed with vaccination because you *know* that is what you want to do? In other words, don't just vaccinate because you can't decide. If you can't decide, then don't start. In my experience, virtually every parent who begins vaccines with the wrong mindset ends up regretting it later. Not because of bad reactions, in most cases. They are mad at themselves because they didn't really want to do it, but someone pushed them into it, and they figured, 'Oh, that's just what I'm supposed to do.' But in their hearts they didn't want to, and most end up stopping the process once this reality hits them.

"Instead, look at this decision another way. Your baby is born, pure and healthy, and is getting a natural start to life. You *then* have to decide if you should intervene with a complex medical procedure. The default should be no vaccines, and *then* you do vaccines if you consider them to be important, *and* you are comfortable with their safety. If you don't think they are safe or important enough, then what should your default be? Just let your baby continue on his or her healthy, natural, and merry little way, or begin an intervention

433

you are uncomfortable with? That's your choice. But I'd like you to approach that choice from the right perspective. So, right now you all have unvaccinated babies. Let's now walk through all the pros and cons of changing that condition to one in which you accept the immunities, and the side effects, that vaccines can offer. But instead of deciding to opt *out*, you are deciding whether or not the right decision for your baby is to opt *in*."

The quarter-hour Q and A session ended up lasting two … hours that is. They always did, and Donald and his wife were always ready with coffee to keep people talking. Babies were nursed. Bathroom breaks were taken quickly. Plates were re-filled with snacks. But the talking never stopped. Because parents never could get enough information. That's all they really wanted. Truthful, complete, objective medical information that would allow them to make what they feel would be the best and safest choice for their child.

And Donald knew that such meetings were taking place nationwide as he spoke, groups that provided education about immunity, led by trained volunteers just like him. Because no one else was doing it, and it had to be done. And that was all the reward he needed.

Epilogue

John watched his toes wiggle out from under the cool sand, not yet warmed by the just-risen sun. The bay was quiet, as it was every morning. The waves gently lapped the edge of the beach in a rhythm that he found peaceful – far more peaceful than his mornings used to be. He loved to start each day sitting in the sand with his coffee, gazing out at his new "back yard" while his wife slept the extra few morning hours he'd never been able to. Which was all good to him, because morning was his writing time, when the words flowed effortlessly onto the pages. And writing while his wife slept meant that she wouldn't be condemned to living this new life alone while her husband spent all day staring at his computer.

John stood up and stretched, walked the ten paces back to the covered deck that was his new "office," and sat down at his "desk." The old wooden picnic table had come with the place, and its stark contrast to the desk he'd left behind pretty much nut-shelled his new life compared to his old one. The one-room beach house – well, shack was a better word – was just icing on the cake. A very thin layer on a cupcake, maybe. Lucky for him, John liked thin icing and cupcakes.

The quiet bay started its morning around John while he weaved a story in chapter 3 of his second book. Fishermen pushed their little skiffs out into the water to hunt down the morning's catch. Children splashed quietly in the calm water. Dogs roamed the sand looking for John-didn't-know-what. Boats sailed past on the morning breeze. The occasional beach walker strode by, wondering who this new light-skinned man and woman were who had recently joined their community.

John had made sure his wife would be okay with having to start a new life before he'd gone ahead with his plan. He'd known it was a risk, but he'd also known that people needed the truth. They deserved it. Their children deserved it more. Some of his colleagues had warned him not to do it, and part of John had never really thought it would come to this – that he would lose so much and have to leave it all behind. But his wife had assured him, "All I need is a shack on the beach – and you." And that's exactly all they had now. That, and the book. And The Project. They could fly back to the States to visit their grown kids as often as they liked, especially when the grandbabies started coming. And to help keep The Project going. He knew that would be enough to fulfill his life. He also knew he'd soon be able to start practicing in the community here once the local medical board approved his license. They sorely needed a pediatrician here, and John was eager to serve. Meanwhile, a second book was already writing itself in his mind, and it should only take a few months of mornings to get it down on paper …

Sandra couldn't believe the results of the latest round of side-effect data – oops, I mean "adverse event" data, she corrected herself. Seven out of every 100 had reported screaming. That can't be right. Not again. Every group they'd given the new product to had shown an unusually high rate of what sounded like encephalitis. Oh well. Her boss would know how to reconfigure the data into something palatable. Sandra was hoping to be promoted to the Phase 3 research group, and only those researchers who helped get the new product to that phase would be promoted. But she knew all the study groups were getting similar results, so it would be up to the higher-ups to come up with a solution … unless … Sandra suddenly had an idea. Yes, that might work. If she could …

The creaking of the floorboards behind John announced that writing time was over, and he didn't need to turn around to know his wife was up and headed toward the kitchen corner to pour the coffee that he'd left for her. She'd take a few sips just to wake up, then he'd brew her something fresh for her to really savor. That was their routine. That, and other things. They had a whole island to explore, and a whole island full of people to get to know. And they had nothing but time now.

His fingers quickly summed up Sandra's new idea before he closed his computer. John knew *he'd* forget what it was by tomorrow morning, and he didn't want Sandra to forget either. So he typed out a few last words that would jog both their memories tomorrow, hit "save," and closed his laptop as the creaking steps reached the doorway out to the back porch. He stood up to greet the thing he loved most in this world.

"Good morning, Mrs. Ryan."

"Good morning, Dr. Ryan."

Resources

Vaccine safety research is ever-changing. Instead of listing all resources here, you can find links to all the research studies, articles, and news reports presented in this book, and more, at www.JohnPhillipRyan.com.

And follow John Phillip Ryan on Facebook, Instagram, and Twitter (@JohnPhillipRyan).

Do not keep this book on your shelf!

When you are done reading, give it away. This work was meant to live, to roam far and wide, and to spread love and understanding. Don't let it gather dust next to all your other novels. Sure, read it twice if you must. Or three times. You may find yourself among the many characters and stories whose lives will seem all to familiar. But don't let your tears smudge the ink, or the fire of your anger singe the edges. If you need to tear some pages out, please tape them back in. Because you'll want the next reader to see every word. Share this book with everyone you love and, even better, with those who don't understand the choices you have made. Perhaps they will come to see that there doesn't have to be two sides to this tale after all.